TEN GOLD WATCHES GIVEN AWAY AS PRIZES.

GUY FAWKES

OR THE CONSPIRATORS BRIDE

REMEMBER!

Given away with No. 1 of this Story, No. 2, and a Large Sheet of Characters for the New Play,

"THE FIFTH OF NOVEMBER; OR, GUNPOWDER TREASON AND PLOT."

NOTE.—The whole of this Grand Play, Scenes, Sets of Characters, Wings, and Drop Scenes, Book of the Play, Handsome Stage Front, and Instructions how to Make a Stage—Gratis.

OFFICE, 81, FLEET STREET, LONDON, E.C.

THE

YOUNG ENGLISHMAN'S JOURNAL.

TALES BY MOST POPULAR AUTHORS.

CURIOSITIES OF NATURAL HISTORY, SCIENCE, AND BOTANY.

DOMESTIC PETS, AND HOW TO REAR THEM.

BEEHIVES AND BEES.

SKETCHES FROM THE CLASSICS.

TALES OF OUR PRINCES.

ADVENTURES, TRAVELS, ETC.

BIOGRAPHIES OF BOYS WHO HAVE BECOME FAMOUS MEN.

"RAMBLES BY THE SEASHORE."

"OUR AQUARIUM AND VIVARIUM."

"OUR YOUNG ARCHITECT AND BUILDER."

LESSONS IN ROWING AND SAILING, SWIMMING AND ANGLING.

GYMNASTICS.

ALL ENGLAND GAMES.

HOW TO REAR SILK WORMS.

HOW TO MAKE A MODEL ENGINE.

ORDER No.

YOUNG ENGLISHMAN'S JOURNAL,

IN WHICH BEGINS

THE GRAND SEA STORY,

ENTITLED,

THE WAR CRUISE OF THE MOSCA.

CHAPTER I.—Fitting Out.

CHAPTER II.—The Six Fighting Mids.

CHAPTER III.—The Schooner with the Yellow Flag.

GUY FAWKES
OR
THE CONSPIRATORS BRIDE

"GUY, GUY! DARE NOT THIS DESPERATE DEED!"

CHAPTER I.
ANNO DOMINI 1604.

A QUIET summer's evening was drawing to its close, and the soft golden sun was slowly sinking from a pale horizon, emblazoned even at this early hour with a few silvery stars, when two youthful travellers, traversing the road to Hounslow, approached an antique hostel, upon whose gabled roof and quaint windows the sinking sun still threw its fading streaks of light.

The two wayfarers were apparently of equal age ; their height was similar, and there was little difference in their figure, save that one stepped with the buoyancy and grace of untired youth, while the other's stride was statelier and more austere.

In features they presented a marked contrast : the more youthful of the two had a fair frank face, eyes of hazel, very gentle in their gaze, and nut-brown hair.

The elder's face, bronzed, bearded, and grave, was singularly sombre in its settled look of thoughtful earnestness ; his eyes were darkly piercing, and his hair was as richly black as the plume in his steeple hat.

Each wore a semi-military attire, and each carried a long rapier by his side ; and as they entered the wayside inn their huge boots rang heavily on the oaken threshold.

Making their way to the snug parlour of mine host, they seated themselves by the open window, and laying their hats on the table, stretched out their legs with an air of fatigue, while they awaited the advent of a ripe flagon of good Hungarian, the which they were speedily discussing with evident relish.

But little conversation was kept up, the elder soldier—for campaigners their attire and aspect unmistakably bespoke them— seemed moody and taciturn, and made but slight reply to the frequent sallies of his more mirthful companion.

This dulness on his part provoked the younger to be more demonstrative in his outbursts ; but finding that, in spite of all challenge to discourse, his comrade remained absorbed as ever, he clapped down his goblet on the table suddenly, and pushing the wine forward, exclaimed—

"Why, Guy, what ails thee, man ? Thou art as dull as the devil at his prayers—even the wine, and 'tis rare of its sort, lacks all relish for thy palate."

A bright gleam of affectionate regard illumined his visage, and he turned towards his companion, saying, with a half smile—

"Indeed my mood is sober, Hugh, yet let me not lack courtesy with thee, good friend : so fill and drink a health. Tried comrade of many a hot hour of strife, if I be grave of mind, let me be mirthful while with thee."

"Which will be while both have our stay on this fair earth, I trust," Hugh said, extending his hand.

The soldier comrade grasped the outstretched hand warmly.

"With all my heart, Hugh," he answered ; "we have been many a year together, and side by side have fought as brothers. I would have none of those things I sometimes fear to come between us."

"Nothing can sunder our friendship, Guy ; let what betide, our hearts shall beat as one." A milder softer look beamed from the dark stern eyes for an instant, but an afterthought seemed to flash suddenly to Guy's brain, for

his face instantly wore an expression of sombre sadness, and with something like a sigh he gulped down his draught of wine.

"I am thinking," Hugh said, as they set their goblets on the table—well drained of their contents—"that our life in Spain was, after all, our happiest time. Those were stirring days— days of spicy broil and danger. Perhaps I love the scenes the more that our friendship was born amidst them. You know, Guy," he added, a gentle fervour in his soft brown eyes, "I ween Hugh Wardour had not been here at this hour but for that trusty stroke of thine, that saved his life on the red field by the Guadalquiver."

"A stroke a hundredfold repaid. Yet I think with you, those were less moody times. I have not been myself since I came hither ; 'tis the chill of this cold isle ; there was a heat in my own sunny clime that sent my blood hot through my veins. Yes, I am chilled at heart, and only the stir of strife can rouse me to my wonted humour."

"Why, marry then, thou wilt be roused anon, for an' I mistake the times, there will be broils and troubles enough to set even this cold isle on fire."

"Ay," the elder soldier said, the fervour of an enthusiast in his looks, " there will be changes strange, and things that now seem firm as the rock shall crumble into dust."

"In which case, Guy, we will fight the foe as of old, and on the tented plains I shall again see the wonted sparkle in thine eye—the wonted joyousness in thy looks."

"God grant it so. Yet I have misgivings it will not be so."

"How! is't my friendship that's in doubt ?"

"No. I am sure of *that*, but I have a hatred to this isle—it is fatal to my race. My proud ancestor had warning not to cross the seas that rolled between this land and Spain. He did— and died !"

"Died ?"

"With the Armada. His was the foremost ship, and all went hurling to the grave the ocean found them. I have a clinging doubt— nay, almost a surety—'twill be fatal to me !"

"Better experience will make thee more hopeful ; this is mere weakness. I know 'tis not that thou fearest death."

"No. I fear not DEATH ; but there is a darker destiny than the sternest death—an everlasting *kill* ; and if aught I fear 'tis that. Hugh, these are changeful times—changeful, ay, accursed—accursed for our creed, since those of our faith are down—trodden by the minions of that Scotch craven whom fate has placed on England's throne. 'Tis a dark hour when to be known to be of Romish faith is to be hunted like a dog—when heretics fatten on the spoils of martyrs—when gray-haired priests are butchered for their sanctity—when helpless babes and hapless innocent wives and maidens are tortured by fires on earth, as they who torture them shall be by fires in hell. Yes, if a hand be not raised to hurl this impious spawn of Satan down to his heretic doom—if blood flow not freely over this land till it quench the fire lighted for the victims of our religion—if there be not violence, hate, and deeds of bloodiest vengeance—then my dreams are false, and they who whisper to my brain night after night are lying demons—not the ministers of the Holy Virgin as I deem them. No! no! 'twill come, and in those desperate changes no man's part shall be more desperate than mine."

His younger comrade seemed startled by this sudden outburst; he glanced anxiously towards the door, then laid his hand on the speaker's arm. "Let us not be rash in speech,"' he said; "these walls have listening ears, and though I own not to the knowledge of fear, yet there be times of cunning need, when the enemy is watchful, as at present."

"Right," Guy said, abruptly changing his manner, "I am possessed to let my mood break forth incautiously; let us to other themes—thy love business, Hugh. Hast gained tidings of the fair maiden, to follow whom you made such haste to England?"

"None—I have gained no tidings since the night when we rescued her from the convent in Spain."

"'Twas an impious deed, Hugh, and has its judgment. Well, well, I have slight favour for the sex, and doubt that their fairest charms will touch mine heart."

"I would it were otherwise, for then I should see thee happier; nevertheless, let us fill a health to Constance, whom if I find not, and rescue not, to make my bride—ay, if I enter fifty convent walls—may I deserve worse fate than ever befel the meanest rapscallion whose brutal throat was girded by a halter."

They had drawn their table to the window, and with a second flagon before them were gazing on the scene without; Hugh watching those who came to or went from the inn, Guy absorbed in thought as he gazed on the sun-illumined and starlit heavens—scarcely yet tinged with twilight's deepening shade—when the door of the room was quietly opened, and a boy dressed as a retainer hesitatingly entered.

"Please you, my masters," he said, looking hurriedly from one to the other, "I am to seek a Spanish soldier-gentleman, whose name is Guy."

"And when thou hast found him?" interrupted Guy.

"I am to give him this," the messenger said, advancing with a letter in his hand; "if you be he, 'tis for your reading."

He laid the letter on the table before them, and, retreating to the door, departed, as if glad of having executed an unpleasant mission.

"For the Spanish soldier-gentleman, whose name is Guy," said the elder, taking up the missive; "who knows me by that title?—who can know that I am here?"

He took up the missive, and cutting the silken string with his dagger, opened it, and perused its contents.

A strange puzzled expression settled on his features as he read. Hugh, curiously watching him, saw his left hand extended to his sword hilt till he read the last line, when a half smile played about his lips, and handing the letter to his companion, he said jestingly—

"So, I am yet to be a mark for woman's wiles—read."

Hugh took the letter, and read with surprise the following:—

"*Guy,—Confiding in your honour and courage as a soldier and a gentleman, I desire your presence this evening at the hour of nine, at the house below Whitehall, on the river bank, in one window of which a taper will burn as a signal. Let your boat be made safe; you will need it to return. Means of ascent to my chamber I will find. Come alone.*

"CLAIRE."

"Brief and pithy," remarked Hugh, as he handed back the letter. "You will attend?"

"Yes, the adventure may be curious."

"Not alone; I will be with you, at least on your journey."

"Not so; it is enough you know whither I am bound. The lady shall not have misjudged me; save for this good friend"—he tapped his sword-hilt. "I go alone."

"And Hugh were indeed weak-hearted in thy cause if he were not near," thought the younger soldier, who then added aloud; "in this case I should go too—yet not from curious motive—trust me there is much secret meaning in that epistle. Marry, what have we here? —a sudden brawl as I live—forth, Guy—but us to the scene of tumult!"

A sudden and loud tumult had indeed broken in upon his speech. The voice of troopers in angry tumult, the shrieks of women, a timid plaintive cry, and a husky beseeching voice mingled in one uproar.

Darkly stern grew Guy's brow as he heard the troopers' voices.

"Some unfortunate of our faith in the power of these wolves," he said, bitterly, as he strode to the door; "but, an' I die for it, they shall know that there are hearts to dare and hands to strike even amongst the persecuted Papists."

As they strode to the door they beheld the cause of the sudden uproar.

Half a dozen armed troopers, acting under the directions of an ill-favored fellow who seemed their leader, were surrounding a priest, who, with his hands outstretched imploringly, was endeavouring to screen a fair faced effeminate-looking boy, now cowering to the ground in terror of the soldiery.

Humbly clad as the boy was, there nevertheless was something in his aspect that bespoke him neither poorly born nor lowly reared. His skin was wondrously fair; his figure was slim; and long hair of a golden hue hung in disordered tresses, escaped from his apprentice cap, which had got knocked off in his struggle to resist his intending captors.

When Guy and Hugh appeared upon the scene the priest was brutally hurled aside, and one of the troopers laid his heavy hand on the boy's slender arm.

"Spare him, spare him," the priest cried frantically, and falling on his knees; "lead me to prison—torture me, KILL me—but spare him !"

"Oh, we'll take you as well; the cub as well as the he-wolf; and if it's any comfort you'll burn together."

The priest sank with a groan, but swiftly rousing himself, sprang to his feet.

"This is merciless villany," he cried. "Oh! that I had a weapon to wield in his defence. Cowards — heretics — *damned* in life, worse *damned* in death ; release this boy, or dread the curse of heaven."

"Ha, ha, ha," laughed the troopers derisively ; "you can give us more of this when you're at the stake."

Their leader, however, was not so easily disposed.

"Gag the foul Papist," he cried, angrily ; "drag him and the cub hence, to prison, where I hope their limbs will rot till it be time to roast them."

The boy, pale as death, and trembling in every limb, uttered a piteous cry, and shrank from the troopers' grasp.

"Spare me, I am innocent," he moaned. "Oh, have mercy ; I am not what I seem. Oh, help—will no one make these brutal men treat me less cruelly ?"

"I WILL."

The words, clear and stern, rang loudly in the air.

The Spanish soldier had spoken them.

Now he stalked gloomily to the midst of the troopers. A fierce light—the gleam of a panther's fury—shone from his flashing eyes : his brow was knit, his hand clenched tightly on his sword hilt.

"Now," he cried, "tell me on what charge this helpless boy, and that poor weak old man, are dragged to death."

"Treason, treason," exclaimed several voices ; "treason to the King."

The leader of the troopers stepped up to Guy. "They're Papists as well as traitors," he said, "so be warned—don't interfere : they'll have fair trial, and a fair burning too, I'll warrant.

Darker grew the look on the soldier-gentleman's bronzed visage.

The priest, who had been anxiously and furtively gazing upon his lineaments, now uttered a low and beseeching cry.

"For the love of the Blessed Virgin," he cried in Latin, " by the Holy Church, rescue him from their hands ! My limbs are old and withered—I care not that they perish at the stake—but save him from this fate !"

Guy was striding forward when the priest, who had till now seemed in a stupor of doubt, uttered a wild and joyous cry.

A few words he spoke, but those were uttered in a tongue that none present appeared to understand.

None except the Spanish soldier : on him the words had a magical effect.

Uttering a responsive word—a cry in the same strange tongue—he drew his sword.

One dash of the hilt in the nearest trooper's face sent one opponent to the ground.

A second, stunned by a fearful blow with the flat of the shining blade, reeled helplessly.

A third had his weapon beaten from his grasp—and the boy was free.

While Guy stood fiercely defying the onslaught he expected—Hugh, with ready blade at his grasp, stepping to his side—the priest, on whom Guy's swift action had exercised a magical influence transforming him from a shaking supplicant to an exulting victor, broke suddenly from the grasp of the remaining troopers, and clapping his hands wildly together, said loudly—

"Saved, *he* is here! Saved! Guy the Chosen, retire—escape for your life."

Guy looked up : the priest was wildly waving his arm towards a horseman who was galloping madly towards the scene.

A tall swarthy rider, mounted on a steed of raven blackness.

A heavy sword swung at his side, but he did not even essay to grasp it as he dashed into the midst of the animated scene, bearing to the earth beneath his horse's hoofs one or two of the troopers who were too late to get out of his way.

Bending in his saddle, he reined in his impetuous steed for a moment, as he reached the spot where the boy stood.

With one movement forward, he encircled him by his left arm.

Gladly springing towards him, the boy, with a cry of excited joy, sprang from the ground, and was in the saddle beside his new deliverer before even Guy could well understand what was taking place.

The next moment, horse and rider, with the rescued boy's slight additional burden, were galloping on as madly as before.

By this time the leader of the soldiers had recovered his presence of mind.

Leaping forward with a hastily grasped pistol in his hand, he cried—"Halt! in the King's name.—Stand, or I fire !"

A mocking defiant laugh came back borne on the wind in answer to his challenge ; and, taking deadly aim, he fired.

He seemed to have covered, point blank, the body of the daring rider ; yet, without a momentary pause, steed and horseman fled on, and before another shot could be fired were hidden by the bend of the road and speeding far away from pursuit.

The priest, who had during this incident made no effort to escape, joyously proclaimed his exultation at the boy's escape.

"You cannot harm him now," he said, "and I care not what you do to me, since he is safe. *My mission is fulfilled*," he added, in an undertone, and with a meaning look at Guy.

"Silence !" roared the leader of the troopers, at the same time giving utterance to a fearful oath of blasphemy. "You at least we will keep safe enough ; and you," he added, turning to Guy, "I arrest in the King's name as a traitor and a Papist !"

The young Spanish soldier, who had been standing in an easy posture of self-defence, at the first part of the other's speech smiled contemptuously, and returned his rapier to its

THE FIFTH OF NOVEMBER
OR GUNPOWDER TREASON AND PLOT.

GUY FAWKES I

GUARDS

KING JAMES'

OFFICERS

CONSPIRATORS

POWDER AND FAGGOTS

GUY AND LADY

2

GUY FAWKE, 3

ORD MONTEAGLE

FIRST SHEET OF CHARACTERS GRATIS with No. 2 of the NEW STORY, "GUY FAWKES; or, THE CONSPIRATOR'S BRIDE."

sheath; but at the insult conveyed in the final epithet a hot flush suffused his face, and his hand clutched his sword hilt.

"Heretic and craven," he began; when Hugh Wardour, who happily had hitherto taken no perceptible share in the recent occurrence, stepped between him and the object of his suddenly aroused passion, and said to the latter—

"Tut, man, he is chivalrous, and cannot keep from meddling in other people's quarrels; leave him to his reflections—they will be sober enough presently, I'll warrant; meanwhile I pledge myself to answer for him, as a true and loyal soldier of the King and servant of that State as I myself am known by you to be."

"Such as he were better left to ponder on their ways in a cool prison; but nevertheless, Master Hugh, though I take your word for him, I shall demand him of you to answer for this even's violence. Follow me, men; look well to your prisoner—no meddling fool at least shall set him free."

Guy, to whom the speaker's glance was meaningly directed, uttered a disdainful exclamation. The priest, who appeared now only anxious respecting Guy's safety, gave himself complacently to his fate when he saw that the young Spanish soldier was, for the present at least, relieved from the consequences of his interference.

A serene placid look was on his countenance as he allowed himself to be placed in the hands of the troopers, some of whom had not yet got over the effects of the rough treatment they had experienced at the hands of Guy and the mysterious horseman, and would gladly have made the young Spaniard bear the priest company.

Guy would even now have interfered to save the priest, but a meaning look from the latter, and a significant gesture from Hugh, cautioned him to refrain.

The leader of the soldiers cast a scowling look at Guy as he gave the order to move forward with the prisoner.

"There is one vile Papist the less," he exclaimed, indicating the priest, "and it will go hard if I see not another beside him at the stake. You'll rue this day's work, I'll warrant, and I'm known to keep my word; you'll know me then."

"Pshaw!" Guy said, "why not let me know you now?"

"As you will; know, then, my name. I am Kit the Keeper, and now, Papist, what name is yours?"

"My name," the young soldier answered angrily, "is GUY FAWKES."

CHAPTER II.

THE HOUSE BY THE WATER-SIDE—THE JESUIT —THE WOMAN AND THE LOVER.

IT was antique and quaint, even for that period, the house by the water-side; gloomy in its solitary quietude, for the houses by the river bank were few and far between. It would have seemed untenanted, but for the solitary taper glimmering at the upper window, through whose diamond-shaped panes the hazy starlight gleamed.

Within the chamber, near the open casement, were two persons, male and female; and no greater contrast could be conceived than was afforded by their respective appearances.

A meagre stooping form, clad in sombre garb—a sallow visage, pinched, keen, and shrivelled into hard lines—thin bloodless lips compressed like iron—small piercing eyes, grey and shifting—it needed not the closely-shaven face, bare head, and cross and girdle, to proclaim the male a priest of the Jesuit order.

His companion occupant of the room was a lady, apparently in her twentieth year. She was richly though plainly attired; her dress of black velvet displaying the perfection of her small rounded arms, white as virgin snow. Her features, exceedingly beautiful, were pale —strangely pale; dark massive waves of hair clustered above a forehead coldly white and polished as marble; and there was a wildness in the gaze of her dark matchless eyes, as they flashed alternately from the motionless face of the priest to the half-open window, while she listened anxiously for some expected sound.

The priest's eyes followed hers with a restless gleam. He, too, seemed listening in inquiet suspense, and took a pace towards the window as the young girl spoke—

"It is the hour, father. Will he come?"

"The hour should bring him here," muttered the priest; "he cannot falter—no, no— he will come."

"Is all prepared?" he asked, after an interval of silence.

"All."

"May it prove him ours; pray the saints strengthen him in the cause. Once sealed by that oath, no power on earth can shake his faith."

"Alas! I pity him."

"Pity!"

"He is young, brave, handsome, and this world is no longer for him when he has taken the vow."

"What is this world to the next? It is his destiny."

"His DEATH."

The priest started.

"A martyr's crown—a welcome before God's throne. Daughter, 'tis a noble destiny, even if it so end."

The young girl sighed, but made no answer. The Jesuit, absorbed in his reflections, strode past her, and peered out at the window.

"I hear the plash of oars," he said presently, "above the moan of the river; a dark speck glides near us—it is he!"

She crept to his side and peered out; there was a moving object on the glistening water; the plash of oars came distantly on her ears— the priest was right. It was Guy.

"Daughter"—the Jesuit laid his hand lightly on her shoulder as he spoke—"time is brief; use all arts to bind him to the cause. I would join in the task, but it is in fittest hands with you; forget not—the oath must be sealed."

A slight shiver passed over the young girl's frame as the priest withdrew his hand from her shoulder.

There was a panelled door at the extremity of the apartment; making his way towards this, he pushed it open, and for a few seconds gazed within. As he gazed, abstracted and motionless, a curious expression settled on his visage, a singular lustre shone in his eye, and his thin lips moved in inaudible communion with himself. He was aroused from his reverie by the young girl moving towards him.

"I hear his boat ground on the bank," she said; "it is time."

"The Saints be with you; be of stout heart; I shall be near to hear and know."

He lifted the arras at the other end of the room, and, pausing a moment to place his finger on his lips in a gesture of caution, quitted the chamber, leaving the young girl alone to execute the mysterious task allotted her.

While this scene was taking place, the young soldier had swiftly propelled his boat towards the house, conspicuous by the signal taper burning at the casement.

On coming close to the bank he stepped lightly on shore, and hastily moored his boat.

Satisfied that no prying lounger observed his movements, he drew his cloak over his rapier, and strode to the terrace beneath the overhanging balcony.

While he hesitated, wondering what means of ascent were to be provided him, a small hand and arm appeared at the window above, and a coil of stout rope was shaken out, one end of which almost touched the ground, the other evidently made fast at the casement.

Understanding that he was to ascend by it, he grasped the rope with both hands, and, springing from the terrace, rapidly and dexterously climbed to the balcony, and sprang into the room.

The young girl, uttering an involuntary cry, drew back at his entry; but immediately recovering herself, pointed hurriedly to the dangling rope.

Guy read the meaning of the movement, and in a second or so drew the rope up and let it fall in coils at his feet. This accomplished, he closed the window, and taking a step further into the room, silently and somewhat proudly faced the young maiden, who, despite her affected self-control, appeared to lose all firmness now that she was confronted by the soldier whom she had summoned to her chamber.

Guy was the first to speak, and there was something of irony in his tone, while his stern gaze was fixed on the pale girl, as producing the note he said—

"I am bidden hither by this missive—will it please you to speak why I am here?"

The young girl raised her eyes to his; her hands were clasped, and she shivered slightly.

"Guy Fawkes," she answered, "you are brave as a soldier—honourable as a gentleman. I asked your presence here, not from weak love but for a solemn mission. If there be aught of levity or reckless misjudging of my meaning

in your heart, dismiss the very thought with the sacred presence before which you shall presently stand. You can come only with pure thoughts and guileless breast."

"Presence!" Guy exclaimed, slightly moved, "and sacred!"

"Question not—but heed. You have a mission here affecting your faith; if you are prepared to champion it heart and soul, remain; if, only in thought, you falter, depart, and let none know you have come."

The young soldier uncovered his head.

"For my faith," he said, a gloomy look settling on his features, "I would peril life and soul."

"I doubt it not; follow, and be silent."

She stepped towards the cabinet, the door of which she pushed open, and indicated that he was to enter.

Guy started as he gazed into the closet-like recess; a sudden spasm passed over his frame, his features blanched, and for an instant he hung back on the very threshold.

The hesitation was only momentary. Without a word he passed into the recess, and the young girl followed him.

Before the door closed upon them it revealed a glimpse of some part of the mystic character of the apartment.

A narrow, cell-like chamber, hung with black—a table draped in the same sable hue; upon that table a white crucifix; two candles shedding a ghastly light on an object ghastlier than could be conceived.

Laid in a slanting coffin, the shrunken form and shrivelled skull of a mitred corpse, a crosier by its side, and the grave-clothes wrapped like a vestment above it.

The relics of an exhumed saint, before which Guy had to take a solemn vow.

All was silent for some minutes after Guy had gone in; then something like a groan—as of a strong man in deep heartfelt agony—sounded from the recess.

An instant after, the door opened, and Guy came reeling forth.

His face was ghastly—his eyes stared wildly—his hands clenched, as if seeking something to grasp in support. When the door closed, a shudder shook his frame.

His conductress walked by his side. Taking him by the wrist, she led him towards the window, and flung the casements wide apart.

The cool air refreshed Guy a little. He returned the pressure of the small soft hand that had locked itself in his unconscious grasp.

"Guy," she asked, looking tearfully into his face, "are you sure your heart is wholly in the cause?"

"I remember my *oath*," he replied hoarsely.

"Nothing will sever you from your mission —not even the certainty of *death*?"

"I am the Champion of my Faith," Guy answered gloomily.

"Once more. You will never disclose the secret of your coming here?"

"The rack shall not wring the disclosure from me."

At the mention of that dreaded word the

young girl shivered and looked pityingly up into Guy's face.

"The saints preserve you from this," she said, in a low tremulous tone.

"It shall not move me."

"You must swear it. Swear that not the perilling of your life—not even if you seem to peril your *soul*—shall make you forsake your oath; swear it by the presence you have seen—by the sacred relics of that saint upon whose bones your blood has trickled like tears—swear."

"*Swear*," came in hollow tones from the vicinity of the recess.

Guy started visibly. His voice was husky as he replied—

"*I swear*."

"Enough. Go now; you are firm as the unshaken rock. A word of caution: in whatever presence you chance to meet me, know me not, unless I bid you so to do."

"I shall attend."

"For this hour farewell."

"A moment," Guy paused; "dare I know you by a name?"

The reply came in a whisper—

"Claire of Grace."

A slight pressure of the hand accompanied the words.

Guy returned the gentle grasp, and sprang to the window-sill.

Dropping the rope to its full length, he slid quickly down.

The white face of Claire peered after his descent—peered till he had touched the ground, when the anxious tearful gaze gave way to a sudden look of horror, and a sharp agonised cry, hushed in its intensity of agony, escaped her lips.

Let us see the cause.

Guy dropped to the terrace in safety. Unstrung as his nerves were by the dread ordeal he had endured, his iron strength did not fail him in his descent.

But he had hardly steadied himself on his feet, when he made the discovery that he was no longer alone.

CHAPTER III.
DEATH.

THE cry that escaped Claire's lips, though unheard by those who were beneath, brought the Jesuit to her side.

He divined the cause of her horrified looks, and his sunken sallow face peered out at the casement beside her.

"It is *he*," she whispered hoarsely; "there will be murder done! Oh, Holy Virgin save them!"

"Hush!" the Jesuit said, "they meet!"

The first surprise of the unexpected encounter over, Guy looked to see what foe confronted him.

His gaze met a glance as unquailing as his own. Two dark fiercely flashing eyes, a proud imperious face—pale with intense passionate hate; a figure about his own height, and like his wrapped in a cloak, from underneath which protruded the hilt of a long sword.

"A word, sirrah," the new comer said, grinding the words between his gnashing teeth; "that chamber whence you descended—was't not the Lady Claire's?"

"Softly—mention no names," Guy Fawkes said quietly.

"Foul dishonouring hind!" the other cried, stamping his foot with deadly passion. "She has admitted you—but it shall be your DEATH. Oh, Claire, Claire. I who have loved so madly have gained only your coldest rebuke, and this accursed villain steals away your favor! It shall not be his boast; out sword! Draw and defend yourself, before I kill you without mercy."

"Aside," Guy exclaimed, taking no notice of the menacing blade; "I am in no mood for trifling."

"Mock me not, craven; thy foul looks bespeak thy cowardice."

"If there be a ministering demon on your side," Guy said bluntly, "let him warn you that in encountering me you meet your fate."

"Minister to this," was the hot reply; and a sudden blow brought the blood to Guy's cheek.

At the same time a lunge was made at his breast; but the blow had stung him into action, and his own tried steel crossed the shining blade.

The white face at the casement grew more rigid in its frozen look of horror. The sallow priestly visage wore a more sinister and subtle expression.

The two combatants seemed almost equally matched. Guy perhaps displayed superior strength, and was less impetuous than his opponent; whose passion did not, however, cause his evident skill in swordsmanship to fail him.

But Guy—cool, wary, and angered—met his attacks well, and all at once, by a swift stroke, hurled his weapon from his grasp.

"Go," he said, returning his sword to its sheath, "this is no time for words; escape with your life."

Either the taunt implied, or mortification at his defeat, blinded the unfortunate lover to the wild recklessness of his acts, for, leaping to the water's edge, he cried aloud—

"Help, help, help; a Papist, a Papist fleeing from Lady Claire's chamber! Stop his way; bring them to shame——"

"Hold!" Guy exclaimed, stepping quickly forward; "for that foul speech you die. Pick up your sword; I must be speedy in silencing thy dastard tongue."

Only a moment's renewed combat after their blades had again crossed. A swift lightning lunge, and Guy stood with extended right arm, the sword he held completely transfixing his enemy, whom it pierced from breast to breast.

Only a moment's awful pause; a ghastly, clammy face, gasping horribly in the soft starlight—a sword dropping from a quivering hand, and then a red blade plucked sharply forth—a choking groan, and the cloaked form fell heavily to the earth.

Only a moment's work, but it had been seen from the casement above. The priest, feeling himself clutched wildly by the arm, turned, but too late, to support the swooning form of Lady Claire.

"O God," came from her pallid lips, as she dropped to her knees, "it is done—it is *murder!*"

"A first sacrifice to try his faith," replied the priest; "may his arm be ever as true and firm. She is right—*that stroke was death.*"

Remorse for what he had done was now filling Guy's breast.

He knelt beside the stricken lover, and raised him to look on his face.

A handsome daring face it was—resolute and defiant even in its ghastly stare of death; noble, too; and Guy noticed that the rigid hands were white as a woman's.

"It is fate," he muttered, laying down the dead lover's hand.

Unconsciously wiping his sword on the fallen man's cloak, he marked it with a blood-stained cross.

The Jesuit, watching from above, clasped his hands in religious fervour when he marked the sign.

But now there came the cries of advancing men. The slain man's cry for help, then, was heard.

Guy sprang to his feet.

As he did so, a voice from above cried aloud, "To your boat; your pursuers are armed; haste for your life."

CHAPTER I

TAKEN.

IMMINENT as Guy's danger was, he was powerless to avail himself of the only chance afforded by the few moments' interval that must elapse before he was surrounded by those who came to take him.

The sight of his lifeless opponent, as he lay with his pallid face upturned to the starlit sky, held him spellbound; the encounter had been so sudden, its result so fatal, that it seemed more like murder than aught else.

He had taken life in the midst of the fierce conflict on the red field of battle, and in more than one deadly duel had left his opponent slain on the green sward.

But the taking of the young lover's life—slaying him because he fought for the honour of his mistress—appeared so cruelly merciless, now that the deed was done: and so he stood with his blood-stained blade idly, resting on the earth, his gaze riveted on the white face of his victim, his limbs refusing to fulfil their office in aiding him to fly from his pursuers; and he might have stood in that motionless posture until taken, had not Hugh Wardour, who had followed hard on his track, suddenly come to rouse him from his stupor.

"Quick, Guy, flee; I will guard your escape," he exclaimed, grasping him by the arm. Guy shook him off.

"Leave me, Hugh," he said, morosely, "my hands are steeped in blood. Leave me to my fate."

"Guy, Guy! does the sight of a slain foe unman you?"

"In such a case as this," Guy answered, bitterly. "He was her lover. I might have reasoned with his jealousy; but I slew him."

"This is no time for repentance. Escape—reflect hereafter."

"It is too late," Guy exclaimed, moodily, as he and Hugh were surrounded by a body of men, some of whom seized him, whilst others stooped down to raise the slain man.

"Here's foul work, men!" exclaimed one, angrily, gazing at Guy's blood-tipped sword-blade; "secure the cut-throat; put cold steel into him, if he tries to escape us."

"Guy," whispered Hugh, anxiously, "do not allow these hounds to take you. They may call this deed *murder*, and make you answer for it with your life."

Guy shivered.

"It rests on my soul like murder," he muttered. "I cannot steep this crime-stained blade in the blood of fresh victims."

As Guy spoke, a solemn chant was heard proceeding from the casement above. It was in Latin; but Guy understood this—that it bade him make good his flight. The chant concluded, and a solemn, sonorous voice said, warningly,—

"*Remember your oath!*"

Guy started; his iron frame shook in every limb, and he glanced terribly from face to face.

Those who held him heard his set teeth grind harshly, and felt him strain every limb; but they were not prepared for the sudden effort with which, all in a moment, he hurled them off and bounded towards the boat.

Standing with one foot on its plank, the other on the shore, Guy shook his sword menacingly—"I am not to be taken with life," he cried, springing into the boat.

The men made a rush towards him, but Hugh Wardour, with drawn sword, barred the way.

Half a dozen swords and staves instantly menaced him, and spite of his excellence in fence, it might have fared badly with him and Guy if unexpected succour had not come in the person of a gay, careless-looking young gallant, who, attracted by the chink of steel, hastened towards the scene.

Seeing how matters stood, he at once pushed his way to Hugh Wardour's side, to aid in covering Guy's retreat.

"What now, varlets!" he cried, drawing a ponderous sword, "cannot a gentleman pink his adversary in fair fight without being attacked by you for his pains? Stand off, or some of you will get a broken pate, and something in your carcases in the way of pointed steel."

"It is murder;" "We saw it done, and will charge him with the crime;" "Let him prove his innocence," were the cries that rose on all sides.

A dangerous look deepened on the new comer's features.

"Oh," he said, "you mean to take him,

GUY FAWKES; or, The Conspirator's Bride. No. 1. PRICE ONE PENNY. NOTICE.—Presented GRATIS with this Number of "GUY FAWKS,"

GUY FAWKES
OR
THE CONSPIRATOR'S BRIDE

GUY'S ESCAPE DEFENDED BY HUGH WARDOUR AND HIS NEW FRIEND.

do you? Well, you've a good stomach for cold steel. Come on, and I promise you your fill."

Using the flat of his sword only, he com- menced instantly laying about him with such goodwill that he, and Hugh, who had followed his excellent example, so belaboured the heads and arms of his would-be captors, that half of them hurriedly beat a retreat, while the rest tried all means of getting out of the reach of the swooping steel.

This timely aid afforded Guy the opportunity of leaping into his boat and pushing off from the shore, and he was already bending to the oars when Hugh Wardour and his new friend, having hotly chased the myrmidons of the law out of sight, returned to the river bank.

Seeing Guy safely making for the middle of the stream, the new comer sheathed his sword, and lightly laughing, said—

"By Jove, how the rascals ran! We peppered their backs, though, to a pretty tune, the rapscallions. Your friend is safe, sir; his captors, —ha, ha—are far off his track. Do then a stoup of wine with me."

Hugh returned his own sword to its scabbard, and he heartily accepted the invitation, saying, "With all my heart: but first accept my thanks for thy timely aid."

"Say nought upon it: your friend is safe; let us look at his handiwork. Jove, but he has done his work cleanly; that was a mortal thrust," he added, examining the direction taken by the blade in passing through the dead gallant's body. "One such stab, I take it, were enough to give any one his quietus."

He stooped down to look at the pale rigid face.

"Thunder of Jove," he cried, starting back aghast, "your friend has made a lucky flight! 'Tis the young Lord Melville he has slain: had he been taken, it had gone hard with him—a short shrift and a hasty passage to the next world. What caused the quarrel?—ah! you open casement! The Lady Claire. Poor bleeding wight, thy love was hot in its passion, but it has grown cold enough in thy lady's sight."

He linked his arms in Wardour's.

"Come. Let us leave him to the varlets who will presently be here: the dead can need no succour; he'll rest quietly enough. Come, we will fill the bowl, for to-morrow who knows what may be?"

Guy watched his friend Hugh and the young gallant sally forth arm-in-arm from the river side. He would have pulled ashore and joined them, but he knew the bloodhound-like tenacity of the men he had escaped from, and to be on the safe side in case they should be lying in wait for him. He thought it advisable to go a little farther down the stream before he landed, which he did. Keeping well in the middle of the running current, he laid to with good will, and the boat, creaking beneath each powerful stroke, skimmed like an arrow along the surface of the water.

Arriving at Bankside, he stopped the boat and looked round to see that there was no one of a suspicious character lurking about. Being perfectly satisfied with his scrutiny, he pulled ashore and landed.

While hauling the boat up, to prevent it from being carried away by the rising tide, in case he should want it again, he felt himself suddenly seized from behind.

Unexpected as was the attack, he did not lose presence of mind. In an instant the passion of his impulsive nature was raging in a fearful tumult. Springing erect, with his hand clasped on the hilt of his sword, he broke from the grasp of his captors, and turned upon them like a tiger, with a cold pitiless glitter flashing from his dark eyes.

A dozen ruffianly looking men stood around him, and Kit the Keeper was their leader, his ill-begotten features gleaming with a cynical triumphant smile.

"Guy," he said, tauntingly, "I told you I never broke my word. Kit the Keeper's so very fond of tripping papists!"

Guy made a spring of a panther at him, and his weapon, quivering like a blue serpent of fire, darted like lightning at the taunter's breast.

Kit the Keeper, in stepping back to avoid the thrust, fell over a piece of timber that lay behind him, and measured his length on the slimy earth.

The Spanish soldier threw all the power of his body into that terrific lunge, and his impetuous blade not being stopped by the body of his foe, it dragged him forward, and he fell across the prostrate man.

The caitiff gang lost not an instant of the advantageous time of their prisoner being down. They were upon him like a pack of wolves, and let fall their staves about him unmercifully, until every bone in his body must have ached acutely; and then he was dragged to his feet and his arms pinioned behind him.

"Fool! did you think to escape me?" said Kit, menacingly, the more vindictive because of his miserable plight. "I might have spared you a little but for thy daring to raise an arm to endanger me. Thy career will close on the rack!"

"Braggart! dolt!" exclaimed Guy, accompanying his words with a look of deadly hate; "my career has not yet commenced. Thou art to hear more of Guy Fawkes anon; and then look to it, for whenever again I get my hands upon thy throat I will not release thee till thy soul has reached the pit of hell!"

The man laughed to scorn the threat.

The hirelings formed a line on either side of their captive, and in that way Guy Fawkes was taken to prison.

That night, for the first time in his life, he was confined in a dungeon cell of the king's prison.

He did not fall into a paralysis of fear when the iron-plated door was closed upon him, shutting out both light and air from his most loathsome prison.

Not a moment he spared to dwell upon the dangers of his situation; his mind was occupied with other thoughts—thoughts dark and vengeful. A sombre cloud gathered over his handsome face as he pondered over the destiny allotted for his future by the oath he had taken over the relics of the saints.

————

CHAPTER V.

THE BULLY COUNT FINDS HIS MATCH.

HUGH WARDOUR and Captain Frank, his new acquaintance, having left Guy safe, as they thought, out of the reach of his foes, they sauntered towards Whitehall, and entered a fashionable gaming saloon, where prince and beggar, the gamester and the reckless gallant, were to be found assembled.

The gamesters were gathered in various groups round the tables, on which were scattered piles of gold and notes heedlessly, and taken from or added to, according as the players won or lost.

Two in particular attracted the attention of Hugh and his companion.

One was a man of about thirty years, tall and muscular, with shoulders broad, and limbs the size and strength of a lion. His face was well formed, dark, and not unhandsome; but there was a cunning cynical expression about his features that at once proclaimed him one of those men who prefer to live by their wits to that of work by honest labour.

The other was a young handsome fellow, with a fair face, much distorted with despair by his heavy losses.

At every throw he lost, and his companion, with greedy exultation, kept drawing the stakes to his side.

Seeing that the young nobleman held the dice in hesitation, he said,—

"Throw again, my lord; the game must change presently; 'tis strange that I should have such a run of luck to-night."

"'Tis no good, Count," said the young gallant, despairingly; "if I lose at this throw, I shan't have a penny left!"

"Never say die! Come, throw again; the game may change; it often does at the last throw."

Urged on by his opponent's words, and loth to leave the table while a coin remained, the young man threw again, as his last chance, and turned up two fives and a six.

The Count threw two sixes and a four.

"A tie!" he said; "you see, hope still remains."

"The youth, inspired by his last throw, rattled the dice, and threw fifteen in all. His companion threw seventeen, and won.

With a deep groan of sorrowful despair, the young noble sank back in his chair.

"Three thousand pounds I have lost," he murmured; "and now I am a penniless outcast."

The exultant gambler laughed harshly at his victim's weakness, and pocketed the winnings.

The ruined youth rose, and was staggering out of the saloon, when a gentleman laid his hand on his shoulder.

"Do you know with whom you have played and lost?" he asked, as the other looked up.

"A count, I believe," faintly answered the youth.

"True, the Bully Count, chief of the Bravoes," said the other; "he has long been suspected of cheating, but he is too dexterous to let any one detect him."

"'Twas he who first drew me into this den of vice, and by the rood, I will be avenged for the lesson taught."

He cast a look back at his opponent of deadly hate, and left the place.

Hugh and his friend had been close observers of the game, and spite the adroitness of the bravo's efforts to avoid detection, they discovered his villainy.

His dice were clogged.

Although many suspected that such was the case, not one ever attempted to charge him with the fraudulent trickery; but the suspicion was whispered from ear to ear, and those who heard it took good care not to play with him, and his only victims were the inexperienced youths who wished to see life and paid for it.

The Bully Count began to feel uneasy: he had several times encountered the steady gaze of Captain Frank fixed upon him with a look of meaning, more than he could interpret.

As Captain Frank went to the table where the bravo sat, and proposed a game, the bravo put the dice he had been playing with in his pocket, and drew out another set.

The Captain saw the act, though the Count had not intended it to be seen by anyone.

"I would fain try a throw with thee," said the young gallant.

"With all my heart; what shall be the stakes?" the Bully said.

"Oh, fifty aside."

The money was put down: the Count threw. Captain Frank followed his throw and won: at nearly every throw he won.

It could be plainly seen that the Bully Count was growing angry at his heavy losses: for it to continue thus would never do.

The game was going on with great spirit, and the novelty of the Count being beaten brought a group of idlers round the table.

"'Tis strange that your luck should have changed with me," the Captain said in a sarcastic strain; "but let not thy fickle fortune damp thy courage; you know, Count, the game must change again in thy favour."

There were many scowling faces besides the Count's turned towards the speaker; the victimized gambler took the observation as a taunt, and he did not misconstrue its purport.

He rattled the dice hastily, and in turning the cup he gave it a twist that hurled the ivories on the floor.

While stooping to pick them up, he changed them for those he had in his pocket.

"Then," he said, "let's double the stakes. By, thunder, if I don't win I shall lose!"

"That's a certainty," replied the young Captain with a quiet smile; "but the stakes will do very well as they are."

In a careless manner he threw the dice and turned up twelve.

The Count won by two, and put out his hand for the stakes; but Captain Frank covered the money and clutched the cheat's loaded dice.

The Bully sprang to his feet and drew his sword.

"Insolent!" he exclaimed, "what mean you?"

"Sit down and ye shall see," was the cool rejoinder; "I am going to show you a trick."

There was a commotion amongst the lookers on, and many hands went under the long cloaks of the wearers to grasp a dagger or sword-hilt.

The Count Chief cast a meaning look around, and the commotion ceased.

All waited wondering what the daring youth was going to do; and the detected impostor stood defiant and vindictive, his face distorted with baffled rage. Hugh Wardour was upon his feet watching the proceeding, and ready for any instant emergency.

"Gentlemen," proceeded Captain Frank, addressing the company; "I watched this man," alluding to the Bully, "while playing with a gentleman, now not present, and saw him win at every throw. I know it was by no fair play that he won successively. I challenged him myself; we played; he lost with me as he had won with his victim. When he threw the dice on the floor, it was for an opportunity to change them for these I now hold possession of, and believe to be clogged; and if I am wrong in my judgment I will stand the consequences, but if not, by thunder of Jove he shall!"

He laid the three dice in a row on the table. The Bully made a spring towards them, but his intent to regain possession of them was frustrated by Hugh, who stepped before him.

The bravo did not resist thus being baulked: perhaps it was the threatening looks of the company that held him quiet.

The Captain took his sword and struck each ivory a sharp cut that split them in twain.

"As I thought," he said, taking them up, "loaded with lead! What should be the penalty of the cheat?"

"Pink him—pitch him out of window—make him run the gauntlet."

Such were the suggestions that arose from all sides; but before any could be decided on the Bully sprang amongst the crowd, foaming with baffled rage, and singled out his exposer.

A dozen ill-looking ruffians, of whom the Bully Count was leader, went to their bravo chief's side, and the rest of the company opposed them, with Hugh.

A general encounter then ensued, but Captain Frank stuck to his foe, the Bully Count.

They were both masters of the sword, and fenced well. The bravo laughed scornfully at the daring youth.

"Insolent varlet!" he said; "I shall make short work of thee."

"Braggart dog!" exclaimed Captain Frank, his pride stung by the other's words; "thou liest, as thou shalt discover."

The bravo laughed again. He had more faith in his superior size and strength than he had in his opponent's matchless skill; and that, he thought, if he knew not how to use a weapon, would be sufficient to vanquish the slim youth who stood before him.

But he made an error, as he discovered the slim youth was a very stiff match for him: the rapid strokes dealt about him took him all his time to guard and parry.

He knew—or rather fancied—his antagonist could not keep on long at that play without his arm tiring; and he waited for an opportunity to deal the fearless young gallant his quietus.

He waited, and Captain Frank kept on at the same rapidity; his arm, though slight and delicate as a lady's, was as strong as iron, and marvellously flexible. Stroke after stroke he dealt, touching his opponent in twenty places, and drawing blood.

"'Sblood!" exclaimed the bravo fiercely, beating the Captain's weapon down, and making a lunge forward.

Frank stepped aside, and with an imperceptible move of his arm, his sword twined round the blade of his assailant's, a slight turn of his wrist, and the bully stood disarmed, his weapon flying to the other side of the saloon.

"By thunder!" said the victor, "I have a mind to make short work of thee, but I should be robbing some one else of the job!"

The beaten bully, with a cry of rage, darted towards his sword; but Hugh was there first, and put his foot across the blade.

"Foul hind, stand aside!" fiercely demanded the Count, grasping Hugh by the throat to move him.

Hugh, without making any resistance, hit him over the head with the pommel of his sword, and in another moment his feet were level with his head.

Just then a cry of triumph arose from the gentlemen—the last of the bravoes were down.

"Pitch the rapscallions out of window," cried one of the conquerors.

The suggestion was unanimously carried, and they commenced with the Bully Count, who was seized upon by as many hands as could conveniently get at him, and dragged to the window. He was stood outside, and told to jump.

But the force of that he did not believe in.

"By thunder of Jove, the varlet merits a pointed invitation to go!" said Captain Frank, drawing his sword and inserting about two inches in that part of the blackleg's person where the flesh was most prominent.

The bravo gave a sudden yell and sprang into the air; there arose a dismal groan as he landed heavily below.

Best part of the discomfited gang had crawled away to avoid a like exit, but those who did remain were assisted out at the ends of a score of keen-pointed swords.

Our two young friends then retired.

"By Jove, the fellow won't forget our meeting in a hurry!" said the reckless captain. "I wonder how he feels,—more uncomfortable about the latter end, I vouch!"

"I almost wish you had not interfered," said Hugh.

"Why?"

"Because he won't rest until he has had revenge for the exposure you brought on him. I have heard of him before. He is the chief of a band of ruffian desperadoes who would kill a fellow in wanton sport."

"Bah! man, think you I am craven enough to tremble at the sight of steel, or fly because I've made a foe? Nay, by St. Mary, I fear no living being!"

"I doubt not thy courage, but would fain warn thee of those Alsatian assassins; they are relentless brutes, and when once set on your track they won't leave it until you are stretched dead with a dagger quivering in your heart."

"Then, friend, they will follow for some time. I have no intention of falling by steel just yet, and when I do it won't be by the hand of an assassin, while I have a trusty blade at my side!"

"These Alsatians can use their weapons," Hugh went on, gloomily; "and another advantage they have over you is that they always strike unexpectedly and in the dark."

"Let them strike when, where, and how they will, I shall be prepared for them," answered the gallant captain; "but come, enough of this! it is not the strain suited to my present mood. I should be thinking of things more joyous, bright, and glorious."

Hugh gave him an enquiring look.

And his friend replied to it.

"I have an appointment to keep!" he said.

"With a lady?"

"Even so."

"Fair, is she?"

"As a lily!"

"Young, pretty, and so on?"

"Everything!"

"And loves you?"

"That I have to learn."

"Then I shall be in the way?"

"By my faith, I didn't say so; and you won't be in the way, because if I fail, you may please her."

"And that would make us rivals!"

"Not so. Hush!" Captain Frank clutched his companion by the sleeve, and both stood without breathing.

The stillness around was profound, and remained unbroken until Captain Frank spoke again.

"Did you not hear anything?" he inquired.

"No; did you?" his companion replied, in the same low tone.

"By St. Mary! yes. I could have sworn some one was following."

Hugh looked behind; the place was apparently deserted, save for themselves. Satisfied that they were not followed, the two friends proceeded, attributing the fancy of some one following them to the fault of a heated imagination.

They had not got far when an incident occurred that proved the Captain to be correct in his conjecture: some one was following them.

Frank stopped short in his walk, and held Hugh back, pointing to a shadow on the wall. The reflection of a man cast there by the faint glimmer of the moon, as it broke through a drifting cloud.

"I knew my suspicions were not ground-less," Captain Frank said; "but I wish the varlet had kept out of the way. I did not mean to visit the lady with my hands stained with a fellow-creature's blood; but what's to be done? For the safety of some poor devil on whom he may be tempted to try the temper of his steel, it will be a charity to stop him ere he does any harm."

"'Tis as I foretold thee—an Alsatian on thy track!"

"By thunder! if 'tis as thou sayest, I will set him an example for the rest;" saying which the daring young fellow bounded across the road, and pulled the crouching ruffian out of a recess in the wall, where he had concealed himself.

"Out with thee, devil's cub!" cried Captain Frank, seizing the bravo by the collar, and hoisting him into the road by a hearty kick. "What would thee have—a bellyful of steel? By the rood! it is at thy service! Draw and defend thy ugly carcase, or I give thee no quarter but of my sword."

The bravo saw how things stood.. There was no chance for him of escape without he could fight his way, and that was rather doubtful, as he only possessed a dagger, and his opponent had a sword.

A long gleaming blade flashed from under the bravo's cloak; an instant more his arm was raised menacingly; he sprang at his dauntless assailant, and dealt a rapid powerful blow for his head.

Captain Frank's danger was imminent, the onset had been so sudden. Quick as a lightning-flash his sword left its sheath, and flashed up and met the descending aim of the desperado. There was a hissing of a moment as the two came in collision, a cry from the victim, and a severed hand, clutching the dagger, fell at the combatants' feet.

Captain Frank recoiled with a feeling of sickening horror. The sight of the maimed ruffian, with his handless arm outstretched menacingly, the agonized look of terror that overspread his swarthy face, might have touched a heart of stone to pity.

The young gallant sheathed his sword: he felt remorseful for what he had done. He took his handkerchief from his pocket and approached to bind up the wound of the man who in cold blood would have taken his life, when the suffering wretch hurled a selection of the most forbidden epithets at him with fierce emphasis.

"Graceless dog! ungrateful hind!" exclaimed the youth in disgust, and turning upon his heels to rejoin his companion, he left the bravo roaring like a lion.

"I didn't intend serving the fellow like that," he said to Hugh Wardour.

"Repentance will not mend it," said Hugh; "he deserved his fate. Had I attacked him I should have slain him."

They drew up under a window—the window of a mansion.

"The above casement, with the light, is hers," Captain Frank said, pointing to a window through which straggled a faint orange gleam,

"I am somewhat behind my time : she may be angry with me. I will give her a serenade : you will be at hand, Hugh—the lady has a sire : he is gouty and awfully vicious, and has sworn to crack my pate if again he catches me wooing his daughter, so you may be wanted."

"I shall be ready if there is an occasion."

Captain Frank commenced a pretty ballad ; his voice was rich and clear as the note of a bird, and floated on the still night air in low sweet thrilling accents.

The casement opened, and a rope ladder was lowered by an unseen person, whom the lover supposed to be the lady he sought.

He tried by a mighty tug to ascertain its strength : it was firm, and he ascended to the lady's chamber with graceful agility.

He had hardly entered the room when Hugh was aroused from his hiding-place by the clash of steel, and the clamour of voices that proceeded from above.

"By St. Mary, if this is a specimen of the reception the fair maid gives her lover, my friend is welcome to her," laughed Hugh.

Captain Frank reappears at the window surrounded by a group of sturdy retainers, armed with huge staves, which they wield in a playful manner above their heads, and drop on the entrapped lover with the weight of both hands.

"Keep the varlets back," shouted Hugh ; and he began to ascend the rope ladder to rescue his friend.

Captain Frank, fighting like a Titan to keep his assailants at bay, got his back to the window.

The men press round him with determined resolution ; their intention is to hurl him out of window. The gallant intruder knew all this, and managed to keep them at the length of his sword.

One of the men, a big burly fellow, with a ponderous club, had beaten down the youth's sword, and stood with his formidable weapon raised threateningly above his intended victim ; but ere he can carry his intent into execution, his arm is stopped in its descent by the blade of a sword, that darts over Frank's shoulders and enters his wrist.

With a cry of agony the knave dropped his stave, and jumped back. Captain Frank followed up the retreat, and pricked his nearest opponent in the stomach as Hugh sprang into the room.

The man, giving vent to a dismal groan, doubled over like a reed, and clapped his hands over the perforated part to stop the effusion of —what ?—a mixture, perhaps, of all that he had eaten and drank that day, at least.

The fight was renewed vigorously. The men dashed upon the daring intruders impetuously, and drove them to the window.

Our young friends did not find their slight rapiers of much avail, as they had no intention of killing their antagonists. They acted merely on the defensive, and the sundry unmerciful hard blows that fell about them made them writhe again.

Hugh Wardour watched an opportunity to possess himself of one of his assailants' weapons.

An opportunity came in the person of the big burly retainer whom Hugh had wounded in the wrist. He grinned maliciously as he aimed a terrific blow at the youth's head.

Hugh stepped aside ; the stave reached the floor with a crash, and the man staggered over it.

Hugh pounced upon him on the instant, dealt him a sharp blow under the ear, wrested the club from his grasp, and gave him a tap on the head with it, by way of a gentle reminder not to interfere.

Hugh then went triumphantly amongst the others ; skulls rang at each blow, and many must have felt sorely the effects of the contest for days afterwards. He kept the retainers actively at work, and Captain Frank took the opportunity to escape.

He slid down the rope, and when safely landed called on his companion to follow his example. Hugh heard him, and wanted to do so ; but now he wished to end the fight, the retainers seemed more determined than ever to oppose him.

Their resistance raised his ire. He fought desperately, and reached the window. The fellows closed around him, and he kept them at bay, and getting one hand on the rope, he sprang out ; but before he reached half way down some spiteful brute cut the ladder, and the remainder of his descent he made very rapidly. At the same moment a petronel was fired at him.

But it missed, and the companions escaped.

"Is that the way the lady generally receives you?" inquired Hugh.

"'Tis no doings of hers," replied Captain Frank, ruefully. "I anticipated a revel of bliss in a dovecote, instead of which I fell into a den of tigers, and had to fight! By my faith! 'tis a sorry end to a love adventure ; but never mind, I shall be even with the old boy who put these cursed knaves in ambush to receive me."

The measured tramp of feet of many men was heard approaching.

Hugh and his companion drew aside as a body of soldiers came on.

Captain Frank and the commanding officer knew each other, and returned the military salute.

"Have you heard of the arrest, Captain?" asked the soldier.

"No. Who is it ?"

"Guy Fawkes."

"Guy Fawkes!" iterated Hugh Wardour, starting with astonishment.

"You knew him, then ?" the soldier said.

"Yes, yes ; he was my comrade in many a long campaign. For what was he arrested ?"

"The murder of Lord Melville and suspected conspiracy."

"'Tis a lie !" cried Hugh, hastily. "Lord Melville fell in a fair duel, and I can vouch the loyalty of my friend to his king."

"Likely ; but that has nothing to do with me. Gentlemen, good night."

He raised his hat, the soldiers went on, and Hugh, linking his arm through the Captain's, said—

"Guy must be saved; he is my friend."

"Thunder of Jove!" cried Captain Frank, "your friend taken! then I vote we get him out."

"It must be done; but we want the means."

"I have it! We will disguise ourselves. I can get an order of admission to the king's prison."

"Many get in without an order," put in Hugh.

"And would give one to get out again; but this is no time for jesting—our business is more serious."

"This is unfortunate, indeed; I thought we left him safe out of reach."

"So we did; but I suppose he was waited for when he landed."

"We must not lose more time in talk; my friend's life is at stake."

"It may be," put in Frank.

"At the peril of our lives he must be saved."

"That is my intention. When once we get inside the prison, we will not leave it without Guy Fawkes."

Resolved on the rescue of their friend, the daring youths lost no time in preparing for their dangerous undertaking.

CHAPTER VI.

LORD CECIL TRIES TO LEARN THE PRISONER'S SECRET.

ONE night Guy had passed in captivity, and the morning dawned in rich majestic beauty, but the prisoner saw none of it; he remained in the oblivion of obscurity—day and night were the same to him.

Every hour of his confinement dragged on like a dreary month. He had not yet closed his eyes—he could not; his mind was troubled with sleepless dreams—dreams that rose vividly before him of his future career in all its wild daring.

How much longer would they keep him there? he thought, rising from his hard rude seat, and pacing his cell.

The grating of the lock being turned from the outside caused him to pause. He stood erect, with his gaze fixed on the door, as it slowly opened, and revealed two persons standing on the threshold.

One was the gaoler, the other a gentleman, by his rich dress and courtly bearing, verging close on to his thirtieth birthday; his complexion was fair, eyes blue and restless—they could not look a person in the face long before their gaze dropped; his nose was well formed, and his mouth might have been faultless but for a cynical expression playing about the lips.

Dismissing the gaoler, he entered the cell.

Guy Fawkes received him coldly, and in a haughty tone, said—

"I did not send for you, Lord Cecil."

"I know you did not, but I thought you would like to see me; besides, I have something to say!"

"Of aught that concerns me?"

"Yourself and others. You were arrested last night for the murder of young Lord Melville. Was it not so?"

"'Tis a lie!" cried Guy, angrily, "and those who say I killed Lord Melville in any way but fair fight shall recall their words or answer me with the sword."

"When you are free," said his visitor, sneeringly.

"The time is not far distant when that will be: and when once I am at liberty let those look to it who have used my name with calumny."

"You forget where you are," said Lord Cecil.

"No, I do not. These walls will not keep me from liberty."

Guy had a peculiar sort of faith which he strongly believed in when once an idea entered his head. He had made up his mind that he would escape, but how he knew not; he had no intention of trying to escape without an opportunity offered itself advantageously. He did not anticipate that Hugh Wardour would risk the peril of an attempt to liberate him, and in what way it was likely for his flight to take place he had no idea; but still he had hope.

Lord Cecil laughed incredulously at the prisoner's idea of liberty.

"If you can vindicate the validity of the charge of murder with which thou art accused, do so—give me a reason why you killed Lord Melville."

"Why should I plead to you?"

"Because I alone have the power to save you! Oppose me, and thou shalt be consigned to the tortures that await thee."

"A threat!" said Guy.

"Ay! a most terrible one. Make a friend or foe of me as thou wilt."

"One is just as much value as the other, my lord; and either way it would be a sorry bargain for any poor devil."

Lord Cecil bit his lip to keep down his rising anger; he had a purpose in visiting the prisoner, and he thought by perseverance he would gain his point.

But he was mistaken. Guy was a keen judge of faces, and he read his visitor's purpose as plainly as though it had been written on paper.

"Guy Fawkes," said Lord Cecil, looking the dauntless fellow full in the face, "your liberation depends upon the answers you give to the questions I ask thee."

"If that's the case," replied Guy, calmly, "I shall remain where I am—at least," he added, "if my liberation depends upon thy intercession."

"Then you defy me?" exclaimed Cecil, his rage bursting forth in a fearful strain.

"No, I merely refuse to answer questions."

"You have some cause?"

"Very likely."

"You are concerned in a dark hellish plot

of conspiracy," Lord Cecil went on, with increasing rage : " but it will be baulked. Thou wilt be set up as an example on the rack—the rack, ha ! ha !—that torturing instrument that will unbind the firmest oath and wring the secret from thy very soul."

Guy shuddered, and his cheeks blanched with terror. Whether it was the accusation of being concerned in a conspiracy, or the idea of being condemned to the rack, that caused this change to come over him, we shall see as we progress.

"Ha ! ha ! you quail ! You see I know more than you thought," continued the fiery Cecil.

"You know naught that I fear," defiantly replied Guy.

"Thou liest, braggart !" thundered Lord Cecil, chafed to madness by the taunting coolness of the prisoner. "I see terror stamped upon thy devil's mug. Think you I knew not thy movements—thy secret visit to the Jesuits at midnight, the ascent to the window, and the assassination of Lord Melville, the witness—is there nothing in this ?"

"Nothing that I care about ! "

"Dauntless devil, brave me as thou wilt, the rack shall draw the secret from you to-morrow, and then the stake at Smithfield."

Shaking his fist menacingly at the prisoner, he gave him a look of deadly hate and revenge, and left the cell in a terrible rage, fully bent upon the destruction of Guy Fawkes.

The gaolor closed the door when the visitor retired, and Guy instantly fell into a gloomy reverie.

Although he had audaciously braved Lord Cecil, he was well aware of the power he possessed : he was the king's chosen friend, and his word would condemn a man to the stake or liberate him as he wished.

Guy began to reflect that he had gone a little too far, and unless some good genius aided his escape that night, his death would be inevitable on the morrow : for he knew the nature of the man he had angered.

CHAPTER VII.

TRAPPED.

DAY was drawing to its close, and evening began to throw its shadow over the earth, when two persons might have been seen hurrying along, as if to escape being benighted. Their dress marked a distinction between them. One was attired as a state messenger ; the other a prison official ; and yet they talked familiarly together, as though on equal footing with each other.

Arriving at the King's prison, the state messenger produced a pass, when inquired by the gaoler the nature of his visit.

"You wish to see the prisoner privately ?" the man queried, reading the information on the scrap the messenger had handed him : "follow me, please : I'll tell Jackson to come."

The man conducted them to a reception-room : it might have been taken for a large stone cell, but for the few articles of uncouth furniture with which it was adorned, and the large cheerful fire of wood that burned in a huge aperture in the wall.

This was Jackson's abode ; and the pretty dark-eyed damsel, who rose blushingly as the two young men were ushered into her presence, was Jackson's daughter. The state messenger was a very handsome gallant-looking fellow, and she evidently thought so by the sly look she gave him askance.

"Are you Master Jackson's daughter, my pretty maid ?" asked the state messenger. The girl answered in the affirmative by a curtsey.

"Come, give me a kiss," the young man said, gliding his arms round her waist and drawing her voluptuous face to him.

A slight struggle ensued ; but he stole a kiss, and she returned it by smacking his face soundly, and was running away when the messenger's companion caught her in his arms and helped himself from her pouting cherry lips without permission. The girl's paternal relative entered just as she was released, and his brows gathered angrily, noticing the girl's confusion.

"You have an order for the cross-examination of the prisoner Guy Fawkes ?" he said to the state messenger, looking at him officiously.

"'Tis here," said the young man, giving Jackson the document.

An uneasy expression came over the messenger's countenance, while the gaoler was studiously examining every line of the scroll. Having read the words over several times with anxious interest, Jackson carefully scrutinized the impressions of the seal. He raised his head and fixed a steady searching glance on the young man's face.

His look was met and returned with as steady and searching a one as he gave.

"And this is your witness ?" said Jackson, alluding to the prison servant who accompanied the young messenger.

"He is, good master Jackson, and if thou art satisfied, I shall be nothing loth to see the prisoner, and make a speedy exit from this gloomy tomb."

The gaoler took them to the prisoner's cell, looked from one to the other, but there seemed nothing to strengthen the suspicion he had of the visitors ; yet when he left them there was a cunning leer on his face, and rubbing his hands together, he chuckled triumphantly.

Guy received his visitors moodily, and the three stood for some time in silence.

"Guy !" said the supposed prison official.

The prisoner was roused into animation, and he looked at the speaker searchingly, but he did not recognize any friendly countenance, though the man's expression was full of sympathy ; and his gaze dropped to the ground in disappointment.

"Guy !" repeated the man, " know you not thy comrade Hugh Wardour."

"Hugh !" exclaimed the captive, jumping up, and grasping the young man's hand.

"Hush ! I have not much faith in the varlet gaoler ; he is suspicious : and if we give him the least cause for his suspicion, the game will be all up."

GUY FAWKES
OR
THE CONSPIRATOR'S BRIDE

THEY STOOD UNSEEN BEHIND THE MASSIVE PILLARS.

"But why in this disguise?" inquired Guy.

"We shouldn't have got admittance in any other," said Hugh. "You quite understand?"

"No, I don't."

"Well; Captain Frank being state messenger, comes to learn your secret privately. I accompany him to bear witness to what I say, and prevent you from doing any mischief."

"I am sure, for such kindness, I am deeply indebted," Guy said. "I have had another visitor who seemed to take a great interest in my position ; a very dear *friend* of mine, Lord Cecil. You know him, Hugh."

"He here !" exclaimed the youth, in surprise.

"Yes ; and if I don't get out of here to-night, he has very kindly promised me the rack to-morrow."

"Thunder of Jove ! Friend !" exclaimed Captain Frank. "By St. Mary and the memory of my great grandfather, we won't give his lordship the trouble to make an exhibition of a fellow. I object, too. Come, Guy, let us change dress, and I will take your place for a time."

Guy Fawkes looked at the reckless speaker in blank astonishment : the proposition was put so cool and earnest. But it left no doubt as to the proper meaning of his words.

"What !" said Guy ; "flee like a coward knave, and leave you to suffer for me ? No !"

"No no," put in Hugh. "Guy will change dresses with me—the exchange won't be a very profitable one."

"No," said Guy, "it won't for you."

"I shall have the best suit, and you will escape."

"Not without you, I don't," replied Guy, determinedly.

"No, decidedly not," Captain Frank remarked generously. "It wouldn't be the thing to part you. If ye will let me have my way, things will be all right : you are boon companions, and neither would be comfortable while the other was in danger. So let me mount sentry here, and you two go hence in peace."

"Nay, nay," objected Guy ; "I cannot go and leave you in danger."

"By thunder ! Now, why the devil don't you let a fellow have his own way !"

"No, no, my dear captain," Hugh Wardour said ; "it is not to be supposed that we should leave you here."

"Why not me ? One of us must remain ; and ye being old comrades, I don't see why I shouldn't give you an opportunity to get away together."

"And leave you here to brave the danger which is mine ?"

"Something must be done, and quickly," Captain Frank said, appealingly. "My friends, if we lose much more time I'm thinking we shall not have the opportunity of getting away."

"By my faith," put in Hugh, "thou hast spoken the truth. So come, Guy, let me take thy place for a time. I warrant they won't keep me when they find you have taken wing."

"Friends," Guy said, determinedly, "'tis no use to argue longer. Neither of you I intend to take my place."

"Know ye the danger you incur by your obstinacy ?" Hugh said, in an angry tone.

"To-morrow your life is threatened with the rack, and yet you resist a kindly offer to escape. Guy, remember your *visit* to the Lady Claire's."

The prisoner's cheeks paled, and his eyes wandered from his friends to the door, and he hesitated.

"Yes, I remember," he said. "I shall yet escape without endangering either of you."

"Thou knowest well the nature of the man thou hast offended : an unrelenting demon, who would glory in your destruction. Remember, comrade, thou hast a greater cause to wish for life."

A momentary shudder shook the soldier.

"Hugh," he said, in a pained voice, "thou hast placed me in a difficulty by thy words : your own destruction alone can save me from "——

"And only too gladly I accept thy fate to save thee."

"Think ye I will see two faithful comrades murdered, while I can prevent it ? Gentlemen, resistance is useless," said Captain Frank. "I mean to take the part of prisoner, and you, Guy, will be state messenger."

"No ; I cannot allow that," said Hugh. "Comrades ought to share each other's danger."

"Well, am not I a comrade ?" Captain Frank said, assuming a hurtful tone. "And havn't I as much right to share his danger as thou hast ? Well, look here ; I'll toss you for it."

"Gentlemen," began Guy, in objection, when a sharp, gruff voice from without interrupted him.

"You need not wrangle any longer. I'll settle the matter for ye."

The words fell ominously on the ears of the conversants ; and, turning round with a look of startled surprise on their faces, they confronted Jackson.

"Marry, gentlemen," he said, chucklingly, "the place is so inducing that ye are all loth to leave it. Well, well. I'll settle the matter for you, by keeping ye all."

The three friends looked at each other in blank despair, and their faces lengthened visibly.

"It would be a pity to part such loving friends," said the gaoler, sarcastically. "Ye shall keep each other company."

He clapped his hands together, and four of his companions entered.

Jackson pointed to the disguised gallants.

"Prisoners in disguise," he said. "Let's see what they are made of under their kirtles.",

The gaolers fell upon the astonished captives, and unceremoniously tore off their disguise.

"A state messenger and prison officer," said Jackson. "Capital company for one another. I hope ye will rest comfortably. Good night."

And, going out, he fastened the iron door upon the three friends.

CHAPTER VIII.

THE COMPACT.

LORD CECIL was not so much affected by the death of Lord Melville as one would have imagined by his apparent interest, which he assumed while with Guy Fawkes. His only cause for seizing the prisoner was to learn if the young nobleman had fallen in a love quarrel, for he fancied that Guy was in love with the beautiful Lady Claire of Grace.

Not that he had any intentions of revenging his death, on the contrary, he was delighted that he had been removed so effectually from his path, for he loved the lady with a strong secret passion; and, should Guy prove another rival, it was in his power to keep him quietly out of the way.

Brooding over these selfish reflections, he made his way to the Jesuit's house, and sought an interview with the Lady Claire.

The Lady Claire of Grace received him with marked coolness. She felt a natural repugnance for the man, who tried to be particularly amiable to her; and Lord Cecil shifted about on his chair uneasily whenever he encountered her gaze fixed searchingly upon him.

On the evening in question he tried to be more gallant than ever, and the lady tried to avoid him as much as possible.

Lord Cecil observed this with a feeling of anger.

"I shall yet bring you at my feet, my proud beauty, in submission," he muttered, his evil eyes following her magnificent form, as she crossed the chamber and went to the window to escape him.

But he was not to be done. He had gone there with a purpose, which the lady partly guessed; and, in spite of everything, he was determined that his premeditated plan should not fail. Rising from his seat, he went to the window, and made a few casual remarks about the beauty of the night.

The cold, disinterested remarks he received piqued him.

"You are not well, dear lady?" he said, winningly.

"Don't you think so, my lord?" replied Lady Claire, quietly.

"My lord—the deuce!" exclaimed Cecil, pettishly. "Abolish that formality. We have known each other long enough now to drop that courtly etiquette. Call me Edward."

"But, my"——

"Edward," put in Cecil, quickly.

The lady's face flushed, and Lord Edward bit his lip on seeing the change.

"I have angered thee," he said, pleadingly, "by my familiarity. I have thy pardon for my boldness?"

Claire of Grace turned to leave him, but his arm he held behind her twined round her waist, and he drew her towards him passionately.

The lady turned haughtily upon him.

"Shun me as thou wilt, dear Grace!" he exclaimed, in a tremulous voice; "banish me—spurn me! but thou must—thou shalt hear my love. Lady Claire, dearest lady!" he went on excitedly, falling on his knees, and clasping her hands. "I adore thee to madness! Long have I kept my love a secret—a torturing fire kept down within my breast, growing fiercer every day, not daring to breathe my passion, for I saw that thy heart was given to another; but now these fetters are sundered, and death parts ye, I hoped—I do hope, that thou wouldst listen to my adoration!"

"My lord," said the astonished girl, trying to release her hand, "this is dishonourable, ungentlemanly, cowardly! Release me instantly, I command thee, or I will call assistance, and have you thrust from this house disgraced."

"Listen, dearest," persisted Cecil, clasping her hands still firmer, and now and then pressing it to his hot lips. "Listen to me, I beseech thee, in the name of the Virgin! Give me but a look of kindness—say that thou dost not hate me, to save me from distraction, from madness—from destruction! Oh! dearest Lady Claire! my idol worship! if you but knew the sincerity of my love, thou wouldst not torture me by this cruel indifference. What have I done to merit this unkindness?"

"Lord Cecil"——

"No—no! not that name!"

"Leave me, then. If you would have me look upon you with aught but of abhorrence, persecute me no further."

"No, no, I cannot leave thee until thou hast told me that you love not another."

"Lord Cecil!" exclaimed Lady Claire, breaking from him.

The courtier sprang to his feet, and advanced towards her, but the haughty look that met him restrained him from taking another step forward, and he fell back abashed.

"Oh, lady!" he exclaimed, distressingly, "if I have dared too much, forgive me! Distraction has driven me beyond prudence, and I must throw myself upon thy gentle mercy. Judge me as thou wilt—condemn me to any punishment, but do not banish me for ever from thee!"

"Lord Cecil, this is getting unbearable," Lady Claire of Grace said, haughtily, her face flushing indignantly. "If thou wouldst be forgiven, leave me instantly, or I will call assistance to have you thrust forth."

The lady's words stung him to the quick, and re-called him to his senses. The change in his demeanour was wonderful, and he confronted the poor girl almost fiercely.

He had acted the part of the despairing lover with all the effects of a dramatist, but neither his touching voice nor distressing looks brought pity from the gentle girl. She knew too well his nature, and the worth of his protestations.

Finding that his device failed to move the Lady Claire, he would try what harsher means would do to make her submit. Her words had given him cause for anger and he grasped at the chance with rage, his breast heaving with an unholy passion to get her in his power.

"Scoff—scorn me as thou wilt for my weakness!" he said, beginning quietly; "but by the saints, thou shalt be mine! You have no lover now to defend you. Guy Fawkes has been arrested for the murder of Lord Melville."

"Will he keep the secret?" involuntarily asked the fair lady.

"What secret?" inquired Cecil, quickly.

Lady Claire of Grace looked confused. The words were spoken unintentionally, and what sacrifice would she have made to recal them. But it was too late now. They had hardly left her mouth, when he eagerly caught at them, and looked at her suspiciously.

"What secret did you allude to?" he asked, cunningly.

"Oh, nothing," said Grace, her cheeks changing the colour of alabaster.

"Nothing!" iterated Cecil. "Lady Claire, thou hast made a step too far. I am now quite convinced that you, as well as he, are concerned in some diabolical plotting. 'Tis no good of thee to try and dissuade me differently."

The poor girl had certainly placed herself in a dangerous position with the crafty man by that innocent slip of the tongue. She strove hard to keep a bold countenance, and looked her accuser haughtily in the face.

Lord Cecil could not stand her fascinating gaze, and his eyes dropped to the floor.

"Think what you will," said Lady Claire; "but be careful what you say, for even you, Lord Cecil, might say too much, and get into trouble."

"You threaten me?" he said.

"Against perjury I do."

"Who caused the death of Lord Melville?" Cecil said.

"He caused his own death."

"No, no, Lady Claire; he knew too much for the safety of you and thy lover, so he was silenced; but to-morrow the murderer, Guy, will be put on the rack, and the secret torn from him."

"No, no! not that fearful torture!" cried Lady Claire, pleadingly. "Spare him that, Lord Cecil!"

"So, so that moves you. Well," said Cecil, triumphantly, "there is one condition on which he may be saved."

"Name it, and if it is ought that lies in my power, he shall be saved."

"You must consent to be mine," was the next proposition.

Lady Claire covered her face in distressed agony.

"Say the word," he said.

"Oh how heartless thou art!" murmured Claire. "Is there no other condition on which his life can be spared?"

"None."

"You must give me time to consider."

"I should think it did not require much consideration. If you don't give me an answer now, to-morrow morning your lover suffers."

"I cannot! Oh, I really cannot! Oh, how cruel you are!"

Cruel and unrelenting as he was, he loved the lovely Lady Claire of Grace tenderly, and it was impossible for him to stand unmoved by her sorrow. Her sweet, sad, pleading voice melted his resolution, and he said, in a husky voice—

"Promise to see me at this same hour to-morrow night, and I will promise you in return that he shall live until that time. If then you have not made up you mind to consent, he must die."

Lady Claire promised the interview, and he departed to visit the Bravo Chief to arrange some infernal plot, and leave Guy to the fate he had doomed him.

CHAPTER IX.

HOW AN ABDUCTION WAS PLANNED, AND WHAT AN INFORMANT GOT FROM THE PRISONERS FOR HIS INFORMATION.

WHITEFRIARS, in the time of this story, was a place of vile resort for a gang of lawless ruffians, blood-thirsty men, whose long, thin pointed daggers were ever ready to take the life of a fallen being, if there was a chance of being repaid for their trouble.

To this vicinity of notoriety Lord Cecil, disguised in a long, slouching cloak, wended his way after leaving his anticipated victim.

On entering a lone, dilapidated inn of evil repute, he was encountered by the savage glaring of a dozen errant caitiffs, who were lounging about the dirty bar, imbibing bad beer and calling one another anything but gentlemen.

Their noise ceased when the stranger entered, and sundry meaning glances were exchanged amongst them. Daggers were seen to leave their sheaths, shaggy beards were stroked meditatively, and little fierce eyes scowled threateningly upon the intruder from under a bush of thick eyebrows and a protruding forehead.

In a disconcerted manner Lord Cecil approached one of the biggest.

"Count Basco—is he here?" he asked.

"Who are you?" inquired the desperado, scowlingly.

"That's nothing to you I want your master—is he here?"

The ruffian scanned him savagely from top to toe, and then glanced at his companions inquiringly, as though to ask if he was to comply with the stranger's command. He received nods and winks approvingly, and then, giving his interlocutor another uncomfortable look, he said, in as polite a voice as before—

"No, he ain't."

"Do you know where to find him?"

SECOND SHEET OF CHARACTERS and SCENE I. GRATIS with No. 3 of the NEW STORY, "GUY FAWKES; or, THE CONSPIRATOR'S BRIDE."

"Yes."

"Then perhaps you will conduct me to his presence?"

The bravo obeyed doggedly. The stranger's tone of voice was commanding, and the fellow felt bound to submit, much against his inclination.

The Bully Count was found in his den—a house by the water-side, of a mysterious character, with many mysterious ways of ingress and egress.

Lord Cecil wondered when his guide was going to bring him to the end of the dark, winding staircase, and along dark passages, through which they traversed and were challenged at every fresh entrance by a dark form, who mounted guard.

At last, the chamber of the Bravo Count was reached, and the guide dismissed.

The Bully looked none the better for his late encounter with Captain Frank.

He raised himself on his elbow from the couch on which he reclined as the stranger entered.

"You appreciate luxury, Basco," said Cecil, sneeringly.

The Bravo grinned spitefully when he thought with humiliation of the cause of his indulgence.

"Basco, thou dost seem in a good humour," remarked the courtier, in the same taunting tone.

"'Sblood!" hissed the bravo, grinding his teeth viciously, and darting a glance at his visitor of wild anger, "if thou hast anything to say, say it, or stop thy banter, or thou wilt soon discover the nature of my humour."

Cecil looked at the speaker studiously.

"Know ye to whom you speak?" he said, in a lofty tone.

"'Sblood!" exclaimed Basco, jumping up. "I speak to Lord Cecil, if I mistake not. And think you, like a mongrel cur, I will be snarled at because thy infernal gold buys I and mine like slaves to do thy hellish work, from which thou shrinkest away. No; if you want me, be civil, or you may find it difficult to get out of here again."

Cecil looked rather surprised. He did not expect a rebuke so sharp. He might have resented the words harshly, but the fellow's services were indispensable, so he was bound to hold himself in bounds to come to an agreeable arrangement.

"I must pardon you for this outrageous speech," said Cecil, forcing a laugh to hide his annoyance. "I suppose thou hast been angered, and I was the first on whom you have had an opportunity to vent thy spleen?"

Basco's lip curled contemptuously at his employer's want of spirit to turn an insult off like that.

"You have something for me to do?" he said.

"I have. Art thou willing to do it?"

"It depends upon the nature of the undertaking."

"'Tis this, then: I may rely upon thee for secrecy?"

"You may."

"I don't want it known to any of thy companions."

"Your secret will be as safe with me as with the dead. Shall I swear it?"

"No, I will take thy word. To-morrow, at midnight, I shall want you to be ready with a boat, to convey myself and a lady from Southwark to Richmond; but, in the interim, I shall want you to go to the king's prison and taunt Guy Fawkes with the tidings of his mistress's elopement with a cavalier. Dost thou understand?"

"Perfectly; but how am I to get admission to the interior of the prison?"

"I will supply thee with a pass. You must then come to me and let me know how he takes the news?"

"It shall be done."

"Thyself, alone, must be the one; no other ear must hear a word. Can I trust you?"

"If thou thinkest I am not capable of doing it, get someone else."

"Methinks, Basco, thou art getting very arrogant."

"Think what thou wilt. If I don't suit thy purpose, get someone who will."

"I think we suit each other," and, throwing a purse of gold on the table, Lord Cecil rose to depart. "I shall expect to see you at noon to-morrow?"

"I shall be there."

Basco threw himself down on the couch again, when his visitor had gone, and was soon in a sound sleep.

*   *   *   *   *

The three prisoners of the king's prison did not feel the gloomy monotony of their situation they otherwise would have done had they been separated.

In the morning, when they awoke, after a night of restless sleep, they exchanged a mutual greeting, and Captain Frank broke the dead silence with his lively voice.

"We are in for a nice thing, ain't we?" he said; "this is all through Guy, this is. I say, comrades, I wonder how much of this they give a fellow to drive him mad? Have ye any appetite for a feast? I have. I wonder what they'll bring us for breakfast?"

"Cold water and bread," said Guy; "all mine's here."

"Keep it, then, and we'll shy it at the fellow's thick head for daring to bring such rations to gentlemen. Here he comes; be prepared for the charge."

Before they could prepare for the intended attack, the prison door was swung open, and Jackson and the Bully Count stood before the captives.

Captain Frank fell backwards, dumbfounded, to see his old enemy standing triumphantly before him, and Hugh and Guy looked on in speechless surprise.

"Well, arrant knave," exclaimed the

young captive, recovering his perpendicular, "for what cause may we flatter ourselves for this gracious visit ?"

"I have brought news for Guy Fawkes," replied the Bravo Chief. "Gaoler, you may go."

The gaoler went with a cunning leer, he mentally calculated upon having trapped another captive.

"Well," said Guy, "what news hast thou for me?"

"That, if I mistake not, which is welcome news to a lover." The chief of the bravoes smiled maliciously.

"Give us thy news quickly and quit," Captain Frank said, getting behind his comrades to prevent an involuntary attack upon the ruffian.

"I thought I would let you know how *devoted* she has been to you," said Basco, sarcastically.

"Come to the point, that's the thing," Guy said, unmoved, for he could plainly see, by the manner of the Bravo, his purpose in coming.

"At midnight a cavalier ascends to the lady's chamber," he said, gleefully, "a boat will be in waiting to bear them hence— Lord Cecil and Lady Claire."

"I will be there to see it," Guy answered, quietly.

"So will I," said Captain Frank.

"And I too," put in Hugh Wardour.

"Braggarts! Why, to-morrow you will all be stretched," said the Bully, disappointed with the coolness with which his information was received.

Captain Frank could no longer master his feelings.

"Lying hound!" he yelled, and sprang upon the big Bully.

Count Basco's arm was raised as his assailant came upon him, and a long dagger gleamed in his hand.

Guy, seeing the danger of his friend, dashed upon the Alsatian, to wrest the dagger from his grasp, but Hugh was before him, and his clenched hand fell, with a dead, heavy weight, on the ruffian's arm, and the weapon went spinning across the cell.

A general rush was made to regain it, but Fawkes was first this time, and he concealed the dangerous weapon in his breast. He had a use for it.

Captain Frank clung to his opponent like a cat. They struggled, swayed to and fro, and fell; and then they renewed the contest with terrible fury, their limbs locked together like snakes, and each endeavouring to destroy the other. It is doubtful whether either would have ever again risen, had not Guy parted them.

The instant the Bravo felt himself released, he sprang to his feet and made for the door; but ere he had hardly regained his footing, Captain Frank had secured him by the collar, and, with a mighty push and a helping kick, sent him flying on his face across the prison yard.

Frank was returning to his companions, flushed with victory and exertion, when a heavy hand grasped him by the shoulder, and held him in a grip of iron.

Frank turned to see who his captor was, and encountered the grinning face of the gaoler, Jackson. Without a word, he took a pair of handcuffs from a capacious pocket, and, to the astonishment of the youth, slipped them round his wrists in a moment.

"There," he said, with a satisfactory grunt, "you can remain quiet till you are wanted."

Again the captives were shut up in the dungeon, without hope of escape.

CHAPTER X.

THE FACE AT THE HOLE IN THE WALL.

HUGH WARDOUR sunk into a reverie of gloomy misgivings that made him feel wretched. He might have borne his confinement more cheerily had it not been in such impenetrable obscurity ; but to have the blessing of light, that is sent for all to share alike, shut from him, was more than he could bear without a sigh of despair.

Captain Frank, too, remained in silence ; his astonishment at being secured so suddenly put a veto on his hilarity, but not for long. He startled his companions by suddenly exclaiming :

"Diavolo! What need had the varlet for securing my hands? Faith, I would it had rather been my mouth."

"Marry, comrade! methinks 'tis better as it is," said Guy. "I can liberate thy hands of the fetters, but thy mouth I should not care to say as much for."

"Comrade, I doubt not thy promise, but I should not like to vouch the truth of thy assertion without thou givest strong proofs."

"I picked up the dagger our late visitor dropped."

"But that is not a key to my fetters."

"It will make a good substitute, though."

"I don't see it."

"I don't suppose you do ; 'tis too dark."

"What, the force of thy argument?"

"To you, perhaps. Give me thine hands, and my promise I will show. You can then vouch what thou wilt."

Frank put his hands forward submissively. Fawkes felt for the lock, and inserted the point of the dagger. There was a click, and the fetters sprang open.

Captain Frank was again free, and he heartily thanked his liberator.

"I have an idea of escape," said Guy.

"I wish I had," put in Hugh, gloomily.

"Cheer up, comrade, we shall yet escape."

"I wish we could. I've had enough of this."

"I have surmounted one difficulty," the Spanish soldier said ; "and the same means may lead to our liberation."

"I don't care how soon then it leads me out of here," said Hugh.

"Patience and perseverance, comrade, are the greatest powers in existence."

"Very good things for the saints to be blessed with, but they don't do for a fellow standing on the brink of eternity."

"You have no faith, Hugh."

"By my faith, I don't want any, if this is its reward," said Guy.

"I have a dagger."

"I haven't; but what's the use of that?"

"To excavate a way out of here."

"I should like to see it done."

Guy Fawkes began to do it. The mortar was soft, and seemed to promise a favourable progress, by the way it fell from the crevice round a large stone.

"Silence, Guy, the gaoler comes," said Captain Frank, who had mounted guard at the door. "Can't you stop that rattling? it will attract the fellow. Put your coat underneath, for the mortar to drop on."

Guy did so, and recommenced to dig away with increasing hope. He had already excavated a hollow round the stone, of two inches deep.

The gaoler's tramp was heard to pass the door; then Guy went on again with his work, with less caution, and made more noise as he got deeper, for the cement got harder, being drier than the outside coating.

Chip, chip, chip—scrape, scrape, scrape, became louder; and every now and then the dagger would miss its mark and scrape down the edge of the stone, sending a ringing echo through the cell.

Again Guy was arrested in his work by the voice of the sentinel, who had caught the creaking sound of the gaoler creeping back to the door of their prison. He stopped outside.

Frank was looking through the keyhole, and saw him stoop down, and place his ear at the little crevice.

Within and without silence alike prevailed. Not a voice disturbed the stillness.

Guy waited anxiously for the man to go. The loss of a moment might prove fatal to them in their undertaking to escape.

The gaoler was heard to rise.

Guy gave vent to a deep-drawn sigh of relief, thinking that the man was going his rounds; but they were disappointed, when they heard the lock shoot back.

The door opened, and the man, putting his head in, looked around the cell suspiciously.

The three friends looked at him most innocently.

Frank had replaced the fetters round his wrists, and Guy had put on his coat, after shooting the rubbish in a corner, which he took good care to conceal from the inquisitive gaze of the gaoler by taking up his position before it.

The fellow, not being able to discern any cause for his suspicions, left the prisoners with a dissatisfied look.

When his heavy step had died away, the work for liberation was renewed vigorously. Not an instant was lost. When one grew tired, another took the weapon and dug away with inspired hope, and so the excavation continued, each one working in his turn incessantly.

At last the stone moved, and every heart bounded with the joyous hope of freedom.

It was a big one, and took the three friends to dislodge it.

Cautiously it was lowered to the ground, and when the captives rose, they were confounded to see a malicious, grinning face at the hole in the wall looking upon them triumphantly.

Quick as lightning, Guy's arm went through the aperture, and the man was seized by the hair and dragged forward; his broad shoulders prevented him from being pulled into the cell, which was a sell for Guy.

"Cut off his head," suggested Captain Frank. The gaoler screamed miserably.

"Remove another stone," said Fawkes, tightening his hold on the man's throat.

Hugh set to work with good will, and the second stone soon fell out.

The gaoler was dragged in, gagged, stripped of his dress, bound hand and foot, and pitched helplessly into a corner of the cell.

Guy assumed the prison garb, and mounted guard outside, to watch a favourable opportunity for their escape.

Evening was casting its shadows around, when a light step was heard approaching the captive's cell.

Guy waited boldly for the comer, prepared to meet the worst. The life of himself and comrades depended upon the part he had taken; and it would not do to stand at trifles, even if one or two lives were sacrificed; but they wished to avoid bloodshed, if possible, and when Jackson's daughter came in sight he felt relieved.

The girl shrank back when she saw him, and would have turned and fled, but Guy caught her round the waist and detained her.

"Leave me alone, Hawk," she exclaimed, struggling to break away from her captor.

"That's good," muttered Guy; "she takes me for the other fellow. Come, come, lass," he said, aloud, endeavouring to get a kiss. "Marry, girl, thou art wayward as a child. Wont 'ee give me a kiss?"

"Let me go; I'll tell my father," she said, quite indignant at the presumption of the fellow wanting to kiss her. "Leave me alone, I say, you big brute."

"Give me a kiss, then. Come, don't be silly." Guy drew her face to his and stole the kiss.

The girl began to cry, and struggle to free herself.

"I will tell my father of this," she said, simpering. "Thou art always insulting me. I've never told my father before, but I will now, and you will be put in a cell."

"I have only just got out of one," said Guy, in altered voice.

The girl looked up, and the expression of terror on her face turned to one of sly pleasure.

"So the varlet, Hawk, is always insulting you, is he?" Guy said, persuasively.

The girl looked at him embarrassed. He was a stranger, evidently; but how he got Hawk's dress entirely puzzled her.

Guy saw her bewilderment, but he could not relieve her, because he did not know whether she was a friend or foe to his comrades.

"I have taken Hawk's place to guard the prisoners—Guy Fawkes' friends," he said, watching her closely.

The girl looked disappointed.

"Let me go, please," she said, coldly.

This change Guy took as a favourable sign. The girl evidently took an interest in the captives.

"I don't like my part," Guy remarked.

"Don't you?" eagerly queried the girl. "Why not?"

"Because I don't think the poor fellows deserve such a fate. If I had it in my power, I would help them to escape."

"It is all through father," said the gaoler's daughter, sighing. "They are so handsome. I am sure they are not bad men."

"It was very wrong of your father to make prisoners of them because they came to see their friend."

The girl sighed sadly; she had quite lost her little heart.

"Father is very cruel," she said, sorrowfully.

"Very," echoed Guy, bending his head to kiss her.

She took it quite passively, and faintly murmured—

"Ah! if I only had a friend in whom I could trust, I might be able to save the poor gentlemen from their cruel fate. Alack! alack!"

"Trust me, my pretty lass," said Guy, drawing her to his breast.

"Can I trust you?" she asked, eyeing him askance.

"I am their friend—one of them."

"One of them?" repeated the girl, not quite understanding his meaning. "What do you mean?"

"I am Guy Fawkes."

"You!" exclaimed the girl, in astonishment.

"Even so."

"How did you get Hawk's garb?"

"I and my friends cut a hole through the prison wall, and when we removed the stone the warder was standing there; we pulled him in, secured him, and I assumed his dress."

The girl clapped her hands with delight.

"Oh! I am so glad!" she said. And she even went so far, in her joy, as to put her arms round Guy's neck and kiss him.

"You said you could help them to escape if you had a friend in whom you could trust?"

"So I will. When father has drunk himself to sleep, I will take the keys from his girdle; but, in case I should not be able to conduct you out, I will show you the way you will have to take."

"Generous, kind girl! Tell me thy name, that I may ever think of thee with a kindly thought; and take this ring, as a token of my gratitude."

He drew a magnificent gem from his finger, and placed it on one of hers.

"Thou art very kind," said the girl, blushingly. "My name is Jessie."

"A name sweet and pretty as the owner."

"Tread carefully, and do not breathe a word," she said, taking his hand, and leading him to an open gate. "Should any of the warders be apprised of your escape, we shall have all the prison servants down upon us, and I shall be ruined."

"Fear not for my discretion, Jessie, love. A cat cannot tread lighter than can I; for not a feather would the breath that passes my lips disturb."

She led him on through long corridors, down flights of spiral stone steps, and along dark, narrow, underground passages.

Presently she stopped.

Guy thought he heard a scuffling, and his heart leaped, like a ball of fire, to his mouth.

"What is that?" he asked, in a suppressed whisper.

"Rats only."

Guy breathed freely.

"Don't move," said Jessie, gliding from his side.

The darkness was too intense for Guy to see where she had gone to, and he was left wondering, when the grating of bolts being drawn told him that she was not far off. A door was opened, and the evening twilight struggled through the gloom, revealing the form of the gaoler's pretty daughter standing in the opening like an angel of light.

"If you can reach this door with your friends, you are free," said Jessie.

"How can I thank you?" said Guy.

"No thanks; follow me back cautiously, and I will get the keys for thee, if my father is asleep."

She closed the door, and they returned to the prison.

Guy mounted guard outside his comrades' cell, while Jessie went for the keys of liberty.

She crept quietly into her father's room; and, as she had anticipated, found him in a state of happy ignorance, with numerous empty bottles scattered around him.

She stole stealthily towards him, her little breast palpitating with guilty terror as she undid his girdle and took the bunch of keys.

It was a moment of fearful peril and anxiety, for had he awoke and caught her in the act, he would have slain her in remorseless anger; but, thanks to the power of the liquor he had so freely imbibed, he was for a time dead to all around him, and the trembling girl escaped freely with her trophy.

GUY FAWKES OR THE CONSPIRATOR'S BRIDE

THE MEETING OF CONSPIRATORS.

Guy welcomed her gladly, but it suddenly occurred to him that she had achieved a dangerous undertaking for no purpose, since she had shown him the way out without the use of keys.

"Take the keys and fly," she said, "my father sleeps, lose no time, escape ere he awakes."

"The keys," Guy said, "I do not want, if

I am to take the same route as you have shown me."

"The doors through which we passed," answered Jessie, "have been reclosed by this time. This key," she added, taking one from the bunch, "will give you free passage."

He kissed her, and she, wishing him and his companion every success, tripped lightly away to replace the keys in her father's girdle, so that when he awoke he would be none the wiser of what had transpired.

Guy went to his comrade.

"Come lightly," he said.

The captives were free of their prison in an instant, and the daring trio were traversing a corridor when the distant tramp of many feet broke upon their ears, and sent a chill of misgiving to their hearts.

Guy put his comrades aside, as a body of soldiers came in view, and they stood unseen behind the massive pillars.

"Back to the cell," he said, in a whisper ; "I will meet these men."

Hugh and Captain Frank returned to their cell dreadfully crestfallen. Fate seemed dead set against them ; every time an opportunity of escape appeared favourable, they were impeded by some fresh danger.

"Who goes there ?" challenged Guy, acting as gaoler as the soldiers came on.

"The conspirators," was the password given ?

"Pass on." And Guy stepped out from behind a stone pillar.

"Thou art the gaoler ;" said the officer.

"I have that honorable post," answered the disguised prisoner. "Is there anyone important expected ?"

"We were sent here by Lord Cecil, to prevent a premeditated escape of Guy Fawkes and his companions," the soldier said, taking the purport of the other's words.

"Premeditated ! In what way ?"

"Lord Cecil was informed by his messenger whom he sent here to see them, that all three had promised to meet him at a certain place this evening ; and he, fearing that they would keep their word, sent us hither to stop them."

Guy laughed heartily at the idea of the prisoners escaping.

"His lordship appears particularly careful about the safety of the prisoners," he said ; "but I don't think he need have troubled you to look after them. I don't think they will get out of their cell in a hurry. However, we may leave them safely while we hold a carouse. I suppose thou art nothing loth to taste a good drop of grape juice ?"

"Nothing, friend ; we have had a long march, and our thirst is somewhat keen."

"Enter here, and rest thy weary legs, while I fetch a bottle or two of fine old stuff that will take the edge off your thirst, I vouch."

Guy pushed open the door of Jackson's room, that worthy still lay snoring loudly in his drunken sleep.

Jessie sprang from her seat, and shrank back in terror ; she instantly imagined that they had come to arrest her as an accomplice in aiding the prisoner to escape.

"Jessie," Guy said, going to her relief ; "I want you to accompany me to fetch some wine for these gentlemen."

Jessie obeyed readily ; and when they got outside, Guy said—

"How can we detain these men while I and my comrades escape ?"

"I will take them some wine, and tell them that you are coming with more," answered the girl, readily ; "in the meantime, escape as quick as possible, or it will be too late."

Another kiss, and Guy left her. He went for his companions and again the three friends were on their way to liberty when a voice charged them to stand.

A big burly fellow, a prison servant, stood boldly before them.

Guy caught him by the throat and hurled him aside, and made for the door. Hardly had they reached the other side of the threshold when the alarm-bell was rung. The escape had been discovered, and an exciting commotion prevailed throughout the prison.

Guy had scarcely divested himself of his disguise when the scampering of feet could be heard echoing through the stone corridors, and presently the soldiers, with the addition of the prison officials, came helter-skelter into the bye lane, in hot pursuit of the fugitives, who at that moment were seen to turn the corner with the velocity of a whirlwind.

The soldiers raised a shout, and dashed after them. An exciting chase was then began vigorously. The daring trio were hunted from street to street, where their pursuers gathered strength from a noisy rabble, who were always ready to hunt down any unfortunate being for the mere sake of excitement.

The escaped captives kept well in advance of their eager followers ; but it was not likely that they could keep the lead much longer, for there were many of the pursuing party fleeter of foot than were they.

On, on, they went, driven by the yelling mob, and felling all who tried to obstruct their flight. Suddenly they came upon London-bridge, and, without hesitation, flew down the steps to the waterside.

Three boats were lying moored on the banks of the Thames ; these they cut adrift to prevent their pursuers from following, and, springing into one of them, pulled away as the yelling mob reached the waterside.

CHAPTER XI.

THE CHASE ON THE THAMES.

THE glare of torches flashed on the water, and revealed the fugitives in their frail barque, going along in grand style. Guy pulled stroke, Hugh bow, and Frank acted as coxswain.

One of the troopers plunged into the water, and swam for the drifting boat. There was only one in sight; the other had been carried away by the tide. Catching hold of the bulwarks to draw himself up, the boat capsized, and he disappeared underneath it. In a moment more he rose again, and turned the boat over to its proper position. He then swam after the oars that were floating down the stream. Having overtaken these he returned to the boat, and putting the yoke lines between his teeth, brought the barque ashore in gallant style, and was received with a round of applause from the lookers on.

In a few seconds the boat was manned, the oars were thrown out on either side, and the soldiers, bending forward, took one mighty pull altogether, that shot the boat forward like an arrow.

"Pull, comrades, pull!" said Captain Frank, urgently; "the varlets are gaining on us."

His comrades did pull with power and velocity astonishing; the boat completely jumped out of the water at each stroke, and the perspiration rolled down their faces in big drops.

But still their foes gradually gained upon them, and there was little hope of escape without their strength could outlast the soldiers, and that seemed wholly improbable; from the start they had exerted themselves too much, and it was impossible for them to last much longer, for already they were panting with exhaustion.

Captain Frank saw how hopeless was their chance for deluding their pursuers on the water. If an opportunity of escape remained, it was on land, he thought, steering the boat shoreward, when a shot was fired by the hostile party that struck their little craft astern.

The shock unshipped the rudder, and caused the boat to lurch aside with a jerk that nearly shot the little crew overboard.

When the boat steadied herself again, she was half full of water and sinking fast. The shot had entered below water-mark. Guy threw his oar out of the rowlock despairingly, and seizing a petronal he had taken from the jailer, he turned in the boat and fired at his pursuers.

A crash and a cry of agony followed the report. The bullet shattered the bows of the pursuing boat, and entered one of the soldier's legs.

The boats sunk simultaneously, and the hostile crews were left struggling in the water.

Guy Fawkes and his friends were the first to reach the shore. The ducking had refreshed them, and in that miserable, saturated condition, they beat a hasty retreat, while the soldiers were struggling with their drowning comrades.

It was a deplorable sight to see the poor fellows who could not swim, plunging about frantically to keep themselves up, their faces haggard and terror-stricken with the fearful thought of coming to such an untimely end.

Pitifully they called upon and entreated of their comrades, who were blessed with the knowledge of the invaluable art of self-preservation, to save them.

Some turned and went to the rescue, while others turned a deaf ear to the cries, and swam ashore.

They were all saved but three, and they found rest in a watery grave.

One, who had clung to an oar for life, darted eagerly forward as a comrade came to his relief, lost his hold, and sank. He rose again, clutched desperately at the oar, but it rolled away from his touch, and he sank, never more to rise, just as his would-be-preserver arrived at the spot.

The soldier dived after his sinking comrade, and brought him up by the hair. He might have saved him, but at the moment he reappeared above the water, another drowning wretch threw his arms around the gallant fellow's neck in wild desperation, and so rendered him helpless; and in that way, clinging to one another, the three went down to eternal rest.

Those who had safely reached the shore did not wait to see the fate of their comrades, so eager were they to recapture the escaped prisoners; and although they had lost sight of them, they commenced a vigilant search, with the determination of having them again in their power before the night expired.

By this time Guy and his friends had reached the Jesuit's house.

The midnight hour tolled forth from the surrounding parish church clocks as they drew up under the window of the Lady Claire's chamber.

"By Jove! I did not think we should keep our word," remarked Captain Frank, "when we said in jest we should be here at midnight to witness an elopement. Do you remember, comrades?"

"Oh, yes," said Guy, looking around. "The preparations are nicely arranged for the flight. There was some truth in the fellow's words, then?"

'Yes; but I can't make out why he visited us," Hugh said.

"To taunt me with the news of the lady's falsity," Guy answered, his olive complexion growing darker with an angry frown. "He was a faithful messenger. He delivered our reply to Lord Cecil—he took our word for the deed, and sent a body of soldiers to intercept us, but they failed, and we escaped. Lord Cecil is up there." He pointed to the window of Lady Claire's window, from which was suspended a rope ladder. "That's his boat," he added, pointing to a wherry lying on the shore. "Comrades, you will take that boat, and wait for me. If I want you, I shall beckon from the window, after pitching out my rival; and if

I don't want you, I shall wave my hand to indicate as much."

"We shall lie out opposite the window," said Hugh, "and wait for your indication ere we move."

"Thanks—do."

"Don't spare the varlet, Guy," said Frank, taking his seat in the boat as Hugh Wardour pushed off and jumped in.

The foregoing conversation had taken place in an under tone, only audible to the conversants.

Guy looked up to his lady's window, doubtfully. "Had she been false, and permitted his rival to visit her with the intention of eloping with him?" he thought. The rope ladder hanging from the window looked very suspicious. It was certain that this meeting had been previously arranged, but in what manner Guy did not wait to ask himself. Lady Claire was harshly condemned, and his jealousy grew into bitter hate.

He was standing wondering how to act, when a cry of distress rang from Claire's room.

Guy's resolution was settled instantly, and mounting the ladder of rope, he dashed open the casement, and sprang into the chamber.

Lady Claire of Grace was no longer judged of falsity when he saw how she was struggling with her villanous persecutor to break from him.

Guy understood the meaning of the scene at a glance, and before Lord Cecil was aware of his presence the Spanish soldier had grasped him by the nape of the neck and hurled him across the room.

"Hound! despicable wretch!" exclaimed Guy, "I would I had a weapon, thou should not escape me thus."

Lady Grace ran into her protector's arms with a cry of joy, and Guy drew her fondly to his heart.

The discomfited nobleman looked at the lovers maliciously, he was somewhat astonished at the soldier's appearance at such a time.

Guy glanced at him hatefully, and his gaze wandering round the room, fell upon a pair of rapiers crossed under a shield standing against the wall.

"Rise, coward knave," exclaimed he, gently putting the lady aside and taking one of the weapons from the wall.

Cecil's face flushed indignantly, and rising hastily drew his sword.

"You have escaped to meet thy death," he said.

"I escaped," said Guy, with a quiet, spiteful smile, "to keep my appointment and save this lady from thee, base knave."

Their swords crossed with a clash, but the fight was not of long endurance. Lord Cecil's effeminate-like wrist bent like a reed under the superior strength of his adversary, and, ere he had got one point, Guy had pinked him in several parts, and disarmed him.

Cecil stood weaponless, and at the mercy of his opponent.

Guy's sword was raised to strike the death-blow, when his arm was clutched by the trembling hand of Lady Claire.

"Do not kill him," she said.

"Not kill kim?" iterated Guy, "why, it would be a charity to rid the world of such a villain."

"For my sake—for thine own—do not kill him."

"It would be mercy to us both were I to bury this blade in his black heart; but, for thy gentle sake, he shall live."

Guy was about to show the beaten scoundrel the way out, when a loud clamour arose under the window.

The soldier looked out. The house was surrounded with troopers, who had tracked him out, and some had already begun to ascend the ladder.

Guy was not prepared to meet them just then. He had a matter to settle with his vanquished foe, ere it would be agreeable for him to receive them; and, to prevent them from forcing their company upon him, he cut the rope with his sword, and they made a rapid descent amongst their companions.

Then he turned to Lord Cecil, and said—

"You must change dress with me quickly."

"For what purpose?" queried his lordship.

"For mine," was the cool rejoinder.

Lord Cecil seemed most unwilling to comply with the other's demand. He stood in dogged resolution to resist, with his arms crossed over his breast. The humiliation of his defeat, and his hate for the daring fellow who had prevented his base design to abduct Lady Claire, had eaten a torturing canker in his heart, and he thirsted like a tiger for his conqueror's blood.

More than once he meditated an attack upon his foe. But the thought of his treachery failing, kept him back.

Guy Fawkes saw that he would not submit to the exchange of costume unless forced to do so; and that force was the only chance he had for accomplishing his plan; and unless Cecil yielded quickly, harsher means would have to be resorted to, as the soldiers were growing impatient, at not having received any response to their summons, they began battering away at the outer door to force an entrance.

Guy knew the door could not resist their furious attack much longer, and he had no time to lose.

Putting the point of his sword in the hollow of Cecil's throat, he said—

"I want your coat and hat."

The courtier stood unmoved, and looked coldly into his enemy's face. He did not show the least fear at the cold steel breaking through his skin.

His manner exasperated the soldier to madness, and in his anger he would have slain him. But such an act, he knew, would be signing his own death-warrant, and he could not afford to die just yet. So, masters ing his impulsive desire, he threw his sword aside, and seizing Lord Cecil by the throat, bore him to the ground.

A slight contest ensued, but was soon overcome by Guy, who divested his opponent of his coat, which he put on himself, and then forced Cecil into his.

The soldiers had broken into the house, and were now rushing upstairs.

Lord Cecil rose with a malicious grin, put on Guy's hat as the door was burst open and the besiegers swarmed into the chamber, armed with pikes and halberds, and other formidable weapons which they knew how to use.

"Guy Fawkes, the traitor!" said the pursuivant, looking inquiringly at the two men.

Lord Cecil's wild, haggard expression, and the wet garments he now wore, proclaimed him as a desperate character they were in quest of, and the soldiers' suspicions naturally fell upon him.

"There," said Guy, pointing to Lord Cecil, "stands the traitor."

The soldiers closed around the baffled scoundrel.

Cecil glared upon the men contemptuously.

"There stands your prisoner," he said, pointing to Guy. "He has forced me into these clothes. I am Lord Cecil."

"That's a likely tale!" said the pursuivant, laughing incredulously.

"That's your prisoner," Lady Claire said, alluding to the discomfited Cecil. "Do your duty. Had this gentleman not arrived so opportunely, he would have carried me away from here by force."

"Away with him, men!" Guy Fawkes said, in an authoritative voice. "Let him be well secured, and mind he does not escape again."

No doubt could now exist as to the identity of the prisoner; and, in spite of Lord Cecil's strong protestations to the contrary, he was manacled and led away like a common felon.

When the soldiers had left the house with their prisoner, Guy went to the window, and nodded to his friends.

The gallant young fellows, from their position on the water, had seen all that had taken place. They recognised their comrade's indication of safety, and rowed away, leaving him with the beautiful Lady Claire of Grace to create their first dream of love.

CHAPTER XII.

THE MEETING OF CONSPIRATORS.

CAPTAIN FRANK and Hugh Wardour had not proceeded far down the river when the splash of another boat following close behind them attracted their attention. They, thinking it might be a crew of their late pursuers, pulled vigorously to escape.

"By thunder!" remarked Frank, "I thought we had got clear of them. The varlets keep on the scent with the untiring vigilance of bloodhounds. Pull, Hugh! 'tis for liberty or death!"

"Cease thy fears, Captain "——

"George, comrade, please," interrupted the young captain.

"Is that thy name?" inquired Hugh.

"It is, comrade. Say what thou wouldst."

"'Tis but a boat with three occupants bearing down upon us; and methinks I have seen them before, if my eyes deceive me not."

"And yet they seem to be following us. Who are they, think ye?"

"Catesby, Wright, and Percy, if I mistake not," replied Hugh Wardour, seriously. "There is some evil work afloat, and I would fain watch their movements. Three such men seldom meet together at such an hour for any purpose of good. George, we will land where we can conceal ourselves and watch."

No more was said. They pulled ashore near Lambeth Stairs, and got out of their boat at a solitary spot; and pulling their little craft up on the Thames-bank, concealed themselves behind some old lumber.

The other boat came on, and was rowed ashore at the same spot. The three men that landed were concealed in long dark cloaks, and since they were seen by our two friends had adjusted masks over their faces.

Each drew his sword, and, in a cautious manner, moved about the shore in search of the hidden fugitives, pressing the points of their swords behind the stack of rubbish where Frank and Hugh were crouching down from observation.

"I wot they are spies," said one of the strangers, in an undertone; "and we are not safe while they are about."

"I think not," said another. "They are but some poor devils escaped from the myrmidons of the law."

"But they are hidden somewhere about here," the first speaker persisted.

"Not they," said the other, in a confidential tone. "You may stake thy soul upon it that they have flown, as if the devil was behind them, when they saw us coming down upon them. No doubt they mistook us for some others."

"Oh, no, we didn't," thought Hugh Wardour, who had taken in every word with an apparent relish for mystery.

Hugh and his friend were relieved when they saw the three strangers depart. They then crept from their hiding-place, and followed at a distance, from which they could distinctly distinguish the dark forms as they traversed on, without being seen.

The men halted at the foot of Lambeth Stairs, and looked back to ascertain that their footsteps were not dogged by anyone their guilty minds conjured up.

Captain Frank and Hugh had fallen back under the shadow of a high wall, and were undiscernible in the gloom, where they remained until their precedents had ascended the steps ; then they hastily followed, and were in time to see them turn the corner of a wretchedly narrow street.

The young friends were playing a daring part by following these three renowned men ; and, had they been discovered, nothing would have saved them from a speedy death.

To avoid suspicion, in case they might be seen, they parted. Captain Frank, in a careless manner, followed closely behind Percy of Northumberland and his friends, and was even bold enough to hum a popular air of that period.

Catesby turned his head and gave the young gallant a searching glance. Frank pretended not to notice it, and in an independent manner went on humming his tune.

The noblemen, thinking him a casual passer by, troubled themselves no further about his presence.

Hugh Wardour, following on the opposite side of the road, saw the three men stop at a dark house, and give a gentle summons at the door for admittance.

Captain Frank passed on, but Hugh stopped under the window of the house where the nobleman waited for admittance to see something to his face.

The fictious fault was instantly repaired as the muffled gentlemen entered, and Frank beckoned for his comrade to come over to him.

"We have had our trouble for nought," said Hugh.

"Not so, comrade. We can get admittance," replied Captain George Frank. "I heard the password."

"Good. But the risk will be great."

"Bah ! What is life without danger ! Give me plenty of excitement — that's the thing."

"We shall have enough of it, I wot not. When once we get in we shan't find it as easy to get out again. It is confoundedly exciting that these prison knaves should have our arms away."

"Our defencelessness will make the excitement the more delicious," said Captain Frank. "Pull your hat over thy brows, and we will enter."

Hugh drew his hat over his face so as to completely disguise his features, and Frank gave an imitation of the summons at the door of the dark house the three noblemen had used.

The door was cautiously opened a few inches only.

"Who comes ?" demanded a voice on the other side.

"Rome," responded Captain Frank, using the password he had overheard.

The door was then thrown open, and the daring intruders entered a long, dark passage.

When the door was closed again, a feeling of dread crept over them, but it was banished instantly. They had gone too far now to retreat without discovery, and they would have to face the worst.

They were prepared for it. With a cool, indomitable courage, they traversed the passage, and ascended a flight of stairs, which Hugh discovered by kicking his foot against the bottom one, and embracing the rest.

They were now in a sort of gallery, dark as the passage from which they had just ascended. A buzz of voices broke the stillness, and a few rays of light straggled through the crevices of the doors.

Their position was a critical one. Should anyone come out from the surrounding chambers, they had nowhere to hide from observation.

Hugh knew the danger they incurred by remaining listeners outside the chamber from whence came the buzz of voices. Not a word could be distinctly discerned, and it was not likely they would gain much without their position altered. It would be more advantageous to gain a chamber next to the one occupied, which appeared nearly deserted, by its silence and the dim light that shone through the crevices of the door. This Hugh quietly opened.

The room was unoccupied, but it communicated with the one in which the meeting was held.

Captain Frank followed his young friend. They closed the door and secured it on the inside to keep out any intruders, and took up their positions behind the heavy tapestry that separated the two rooms.

Captain Frank drew the hangings aside and took a survey of the chamber and its occupants.

It was a room of enormous dimensions, magnificently decorated, the rich tapestry of the walls was emblazoned with costly emblems of the Catholic religion. Ranging along the centre of the room was a large oaken table, richly carved, and around it sat many noblemen. At the head of the table was erected a dais ; this was occupied by Percy of Northumberland, Catesby, and others.

A whispering conference was taking place, and every face wore a determined expression.

The hidden witnesses and listeners of this strange scene held their breath to catch a word of the conversation ; but the voices only reached them in an indistinct manner as yet.

"Redemption is near at hand," said Catesby, and the listeners caught these words. "Our suppressed religion shall again assume its mighty stand ; the tyrannical infidels shall no longer butcher our priests and defile our church."

Here he lowered his voice, and our young friends were unable to hear any more just then.

"Conspirators," whispered Hugh. "I knew some infernal work was at hand when I saw them."

"Hush!"

And Frank grasped his comrade's arm for silence.

"Is every gentleman here true in our cause?" asked Percy of Northumberland.

Everyone rose and answered solemnly in the affirmative. Brimming goblets were raised, and an oath of fidelity sworn by the conspirators.

"We have undertaken that which, if known, would throw our lives into the hands of the executioner," continued the speaker. "The utmost secrecy must be kept—an eternal seal placed on the lips of those engaged in the plot for the success of our scheme—a mighty undertaking; it is for the restoration of our Church and the peace of England; but while James wields the sceptre we cannot hope for much success."

"Down with James!" shouted the company.

Captain Frank sprang forward—an angry exclamation broke from his lips—with the intention of hurling Percy from his throne; he dashed aside the heavy hanging; but ere he had taken a step Hugh grasped him by the arm, and held him back.

"Patience," said the youth. "Your indiscretion will be our ruin. Wait. We shall do more good by warning James of his danger. There is more to be learnt from these traitors."

The noise of Captain Frank's movements was heard by the conspirators.

"A spy! death to the spy!" was the cry that rang through the chamber, and every one was on his feet in a moment with drawn swords, hunting for the spy.

Captain Frank's and Hugh's danger was imminent. The conspirators were coming towards them, and should they be discovered, their death was certain. They knew not where to fly for safety.

"The window," suggested Captain Frank.

The words were scarcely spoken when the curtains were torn open, and they were menaced by the enraged conspirators.

"Death to them!" cried those behind.

"Follow me!" cried Captain Frank, to his friend, and dashing through the conspirators, he made a flying leap for the window.

There was a crash as he disappeared through the glass.

In the position of a ball he descended to the ground, and rolled against the door of a shed, which was partly open, he fell into a sort of vault three feet deep.

In an instant he was upon his feet. Just as he got into the street again to look for his companion, there was a crash and a tremendous shouting, and the conspirators appeared at the window as Hugh, like an eel, slipped through them and followed the example of his friend.

Directly Hugh reached the ground, Frank took him up and carried him into the dark vault.

"Thunder of Jove!" exclaimed the reckless captain, putting his companion down to secure the door, "it was a mighty jump from that window, friend. How fares it with thee?"

"Quite serene, but a little sore; the varlets helped me out with their swords. Where are we?"

"I know not, more than when I left the room I found myself here; but I would fain like to know its locality. Can we get a light?"

"I have a dagger, we must see what can be done."

They were in a vault of total darkness—a vault under the house from which they had just escaped, but they knew it not.

Hugh Wardour struck the blade of his dagger against the stone wall, the sparks that were caused by the friction fell upon a cambric handkerchief he held, and it ignited.

Keeping the smouldering rag in a flame by puffing it, Hugh went round the vault in search of something that would serve for a light, and discovered a torch stuck in an iron ring against the wall.

This he lighted, and with Frank, began to explore the vault. The first thing they found was a stack of barrels.

These Frank eyed curiously.

"Wine, Hugh," he said, "a beautiful find; delicious beverage. How I long to moisten my parched throat with its refreshing juice! Hugh, give me thy dagger, to excavate an entrance to this treasure."

He took the proffered weapon, and drew the blade up and down the wall to sharpen the point, and then bored a hole in one of the barrels. Blowing the dust from the perforation, he put his mouth over the hole and began to draw; but he drew in vain, nothing came, and with a wry face he turned to his friend.

"Have a try, Hugh," he said, "it may be that my bellows are not strong enough."

Hugh had a draw, and began to spit and splutter as though he was poisoned.

"Gunpowder, as I'm a sinner!" he exclaimed, in surprise and disappointment. "materials for the consummation of their infernal plot. George, I think we shall be safer if we get out of here."

"They want to dethrone our king, do they?" Captain Frank said, his loyal blood rising with indignation at the dark scheme of the conspirators. "They want to divert the power of our King James to establish their hypocritical church in this land of freedom. If it lies in my power to prevent their hellish work, nothing shall be left undone to bring them to judgment."

The creaking of a secret door being opened warned them that someone was near.

Hugh extinguished the torch, and they had only time to crouch down behind the barrels when the conspirators entered with drawn swords and some bearing lanterns.

"I saw them enter here from the window," said one of the conspirators; "they must be hidden somewhere." The speaker sniffed. "They have had a light: I can smell the burning of a torch."

The hidden spies felt an icy chill creep over them ; they had no way of escape ; the conspirators had taken up their positions in different parts of the cell, and some stood before the door. Their discovery was unavoidable, and Frank regretted that they had entered the accursed place when they were free.

Hugh could see, through the crevices in the barrels, their foes coming towards them, he crouched down, and restrained his comrade from jumping up and springing upon them as was his intent.

The noise of Frank falling brought the conspirators upon them like a pack of wolves and just as a shout of " Here they are !" arose, the young men pushed the barrels of powder over, and sprang out of their concealment amongst the assailants.

They were soon overpowered and forced against the wall, with twenty deadly weapons levelled at their breasts, menacing them with death.

"Who are the spies ?" said Catesby, coming forward, with a lantern raised above his head, to examine the prisoners. "Strangers!" he cried. " Let the varlets die ! "

Captain Frank made a spring forward, knocked the speaker over, and snatched the light from his hand.

This occurred in a minute, and Hugh, inspired by the daring of his companion, dropped to the ground, hurled his captors on their backs by pulling their legs from under them, and, with a dozen of the angry noblemen chasing him round the vault, he picked up the torch, and threw it to Frank.

' Light it,' he shouted. "Blow the traitors into the air !"

A dash was made to secure the torch, but Captain Frank had possessed himself of it when the conspirators fell upon him to take it from him.

Regardless of the spiteful digs he got on all sides, and the danger of being run through, the daring youth hurled his assailants from him, and lighted the torch. As the attack was renewed, he made a light spring with the agility of a cat, and landed amongst the barrels of gunpowder.

"Back !" he exclaimed, his voice ringing through the vault. "Back ! take another step towards me, and I will blow you into the air !"

The red glare of the torch lighting up his excited features made him look terrible in his determination—a fiend he looked, standing fearlessly in the midst of the destruction, with the burning torch held in his hand. Should a spark fall, there would be an instant explosion, and everyone would be blown into the air.

The conspirators stood panic-stricken, expecting every moment the fearful catastrophe to take place.

CHAPTER XIII.

THE BLACK RIDER.

HUGH WARDOUR was the first to break the spell of terror that held all powerless.

"Hold your hand," he said, making towards Frank ; "if a spark fell we, too, should perish."

"Our death will save many others from a like fate," replied Captain George, resolutely, "and keep the peace of our country."

"We may do more good by living," said Hugh. "There are others besides those here connected with the conspiracy, and to blow up this place would only be sacrificing our lives for a useless purpose. Come, Frank, forego thy intent, and we will leave in peace."

"And leave these plotting villains to carry out their diabolical scheme ? No."

"Gentlemen," said Catesby, "let us have an explanation."

"With all my heart," said Hugh, " if your friends will put aside their swords. What would you know ?"

"You were the two gentlemen, I presume, who preceded us on the river ?"

"We were," answered Hugh.

"You were waiting for Guy Fawkes, who had entered a house at the river side ? He is a companion of yours ?"

"He is," was the laconic reply. " What know you of him ?"

The conspirators exchanged meaning glances.

"He is a friend of ours," replied Catesby; " a true brother ; his heart and soul is given to our cause."

"What ? " exclaimed Captain Frank ; " Guy Fawkes a conspirator ?"

"Even so, and wherefore not ? You, too, would be one if you were acquainted with the secrets of the conspiracy."

"Never!" firmly responded Frank, changing his dangerous position.

"Bah ! why not ?" asked Catesby.

"Because I am a loyal subject."

"And you ?" inquired Catesby of Hugh.

"Have no inclination to mix with the country's feuds on one side or the other."

"Then you cannot leave here."

"Who will stop us ? " asked Frank, angrily.

"We ! " The voices of every conspirator rose as one.

"Try it," said the daring fellow, making his way to the door.

Instantly, several of the conspirators stood in his path with drawn swords. Hugh was by his side ; Frank suddenly sent out the flaming torch, and hit his assailant in the face.

Hugh took the opportunity of excitement to wrest two swords from the astonished men, one of which he instantly gave to his comrade, and they began to fight like very demons.

GUY FAWKES
OR
THE CONSPIRATORS BRIDE

DEATH FOR LIBERTY.

The conspirators, who had not liked the meanness of attacking two defenceless men, now commenced in earnest.

Hugh and Frank were driven back, de-

spite their indomitable courage, and forced to give in.

"We do not wish to take your lives," said Catesby; "but we cannot let you go at large with the possession of the secret you over-heard."

"You can't get the secret back again," Frank answered.

"No; but if we get your word on oath not to divulge anything, you may have your liberty."

"I never take an oath."

"Then you must die."

"Sooner or later. As you like; kill me, if you think it worth while."

"It is for our safety, without you will swear not to reveal what you overheard."

"I will give you my word not to divulge anything; but I will not swear to it."

"Can we trust him, think ye?" asked Catesby of his companions, giving them an insinuating wink.

"You can do as you like about it," Frank said.

"I think he will keep the secret," said Wright.

"You can think what you like."

"Give them liberty," said Percy; "for the sake of their friend, they will not reveal any-thing."

"Guy Fawkes is no longer a friend of mine," said Captain Frank, "if he has forfeited his life for thy devilish plot; and I would as soon see him writhing on the rack as I would any of thee."

"Thou speakest boldly, but we doubt not thy word," said Catesby. "Go; freedom is thine—*for a time*." He added to his companions, as the young men left the vault, "*They are bold, daring men, such as we want, and ere long they must be of us.*"

It was only the thought that they might be able to get them to alter their opinion of the conspiracy and join them that they were allowed to go.

The fatigue and excitement the young friends had undergone now began to tell upon them, and they were forced, from ex-haustion, to seek some place of rest.

Morning had dawned, and the sun's first golden streaks chased away the shadows of night, when they stopped at a hostel and knocked for admittance.

It was some time before their summons was answered; and then the host thrust his nightcapped head out of window and in-quired what they wanted.

"Rest, confound thy impertinence," cried Captain Frank; "come down and let us in, or we will let ourselves in."

With a dissatisfied grunt, the head disap-peared from the window.

"I wonder whether the old scoundrel means to admit us," wondered Hugh, keeping up an impatient tapping at the door with the hilt of his sword.

The pattering of naked feet coming down the stairs indicated the approach of the inn-keeper. The door was unfastened; and while it was being slowly opened, Hugh and Frank pushed their way in.

The landlord fell back from their path sus-piciously nervous, and looked upon them uneasily; not that there was anything in their character to cause alarm, but still the host did not appear comfortable.

"Now, landlord, we want a bed; but firstly, get us something to eat," said Captain Frank.

"Right, sirs," replied the host, sighing with relief. "Thou art gladly welcome to what my humble abode can afford thee."

Wherewith the landlord conducted them to a room, and set about preparing a meal, which was gladly hailed by the weary guests, and diminished ere they rose from the table.

Half-an-hour later they had retired to rest; but they did not enjoy many hours repose when a tremendous banging at the door awoke them.

It was yet early, and the young friends wondered at this disturbance.

"It can't be any traveller seeking refuge," said Frank. "Jump out of bed, Hugh, and see who it is."

"No, I'm deuced if I do. Let them knock, it's nothing to do with us."

"Only that they disturb our rest, and I want to sleep."

"Then get out of bed and tell them to go away."

Frank thought he would serve him out for his selfishness. Planting his feet in the middle of Hugh's back, he shot his legs for-ward, and sent him flying across the room.

"You can see, now you are up," he said, coolly.

Hugh returned to the bed, and, suddenly clutching Frank by the feet, lugged him out on his back.

"You can see now," he said, jumping into bed, and diving under the clothes.

Frank looked out of the window, and directly his head appeared in the street, a shout arose from below.

"Hugh!" he exclaimed, pulling the clothes off the bed, "get up, the house is attacked by soldiers."

"Well, they don't want us," Hugh said, sullenly, sitting up with his hands clasped round his legs, and his chin resting on his knees.

"Perhaps not; but it is certain they are after some unfortunate victim, and it ain't in us to stand inactive while these brutal caitiffs walk them off."

The banging was kept up with increased vigour, and the battering of the attack vibrated through the house.

"Open the door, in the king's name!" yelled a voice; "open, I say, or we'll pull the house down about your ears."

"Likely, likely," muttered a gruff voice, outside the chamber of our friends, "but while there stands a stave to resist thee, ye'll not get admittance by me, ye varlets."

Captain Frank went to the door.

"What's the meaning of this uproar?" he demanded of the landlord, who was at that moment entering a chamber opposite the one occupied by Hugh and his friends.

Before the landlord could answer, a boy ran out of the room in great alarm. His fair, beautiful face was expressive of fearful terror, and long, golden tresses hung around his shoulders in wild disorder.

"'Tis I they seek!" he exclaimed, taking Frank by the hand, and looking imploringly into his face.

"You, the bloodthirsty hounds seek?" said the gallant fellow.

"Yes, but I know not for why. From place to place they have hunted me like a common felon. Thou wilt protect me?"

"Ay. Were their number treble, not a hair of thy head should they harm!"

"Oh, thanks! thanks! a thousand thanks!" cried the boy, gratefully, as Captain Frank led him into their chamber.

"My God!" exclaimed Hugh Wardour, jumping from the bed. He seized the boy by the arm, and looked searchingly into his upturned face.

"Strange!" he muttered, wonderingly, as though trying to call to mind some bygone scene. "'Tis strange that the sound of his voice should have awoke those slumbering recollections of the past I would fain forget, since I can never more hope to clasp her to mine heart. Oh, cursed, unhappy hour was it when I left my native land." He seemed to become abstracted in his cogitations. Even the battering sound of the besiegers was lost upon him, as he glanced at the boy, whose bright, blue eyes were fixed upon him with a strange expression that sent a thrill of wild emotion through Hugh.

"How like!" he continued mentally. "Were he dressed in the garments of the other sex I could stake my life on't that thou wert the same; and yet," he went on, with another look at the boy, "he is marvellously fair for a boy."

"Hugh, dress thyself," cried Frank, "and give not way to absurd wonderings. What is it that casts the cloud upon thy brow? Come, comrade, pull thyself together, and lend thy sword in defence of this lad."

Hugh felt ashamed of himself for standing in his *robe de chambre* before the strange youth, and hastily began to pull on his clothes. He was buckling on his sword-belt when a mighty crash shook the house. Then was heard a triumphant shout as the besiegers dashed into the passage, and commenced their destructive work.

Rooms were broken into, furniture pulled down, things hurled about and broken. People pulled unceremoniously out of bed, regardless of sex, and subjected to the vile, brutal jest of the coarse, pitiless ruffians, and anything of the slightest value the villains could lay their hands on was seized, and the owners maltreated, if they laid a claim to the property, or objected to go under an examination.

The landlord came rushing into the room of our young friends, and, in an excited manner, cried:—

"Save the boy! Fly! The villains have entered. Fly!—fly!"

"Whither?" inquired Frank, looking round for a way of exit.

"The window!" said the landlord, putting into the querist's hands a coil of strong rope. "Fasten this to the bedpost, and slide down into the street."

Captain Frank was in the act of explaining the impossibility of such an act, when Hugh took the rope from him, and did as directed by the worthy host; then, returning for the boy, he took him up in his arms, as though he had been but a mere child, and getting out of the window, called on his comrade to follow. He slid down the rope.

The troopers rushed into the room and seized the astonished landlord roughly by the throat, just as Captain Frank disappeared out of the window.

"The boy—where is he?" demanded the leader, shaking the innkeeper. "Bring him out, trembling dog, or we'll take you for harbouring Papists."

"Hands off, scoundrel whelp!" exclaimed the landlord, shaking his captor off, and striking him to the ground by a well-aimed blow from the shoulder. He then made for the door, as quick as his legs could carry him, as the troopers rushed after him, and locked them in the room.

The baffled ruffians swore as only troopers can swear at being thus baffled, and while some were trying to batter down the door, others went to the open window and looked out.

"He has escaped by this window, and is flying down the street!" shouted the men, detecting the fugitives.

The shouts of the soldiers were heard by the boy, and, with a despairing cry, he broke from his friends, and flew on before them with the fleetness of an antelope.

Hugh and Captain Frank were astonished to see how the boy kept in advance of them; but they followed, and kept close upon him.

The shouts that burst on the evening air, as the troopers descended from the hostel by the rope from the window, apprised the fugitives that the bloodhounds were on their track, and they did all they could to delude them. Presently their uneasiness was increased by hearing the clatter of horses following them, and they were about to give up the idea of escaping when the friendly voice of the landlord called upon them to stop.

Hugh Wardour turned, and, to his infinite joy, saw that the landlord of the hostel was thundering towards them on the back of a spirited charger and leading another by the bridle.

Riding up to them, he slid from the saddle, and threw the reins to Hugh, and Frank caught the bridle of the other steed.

"These will aid your escape," the landlord said. "Take them, and save the boy; he was entrusted to my care, and for the wealth of the kingdom I would not have harm come to him. Hurry on. The troopers approach, and I must leave thee. Farewell. God speed thee!"

He drew the boy to his breast, and kissed his fair brow, then disappeared, as the yelling troop came rushing madly on.

The daring youth, sprang into the saddle, and Hugh, lifting the boy off the ground, placed him before him, and raising a triumphant cheer dashed away.

The pursuers fired a volley of bullets from their petronals after them; the shots fell harmlessly in the rear, and the fugitives, with their strange charge, escaped safely, leaving the troopers out of sight, a prey to baffled rage.

The boy nestled to his gallant preserver with remarkable fondness, and the tender glances Hugh cast upon the sad, pale face upturned to his bespoke of a strain of secret thoughts that troubled him much.

"Why is it that thy young life is threatened with such danger?" asked Hugh, slackening the speed of his steed.

"I know not," replied the boy in a sweet tremulous voice; "they condemned me for a Papist, because discovered under the protection of my guardian, Father Oldham."

"Are you a native of this soil?"

"By birth;" replied the boy, "but the greater part of my life was spent in Spain."

Hugh started, and looked at the speaker with a troubled expression.

"Strange!" he muttered. "This is a mystery I cannot understand. Are your parents living?"

"No," was the sad answer; "they died before I was old enough to know them. I am entirely alone in the world without a friend to protect me."

"Have you no brothers or sisters?"

"None."

Hugh mused.

"Who is Father Oldham?" he inquired.

"A priest under whose protection I placed myself when I left Spain."

"Why were you put in the care of the landlord of the hostel from which we just escaped?"

"For safety. When hunted from our home, and my guardian had to fly for life, leaving me in charge of the innkeeper."

Here their conversation was cut short by the approach of a person whom Captain Frank recognised as Guy Fawkes, and welcomed him with a hearty shout.

"Well, comrade," said Hugh; "what brings thee out at this early hour?"

"I?" Guy laughed, drily; "Oh, I am just returning home."

"The deuce you are."

"Why, who have you got there?" asked the soldier, looking at the boy. "The youth I befriended, as I live! By my faith, I thought that strange being who carried him off would have kept him from danger."

"So he would," put in the youth; "but while he was gone to rescue the priest from prison the soldiers discovered my retreat attacked the place, and I had to fly."

At that moment the clatter of horses' hoofs approaching startled the gallant trio, and before they could detect from what direction the sound proceeded, a half dozen troopers, with their leaders well mounted, whirled round the bend of the road, and surrounded them.

The horses the soldiers rode had been stolen from some stable, and owing to the easy pace Hugh and Frank had proceeded after escaping their pursuers, it gave them plenty of time to be overtaken, and the soldiers keeping up a hot pursuit had succeeded in so doing.

"Guy Fawkes, I arrest you as a conspirator," said the leader, drawing his halberd to intimidate the daring fellow.

Guy's brow darkened black as a thunder cloud with anger. He and his comrades were three against seven; the odds were great, but if they meant fight they should have it, mentally determined the Spanish soldier.

"And you, Master Hugh Wardour, I arrest for aiding that boy you hold to escape," the trooper said. "Men, arrest them; if they resist, cut them to pieces."

"That's what you mean, is it?" said Captain Frank. "You low-bred thief, clear off, or by thunder some of ye will meet a hasty end."

His sword flashed from its sheath, and wheeling round his horse, he dashed amongst the troopers in grand military style.

The soldiers charged him with their pikes; but, fearless of danger, he beat them aside, put his sword between his teeth, and clutching one of the pikestaffs with both hands, he wrenched it from its owner, and struck him over the head with it. The man staggered and reeled out of the saddle.

"Guy, here's a horse for thee," cried the daring fellow, coolly, whirling the staff round his head at full length to keep his assailants at bay.

"All right, keep it for me while I settle this fellow," returned Guy.

The fellow he desired to rid himself of was Kit the Keeper. Guy had pulled him from his horse, and they were fighting hand to hand.

Hugh was contending with three of the ruffians under great difficulty, being encumbered by the trembling youth, who clung to him in terror, and the contest was likely to end fatally with him, but, fortunately, at the moment he was being overpowered, Captain Frank unhorsed another of his assailants. The other fled, and the young gallant went to the assistance of his companion.

He rode at the soldiers with his lance held firmly at his side. The point entered one of the men just below his breast brigantine, and, with a cry of mortal agony, he dropped his halberd, and fell forward on his charger, bleeding profusely from the wound.

The others, dispirited by the fate of their companion, turned and fled.

Guy seeing the victory won by his comrades, quickly disposed of Kit the Keeper by a blow that left him writhing in agony on the earth, with his hand clasped over his lacerated cheek.

In a few seconds, Guy was in the saddle of the horse Captain Frank had secured for him, and again the gallant trio were on the road to liberty; but their career was brought to a termination by a second troop of the enemy, who suddenly came upon them.

The three friends drew up their steeds, their swords flashed out, and a furious onslaught was made at the troopers.

While the fight was raging with terrible fury, Kit the Keeper and his small company came up, and set upon our invincible friends.

"Guy Fawkes, I have sworn to be thy fate," exclaimed Kit, maliciously. "Give in quietly. It will be better for thee."

"Malapert knave!" said Guy, between his compressed lips; and, riding towards his foe, a deadly glitter darting from his dark eyes, he aimed a rapid blow at his head.

Kit caught the descending blow on his halberd; and, turning it aside, pressed his horse forward, and the combatants closed. Each had got the other round the waist; and, while the frightened steeds plunged about, they were trying to hurl one another from the saddle.

One of the troopers struck Guy a coward's blow on the head with his lance. His hold relaxed, and he reeled from the saddle to the earth, insensible.

A dozen of the ruffians were upon him in an instant, and his friends being surrounded, they were unable to go to his assistance.

Another minute and the three gallant men would have been helpless captives, but at the moment they thought their triumph was complete, a strange, weird-looking horseman —a being of majestic build, astride a barb of spotless black and of powerful build—rode upon the scene.

The troopers fell back awed by his appearance, and Kit the Keeper gasped in terror—

"The Black Rider."

He had come upon the scene like a shadow, and without deigning to use the ponderous weapon that swayed at his side, his charger made a passage through the troopers to where Guy lay.

He stooped in his saddle to raise the insensible fellow, when Kit, recovering from his fright, exclaimed—

"Being of man or devil, thou shalt not cheat me!" and fired point black at the stranger's breast.

The bullet flattened, and fell to the earth.

The ruffian gave a shriek of horror, and fell back from the withering gaze of the mystic being.

"Beware!" said the Black Rider, in an unearthly voice; then, turning to Hugh and Frank, he said, "Follow me!"

But the furious voice of Kit the Keeper yelling at his men to stop their prisoners, brought the troopers in a resolute body before the fugitives.

The Black Rider drew his huge sword, and turned upon the troopers with a meaning look, the men slunk back cowed, and the young gallants rode away with their mysterious preserver; but they had not gone far, when a volley of bullets was fired by the troopers.

The boy gave a cry of agony, and his body relaxed. He was hit—a shot had entered his side.

Hugh clasped the stricken boy to his breast, and looked despairingly into his haggard face.

"Hugh, forgive me!" murmured the youth, smiling faintly! "I have ever loved you. Say that thou wilt forgive thy Constance, ere I die."

"Constance! my dearest!" wildly cried Hugh! "'Tis you, then, in this disguise! I thought so; yet I dared not cherish such a hope."

The gentle girl clutched his arm, and looked imploringly into his face. Hugh saw the meaning of that look, and kissed her quivering lips.

With a smile on her placid countenance, he eyes closed; and she sank into his arms a dead, helpless weight.

Hugh gave vent to a wild, despairing cry, and leaving his companions with the Black Rider, dashed madly away in search of some one to save the life of his gentle love.

CHAPTER XIV.

LORD CECIL AND HIS COLLEAGUE ARRANGE A PLOT TO ENTRAP GUY FAWKES.

DESPAIR and rage at the loss of Lady Claire, and the humiliation of being shut up in a prison through the clever device of Guy Fawkes, had wrought a wonderful change in the expression of the sleek, well-shaped face of Lord Cecil. His cheeks had lost their healthful glow, and hung down about his jaws like laps of superfluous flesh, and his eyes, once so haughty, now wandered about with a wild and restless glare.

Several times he had tried to make his gaoler understand the mistake that had placed him in such an awkward position, but the man only laughed, and told his discomfited lordship that they were used to that sort of thing, and left him to his reflections, which were certainly not consoling.

Even Jackson refused to visit him, not believing the message he sent, being so often lured by the prisoners with a like request, which, if granted, ultimately ended in a struggle with the captives, who, as soon as the cell door was opened, would make an attempt to escape, and sometimes succeed, but more often fail.

The doom Lord Cecil had allotted for Guy Fawkes was very likely to fall upon himself. There seemed no way left for him to avoid it. Jackson had refused to see him, and the gaolers only scoffed at him whenever he tried to explain the mistake that placed him in such jeopardy.

Nobody but his enemies knew of his imprisonment, and the slightest favour he asked was refused, so he had no chance of sending for a friend to clear up the mistake.

Was he to endure the misery of this horrible confinement? he thought; to be removed, hence to the torturing rack? He shuddered as the idea impressed itself upon him.

He had abandoned himself to despair, and his head was buried in his hands when his cell door was opened.

He raised his head to see who came, and his gaze encountered Count Basco and the prison official, Jackson; the latter turned to go, when Lord Cecil cried—

"Detain that man."

"I sent for thee," said the prisoner, in an angry, indignant tone.

"Well!" queried the man.

"And you refused to come."

"I should have enough to do, if I minded the whims of all the prisoners."

"Know you to whom ye speak?"

"No—nor do I care."

"Insolent man, thou wilt repent this."

"Methinks, sir prisoner, thou speakest rather bold for a man whose hours are numbered."

The presence of Count Basco revived Lord Cecil's fading hope of freedom; and he arose in all his dignity, his cold cynical eyes glittering in the dark like the eyes of a snake.

"And why, sirrah, did you not come when I sent for thee?" he demanded.

"Because I did not think it worth my while," was the cool rejoinder.

The darkness of the interior of the cell where Lord Cecil stood prevented Jackson from plainly distinguishing the person he addressed; so he was totally ignorant of the prisoner's rank, and he wondered at his presumption for calling him to an account for not complying with his request.

"What right hast thou to question me?" he asked, indignantly.

"What right have I to question thee? the right of a superior, insolent varlet."

"A superior! insolent varlet thou art, I know," said Jackson, with quiet irony: "but why that should give thee a right to call me to account, I can't make out."

Cecil took the taunt, and his rage burst forth in violence.

"Braggart! servile hound," he exclaimed, foaming with rage. "Thy daring insolence will cost thee dearly: bitterly shalt thou rue the hour when you braved my authority."

"Who art thou?" asked Jackson, uneasily, a suspicion of the truth crossing his mind.

"Lord Cecil, knave," answered the prisoner, confronting the gaoler.

The change that came over Jackson's features was wonderful. Had a thunderbolt fallen at his feet he could not have felt more astonished than he did at the appearance of Lord Cecil: his head bowed in submission, and he stood an object of abject misery.

"What hast thou to say in defence, for thy unpardonable conduct?" demanded Cecil, haughtily.

"This, my lord," said the gaoler, gathering courage: "that I could not credit that thy lordship had been really captured and brought hither; it seemed so utterly impossible that the men could have been fools enough to make such a mistake."

"But the mistake was made, and thou hadst a right to come, when sent for."

"I should have done so instantly, my lord, but I have been fooled so many times by the prisoners in a like manner, that it has made me careful."

"Yet you had no right to doubt my word. Is it likely that any prisoner would assume my name?"

"They have done the like before, and when I have gone to see them they have tried to escape."

"Yet that does not exonerate you from the crime you have committed by keeping me confined here."

"The fault was not mine, my lord: I acted on my right of duty, and I crave thy pardon for the innocent offence."

"Well," said Cecil, piqued at being defeated, "saying that the fault of my imprisonment was not thine, how was it that the prisoners came to escape?"

"Their escape, my lord, arose through the indiscretion of thy messenger," replied the gaoler, alluding to Basco.

"In what way could he be the cause of their escape? They got away through your indolence. You will not get out of this so easily as before."

"Pardon me, my lord, it was no fault of mine that they got away. Had your messenger been more prudent, and not used his dagger, they would have been here now. You have him to thank for what you have endured."

Cecil gave the Basco a look that sent the hot blood tingling to his swarthy cheeks, and he returned a look of defiant scorn.

"Explain," demanded Cecil, impatiently. "How could my messenger have prevented their escape, or even the cause of it."

"A quarrel arose between them. Your messenger used his dagger. It was struck from his hand. One of the prisoners secured it, and with that they excavated a way out of their cell."

"Where were the gaolers?" inquired Cecil, fixing the gaoler with his cold cynical eyes.

"The one who kept guard outside their cell they overpowered, bound and gagged him. Guy Fawkes put on his clothes, and acted as gaoler, until he saw a safe opportunity to conduct his comrades out."

"Oh!" said Lord Cecil, unpleasantly; "and this is the way the king's prison is guarded! If the prisoners can contrive to get out of their cell, they are allowed to go. Mr. Jackson, you will have to answer for this. It is through your neglect that they escaped."

"But, my lord, hear me."

Cecil moved his hand.

"Conduct us hence," he said.

The gaoler led them to the prison gates, feeling awfully dejected. He held a responsible situation, and the disgrace of being accused of neglect he felt keenly.

Now that he was free, Lord Cecil began to vent his spite upon his confederate.

"Had you been at the place appointed, as agreed upon," he said maliciously, "all this would not have occurred."

"I was there," Basco said, pertly.

"How was it, then, that you did not come to my assistance?"

"You had gone when I arrived."

"And whose fault was that?" fiercely inquired Cecil.

"Thine own, for being taken," replied the Bravo, quietly.

"Had you been there, I should not have been taken by the dogs."

"But as you were, it's no good making a confounded row about what has happened, and can't be undone."

"Is that any reason why you should fool me? I paid you to be there, in case I should want you. I did want you, and you were not there."

"I was there."

"Liar!"

The Bravo's eyes gleamed like fire, and giving the infuriated nobleman a scowling look, he said, in a fierce voice—

"I stand that from no man, be he lord or king. Repeat that sentence, and it will be thy last. Be warned, Lord Cecil."

Cecil laughed ironically at the threat, but he did not repeat the sentence. The Bravo's words left an impression on him, that it would be advisable to smother his wrath.

Count Basco was not the man to be kept under restraint by the tyranny of a master: he was not the cringing, servile slave Lord Cecil would have liked to do his dark, infernal work, and he bitterly regretted having taken him into his confidence; but it was too late now to retract, and he would have to put up with him, greatly to his mortification.

"Well, if you were there, it was not until after the hour named," continued Lord Cecil, not wishing to show any fear.

"I was there at the time specified by you," Basco said, deliberately.

"Then, where were you?"

"Beneath the Lady Claire's chamber window, but the boat had gone, and so had you."

"Then you could not have been there at the time stated," Cecil said again, losing his temper.

"I was there at my time, Lord Cecil," said the Bully Count, impressively.

"Your time," said Cecil.

"The time stated by you."

"Explain."

"'Tis easily done."

"Do, so, then, and taunt me no longer," cried Cecil, impatiently.

"Thus it was then that I obeyed you by being there at my time. Your appointment with the lady was at midnight, as arranged by thee. I was to be there at half an hour later, giving thyself the interim to woo the lady. I was there at my time, but your wooing had not lasted half an hour, through the intervention of Guy Fawkes. Need I tell you the rest?"

Lord Cecil scowled darkly at the mention of his foe, his bitter hate rose in all its maddening tortures. He always bore the daring fellow a malicious spite, but since he had been the cause of defeating his evil project, in carrying off the fair Lady Claire, and the humiliation of being dragged to prison, he was more incensed towards him than ever.

Basco watched his working features with a gleam of triumph; it gave him infinite delight to see him suffer.

"I hope thou art satisfied that the fault of thy degradation was not mine," he said.

"Let the subject drop," almost furiously exclaimed Cecil. "Guy Fawkes has escaped my vengeance, but it won't be for long. He must be caught again, and then he shall know the power of the man he has dared to brave."

"It's very easy to say he must be caught; but the thing is to catch him. How will you manage that?"

"I have an idea which, if arranged with skill, will easily trap him," Cecil said, his malignant features gleaming with evil triumph. "The fool thought to deter me from my purpose with the Lady Claire by his interference. It has made me the more eager to carry out my plan. She must be mine."

"So she shall, if it is possible."

"Possible!" echoed Cecil, astonished that his ally should think there existed a doubt to impede the success of his scheme. "Why not? Do you think it impracticable?"

"I shall be better able to tell you when you have disclosed your idea."

"Well, this it is," began the favoured courtier, "to-morrow night Lady Claire will be lured from her home by stratagem. I shall have a boat ready to convey her to some lone place where I can make her mine, during which time Guy Fawkes must be sought and found out. In case of his mistress's abduction, he will follow. We must have a body of men to secure him at a favourable opportunity, and so I think my revenge will be complete."

"The scheme is good, and likely to succeed, I think; but the worst difficulty is to find Guy."

"You will find him at some of the gambling haunts, no doubt; however, I will leave you to ferret him out, and to-morrow we can further arrange matters."

The two dark-souled plotters parted, and Count Basco went in quest of Guy Fawkes to lure him into the dangers planned for his destruction.

CHAPTER XV.

THE STRATAGEM SUCCEEDS.

LADY CLAIRE OF GRACE was sitting at her chamber window, watching the boats as they glided up and down the river, and expected every moment to see one pulled ashore, and her gallant lover jump out.

Guy Fawkes had promised to visit her on the evening in question, and she waited anxiously for the hour to arrive that would bring him to her arms.

Their love was a secret engagement, unknown to any, save the Jesuit, who had the guardianship of the beautiful girl, and rather encouraged their love than disapproved of it.

Lady Claire was an orphan and an heiress to a vast fortune. She had been placed under the protection of the king by her dying parent, and, unless she married the man his majesty approved of, she would be disinherited, and her fortune confiscated.

The king had put her in the care of the priest, with whom she never resided, believing him to be a true and faithful, loyal subject of the Protestant faith, and the most proper person to bring up a guileless girl of tender years.

But the crafty priest had broken the royal trust, and while his ward was an unsuspecting child, he had poisoned her mind against the Protestants, and made her a confirmed Catholic by the time she had reached the age of maturity, gradually disclosing the secrets of the terrible revolt in agitation, and artfully drawing her into the fearful vortex.

He had his own reasons for the base treachery, and he was pleased rather than otherwise at the lovers' stolen interviews.

The time was drawing nigh when the lovers were to meet; and Lady Claire waited with the yearning hope of her pure, ardent love, longing to hear again the tender words whispered in her ear, spoken by her lover's manly voice—such words as a maiden loves to listen to.

The night was clear and beautiful, and the few gloomy clouds that hung about slowly drifted away, and left a vast, starry vault of calm, blue sky; the stars twinkled out, bright and clear, upon the waters, and the moon threw long rays of silvery light on the black, surging waves. It was an hour for peaceful thought. The old city, with its quaintly-built houses, and the myriads of steeples seemed wrapped in slumber, as their dark shadows loomed dimly out. A silence singularly profound reigned throughout, and was not without its influence upon the lonely maiden, watching for the coming boat of her expectant lover.

A boat came, and was pulled ashore, and Claire's heart leaped with joy, but sank the next instant with disappointment, as a stranger stepped out of the frail barque.

The man looked about as though not certain that he had come to the right place, until his gaze fell upon the pale features of the maiden at the window. Then he stood meditatively and seemed at a loss how to proceed.

Looking up he raised his hat with an awkward grace, and said—

"Sweet lady, I am the bearer of a missive from thy lover, which I would fain give into thy hands."

"Wait, then, good sir, and I will descend unto thee," said the unsuspecting girl.

She vanished from the window, and in a few seconds appeared on the bank of the sluggish waters, through a small door that opened in a recess in the wall.

The man put a note in her small, trembling hand.

"Who sent thee with this?" she asked, her voice quivering with emotion; for the very idea of her lover sending a stranger with a message, filled her with fearful apprehensions of some terrible calamity that might have befallen him."

"Guy Fawkes," said the messenger, in answer to her question; "and I am to wait for thy answer, if it so pleases your ladyship."

"Wait," said the maiden, hastily.

The man waited while she returned to her chamber to read the forged epistle.

Her eyes filled with tears of agony, and her face turned a deathly pallor, as she read the following lines:—

"*Dearest Claire,—*

"*Come instantly, if you would see me in life again. I have been waylaid and attacked by a gang of ruffians, and now lie in a very precarious condition at an inn at Richmond. I have much to say, ere I die, of great importance to thee, and which thine ears alone must listen to. Do not lose a moment in hesitation, but come as thou art, while I have breath to impart the great secret which concerns thy*

THE GUARDIAN ANGEL.

future life. I have sent a faithful messenger in whom you may place thyself in confidence, and he will convey you hither to thine own devoted and expiring GUY FAWKES."

6

The letter dropped from her hand as she read through her tears the last few words, and she stood like a statue, her lovely features marked by the iron hand of grief.

The first cruel blow of her persecutors was dealt with sure and destructive accuracy ; the golden-linked chain of her young life's love-dream was broken, and she stood a wreck—a sad, despairing specimen of what she was even an hour before.

She broke from her lethargy by a sudden start, and hastily taking up her hood and cloak, she hastened to the water side, and rejoined the boatmen.

"Hasten, good boatmen," she said, "to thy journey's end, and thou shalt be well paid for thy trouble."

The men conducted her to the boat. It was then that a misgiving that all was not right crossed her mind. She would have made some excuse to return to the house, but it was too late now. The boat was pushed off, and two men, who had been lying concealed at the bottom of the little barque, sprang up as they reached the middle of the stream, and she was roughly seized, gagged, and bound before a cry could escape her lips.

The three ruffians then took their seat, having hidden their fair captive in the bottom of the boat from the gaze of passers by, and pulled together with all their strength to the rendezvous, where their master awaited them.

Lord Cecil had planned the lady's abduction with clever ingenuity, and his stratagem had succeeded so far. But whether he was going to have the rest of the game in his favour we shall see as we go on.

The boat had hardly receded out of sight when Guy Fawkes appeared upon the spot where the treacherous scene, a few minutes before, had been enacted.

Count Basco had failed in his search to discover him, and Guy was here by appointment, innocent of what had taken place ; but after waiting about for some time, without seeing any signal from the lady, a suspicion that something had occurred flashed through his mind, and his dark, handsome face became darker by the sombre cloud that shrouded his thoughtful brow.

He had noticed a boatman pulling up and down the stream in a short space, and now and then glancing towards him, as though hesitating whether to row ashore or not.

Guy hailed him, and the man pulled in-shore.

"How long have you been about here ?" inquired Fawkes.

"All the evening, sir, waiting for a job ; but nobody seems in want of a boat," answered the man, with a ready lie, for he had only taken up his position opposite the house of the Jesuits as the other boat, with the fair captive, rowed away, which were his instructions from Lord Cecil.

The crafty statesman, on being informed by Basco of his failure to discover Guy, had anticipated that he would be there, and, accordingly, sent out spies to lure him into the trap laid for him.

"Have you seen anything transpire here ?" Guy asked.

"In what way, sir ?"

"Well, has anything unusual transpired ?"

"Well, sir, as far as that goes," and the man hesitated.

"Be not afraid to speak," angrily exclaimed Guy, "I will pay you for thy information," and he threw the man a gold piece.

"Well, sir, as thou seemest interested, something did happen ; but it ain't the likes of us watermen to tell everyone what we see, you know, sir."

"Well, well, what did you see ?" uneasily interrogated Guy.

The man regarded him studiously, weighing over in his mind if there was an opportunity of making any more gold pieces.

Guy interpreted his avaricious thought, and held up two pieces between his fingers.

"Give me your information truthfully," he said, "and you shall have these."

The ruffian's eyes glistened greedily.

"I saw a boat row ashore here," he began, "and the lady that was up in that room, after some talk with the boatmen, came down. She got in the boat ; then two more men jumped up, and the lady was gagged and thrown down in the boat. I followed the boat," the man said, significantly, in conclusion, as though for the remainder of the recital he wanted another gold piece.

Guy was electrified by the intelligence. This was rather more than he had expected. His blood coursed through his veins, turning from an icy chill to a heat of liquid fire.

The boatman was nicely taken in. This time, instead of his interlocutor asking him where he followed the boat to, he said—

"Take me to where they went, and I will satisfy your greed for the remainder of the story."

The very thing the man wanted was to get him in the boat, but his only grief was that he would not get any more gold then. This was the reason he wanted to obtain as much as he could before they came to the boat arrangement, but Guy's sudden request put a damper on his extortions, and he was obliged to obey.

They got in the boat, and each taking an oar, pulled with a will, though against the tide, that astonished many men they passed, who were struggling with the stream.

Neither of them spoke a word. Each was occupied with his own thoughts ; Guy thinking of the poor girl's peril and revenging her wrongs, and his companion chuckling over the dexterity with which he had got him in the toils of his foes, and the astonishment he would feel when they landed at their destination.

The boat shot through Battersea Bridge, and a few minutes later the boatman said—

"This is where they landed."

It was a lonely wretched spot in Battersea

fields, marshy, with patches of bushes, and a few solitary trees growing at a most unfriendly distance from one another, and looming out in the twilight like grim sentinels.

Guy cast one rapid glance around, and as he sprang from the boat the boatman raised an oar and aimed a furious blow at his head, but fortunately his coward arm was diverted from its mark by the hand of Providence, and the daring adventurer escaped being brained.

Directly his feet touched the ground a gang of Cecil's hirelings, who had been waiting in ambush for him, sprang up from behind the bushes, and surrounded him like a pack of wolves.

"A trap," muttered Guy Fawkes, drawing his sword; and, making a leap from where he stood, he took a firm stand in the thickest of them.

"Come on," he said, with cool resolution.

The men dashed at him furiously; the foremost one fell, pierced through the heart.

"One," Guy said, looking round 'to see how many remained, "twelve, thirteen with the boatman; one down leaves a dozen."

He fixed his betrayer with a glance that made the callous wretch slink away, feeling awfully uncomfortable. He was doomed; but Guy allowed him to enjoy the spirit of the fight with the rest.

The bravoes, incensed by the loss of their companion, made a furious onset at his slayer, and Guy was beaten back.

Then he turned, like a tiger, upon them—his weapon, darting about like an electric serpent amongst the slashing blades of his opponents, soon made a path for him; and he singled out the boatman, whom he grasped by the throat. His sword was raised to strike the fatal blow, when the quailing wretch artfully threw down his sword, and said—

"Thou wilt not strike a defenceless man?"

Guy saw the coward act, and it made him the more angry, because of its meanness.

"Strike you!" he said, in a stern, pitiless voice. "Ay, will I. It will be a charity to rid the world of such a dastardly knave as thou art."

"I did but my duty. If I had not, some of the others would."

"You should have let them done it. It would have paid thee better to have put me on my guard, instead of luring me into this snare. You merit death alone for the cowardly act of throwing thy weapon away; then there is the treachery of bringing me here, and the attempt to brain me as I got out of yonder boat. Offer up a hasty prayer for thy black soul—thy time is nigh!"

"Mercy! Save me!" gasped the terror-stricken ruffian.

"As much mercy thou shalt have as thou wouldst have shown me. Prepare! I give thee but a few moments to ask pardon for thy sins."

The ruffian struggled madly to break from the iron grip that held him, and Guy, to end the matter, sheathed his sword in his captive's heart, and then hurled the quivering body from him, and it fell into the murmuring waters with a dull, heavy splash.

The men shivered as their companion disappeared, and looked from one to the other in unutterable horror.

The tragedy had been consummated so quickly, that there was no time for them to interfere, and before they had broken from their spell of horror, Guy Fawkes was upon them again like a tiger that had tasted blood and thirsted for more.

The ruffians shrank from him involuntarily, not that they feared him exactly, for had they been a little more active with their weapons, they would not have left much of him to escape, but they were awkward, and used no skill, and, like all bullies when confronted by any real danger, they were the first to lose courage.

Guy took the opportunity of their embarrassment, and turned on his heels to escape by the boat that had brought him hither.

Directly the bravoes saw that he had shown the white feather they raised a shout, and rushed after him, but before they had reached the water's edge, Guy was far out of their reach, and pulling towards Mortlake, where he had an idea that he would find his lady love.

CHAPTER XVI.

THE SIGNAL SCARF.

THE moon was shining brightly on the rippling waters, and in the wake of Guy's boat, as he glided down the stream, there followed something dark and silent.

The object was not discernible, but there was something about it that transfixed the gaze of the boatman with terror, a pair of fierce eyes he fancied glared upon him from the surface of the water with a look of vengeance.

The solitude of the hour, the gloomy desolation of all around, where nothing was heard save the sudden splash of the water against the sides of his boat, and the melancholy moaning wind blowing through the swaying trees on either side of the Thames, did not console the dread feeling of awe awakened in Guy at the appearance of the mysterious object that followed his boat.

He tried to turn his eyes from it, but he could not; the fascinating glare exerted a magnet-power over him he could not resist, and he pulled frantically to escape it.

He did so, and when he ventured to look, the silver-tipped water was clear, and he breathed with relief.

By this time he had reached Mortlake, and while landing, something came against his boat with a sullen thud that caused his heart to leap to his mouth, and starting round he stood paralyzed at what he saw.

At his feet lay the body of the man he had slain in remorseless anger, and threw into the Thames. The pale moon's rays fell full upon the rigid features, and the eyes, in death, were fixed upon his slayer's face with a look of retribution.

Guy could not repress a shudder; and giving vent to his terror in a piercing shriek, he rushed off as though mad—his stricken conscience at work, peopled the road behind him with a thousand phantoms giving chase.

He ran until his legs refused to take him further, and he sank down at the foot of a tree exhausted.

He soon forgot his fright, and relapsed into a chaos of deep reflections, from which he was aroused by the rustling of the leaves, disturbed by someone approaching.

He looked up and beheld a dark female form gliding silently towards him.

Guy slowly rose from the ground; his hair rose on his head at the same time, and his large dark eyes, full of dread, were fixed upon the sad white face of the intruder.

He would fain have fled, but he could not; the steady gaze of those wild eyes looking into his own held him powerless.

There was not much in the person who confronted him to cause him the uneasiness he felt, but Guy Fawkes was naturally superstitious, and the memory of the late coincidence of the dead man following him on the water, rose vividly before him, and he really thought that he was beset by some unearthly being.

Guy shuddered, and big drops of perspiration rolled down his face as the solemn hour of midnight was borne through the silent air in dismal echoes from a distant church spire; and as the last stroke died away, borne on the wings of night, he expected to see the form before him sink into the earth at his feet—shrouded in a ghostly winding sheet.

But it did not. It stood there in the form of an earthly being, which it was, and not a bad-looking one either. It possessed a figure of grace many might have envied, and a face of faultless beauty, save that there was a wearied expression about the features that marred the calm it once wore.

She was a being of about twenty-five years of age, with a dark complexion, wild-looking eyes, almost ferocious in their expression as you looked into them, and a rich cluster of jet black hair hung about a pair of white round shoulders in wild disorder.

Her features changed to a sorrowful expression after regarding Guy for several moments in silence, and she said, in a low, melancholy voice, raising her hand to heaven as she spoke—

"Be warned, before it is too late. Take the warning of one who can foresee thy fate. Unless you forego the terrible undertaking you have been drawn into, thou wilst suffer a lingering death of fearful torture. Be warned —be warned!"

And giving him a beseeching look, she gathered her garments around her, and fled.

Guy stood stupified for a few seconds, and, when he looked after her, she was nowhere to be seen.

"Some poor distracted maniac," he cogitated, walking away in moody thought.

He was in a desolate part of the country, uninhabited, and he walked on, knowing not whither he was going, but trusting to Providence to put him in the right path, to discover the abductors of his lady love.

A glimmering light from a distant window broke through the clustering trees. This gave him hope, and he hurried on—not with the thought of finding his lady there, but he felt a kind of joy to know that there were some human beings near.

While passing under the window of the cottage—a pretty, quaint building, surrounded with a fairy-like garden—something fluttering above his head attracted his attention, and he looked up.

A silken scarf hung from the window, the window was partly open, and a dim light burned in the room.

"I have seen that scarf before," he thought, regarding it studiously, as though trying to call to mind where before he had seen it.

"If I am not mistaken, Lady Claire had one similar," he went on cogitating; "but surely it cannot be hers; and yet it may be. Why not? The scoundrel may have brought her hither, and she, perhaps, hung this out as a signal by which I might learn her retreat if I followed."

With this thought uppermost in his mind he stood beneath the window, wondering how he could learn if his suppositions were correct, when a white arm was put out of the window between the iron bars, and a pocket-handkerchief fell at his feet.

Guy picked it up, and in the corner was the Lady Claire of Grace's crest. His doubts were now confirmed to realities, and looking up he beheld the object of his thoughts, white and trembling, standing at the window, with the iron bars before her that kept her a helpless captive—a timid bird, caged, shut up from liberty and those she loved—a prey for the brutal monster who had trapped her—a victim in whose delicious charms he longed to revel in, and only waited to see if she would consent.

Guy kissed the point of his sword to heaven and then his hand to her.

Lady Grace understood the token of faith; she knew that her lover would contrive to save her.

Guy went away, and returned to the waterside, where he cut the mooring of the boat to make a rope ladder of, and when he returned it was complete.

Tying a piece of rope to the end of the ladder, and a stone to the other end of the rope, he threw it dexterously over one of the iron bars before the window. The weight of the stone brought the rope to the ground, hauling up the ladder as it descended.

Guy indicated to the lady to make it fast. She did so; and then he tried its strength, mounted lightly to the window, and began with his dagger to loosen the bars.

Lady Claire stood by watching him with admiration, and trembling with fear lest the noise of his digging should arouse her persecutor, who waited like a hungry tiger to make an attack upon his lovely victim.

One—two bars were removed; the third was rather more obstinate than the others. Guy got in a great perspiration; he worked incessantly, dug mortar away, even loosened bricks, tugged and wrenched at it with all his might, but it would not move. He would not give in, though. Though his arms ached so by pulling that he could hardly raise them, yet he persevered, and at last the obstacle was removed, with two long staples at either end, which had been the cause of all his difficulty.

A little cry of joy escaped Lady Claire's lips when the last bar to liberty was removed.

Guy assisted her through the window, drew her to his breast, and kissing her fair brow began to descend.

Clinging to her lover, Lady Claire cast her eyes down the fearful depth they had to descend, and a cry of terror burst from her lips.

She saw beneath Lord Cecil and a gang of hirelings waiting for them. The nobleman's face was radiant with savage triumph; savage because the daring fellow had escaped the snare he had been lured into—triumphant that he had another opportunity to wreak his vengeance upon him.

Guy stopped in his descent, and looked down to ascertain the cause of the lady's alarm.

He saw it. His flight that way was entirely cut off. His only chance was to remount to the window.

The difficulty to remount was great, and the risk dangerous, as he had but one hand at liberty, clasping the lovely form of the lady with the other.

To descend was comparatively easy, but none the less hazardous on account of the ruffians waiting for him. His only chance to reach the window entirely depended upon the lady's nerve. If she could clasp her hands round his neck and trust herself, he could use both hands and succeed in reaching the chamber.

He was about to put the proposition to her, when a gang of ruffians appeared at the window.

His escape was entirely cut off now. Above and below he was menaced by his foes.

Lady Claire gave herself up for lost. Not so with her lover. He was indomitable to the last. His face assumed a terrible expression. He placed his sword between his teeth, and began to descend, when the ruffians above hauled up the rope ladder.

Lady Claire of Grace was torn from her lover, and the ladder let drop again.

The jerk nearly precipitated Guy among his enemies beneath, but he retained his hold, and began to slide down the rope, when the malicious brutes cut the ladder, and he finished his descent with lightning rapidity.

Quick as the caitiffs were to fall to the attack, Guy was upon his feet, despite the fearful shaking the fall had given him, and his sword clashed against the thirsty blades of a dozen ruffians.

Guy was like a caged tiger. He flew at the nearest to him, in ferocious anger, and felled remorselessly all who came within reach of his sword.

"Kill him!" yelled Lord Cecil.

Guy looked round for the speaker, his eyes, blazing like balls of fire, met the gaze of his foe, and Lord Cecil slunk away.

Guy Fawkes watched him, and, cutting his way through the ruffian gang, confronted the white-faced villain.

"Coward knave," cried Fawkes, "defend thyself, ere I put an end to thy miserable life."

His sword was raised to strike; his look was stern and relentless; his foe saw there was no mercy, and drew his weapon to defend his life.

The bright steel crossed, and the two men fought in deadly hate, foot to foot. Eye watching eye, they stood, each waiting for an opportunity to pierce the other to the heart.

Cecil made a straight lunge for his opponent's left side, but his blade was turned quickly aside. Guy ran the point of his sword along his foe's, and, like a glittering snake, it wound round Cecil's weapon, then, with a sudden wrench, it went flying from his grasp.

Lord Cecil stood weaponless, and at the mercy of his foe.

There was no mercy for him, he had aroused the demon of Guy's nature, and he saw the cold blade coming towards him.

Terror took possession of him, and he retreated, shrieking with mental fear, so demoniac did his foe stand before him.

Guy made a stroke at the trembling dastard, and smote him to the earth by a cut across the forehead that would have cleft his skull in twain had it not been so thick.

Writhing in agony, Lord Cecil called upon his hireling crew to attack his assailant.

The ruffians made a rush at Guy to avenge their fallen master.

"Let him not escape, on your lives!" cried Cecil. "Hack him to pieces!"

Guy turned. He had shed enough blood for one night, and without any purpose but that he had defended his own life. He might slay a dozen more of the ruffians and be just as far from saving his lady love as he was then.

And he fled, leaving the lovely girl to the mercy of her enemies, while he sought his comrades.

The ruffians, thinking he fled from cowardice, dashed after him.

CHAPTER XVII.

LIFE OR DEATH.

WHEN Hugh Wardour dashed away, leaving his comrades with the strange horseman, he was half frantic with despair. He held the stricken girl to his throbbing breast, insensible—perhaps dead ; and he knew not in what direction to go for assistance.

Suddenly he came upon a small habitation ; here he thundered loudly at the door for admittance, and was answered by a motherly old lady, who came down out of her warm bed and took the bleeding form of Constance from the young horseman.

Having safely deposited the poor girl on a couch, she awoke her husband, and sent him for medical assistance, while she herself did all that lay in her power to restore the stricken girl ; and when the doctor appeared she had extricated the bullet from the delicate flesh and bound up the wound, and to the astonishment of the medical gentleman, defied him to undo her handiwork.

"But, my dear madam," he began expostulating ; "you sent for me—the lady is in a very dangerous condition, and unless proper medical advice is shown her, the case may prove fatal."

"Fatal, indeed !" sneered the old lady ; "the poor creature might have died twenty times while you were finding your way here."

"Marry ! my dear lady, thou forgettest the journey I have had to come."

"I forget nothing, sir ; but I think you might have made more haste."

"I lost not a minute when your husband arrived ; and if you have dispensed with my services, I may go. To-morrow I shall send in my account, and I hope you "——

"Yes, you dare send in an account !" the old lady burst out, wrathfully. "A pretty thing, indeed, that ! You want to impose upon people for doing nothing."

This feudal engagement was overheard by Hugh, who, in an adjoining apartment, had been waiting anxiously to hear if there was any hope of the lady's recovery. Growing impatient, and wishing to know what all the wrangling meant, he made his way to the scene of strife.

"What does all this mean ? " he asked in a bewildered manner.

"Mean, sir ?" said the old lady, in self-defiance. "It means, sir, that this pretty scarecrow, who calls himself a doctor, came

here an hour after he was wanted, and now wants to send in his bill for doing nothing."

"You won't give me a chance to do anything," the physician said, taking the instant opportunity to put in a word as the old lady stopped to draw breath.

"I wont ? you insolent varlet !" roared the old lady. "How dare you speak to me in such a manner ?"

"By the saints, good dame, thou mayst have forgotten"——

"Forgot what, sir, eh ? Do you mean to insinuate that"——

"I insinuate nothing," the doctor said, raising his hand for peace.

"I must really interfere," Hugh said, who had been looking on in distraction. "This is not the place to quarrel, with a sick lady in the room. If this gentleman is the physician you sent for, I must demand his attendance for the lady."

The doctor bowed, and the good old lady bounced out of the room, overflowing with wrath at being thus defeated.

"Ah !" she muttered, as she banged the door after her, "that's all one gets for being charitable. Never more shall anyone enter my house. No ; not if they are dying. I've sworn it, and I'll keep my word. A pretty thing indeed ! I am to be turned out of my own house by strangers ! I'll see about that. They shall find that I have got a spirit. I'll let them see that I won't be trampled on by them, I'm sure. I wonder what will come next ? George ! George !"—this was in her very highest note for her husband—"George ! come down and protect me."

"Eh, my dear, what's the matter !" came a deep, grunting voice, from some part of the house.

"The matter ! Come down, I say, and see. I shall be turned out of my own house, and all through you !"

"Through me, old gal ! How ! Who's the varlets that dares take liberties with thee, eh ?"

The person who spoke those words descended from an upper room with a heavy tread, and the irritable old lady's lord and master approached his better half in a drowsy state and in half dishabille.

"Ludlow ! Ludlow !" shrieked the old lady, shaking him by the arm, "I tell thee I've been insulted ; an' thou art no man if you don't see me righted."

Ludlow was a huge, easy-going man, who would rather drown his wrath in a stiff glass of grog than risk the danger of seeking the man who insulted him.

A big grin spread over his broad, good-humoured face, at the indignation of his wife, and smacking her sharply on her round, plump shoulder, said—

"Did they, though ? We'll see what the malaports mean by such insolence."

"Mean ! Why they mean to take possession of my house, and turn us out."

"The devil they do ! " said the old fellow,

laughing aside. "Well, well, we will see what they are after."

They entered the chamber of the sick lady. Hugh sat by the side of the couch, watching the sleeping sufferer, with one tiny hand resting in his own. The doctor, who had re-dressed the lady's wound, was waiting to see a change come over her. She lay in a very precarious state, and he knew not which way the change would result until she awoke. But he did not wish to wake her, as the slightest shock might sunder the slender web that held life together, and as the happy pair made their appearance, the physician met them at the door, and enjoined silence.

"Well, I'm sure!" exclaimed the old lady, with an indignant toss of her head. "I wonder what next! I suppose you'll turn me out of my own house!"

"My dear lady, have some consideration for this poor young creature," the doctor said, sharply, annoyed at the irritable cottager's want of discretion; "the slightest noise may prove fatal, and I must beg of you to leave the room, if you please."

This was rather more than the old lady could quietly stand. She fairly danced with rage, and her wrath rose in such fury as to nearly choke her.

Her breath caught, her face turned scarlet; the veins stood out like cords in her throat; she threw her arms about in wild gesticulations, and kept up a rapid tattoo with her feet.

Her husband knew when her breath once got vent, there would be a terrible explosion, and to prevent such a catastrophe taking place in the sick chamber, he took her up in his arms, and carried her out.

Then she found breath, and gave vent to her injured feelings in a prolonged shriek, and being restrained by her husband from re-entering to vent her spite on the doctor, she went into hysterics, overpowered by her uncontrollable passion, and was carried up to her bed, where her good-natured husband left her to recover.

Her screams had disturbed the gentle sufferer from her trance-like slumber, and Hugh sat in torturing suspense hushed in silence of the tomb, watching her slightest movement. He feared each breath she drew would be her last, and big, scalding tears ran down his manly, sun-burnt cheeks in agony.

Constance opened her eyes, smiled faintly at her lover, and glanced round the room.

The doctor thought she seemed as though she wished to say something to him, and he went to her side.

Constance wished to say something, but her voice was too faint to articulate a word. The beseeching look of her pretty soft blue eyes was interpreted by the kind-hearted physician, and he said, with a misgiving at his heart—

"There is hope; but you must remain perfectly quiet."

The grateful smile she gave him as she sank back on her pillow was enough to tell him she had not mistaken the meaning of his look; and though glad that he had been the means of comforting her, he was sorely pained at having to deceive her, for he felt that there was no hope of her recovery.

The doctor's change of countenance, the look of deep concern, did not escape the notice of Hugh.

"Is there hope?" he asked, not daring to look the doctor in the face, for fear of reading there the fearful truth his fears suggested.

"There is hope," the physician answered.

Constance had fallen into a sound sleep; so still did she lie, anyone would have thought that it was her sleep of death. Her pulsation seemed stopped, and a clammy yellow tint settled upon her features.

The doctor watched her uneasily.

"She is worse than I thought," he said. "I have but one remedy, and that will kill her if she is not strong enough to stand its influence."

"And what is that?" asked Hugh, eagerly.

"A most powerful elixir, a potion known only to myself. It has saved many from the jaws of death when no other earthly power could save them. Shall I try it?"

"If you think it will save her."

"It will revive her for a time. But she is so delicate that I cannot say she will recover after the power of the elixir has worked off. But she may. It is a chance of life or death. If she keeps cool there is hope."

"Then, in the name of the Holy Virgin, try it with my free consent," Hugh said. "There is no hope of her recovery in her present state?"

"None," replied the man of science, taking from his breast pocket a small phial containing a greenish liquid.

"Stay!" exclaimed Hugh, grasping the doctor's hand as he drew the cork, "Stay I would not have her sacrificed by an experiment."

"It is no experiment. I have used it oftentimes before to know its influence; but I told you it will be a case of kill or cure."

"I know, I know," said Hugh, drawing his hand across his brow in perplexity. "What am I to do? I would not have her hurried from this world by the draught, in the event of its not succeeding to return life."

"Well, if you doubt the power of my knowledge in the science of physics, try its effect upon thyself," suggested the doctor, a little amazed at the other's want of faith.

Hugh assented to try it, and the doctor poured out a few drops into a glass and added a little cold water to it.

Hugh, without hesitation, drained the glass; and, in a few seconds, the effect it produced upon him was wonderful. His face flushed hotly, his chest seemed to expand, and a strength he had never felt in the best of health was leant to his limbs.

"Zounds!" he exclaimed. "'Tis powerful enough to bring the dead to life."

The doctor smiled approvingly.

"Then you think it worth trying?" he said.

"Yes—yes; and lose no time, in heaven's name!" quickly answered Hugh.

The doctor then mixed a little more of the elixir with some cold water; and, after bathing the fair sufferer's face and temples with the lotion, poured a few drops of the potion in its raw state down her throat.

The glass was barely taken from her lips when a convulsive thrill ran through her body; her eyes opened and glared wildly about the room; her face gleamed with a hectic flush; her bosom rose and fell, and she began to breathe heavily.

Hugh stood looking on in wonderment. He took one of her hands in his own, and her fingers twined round his with a pressure that made him wince, and her eyes were fixed upon him with a curious brilliancy.

The doctor then mixed some more of the elixir with water, and poured it down her throat.

In a few minutes she became calm. The wild look went from her eyes, and soon again she fell off into a peaceful sleep.

"She will live," said the man of science, looking at her with an air of satisfaction.

Hugh squeezed his hand in silent gratitude. He was too joyous with the happy news to find words to speak, for a time at least.

The doctor put the phial of elixir in his hand.

"This may be useful to you; but use it with care," he said, kindly.

Hugh accepted the valuable gift in the same silent gratitude.

"And now," continued the speaker, "I think I may leave her in safety. Look, sir," he added, pointing to the window, through which the grey streaks of morn stole. "Morning dawns; and you require rest, as do I. The lady will not wake for some hours yet, and you may rest with ease."

Hugh gave the sleeper a furtive glance, and mastering his emotion, he found his voice.

"Doctor," he said, fervently, "this is a debt I shall ever owe you my life's gratitude for. Money cannot efface it; though," he went on, taking from his pocket a goodly-filled purse, "you must be paid for your time, and shall."

"Say nought of that," the doctor said, generously pushing Hugh's hand aside, with the tempting purse of gold. "I vouch thou hast no more than thou knowest what to do with."

"I have that much to spare, without missing it," Hugh said; "and I beg that you will take it. 'Tis but a poor recompense for the happiness thou has restored to me."

After some little persuasion, the doctor took the money, nothing loth, and departed.

Hugh then kissed the pale brow of the sleeper, and threw himself on the hearthrug to rest, where he enjoyed some few hours' slumber with greater relish than he had done for many a long day, although it was on the hard ground.

CHAPTER XVIII.

CONSTANCE'S HISTORY.

HE was awoke by the old lady knocking at the room-door, to inform him that it was "very late."

After doing a comfortable yawn and stretching out his arms and legs, to arouse himself, he jumped up, quite refreshed, and, to his astonishment, Constance was sitting up on the couch, regarding him with a quiet, amiable smile, looking far different from the weak, helpless creature of the previous night.

"Constance, my love!" he exclaimed, in ecstacies at seeing her apparently so well. And he bent over her to kiss her glowing cheek. "You are better."

"Oh, much, dear Hugh," she said, sweetly. "I feel quite strong and well. But I suppose I may not get up just yet."

"Not yet, love. You must be content to remain a prisoner here for a few days."

The summons at the door was repeated, rather more loudly than before, by the irritable old lady.

"A fair morning to you, madam," said Hugh, admitting the old party.

"The same to you, young sir; and I hope the lady is better." The old lady was more calm after her fit.

"Much—thanks to your kindness, and the skill of that wonderful doctor you so kindly sent for."

Had Hugh wished to offend the old lady, he could not have touched her dignity upon a more delicate point than he did by speaking of the doctor's skill. She regarded him as ungrateful, using her own thoughts.

"Well, sir," she said, hastily, "I don't know so much about owing the lady's recovery to the skill of the man you are pleased to call doctor. I think if she had been left entirely to his care, she would have fared badly."

"Of course, madam," Hugh said, bowing in apology for the mistake he had made. "I owe you much for your kind, timely assistance."

Mrs. Ludlow was satisfied, and asked what they would like for breakfast.

"I," said Hugh, "will partake of anything you may have for your own breakfast, but for the lady I should like you to prepare something light."

The old lady liked the frank speaking of the young man, and promised to satisfy them both, which she did, for the breakfast she brought in for Constance would have tempted the most delicate stomach to an attack, and the gentle sufferer did not make a bad meal, nor did Hugh, for he ate as only a hungry man can eat with a keen appetite.

GUY FAWKES
OR
THE CONSPIRATOR'S BRIDE

RESCUED FROM DEATH.

"Now, dearest," said Hugh, when the remains of their repast were cleared away, "you had better take a little sleep, as I shall require you to answer me a few questions."

"I am quite able to answer them now, dear Hugh," replied Constance. "You don't know how strong I feel; I believe I could not sleep again just yet, were I to try."

"If you do not rest, the potion you have taken will do you no good," said Hugh.

"What potion have I taken ?" asked Constance, in astonishment.

Her lover then told her all that had taken place. She was no less timid than astonished at the effect the elixir had produced upon her.

"Do you think there is any fear, Hugh," she asked, fearing that her strength was only artificial.

"In what way, dearest ?"

"Do you think that I shall fall into that insensible state again when the power of the potion I have taken is exhausted ?"

"No, dearest ; the danger is past, and you have nothing to fear now."

"I have much to fear, Hugh, dear," said Constance, sadly.

"From what ?"

"From the treacherous priest, Father Guynot."

Hugh's face became stern at the mention of that name.

"What of him ?" he asked, uneasily.

"Much that I have to fear."

"Explain, dearest ; thy vague answers bewilder me."

"You remember taking me from the convent in Spain ?" she inquired.

"Well," answered Hugh.

"It was he who put me there—he with whom I was left in charge by my father—he whom my father trusted as a brother when he left England to fight for his country and his Queen."

The remembrance of the crafty priest's treachery greatly excited the poor girl, and she had to pause, for her breath was short already, she had overtaxed her strength.

Constance Meredith was a pure English patrician lady by birth. Her father, previous to his leaving England at the head of one of Elizabeth's armies during the time of the war with Spain, left his only daughter—his only child, Constance—under the protection of the above-named priest, and bequeathed to his charge the deeds of his vast fortune, which, in the event of him not returning, was to be made over to his child when she came of age.

The priest, an ambitious crafty man, abused the trust of the confiding nobleman by taking his *protégée* to Spain, where he placed her in a convent, much against the young lady's inclination.

His treacherous design was evident ; the property he had the sole control of, should the soldier not return after the campaign, his intention was to take possession of it ; but the knowledge of the lady's escape from the convent coming to his ears frustrated his design, and he set out in quest of the heiress with a deadly revengeful purpose to remove her from his path of ambition.

Constance minutely related the above to Hugh, and he listened to the villanous plot, his breast heaving with indignant rage.

He longed to get the wronger of his gentle lady-love in his grasp, to seek retribution for the wrongs she had suffered.

"Who was it who took you from the people whose care I placed you under after forcing you from the cloisters of the convent ?" he asked.

"Father Guynot," she answered ; "he discovered my retreat, and dragged me to some other place of confinement, where I knew not day from night. He would have slain me, but his heart was not quite void of feeling for the child he had even brought up from infancy under his care ; so he left me in the dungeon of the castle where he had taken me to linger out my days in captivity.

"The gaoler who supplied my daily wants, I entreated to let me see a priest, as I could not live much longer. At first, he would not listen to me ; but at last my supplications touched him, and he granted my wish.

"A priest was sent to me. I told him the miseries I had endured, and he took compassion on my unprotected position, and remained with me until evening—reading prayers, as the men who were put on guard to watch me thought—and that same night, when all was silent, he effected my escape.

"I placed myself under his protection, and he brought me to England, in hopes of finding my father. Our flight got known to Guynot ; he followed us hither, and denounced us to the Government as Papists. We were hunted by the men of law from place to place, and my protector thought it advisable to change my costume for the one you found me in."

"Is that the same priest you named to me ?" inquired Hugh.

"Aldham ? Yes ; he has proved a true and faithful friend. On the night when first we met, and I saw you—though I dared not reveal myself to you—he was taken prisoner by the soldiers, and I was saved from them by a strange horseman—the same mysterious being who saved you and your friends from the troopers yesterday."

"You speak of the night when I and my comrade, Guy Fawkes, fought with the soldiers at an inn ?"

"The same," said Constance. "The man who saved me I have since heard is known by the appellation of the Black Rider."

"'Tis so," put in Hugh. "Where did he take you to ?"

"A house at Hounslow. I was discovered there by the soldiers while the Black Rider was away. I had to fly from them for my life ; and while being chased by my pursuers, I met Father Aldham. He had escaped from the temporary lock-up, where his captors had put him, while they came in search of me.

"We had no time to exchange any words ; our pursuers were gaining upon us, and we had to fly. We sought refuge at the hostel from whence you and your comrade saved me last night."

"Why should the landlord have taken

such an interest in thy welfare?" asked Hugh, curiously.

"I know not. Father Aldham had a long conference before he departed, leaving me in the charge of the worthy fellow, who, I believe, knows more of me than I am aware of."

"Strange!" thought Hugh. "I must see him, and learn what he knows."

"Such is my history, as well as I can remember," said Constance.

Just then there was a clatter of a horse's hoofs. As the sounds approached the little lonely cottage, Constance, in terror, clung to her lover for protection.

The horse was drawn up at the door. Then came a knock.

Hugh and his trembling patient sat in fearful anxiety waiting the issue of the summons.

Presently there was a tapping at the chamber door.

Hugh, in a tremulous voice, called out for them to enter—we say them, because his imagination pictured at least a dozen troopers come to arrest him.

The door was thrown open, and, to the great delight and surprise of the young soldier, Captain Frank entered the chamber; but he went back when he encountered the fair lady, and apologised for his rudeness.

"Where's Guy?" asked Hugh, after an affectionate greeting had passed between him and his gallant friend.

"He left me to keep a love appointment. We were to have met again last night at the Man in the Moon Inn; but he did not show up, so I came out in search of you."

"How the deuce did you know where to find me?"

"I did not know until I fell upon the trail of blood, which I guessed would lead me to thy retreat."

"Why did you think that?"

Captain Frank indicated to the lady, meaning that the blood had fallen from her.

"By Jove!" he said, "what a mysterious individual the Black Rider is."

"Ah! where did he take you to?"

"I was quite disappointed, at least I thought he would have taken us to some wild habitation where one would imagine such a being lives, but he didn't; he merely conducted us to a lone part of the country in silence, and then said in a voice that sent a cold shiver through me: 'Go thy way, thou art safe.' And then he disappeared like a shadow, leaving me and Guy standing in bewilderment."

"Didst thou not see where he went to?" inquired Hugh, in a mysterious manner.

"The words had barely left his lips, when he appeared to die into air, horse and all, Hugh. I shan't seek his company again, if I know it."

"He is not a very lively companion," said Hugh, "but his services are invaluable. I owe him much gratitude."

"So do I; if he had not helped us out of the mess with the soldiers we should now be lying in prison."

"True; so we have much to thank him for."

"Will you return with me to the Man in the Moon? I expect Guy will be waiting for me, if he has not got into danger."

"I will," Hugh said.

The Man in the Moon was the sign of the hostel from which they escaped with Constance. Hugh felt eager to question mine host about the lady he had befriended.

Hugh then saw Mrs. Ludlow, and arranged with her about the keeping of Constance while he was absent.

"No, sir," she said, in opposition to his desire to give her money; "you will only insult me if you persist. I like you, and the dear young lady shall not want a friend while I and my husband live. We have no children of our own, and it would only give us too much happiness to look after her as though she were our daughter of our own."

"My dear lady," said Hugh, warmly, "I cannot express my gratitude in words; but in the time to come I may be better able to reward thy disinterested generosity."

"The pleasure of looking after the dear young lady as a daughter will quite repay us for our humble offerings, if, when she has recovered, she will not forget that such a person as Mrs. Ludlow lives."

"Fear not on that score, madam," Hugh said. "The lady will be too happy to find so true a friend in whom she may confide. She is entirely alone in the world, and requires a mother's care."

"Then—bless her!—she shall find both parents and a home here while we live."

"Watch her well. She has many enemies at work, who would destroy her young life without compunction. Trust not in strangers, for you know them not; and do not let her leave this roof while I am away."

"Fear not, young sir. The lady shall have my strictest attention."

Hugh then departed with his friend, in full confidence of the old lady's fidelity.

As they passed out of the door, a priest crossed their path. He started, and giving Hugh a piercing glance from under the capuche that nearly concealed his cynical features, he hurried on, muttering in Latin the following words, translated—

"He here! *She* cannot be far off. This is fortunate;" and his cold grey eyes sparkled with a cunning triumphant leer as he concluded.

Hugh could not see his face, but the man's suspicious manner attracted his attention.

"I fancy I have seen that man before," he said, looking after the retreating figure uneasily.

"Most likely," observed Captain Frank. And so the matter passed without further notice; but had Hugh known in what country he had met that man before, he would not have left Constance Meredith to the protection of the lone cottagers.

He knew it not. He was innocent of all alike—the terrible sombre cloud of approaching danger that slowly enshrouded him and the gentle girl he loved in its meshes; the treachery of the man who crossed his path like a shadow of evil, Father Guynot, the traitor who was to be the cause of his future great sorrow and peril.

CHAPTER XIX.
GOING TO THE RESCUE.

THE two young friends reached the hostel without having an occasion to recourse to their weapons for defence, which was rather a wonder to them.

Guy Fawkes was waiting for them when they entered, and in a few words he told them all that had occurred. The snares he was unwittingly drawn into; the way he fought himself out of them; the signal by which he found the retreat of Lady Claire; the way he took her from her captors; and the way her captors took her from him.

"I quite envy you the adventure," said Captain Frank; "it must have been delightful."

"It was," answered Guy. "It was so good that I came to fetch you and Hugh to share the second part of it."

"By St. George, I am with you," said the young gallant, delighted at the idea of a good fight.

"And you, Hugh, canst thou spare time?" asked Guy.

"Did you ever know me to desert a comrade in the time of peril?" Hugh said.

"I acknowledge that I did not. By the way, how fares it with the boy you saved?" Guy asked, giving his comrade a sly look.

"A boy!" exclaimed Frank, breaking in. "By my faith, 'tis a boy of the kind I should like to save."

"That's ungenerous," Hugh said, reproachfully. "You should not tell tales out of doors."

"By my faith I said no more than what I saw, an' though I felt inquisitive, I questioned not thee but my own imagination."

Guy laughed heartily.

"It is as I anticipated," he said; "thou at last hast found thy own Constance. Is it not so, comrade?"

"It is," answered Hugh.

"And is the hurt dangerous?"

"It was; but it is better now."

"That's fortunate; and she is safe."

"I left her so; though I know not how long she may remain unmolested."

"What fear hast thou?"

"I know not," answered Hugh, gloomily. "'tis a presentiment I have that she will not be there when I return."

"Bah! thou art as superstitious as a woman. If thou canst trust the persons in whose custody you left her, thou hast nought to fear."

Hugh was silent. He knew to give the cause of his uneasiness would only cause a laugh of derision from his friends.

"Are you with me, comrades?" asked Guy.

"To the death," answered Hugh, and Captain Frank said the same.

"Then, friends, let us away to the rescue of Lady Claire."

The three friends rose.

"How do we travel?" asked Frank.

"By whichever way will take us quickest," said Guy. "Mortlake is the destination; by water is a direct way."

"But horse will take us quicker."

"Then by horse we go," Guy said. "Mine host, prepare us three steeds, and let them be fleet of foot."

"In my stable I have some of the finest animals England can boast of," mine host said, with an air of pride; and he went into the yard to choose the horses for his guests.

The three adventurers saw that the primings of their weapons were all in good repair, and ready for an emergency.

By the time they had refilled their flasks with brandy, and their pouches with a fresh supply of ammunition, the steeds were brought round to the door of the hostel by the ostler.

They were magnificent creatures, black as Arabian steeds, with all the powerful development of limb and fiery spirit of the thorough-bred race-horse.

Guy and Captain Frank vaulted into the saddle of their respective steeds, but Hugh lingered behind; he intended to learn what the landlord knew of Constance Meredith.

"Now, comrade," called Guy, "why linger behind? It is not chivalric to delay time while a lady is in danger."

Hugh said a few hasty words to the landlord, ran down the steps from the door, and, making a leap, sprang across the saddle.

The unexpected shock startled the horse. Rearing up on its hind legs, it plunged madly forward, hurling the ostler who held the bridle senseless into the road, and dashed off like a flash of lightning.

Had not Hugh been a very expert rider, he must have been dashed to the earth. The horse darted off before he had time to secure the reins, and he was obliged to hold on to its mane.

It was a pretty wild sight to see the noble animal going on at its headlong speed, its ears laid flat on its glossy neck, its eyes protruding like balls of fire, and its nostril extended in mad fury. The fearless young rider kept his seat bravely; he had been too used to the sudden flights of horses to be thrown easily.

He was taken out of sight before Guy and his comrade could move a hand to save him. They followed in the direction taken by the frightened horse, and the only guide they had to keep them on the right track was the fresh imprints of the horse's hoofs in the earth.

Miles they followed this trail without catching sight of the runaway. Half-an-hour they had been in hot pursuit of their friend. Guy began to despair. What if they had been on the wrong track, he thought; and he was about to give up the search, when an exclamation from Captain Frank altered his idea.

"That's he, Guy," said the young gallant, digging spurs into his horse. "See—see, there he goes! He leaps a ditch near a hedge. The horse falls. He is thrown. Quick, Guy, quick! to his rescue!"

Guy Fawkes held his breath in dread suspense. Urging on his charger with whip and spur, he saw the leap taken, the horse and rider fall, and his blood ran cold.

Captain Frank was the first to leap the ditch. Guy's horse made a dead stop on the brink of the declivity, and looked down into the sluggish waters hesitatingly. The turf was giving way beneath its two set feet on the edge, and without it retreated it must roll head-foremost in.

Eager to get to the assistance of his friend, and enraged by the delay of his steed's timidity or obstinacy, Guy furiously plunged his spurs into its flanks.

The animal took an involuntary spring forward, missed the opposite bank, and rolled backwards into the thick mire.

A stifled shriek arose from the depths of the slimy waters, as horse and rider disappeared.

The despairing cry was heard by Frank, and he returned to see what had become of his friend. Presently, while looking over the ditch from his elevated position, he was surprised—though he expected as much—to see two animated cakes of mud arise from out of the stagnant water, forming the shape of a horse and man, as they gradually ascended up the side of the ditch.

When they both had reached the top, the four-legged cake of mud took flight, the two-legged cake took flight after it, and jumped upon its back.

Captain Frank indistinctly recognised in the form of the smaller piece of mud his comrade, Guy Fawkes, and he was suddenly seized with a fit of convulsive laughter uncontrollable.

"'Sblood!" exclaimed Guy, in a voice that sounded half choked, "'tis no laughing matter, friend."

"No! oh—oh—oh!" roared Frank, rolling about in the saddle.

Guy turned away in disgust, and drew his hands through each other to clear off the thick mud. Then with difficulty he found his way to his pocket through several inches of sticky mud, drew forth a small dagger, and began to scrape his face; his eyes and ears he cleared out with his fingers, and then looked around for his comrade.

"Where is Hugh?" he asked.

"Gone!" replied Captain Frank, trying very hard to keep a serious face.

"Gone where?"

"I don't know."

"Did you help him?"

"No. I was going to, when his horse sprang to its feet, with Hugh clinging round its neck, and it dashed off again before I could stop it."

"Let us follow him; he may meet with some danger."

"Thou canst not follow in that state," remarked Captain Frank.

Guy made an angry gesticulation with an arm of mud, and giving his steed the rein, leaped the hedge in gallant style.

Captain Frank could not follow. The curious sight horse and rider presented, as they disappeared, caused him to break out afresh in laughter, and it was not until his sides ached and he felt quite exhausted that he attempted to clear the hedge.

Guy Fawkes had got some distance in advance, but it did not take the young gallant long to overtake him. Guy's steed had gone along in gallant style, but as the mud began to dry in a hard crust all over it, the joints of the poor beast stiffened, and its speed decreased.

"Did you want to know the depth of the ditch?" asked Captain Frank of Guy, as he rode up to him.

Guy bit his moustache angrily.

Frank said no more. His friend was in no mood to take jests. His accident had made him malicious.

They were nearing Kingston, when a great crowd of noisy people attracted their attention.

"Hugh's in danger," exclaimed Guy, drawing his sword.

"Is he? then we must get him out of it," and Captain Frank drew his sword.

The two daring fellows took their steeds through the mob to where Hugh Wardour fought with the gang of soldiers who had kindly stopped his horse for the generous purpose of taking him prisoner.

Hugh felt grateful to the man for stopping his horse, but he had no idea of being taken as a recompense for the trouble.

The soldiers had in their midst a pretty-looking young woman, a captive. Her small white hands were fastened together by a pair of rude iron manacles, and two uncouth burly fellows held her between them.

The mob was yelling furiously for the trembling girl's blood. The soldiers had to charge them with their pikes to keep the inhuman brutes from tearing her limb from limb, as they would have done could they have got at her. Hugh hailed the coming of his comrades with a shout of welcome, their appearance inspired him, and he dashed amongst his assailants.

The soldiers met the onslaught coolly. They did not strike; they were content to keep him in their midst at the end of their pikes.

Hugh's blind daring might have been his fate had not his comrades been there. Regardless of the risk, he charged at the soldiers. They did not budge an inch; and, had it not been for the timely aid of Guy and Captain Frank, who broke the rank from behind and made a passage for the escape of their friend, he must have been riddled on the points of the spears.

"Keep them back," said Hugh, meaning the soldiers, as he rode forward.

His friends did their best, and Hugh did what he wanted. He knocked two soldiers over and took the girl from them.

"Down with him!" yelled the mob, closing round him. "Don't let the witch escape! Pull him off his horse!"

Hugh put the girl before him on the saddle. Giving his horse full play of the reins, he galloped through the thirsty brutes, cutting right and left with his sword.

His comrades were behind him. They kept the soldiers at bay while he got off with the rescued girl he had saved from death.

It was all very well while they faced the soldiers; they could not be easily got at. The danger was when they turned to fly, and that they would have to do shortly. The yelling mob were crying vengeance for the loss of their victim, and many had made an attempt to pull the daring adventurers off their steeds and many more would have tried, too, but the thought of meeting with the fate of those who had tried and failed did a great deal towards keeping them back.

The soldiers could not get at the young friends to make them prisoners, but they were determined not to let them follow Hugh.

Guy did not appear to take much notice of this. Most of the enemy were behind, to prevent him from making a retreat, little thinking that he would take an opposite direction. But he did. Touching Captain Frank on the arm, he made a dart forward, scattered the few men who confronted him, and dashed off with the yelling mob giving chase.

They soon outran their pursuers and caught a glimpse of Hugh with his fair burden in the distance.

Hugh Wardour just then happened to turn his head, and, seeing his friends coming towards him, waited for them?"

"What is to be done with this poor girl?" he asked. "She has fainted."

Guy glanced furtively at the pale, placid features.

"Faith, comrades," he said, "'tis the same lass who forewarned me of my future the other night."

"Then allow me to put her under thy protection," said Hugh.

Guy Fawkes gave him an ambiguous smile.

"Why?" he asked.

"Because you knew her before I did."

"I should be happy to enlighten thee, but present affairs make it rather awkward."

"Confoundedly awkward!" put in Captain Frank; "we can't take her with us, that is certain. See yonder inn—can't we leave her there?"

"We will try."

They rode up to an old-fashioned wooden building, dismounted, tied the reins of their three steeds together, and entered.

"I want this lady taken care of for a short time," said Hugh; "hast thou accommodation?"

The landlord informed him he had, and called out his wife to take charge of the helpless girl.

They then cracked a bottle of wine, left abundant money to defray expenses, and departed.

When they got outside, they were astonished at the freaks of their steeds, each had taken it into its head to bolt, and directly their masters' backs were turned, each made a sudden start in a different direction, and all three came in concussion; then they stood in a triangular position, and tugged away with all their might.

"The brutes!" said Captain Frank; "they are making a nice knot for us to undo."

He picked up a stone, and hurled it at them spitefully. The tips of his fingers ached at the very idea of having to undo the knot they were drawing up.

The stone struck one of the horses on the flank; the animal reared up, plunged forward, hurling the others round on each side of it, and the three, neck and neck, galloped down the road, with the three adventurers trotting after them.

How long a run they would have given our three friends, it is impossible to say, had not an accident occurred that stopped their flight.

A drowsy old farmer was coming in the opposite direction taken by the runaways, riding on a sturdy cob, in the centre of the road.

The farmer, being asleep, did not see his danger, and, his cob, not having instinct enough to get aside, or, perhaps thinking that he was going to stop the fugitives, made a dead stop in the road.

What followed can easily be imagined—farmer and cob were rolled into a ditch, where they laid until Guy Fawkes, who, having been served the same way, felt a mutual feeling for the unfortunate farmer, helped him out, while Frank and Hugh secured the horses, who stood over the ditch, looking down at their victims, reflectively.

In a few minutes all was right again, the three adventurers were in their saddles, and the cob was trotting home with a huge piece of animated mud on its back.

"Now, comrades," said Guy, eagerly, "let us to Mortlake. We have had nothing but mishaps to-day."

"Let us hope for better fortune on the rest of our journey," said Captain Frank.

"I say, Guy, you look a most awful sight," remarked Hugh Wardour.

"What can I do," said Fawkes, despairingly.

"Take a plunge into yonder pond," suggested his comrade, "that will clean thy clothes as it will thy poor beast."

"No, thanks," Guy said, shaking his head, "I've got used to the mud. I should not get used to wet clothes until they dried, besides, there is no time to lose."

No more was said; the horses were got into full speed, the three friends were going to the rescue of Lady Claire of Grace, and no time was to be lost.

They reached Mortlake without further adventure, and as they drew up at the pavilion, where the fair lady was kept prisoner, a carriage and an escort of mounted cavaliers drove away.

CHAPTER XX.

THE COUNSEL OF CONSPIRATORS.

A FEW evenings previous to the incidents related in the preceding chapter, a meeting of conspirators was held, under the direction of Sir Everard Digby, who had called together those of his brother Jesuits who were at that time in London.

Their rendezvous was not the sort of place such men of rank would have sought, but the severity of the law against Roman Catholics drove them to endure privations their hearts often revolted at in disgust.

Sir Everard, in this instance, had hired a cellar beneath a miserable, dingy-looking shop in one of those poverty-stricken small loathsome thoroughfares, so abundant in Westminster at the time of which we write.

The conspirators arrived alone, at intervals, to avoid detection; each was so effectually disguised as to entirely baffle recognition of one another.

They entered the chamber by a flight of stone steps running under the shop front.

No time elapsed after the entry of the last before a word was spoken; then Sir Everard looked around and mentally counted those assembled.

"Let the place be secured," he said.

Two of the conspirators rose to execute the command. An iron grating was let down and locked over the stone steps, then a sliding door was drawn across the aperture in the shop front. The men then returned to their seats.

Their council chamber, if it may be so called, was, as we have before mentioned, a large underground cellar. The walls were bare, bricks falling to decay in sundry parts from the dampness of the place; the flooring of the shop served for the ceiling; and from a huge beam that supported it hung an oil lamp with four burners. This was the only light that was ever allowed to exhibit the interior. Of flooring there was none save the loose earth, into which the feet sank several inches. The only articles of furniture with which the cellar was decorated were a large, rudely constructed table, ranging from one end to the other, two forms, and a few empty casks.

Yet such a place, not fit for the keeping of a dying dog, was often inhabited by companies of human beings. Was it from fancy or compulsion? The latter, let us say, when the minions of the law were vigorously on their track, and they had to seek for safety, they found it there.

Often as the place had been suspected of concealing malefactors, and though the place had gone under the most vigilant searches from roof to basement, the refugees had remained in their place of concealment undetected.

Sir Everard knew this when he hired the cellar, and getting the confidence of the landlord by paying him well for his silence. Should their foes even trace them out, there they were safe from discovery.

Sir Everard Digby elevated himself on the top of a cask at the head of the table to address the company.

Before he spoke the conspirators rose, and each removed his disguise, so that they should know no stranger was amongst them.

"Guy Fawkes is not amongst us," said Sir Everard, glancing from face to face. "Think you, Catesby, he is true in our cause?"

"I know not," answered the intriguing noble, with a shrug of his shoulders. "He is a strange being, of a greater depth than we know of. Though he appears to be a devout Catholic, and very zealous in our great undertaking, there is that about him that causes me to suspect his fidelity is not so true as he would wish us to believe."

"Thinkest thou our secret is safe in his keeping?" asked Sir Everard, uneasily.

"I would not trust him too far, we might be safer if he knew it not."

"And yet I can hardly think he would play the traitor, he seemed so eager for the scheme to be carried into effect, and volunteered freely to undertake the most hazardous part of the plot in his own hands."

"Then why should he keep back?"

"He may be watching an opportunity for the institution of some plan of his own for the benefit of our cause."

"Or he may have reflected upon the risk of the part he had volunteered to perform," Catesby said, his brow lowering with a dark scowl, "and discovering the danger he stood in, has abandoned us."

"If thou canst aver thy suspicions he shall be sought, and silenced without further delay. But if you have not cause for thy accusation, we must leave him for a more fitting time, and I will proceed to lay before the gentlemen of the counsel, a stratagem for the obtainment of the Princess Elizabeth."

Catesby was silent. He had no cause for suspicion, nor had he any doubt of the soldier's honesty, but owed him an old spite, and he would not have hesitated at a lie to have brought disgrace upon the honest fellow; but he knew to accuse him of treachery, his life would be forfeited, and he was too valuable a confederate to lose. He knew Guy's indomitable resolution, his daring courage, his deep sympathy for their fallen religion, and his determination to seek atonement for their wrongs, yet he was base enough to cast a shadow of censure on his character by accusing him indirectly of breaking their trust.

Catesby was wondering how to answer, when he caught Sir Everard's eyes fixed upon him searchingly, and in a faltering voice, for he felt the baseness of his own perfidy, he answered—

"Of course I should not wish to condemn him of falsity without I had very strong proofs that such was the case; but still I have not much faith in him, and would advise a strict investigation to be made into his movements."

"Fear not, there," said Sir Everard, "he will not survive long if he has broken the oath of our secret, and if not, I shall be right glad to see him amongst us again ere long."

His speech was received with signs of approval from all present, except Catesby, who with all his subtlety felt that his supposition was doubted, and he did not vouchsafe to raise his eyes to the speaker, though he was the particular person addressed.

A scornful smile curled Sir Everard's lip. He saw the mean spirit of the man with whom he was in league, and from that time he did not trust him more than was necessary.

"It is essential," he began, in the delivery of his new scheme, "that there should be someone in whom we can look forward to as the upholder of our church. Is there anyone you can name of Royal blood to wield the sceptre we shall wrest from the tyrant who now holds it with impunity. Is there one in whom we can place the great power of nations with confidence. Speak ye all; is there, or is there not?"

"There is not!" was the unanimous response.

"Then, this night shall decree the future sovereign of England," Sir Everard Digby went on, with increasing excitement; "too long have we borne the oppressions of a despotic power, our faith opposed by the yoke of a heretic religion, our church destroyed, and our priests slaughtered by the tyrannical monster James, who swore to support our church. He has broken his oath—he is no longer worthy being king—he must be removed!"

"He must!" rose from the conspirators.

"But can we remove him without the destruction of many of our brethren?" asked Percy.

"Certainly not," replied Digby. "We must sacrifice a few of our brethren with the heretics, for the benefit of the cause."

"But should our undertaking fail," Percy said, "not only will our enemies condemn us, but our friends and brethren will turn upon us for treachery."

"It can't fail," said Catesby, "if all who are concerned in the plot are of one mind."

"The time draws near," continued Digby, "redemption is at hand; fear not for our success. God will guide the just, and if we fall it will be by his wish."

"This is no time to hesitate," put in Wright, "and we must dare the worst. The next Parliament meets in November, we have not much time to lay the powder beneath the house, which will send into eternity, by God's good will the King and our enemies, the heretics, the defilers of our faith, and the murderers of our brethren."

"And then," eagerly added Sir Everard, "to whom are we to look for support when our oppressor is removed?—when once again our mighty church takes its grand stand—when our people fall on their knees to bless the salvators of their restored religion, to whom then, shall we give the power we have won? Is another heretic to ascend the throne? No."

"No," reiterated everyone.

"No, I repeat," Sir Everard Digby said. "I called this meeting together to lay before the judgment of my brethren a scheme which, if carried into effect, will be the source of securing the sway of the Catholic religion henceforth. My project is this, gentlemen. That we get the Princess Elizabeth in our power, and place her under the protection and strict tuition of the fathers of our holy church. * Let the Catholic religion be well instilled into her young mind, and when we have achieved the point for which we work, let her then be placed on the throne in her sire's stead, as an upholder of our faith, and a patroness to our church."

His plan met with mutual agreement.

"When dost thou propose to put into effect thy design?" inquired Percy.

"To-night," answered Digby; "too much time has already been lost to admit of a moment's delay more than is necessary."

"To-night will be impossible. Know you that the princess is under the protection of Lord Harrington, and he stays at Chelsea."

"Such it is that makes me the more eager to get the princess in our power, ere she is removed to a more secure place. To-night is the time for our expedition; the priestly cloisters must be laid aside for the weapons of war. We may meet with a strong resistance, so we must be prepared; the Princess Elizabeth must be ours to-night. Are you all ready to undertake a part in the abduction?"

"We are," cried one and all.

"Brethren, it is now time that we departed, to prepare for the carrying out of the project so dear for the benefit of our faith."

"How are we to travel?" asked Catesby.

* Ainsworth.

GUY FAWKES
OR
THE CONSPIRATORS BRIDE

WAITING FOR THE SIGNAL.

"On foot, and not more than two together. We want neither uninvited followers nor witnesses to our proceedings."

"It won't be good for anyone I catch prying into our secrets," said Wright.

The conspirators then re-assumed their

disguises, and the party departed from the secret cellar. They were always prepared with sufficient weapons of defence in case of emergency, so time was not delayed by their having to seek for arms.

They separated in twos when outside, and it was so arranged that they should meet at a certain place at a time stated by Sir Everard Digby, near the house of Lord Harrington, guardian of the Princess Elizabeth, there to further lay their plans for the execution of their meditated assault, and the abduction of the Royal maiden.

CHAPTER XXI.

THE BENIGHTED TRAVELLER.

An hour later the conspirators met at their rendezvous beneath the shade of a giant oak. Eight or ten were there in low converse, and at no great distance from their position there loomed out, by the moon's bright rays, a solitary habitation. This house, in its time, had been a royal residence, and now it was occupied by Lord Harrington and his royal charge, the Princess Elizabeth.

Presently two more disguised persons approached those already assembled, and then came another two.

"How do you propose to proceed?" asked Catesby.

"I," returned Sir Everard, "shall crave shelter for the night. If I am detected, in some way I shall contrive to let you know, and then you must make a sudden attack upon the house; but be careful, keep well out of observation while I try the success of my stratagem."

"Never fear, Sir Everard." Percy said; "if we are wanted, we shall be at hand. How shall we know whether you are in danger, or not, when you get admittance?"

"If I am not discovered, I shall contrive some means to let you know."

"And in the event of your being arrested, how are we to know them?"

"If I make not my appearance within an hour, I shall have been discovered. I must leave it to thy discretion to get an entrance. Then let the princess be your first thought. We must have her to-night. If I am not at hand, do not endanger the safety of our prize by losing time in looking for me."

With these few cautious remarks he drew his long cloak around him, and made for the house.

His summons for admittance was answered by a servitor—a man of a uninviting aspect. He stood before the applicant, glancing at him inquiringly.

"Thy business?" he demanded, gruffly

"Good sir, 'tis shelter I seek," said Sir Everard, blandly, feigning to be overcome with fatigue. "I've travelled far, and still I've farther yet to go; but exhaustion has ended me too faint to proceed, or I would not yet give way, for I am eager to get to my destination."

"Know ye to whom you ask for shelter?"

"Faith, how should I, a stranger totally unacquainted with these parts? but I hope I speak with a Christian who will not deny the hospitality of his house to a weary pilgrim?"

"The house is not mine, messire," the servitor said, with some respect; for though Sir Everard tried to conceal his conspicuous dress, the man knew he spoke to a person of no common birth.

"Marry, friend," the Jesuit said, with as much mirth as his deceit of fatigue would allow him to assume, "I did not suppose it was; but methinks thou canst find a corner to lodge a truly weary being from the miseries of a night like this. The wind blows cold and bleak, and if I mistake not, we shall have a storm ere the dawn of to-morrow's morn."

The man hesitated.

"I would willingly give thee shelter," he said, "did I hold the power."

"And wherefore not?" queried Sir Everard.

"Come ye, enter, and right welcome art thou, for my share."

"Thanks, good friend, thanks," warmly exclaimed the supposed pilgrim; "it may be that in a time to come I shall repay thee for thy kindness."

"'Tis not with a thought of reaping a benefit hereafter that I run the risk of insuring the displeasure of my employers by admitting thee," said the man, frankly, "but from a pure sense of feeling for a fellow creature."

"Thy honesty is deserving of a better reward than lies in my power to give thee at present," said Sir Everard, as he entered, "but take this as a token of my gratitude."

And he gave the man several gold pieces, which the servitor pocketed with an apparent relish.

He then conducted the conspirator to the kitchen, where a large wood fire cracked and sparkled on the hearth of an aperture in the wall.

"A gentleman who has come a long journey, and seeks shelter for the night," said the servitor, introducing the stranger to his fellow servants, who were seated round a long table, doing justice to the last meal of the day.

Sir Everard was invited to partake of the viands, and though he liked not the company of the honest men with whom he mixed, he could not resist the savoury odour that arose from the large joints, and he sat down with a gnawing appetite, and did his part towards clearing the platters. The large earthen pitchers of beer were passed round the table from one to the other, and the foaming liquor ran down the throats of the vassals like soapsuds down a sink hole.

Then came the lighter courses of pastry,

but this did not make such a rapid disappearance as the more substantial food; and when the table was cleared, the men were considerably closer to it than when they first took their seats.

Cards and dice were then introduced by those who felt it beneficial for a little recreation after a meal of such sumptuousness, while others who had gorged to an extent that made them feel uncomfortable, sneaked off, groaning, to some quiet place of repose.

As time wore on, it brought with it uneasiness to the mind of the conspirator. He heartily wished those who lingered behind would follow the example of their fellow servants and retire. It was entirely out of his power to get an opportunity of making known his safety to his companions, and his fear was that they would make an attack upon the house did he not turn up to their view within the expiration of the hour. Two-thirds of the hour had already passed, and two-thirds of another seemed very likely to follow ere he would get an opportunity of being alone. The men were playing vigorously. They were much interested in the game, and Sir Everard sat in torturing suspense, sweating with fear, and mentally praying for the men to go.

The loud snoring of one of the players broke upon his ears like music, and when the others caught the infection, sundry heads were nodding over the table. The game lacked the spirit of interest, and when the only one who survived the strong magnitude, a perfect weasel, who never felt sleepy, but thought it necessary for nature, looked upon his companions with contempt for their weakness, proposed that they should adjourn, Sir Everard breathed with hope.

A pallet was placed at his service for repose, and the servitors retired to their respective quarters.

It was not long after their retirement when the supposed pilgrim arose from his couch, put a lighted candle in a lantern, and began to reconnoitre the course to pursue.

Certain that all was silent, he drew his sword to welcome any one who might feel disposed to intercept his course, and began to ascend the broad staircase that led to the apartments above.

He reached the landing of the first storey without any obstruction. Here arose the greatest difficulty he had to contend with.

In which chamber slept the princess? This was a dangerous thing to discover.

He stood debating how best he could proceed, when the striking of a clock reminded him that he had no time to lose. What he had to do must be done quickly. A few minutes more, and the attack of his friends would alarm the whole house.

This thought dissipated all thoughts of fear, and he cautiously entered the nearest chamber, and without pausing a moment made his way to the bedside, and threw the light of the lantern on it.

Sir Everard was deprived of all power when the light revealed the form of a man lying down, with his eyes fixed upon him.

It was a moment of intense agony, for he knew not what to do. Self-preservation was their law, and drawing a dagger he approached the bed, trembling with horror at the thought of the deed he would have to commit to prevent being discovered.

The countenance of his victim did not change its expression, even when his arm was raised, and the gleaming dagger poised above him, nor had the eyes diverted their position in the slightest degree.

Sir Everard Digby thought this strange, that a man should be there watching an intruder in his chamber, who threatened life, and yet not to make any resistance. Could he be awake? Was he watching him?

The conspirator put his hand over his would-be-victim's face, to ascertain if he really was awake. The eyes did not move; the man must be asleep.

Could such really be the case? a man asleep with his eyes wide open? Sir Everard did not feel satisfied, and he even dared in the impulse of his curiosity to lay his hand on the sleeper, and shake him.

He was confirmed now that he did sleep; but this unguarded act had awoke him.

The man started up in bed, and Sir Everard fell down by the side of the bed, and then rolled underneath, extinguishing the light, and squeezing himself into as small a compass as possible into the remotest corner.

His heart leaped burning into his mouth as the man sprang out of bed. He heard the clanking of steel as a weapon was taken from the wall; and in his fear of being discovered he meditated the foul crime of murder.

"One silent plunge from behind," he thought, shivering at the idea, "and I may have time to accomplish my design and escape; but if he gets a light, and I am found, all will be lost. It must be, though I would avoid it if possible."

He silently crept out on his hands and knees from beneath the bedstead, with the dagger held between his teeth; and, rising up behind his victim, who, in great agitation, was trying to get a light, to search for the disturber of his slumber, he raised his hand with the gleaming blade poised for its fatal work.

At the moment his arm was in the act of descending, the man turned. Digby stepped softly aside out of observation's way, and seeing the chamber door open, he thought it better to make his exit, than to murder a man in cold blood, so he went and entered another room.

A small night-lamp burned on a toilet-table by the bedside; its subdued rays shed a soft gleam on the calm features of a lovely maiden, wrapt in her virgin slumber, unconscious of the evil shadow of danger hovering over her.

The daring intruder stood in the sacred sanctuary, gazing with enraptured admiration on the innocently displayed charms of the royal maiden—one round white arm thrown carelessly over the coverlet, had revealed a throat and bosom of surpassing magnificence to the unholy gaze of the intruder.

A sudden crash, as if a legion of giants were attacking the house, broke the silence, awaking the echoes of night, and recalled the Jesuit to his purpose.

The hour had expired, and the conspirators had come to search for their missing companion, and carry off the princess.

Sir Everard stood bewildered.

"Lost! lost!" he muttered, perplexed, as the noise of the people in the house preparing to discover the cause of the sudden alarm broke upon his ears.

Sir Everard started round; he might have time yet to carry off his fair prize before anyone was about. With this thought, he went to the bed to seize the princess, when she started up in great alarm, and fixed on him a look of wild terror.

The attacks were repeated in quick succession, and with increasing power.

Not a moment was to be lost; the whole house was astir, and unless he flew instantly discovery would be certain.

He took his cloak off to throw over the royal maiden's head to stop her cries.

The terrified child shrieked as he advanced.

Then could be heard the rapid approach of feet nearing the chamber.

The cloak from his hands, and in a bewildered, helpless manner, he exclaimed—

"Lost! lost!"

CHAPTER XXII.

SEIZURE OF THE PRINCESS ELIZABETH.

SIR EVERARD DIGBY stood in breathless terror as the sound of feet came nearer; but nobody entered as he feared they would do, and he breathed with hope as they passed the chamber door.

Something must be done quickly; he stood in a most awkward position of being discovered should anyone come to look after the safety of the princess.

His manner had frightened the royal child, and he knew if he attempted to use force to take her, her cries would bring assistance, and his fate would be sealed.

He looked towards the door; it was open; and he thought how easy it would be for him to escape alone; and he was almost prompted to avail himself of the opportunity, but the remembrance that the fulfilment of the great purpose for which he and his companions risked their lives depended entirely upon the possession of the gentle girl before him. He dissipated the craven thought, with the reso-

lution to stick by his purpose—to conquer or die.

The danger of detection was equally the same should he fly alone or with his fair prize. Whatsoever might befall his daring, he was determined not to forego his purpose.

The princess fixed him with a timid look of bewilderment. She knew him not, either as friend or foe, the light being too faint for her to distinctly discern the intruder.

Sir Everard took advantage of her embarrassment.

"God defend us!" he exclaimed, in a tone of feigned alarm. "Quick, dear lady! dress thyself, the house is attacked by a gang of men who seek thy gentle person! Attire thyself hastily, and let us fly ere they break in, or all will be lost!"

Disarmed of her suspicions by his apparent concern for her safety, the terrified girl nimbly jumped from the bed.

The Jesuit withdrew from the room. He had not waited long when the sound of hurried feet approaching warned him of his danger, and he re-entered the royal chamber, resolved not to relinquish his fair prize while life remained.

The princess was ready for the flight when he entered, and she ran gladly to his arms for protection, trembling like a timid fawn. She drew the long cloak, in which she was enveloped, round her fair shoulders, the hood over her head; and giving Sir Everard her hand, he led her to the door.

He drew his sword, and clasped the royal maiden tightly to his side, to prevent her breaking away, as a gentleman confronted him.

The new comer looked upon the pair aghast.

"The princess and Sir Everard Digby!" he said, confounded. "What means this?"

"Exactly what you see, my Lord Harrington!" Sir Everard said, coolly. "That I am going to take the Princess Elizabeth under my protection, and I trust that thou wilt not obstruct my path, or I shall have to remove thee!"

He flourished his sword significantly, but the other heeded it not; his face grew terrible with rage, and he advanced to take the royal maiden from her betrayer.

Sir Everard held him back at sword's length, and laughed scornfully at his vain attempt.

The princess fully knew now that she had been drawn into a treacherous snare, and raising her face with an imploring look at her guardian to save her, she tried to break from her captor; but she was held beneath Sir Everard's arm as in a vice, and the more she struggled the more he tightened it, and she grew faint beneath the cruel pressure.

"Traitor! relinquish thy hold!" exclaimed Lord Harrington; "or you leave not this place alive!"

"Fool!" hissed the conspirator; "stand from my path ere I smite thee down!"

Lord Harrington stood without a weapon of defence. He had not thought to meet with so resolute an opponent— nor had he thought to meet with anyone, particularly under such circumstances; albeit he could not return to arm himself, because his foe with Elizabeth would escape.

A mighty crash, at the moment the courtier was about to call for assistance, shook the house, and echoed through the room like successive claps of thunder. Then arose on the night air loud shouts of triumph, enraged cries of angry men, shrieks of agony, clash of steel, reports of firearms, and the rush of feet, as the conspirators dashed in, driving their opponents before them.

Although the servitors of the house numbered three times those of the besiegers, and were armed with huge clubs, staves, halberts, calivers, short iron hand-pikes, demi-lances, blunderbusses, and every other kind of weapon, they could not keep the assailants back, who were only possessed with a slim sword and a few small pistols amongst them.

It was a terrific fight; the men kept their ground firmly, and fought bravely in their own rough style; but the superior science of the conspirators, their determined courage, and the thought of the great cause in view, spurred them on, and the vassals were put to the route.

Sir Everard heard his companions coming up the stairs, fighting their way up step by step, and driving the servitors before them.

"Ho, there, men! this way!" cried Lord Harrington.

The men who were coming up the stairs backwards, fighting the invaders, turned at the call of their master, and ran to his assistance.

Their retreat was followed by the conspirators, and the war was renewed when they met with a fresh detachment of opponents.

These were gentlemen of rank, who, having heard the hubbub, had hastily attired themselves with equipments for a melée, and they, too, were well versed in the art of swordsmanship.

The conspirators found a stronger resistance with this small hostile party, who were not more than half their number, than they did with the greater odds of the servitors.

The noblemen kept the top of the stairs well, meeting with cool skill the furious attacks of the invaders, and pitching all who came within their reach headlong down the stairs or over the bannisters.

It chafed the hot-headed soldier, Catesby, to madness, to be thus kept at bay when they had won so much. He called together his companions, and picking up a huge club which one of the servitors had dropped, he led the party for a final charge, and dashed among their opposers. Swinging round the club, he cleared a passage for his followers to follow him.

The gentlemen fell to the attack again with right good will to conquer or die; but they were beaten back. Catesby did more with his club than all his companions put together.

Sir Everard hailed their coming with a shout. The servitors had gathered round him, and held him tight prisoner; but he moved not at their molestation. He had secured the safety of himself by driving into a corner Lord Harrington, and fixing the point of his sword at his throat, to drive it in, if the other gave orders for him to be attacked.

When the conspirators fought their way to his rescue, hurling the servitors aside, he lowered the point of his sword, and gathering up into his arms the now insensible form of the Princess Elizabeth, he turned to retreat, his companions keeping a clear course for him to do so; but he had not got far when Lord Harrington, who had secured a weapon from one of his men, threw himself in his path.

"Stand, villain!" he exclaimed "thou stirrest not another step."

The Jesuit's lip curled in scorn, and he made answer—

"Thou wilt not stop me nor make an attempt, if you value your life."

"Malapert slave!" cried the other, reddening to the temples at the taunt, and he aimed a blow at the daring conspirators.

His blade was caught and turned aside; then a passage of arms ensued between them in angry strife.

A stirring battle was going on with the others, when Lord Harrington lost his sword and fell to the ground pierced by his opponent.

A cry of agony burst from his lips, and brought his noble guest to his aid. Sir Everard was furiously attacked by the angry gentlemen. His danger was imminent, when the conspirators dashed amongst the noblemen and drove them from off Sir Everard.

A fearful combat ensued, attended with great loss to Lord Harrington's followers; but Sir Everard Digby, with the lovely princess clasped to his breast, as a safeguard to his life, cut his way through the enemy and got clear to the stairs.

Then there arose one mighty struggle for the final onset. The conspirators were furiously beset; they fought with indomitable courage, cutting down the thick barrier of men, with little loss on their side, while they left fearful signs of their bloody work behind them.

Catesby seemed to bear a charmed life; he went into the thickest of the strife, and came out unscathed; and he kept the assailants back while his companions picked up those of their party who had been stricken down, and then they beat a rapid retreat, remorselessly cutting down all who stood before them.

They reached the lower part of the house,

keeping back the enemy step by step as they went, and got safely to the door through which Sir Everard Digby had escaped with his prize.

Two of the conspirators had slipped out unobserved, while the fight was at its height and secured all the horses from the stables. The daring abductor had fled on one of these, the other horses were in readiness for instant flight.

Catesby, Wright, Thomas Percy, and others, fought bravely to defend those of their companions who carried the wounded. They did not give way an inch, though pressed hard upon by the overwhelming number of the enemy, until their brethren had got safely in their saddles ; then they turned to follow.

Percy was struck down by a blow from a ....., Catesby heard him ..., and sprang ... like a tiger, ... time to save the conspirator's life.

One of the soldiers was in the act of thrusting his weapon through his breast, when Catesby leaped forward, caught him by the throat, and ..... him back with great power ; then he ..... to raise the insensible Percy.

A man who had felt the weight of his club, and sorely wished to pay the debt, had followed him closely, waiting for an opportunity to wreak his vengeance full. He took the advantage of Catesby being down, and sprang on his back ; but ere he had time to accomplish his diabolical intent of driving a dagger between his shoulders, Catesby threw him off, and pinned him to the earth with his own weapon.

He then raised his companion, and threw the inanimate form over his shoulder, and like a fiend he fought his way through the opponents, who had dispersed the conspirators, and crowded round him.

He received several slight wounds, but they only tended to increase his fury, and he reached the horses, followed closely by his assailants.

His difficulty was now to mount ; he might have managed it with ease, had he not the insensible Percy to defend. But the whole hostile party beset him with increasing fury, he was the most dangerous of all, and they knew to conquer him the rest of the conspirators would fall easy victims.

But Robert Catesby was a matchless swordsman, and a man possessed with that cool indomitable courage so valuable in time of war, and the quick celerity with which he used his weapon, kept off the rapid blows of his combatants.

But he could not ..... against them much longer, he had fought long and unceasingly. His arm now began to tire, his strength was fast failing, and he had to slowly retreat.

His assailants saw this, and followed up the attack with increased vigour.

A moment more and he must fall ; but at that moment, when the sword was beaten from his hand, he jumped ..... in despair

ing cry of rage—his companions rushed between him and his opponents, and, with petronals on full cock, confronted the assailing party.

Catesby lost not an instant to bestride a powerful charger, and laying his friend across the saddle before him, dashed away.

The servitors made a rash attempt to follow the conspirators, fired their pieces (blank cartridge) point blank at them, and then took the opportunity of the confusion to flee, and they all managed safely to escape, two on each horse.

CHAPTER XXIII.

ON THE TRACK OF THE ABDUCTORS.

WHEN the men recovered from the consternation the charge of fire had thrown them into, their assailants were nowhere to be seen, and they knew the utter impossibility of overtaking them on foot, so they gathered up their fallen companions and conveyed them to the house to administer balm to their hurts.

Lord Harrington had been removed to his chamber when his friends returned. Sir Everard's sword had gone well home, and though the wound he had inflicted was not mortal, it was mighty dangerous, and left the loyal gentleman in a most uncertain state of recovery.

The household were left in a dejected state of suspense : their master lying insensible, between life and death, the royal maiden stolen from them, and their only means of pursuit cut off by the daring rebels, who had taken all the horses from the stables, placed them in a position of perplexity.

Nothing could be done without the word of their master, and everyone was kept at a standstill until he should recover. However, the morning following the contest, he was somewhat improved by careful nursing, and he held a debate with his friends on the best course to pursue for the recovery of Elizabeth.

It was finally settled that Harrington should lay the matter before Lord Salisbury, Secretary of State, and leave it to him how to act. He therewith wrote a letter and despatched it by one of the servitors.

When the messenger arrived at the palace he was conducted to the presence of his lordship, who, having made the man quite nervous by asking him sundry questions, read the following letter sent by Lord Harrington.

"*My Lord*,—

At midnight, last night, my house was besieged and broken into by a gang of miscreants, who, after a terrific encounter, in which I got severely wounded, carried off the Princess Elizabeth, and got safely away with the horses they took from the stables, so that our means of following are entirely cut off.

Amongst the rebels I recognised Thomas Percy, Robert Catesby, Sir Everard Digby, and Christopher Wright, all of whom took a prominent part in the attack, besides many other zealous Catholics who acted in concert with their leaders, slaying all who opposed them, and many of my vassals were killed outright. I hesitate not to assert that this is the forerunner of some devilish plot in work, and unless instant measures are taken to bring to punishment the above-named personages, we shall be apprised of some terrible calamity that may be the overthrow of the State ere long.

In the name of God and our King, I entreat thee, my lord, for the peace of the country, to use thy power for the restoration of the Princess, and the apprehension of the rebel Catholics, who have laid such devastation throughout my house, and threaten danger to the State.

(Signed)

HARRINGTON.

Lord Salisbury stood reflectively for some moments after reading the letter. Then he sat down hastily, wrote a note, and sent it to Lord Harrington by his messenger.

Soon as the man had gone, he wrote out warrants for the apprehension of the conspirators named in the letter. The King, at this juncture, being away at Royston, a favourite retreat of James's, his signature was not to be had, so Lord Salisbury stamped the writs for the capture with the Royal Seal, and giving orders for four companies of the Royal Guards to prepare for action, he supplied the officer of each company with documents for the capture of the daring Catholics, and in half an hour the country was being scoured in all directions by the soldiers.

Promptly as all this had been done, there were others on the track of the abductors ere the guards set out.

They were Lord Harrington's guests, who, mortified at being beaten in the encounter, swore to hunt down the daring rebels, not from any inveterate feelings of spite, but they felt, as loyal gentlemen, it was a duty due both to their stricken host and their king to save the princess, and bring to punishment her abductors.

The news of the attack soon got spread about, and many young gallants volunteered to join the hunting party; in many instances their offers were accepted, and when they numbered twelve, they set out—a company of such richly dressed cavaliers seldom seen in a body.

They were equipped for a long route and a stiff encounter, should they fall in with the enemy unexpectedly.

During the search by the cavaliers for the abductors of Elizabeth, a different scene was going on at the pavilion at Mortlake, to which scene we will take the attention of the readers.

After Guy Fawkes' defeat by Lord Cecil's myrmidons, Lady Claire of Grace, as has been before mentioned, was placed in her room, after being taken from her lover's arms.

When Guy had gone, Lord Cecil dispensed with his hirelings, save Count Basco, who he sent to procure a conveyance to take the lady to a place more secure than the one she was in.

He entered her chamber, and the poor girl, hearing his steps approaching, tried to hide from his hateful gaze.

"Anyone might take me for something inhuman," he said, sneeringly, approaching her; "am I so hideous that thou art obliged to hide that pretty head of thine. Come, come, Lady Claire, this is all stupid sham. Thou knowest well how I love thee; and wouldst thou forego the luxury I could give thee to become the wife of an outlaw—a murderer?"

A tremour ran through Claire's frame, she knew well to what he alluded, and she disliked him the more for his manners in trying to intimidate her into compliance by the threat of denouncing her lover.

"Coward!" she said, mastering herself for a trying ordeal. She saw by his excited look he meant to accomplish his base purpose. "Dastardly craven, to take the mean advantage to attack a weak woman! Wouldst thou face a man in anger as thou takest the advantage of me? No, like the dastard coward thou art, thou wouldst hire ruffians to do thy work, mean-spirited reptile! I scorn thee with loathing and contempt."

Lord Cecil was confounded. He had not expected such an attack from the gentle Lady Claire; her words stung him keenly, and he felt the miserable despicable cur he looked. His face reddened with shame; his thin lips quivered with concentrated rage, and for a few moments he stood abashed before the indignant gaze of his victim.

She was no longer the trembling, terrified girl he had thought to find her. The danger of her position gave her strength and courage to protect herself against the villany of her persecutor. She had risen from the ground, dashed the tears from her eyes, and drawn herself up in haughty grandeur before him; her breast heaving with agitation, her eyes sparkling like two massive brilliants, she stood fearless and beautiful.

Cecil raised his eyes towards her, and he thought that he had never seen a being so beautiful. He would have won her with kindness, but he knew how she loathed at his presence, and the knowledge drove him to desperation.

A wild hysterical cry broke from him, and advancing rapidly towards her, he seized her delicate wrist in a nervous grasp.

"Lady Claire," he said, his voice husky with emotion, and his countenance was pitiful, as he looked into her face; "Lady Claire I love thee. I am not cruel, but thy cold contempt drives me to desperation. I cannot bear the thought of losing thee; you whom I have ever worshiped as an idol, living on, hoping one day to win thy love, and now to see you thrown away upon an outcast is maddening to me. Lady Claire, it must never be. Thou shalt never be his while I live. Say that I may hope that thou art only using an artifice to try my love."

"Release me, sir," demanded Lady Claire haughtily; "this is useless. I can never be thine."

"And wherefore not?"

"Because I could never love thee."

Her words sent a thrill through him as though he had suddenly been struck by a dagger. He regarded her in mute agony; his love for her was certainly very great, and he would have sold his soul to his Satanic Majesty to have possessed her.

It was with pain he saw her abhorrence of him. Cruel, relentless as he was, it was not without a feeling of regret that he gave way to his bitter passion and disappointment.

"Lady Claire," he said, in a thick voice of desperate fury, "I have ever loved thee. You must thou shalt be mine! I have sworn it! And, in spite of heaven and hell, you shall be, either by thine own free will or by force!"

"Monster!" exclaimed the fair girl, with wonderful coolness; but her voice sounded harsh, and a ferocious light gleamed in her eyes. "Coward! dog! let me quit this place instantly, or thou wilt repent ere 'tis too late."

Cecil laughed demoniacally.

"Fool, that I should be, to let thee go now that I have got thee securely in my power," he said, bitterly. "No! we part no more! Lady Claire, thou art mine!"

And, throwing his arm around her waist, he drew her to his breast, and showered hot, passionate kisses on her flushing face.

She struggled to break from his grasp, but he held her too firmly, and laughed at her frail attempts, as he drew her face to his; he glued his lips over hers, his heart beating with delirious passion; he held her tightly to him, drawing her breath; and she became gradually quite weak.

Her eyes grew dim, her head giddy, and the room appeared to be whirling round; she felt herself going, and knew she must fall an easy victim to her brutal captor. Nerved to desperation by the wretched thought, she made a last effort with her failing strength to save her honour; and, with a sudden wrench, got her arms free, and fastened her hands on her persecutor's throat.

Cecil gave a gulping gasp, and his face turned a deep purple. He tried to shake her off, but he could not; she held him with tiger-like tenacity, and her beautiful face looked almost demoniac with outraged dignity.

Lord Cecil was choking; his eyes protruded from their sockets, his tongue lolled out of his mouth, and his lips were covered with thick red foam; he pinched her arms and face to make her relinquish her hold, but she tightened her grip; and, as a last resource, he caught her round the waist, lifted her off the ground, hurled her backwards, falling forward as she fell.

Lady Claire shrieked three times for help, while falling, knowing well that he must conquer now, and hoping by her cries to bring assistance to her rescue.

Her hold relaxed; the fall had stunned her: and Cecil rose and stood over his fair, beautiful prize in contemplative triumph, when the rattling of a carriage drawing near the house startled him.

"Basco," he muttered, "this is fortunate."

And he stooped to lift the senseless girl to a couch, when the bravo dashed into the room in a state of alarm.

"Fly!" he exclaimed, "we are discovered. A body of mounted horsemen drew up underneath the window as I arrived with the carriage."

Cecil stood dumbfounded. He did not appear to relish the idea of leaving his victim when he had so near succeeded in his purpose. He stood over her, gloatingly, contemplating her as she lay so innocent and helpless.

Suddenly there came a crash, as the door was forced open, that made him leap round; then came the rush of feet upstairs and the clash of steel.

Lord Cecil was about to take the insensible girl up in his arms, when Basco clutched him by the shoulder and pulled him out of the room.

A few moments after their exit a dozen richly-dressed cavaliers rushed into the chamber, with drawn swords, and looked about as though expecting to see someone.

"By heaven she is here!" said one of the nobles, sheathing his sword. He went to the couch and gently took the insensible girl up in his arms. "Follow, gentlemen, the varlets may be lying about somewhere, and we cannot endanger her life by an encounter, as much as I long to get my sword amongst them."

He left the room with the beautiful girl, and his friends followed him. Reaching the garden where the carriage stood, they placed her inside, and one of the horsemen acting as coachman, the vehicle was rapidly driven away with the rescued girl, and the cavaliers rode on either side as an escort.

Just as they drove away Guy Fawkes and his two friends came galloping up.

———

SEEKING THE MYSTERY.

CHAPTER XXIV.
THE LEGEND OF THE RED-CASTLE.

"FORWARD, comrades!" cried Guy; and, putting spurs to his horse, he followed the abductors of the Lady Claire, as he thought.

And he was not far out.

Without waiting for his friends, Guy

dashed after the company of cavaliers, mad with fury and eager to get at his foe, Lord Cecil, whom he fully imagined to be one of the party.

Captain Frank and Hugh Wardour were close behind him, when the escort turned to see who followed them.

Suddenly Guy Fawkes found himself surrounded by the warlike gentlemen, and a dozen bright rapiers flashed before his eyes, an angry flush rose to his swarthy cheeks, and he drew his sword with furious impetus.

"Is it fight the varlet means?" exclaimed a gay, elegant youth, bringing his horse round to confront the Spanish soldiers. "Come on thou ill-looking sneak! Gentlemen, look after the two traitors you have."

The two traitors the young gallant alluded to were Hugh and Captain Frank, who, while he was speaking, broke through the cavaliers, and took up their position in defensive attitudes on either side of Guy.

"Come on," said Captain Frank, brandishing his sword enthusiastically. "Four to one! that's the thing; nothing like plenty of excitement, and something to fight for."

The coolness of the reckless speaker's challenge won the esteem of the noblemen, save the young gallant, who confronted Guy, and his handsome lip curled with scorn.

"Methinks, braggart," he said, "thou mayest find thy work with one. An' since thy friend seems loth to accept my challenge, I would fain try the temper of thy steel."

"By thunder of Jove! it was thee who called me traitor!" exclaimed Captain Frank, hotly, stung to the quick by the other's sneering manner, "and thou shalt answer for the insult with thy sword; an' it may by that. I do not brag idly, so come on, if thou art ready to be taught a lesson."

"A lesson which may cost thee dearly," said the other, in cold irony, as he whirled round his steed to face his combatant.

They were of a similar build—slim and gracefully formed, moving with that easy elasticity so characteristic to the thoroughbred gentleman. Captain Frank may have been two or three years his opponent's senior, but the difference was very slight, and altogether they were splendidly matched.

The combatants met in real earnest. Captain Frank, deeply wounded by the taunts of his opponent, entered into the contest with a feeling of revenge, and the other fought for honour, as he felt in duty bound to kill the man with whom he fought.

They had merely crossed swords when one of the gentlemen came in between them.

"For what are you fighting?" he asked, looking from one to the other inquiringly.

"I fight because I was challenged," Captain Frank made answer.

"And I because I wanted to have a fight," said his opponent.

"And I," cried Guy, coming in amongst them with sudden energy, "in the lady's defence."

"And I," echoed Hugh Wardour, "Fight for my friends."

"Very capital causes from all of ye," said the nobleman, smiling, who had stopped the duel. "But before we enter further into this dangerous matter let us fully understand each other."

"That's the idea," cried Captain Frank. "What's all the row about?"

"Thy friend there," said the nobleman, speaking to Captain Frank, and alluding to Guy Fawkes, "spoke of a lady, for whom he said he fought. What lady does he mean?"

"The Lady Claire of Grace, the king's ward," exclaimed Guy, passionately, "the lady, scoundrel cavaliers, whom ye have stolen from the pavilion."

"It appears to me," said another of the cavaliers, coming forward in time to prevent Guy from using his sword, "thou art all under a strange delusion. What is thy grievance, my gloomy-looking friend."

Guy looked anything but pleasant at the speaker.

"D'ye call yourselves men," he exclaimed, "for all of thee to persecute an helpless lady?"

"What the deuce is the knave roaring about?" asked one of the nobles.

"The fact of it is, gentlemen," said Captain Frank, "my friend has lost his lady, but he don't like to say so."

This brought a round of laughter from the cavaliers, much to the disgust of Guy, who felt so grateful for the revelation that he would willingly have given the reckless speaker a few inches of cold steel gratis.

"Well," said one of the noblemen, 'I feel sorry for thy friend, but that is no reason why he should stop us."

"'Tis every reason, coward libertine!" Guy was awfully incensed, and his dark eyes grew the brighter with a more dangerous fire as his anger increased, "since 'twas thee who, in concert with Lord Cecil, took her from her guardian's care."

"Marry, sirrah, methinks thou speakest boldly," said the cavalier indignantly, "and were it not that I thought thou wert labouring under some mistake, thou shouldst answer for the insult."

"Perhaps, Guy, thou art mistaken," said Hugh.

"'Sblood!" impatiently exclaimed the hot-headed soldier, "how can I mistake when I saw them leave the pavilion where I left Lady Clare?"

"Let's come to the point, that's the thing," said Captain Frank; "without a doubt we saw the gentlemen leave the pavilion. If I may be so bold, what was thy business there?"

"In good faith I answer thy question," replied the nobleman addressed. "Last night the Princess Elizabeth was stolen from Lord Harrington's house; this morning I and my friends set out to find her. We fell on the track of the abductors, and found the princess at the pavilion in an insensible state."

"Then Lord Cecil is implicated in this affair," said Guy.

"It will be the worse for Lord Cecil if he is," said one of the cavaliers.

"We stopped thee for the traitors," said another.

"Very kind of thee," said Frank, "we followed you for the abductors."

"I feel flattered," good-humouredly made answer a third. "See what a terrible fight a little reasoning has prevented, fortunately for thee and thy friends."

"I don't see it," answered Captain Frank with a great amount of confidence in his own prowess. "Do you mean to insinuate that I can't fight?"

"Not at all, but thou wouldst not have much chance with twelve of us."

"Oh! you think so! Well, try us, that's the thing."

"Why should we fight?"

"Because you doubt my assertion, and I wish to prove to thee that I *can* fight."

"I doubt not thy assertion, my friend, but I see not the necessity of endangering one's life because you want to fight."

"Well, I must have a fight with someone. Ho! knave, where art thou who challenged me? Come out and show thyself!"

The youth with whom he had crossed swords answered the challenge, and a spirited passage of arms ensued.

"Is it a duel to the death?" asked Frank.

"To the death!" answered his combatant.

"I shall disarm you, my sanguinary friend, with the third point," coolly remarked Captain Frank, confidentially.

The youth smiled doubtfully, and watched closely for an opening to pink him.

"One!" said Frank, ripping open the arm-seam of the other's coat with the point of his sword.

The youth took it quietly; he meant mischief. A cruel curl of the lip showed his purpose. He fenced admirably well, but not well enough to compete with his opponent.

Captain Frank was observant of his combatant's maliciousness and, to increase his spite, he toyed with him aggravatingly.

Suddenly, the young noble, with a twist of his wrist, brought his sword in a line with Frank's breast, and made a rapid lunge forward.

"Nicely aimed," said Captain Frank, diverting the blade on his own, "but hardly quick enough. I will show you how to pink a fellow in the stomach."

Crossing swords again, he ran his blade along that of the other's, and through the hilt, thus fixing his opponent's arm, and, with a slight pressure of his hand on the pommel of his sword, he drove the point through the youth's coat, and drew blood.

"Two points!" he said, drawing back his arm and falling into the attitude of defence as the humiliated young noble aimed a furious blow at his head.

The lookers-on now thought it time to interfere, as the contest was becoming serious, and it had every appearance of ending fatally.

"This is neither time nor place for this sort of thing," one of the cavaliers said, interposing with his sword. "Come, my lord, forego this for a time more fitting."

"Yes, stop it. What the deuce dost thou want to fight for?" said Hugh Wardour, pulling Captain Frank back by the collar.

"Leave me alone. I've only got another point to get," Frank said, struggling to break away from his captor's grasp.

"Leave it for another time."

"But I want to fight," Captain Frank said, cutting and plunging forward with his weapon while being pulled back. "Let go, Hugh; I will fight."

"Then fight me."

"No; that ain't the thing, you know. You don't want to fight."

"But I will, to oblige you."

"That sounds very much like a challenge."

"That's what it is meant for."

The captain turned and faced his friend.

"Do you mean it?" he asked, seriously.

"I was never more in earnest."

"'Sblood!" exclaimed the gloomy Guy, coming between them. "Come, come, comrades; let's have no broil amongst friends."

"By St. George! I meant him no ill-will," said Hugh. "I spoke but for his good and ours."

"Thunder of Jove! think you, friend, I stood in danger of that milksop's blade? By my faith! if I could not beat half-a-dozen of such, I would snap my steel across my knee, and get one of thee to bury thy sword in mine heart!"

"Braggart! varlet!" exclaimed the youth, who had overheard the other's speech while being pulled away by two of his friends. "There's my challenge,"—and he threw his gauntlet in Captain Frank's face. "We meet two days hence, at noon, beneath the wall of the ruined chapel, St. Mary. If thou art not a coward, thou wilt be there."

"I shall remember," said Captain Frank, sternly, as he hurled the gauntlet back.

The twelve cavaliers again formed the escort of the carriage, and the gallant company went on their journey with the lovely Lady Claire, whom they had saved from an ignominious fate, but whom they really thought to be the princess.

"That's one fight on hand," said Captain Frank, with satisfaction. "I must try and get two more for the interim."

"Fear not, my friend, thou wilt have plenty of fighting ere the wane of the second moon from this."

"The more the better. I could live on fighting."

"You may die on it some day," gloomily remarked Guy Fawkes.

"Then I should be content to die,
   If by a warrior's hand I fell;
The ring of steel with my life's last sigh,
   Sweet echoes to toll the dying knell."

"Do you remember the old song, Guy?" Captain Frank asked, breaking off abruptly in the melody, for he had forgotten the rest.

Guy shook his head in the negative.

"Then thou canst not help me through with it. Hallo! who comes?"

The three friends drew aside. Three horsemen were coming towards them rapidly, and following behind them came a body of soldiers in hot pursuit, their bright armour and the points of their lances glittering brightly in the moon's rays.

"Guy Fawkes!" exclaimed the foremost of the three riders, as he passed, bearing on the saddle before him the lifeless form of a man, "for thy life follow! We are discovered!"

"Catesby," muttered Guy, wondering what his brother conspirator meant.

While he sat wondering the other two came sweeping past, and they too warned him by exclaiming—

"Follow, for thy life!"

Guy followed, wondering what they meant. A glance at the soldiers thundering towards them was enough to let them know they were in danger, and they did their best to get out of it. Valiant as they were they did not feel disposed to face the warlike warriors.

"No," said Captain Frank, "I would take any half-dozen, but twenty is too many for any fellow. It's all very jolly to fall in the glory of battle, but I have no inclination to fall before my time comes. So come on, and let's leave them to follow. We can give them a ride."

"To eternity," Hugh put in, and away they went—not to eternity.

The soldiers were fast gaining on them.

"This won't do," said Guy, who rode neck and neck with Catesby. "How happened this?"

He pointed to the man who lay across his companion's saddle.

"This is no time for questioning," replied Catesby; "it's like Percy's luck."

"Thomas Percy is it?" queried Guy.

"It is," answered Catesby, who heartily wished it had been Guy instead; "then we must take another route or we shall be overtaken."

Guy and his comrades, Frank and Hugh, turned their horses' heads to the left.

"Meet me at the Red Castle!" Catesby shouted, dashing forward with his lifeless burden.

This manœuvre slightly mystified the soldiers to know which party to follow for the right, but to make sure they divided into two companies, and followed both.

The pursuit was a long one: the soldiers kept close on the heels of our three friends, and they were compelled to dodge about quite out of the course they wished to pursue, and belabour their steeds almost brutally to keep at all a-head of their pursuers.

"If we can only keep up at this pace a little longer we shall give the varlets the slip," said Captain Frank.

Their horses were scudding through the air at racehorse speed, but there did not appear much possibility of their continuing so much longer; the poor beasts were panting almost breathlessly, and they were only kept up at the pace at which they were going by the torturing spur being driven into their sides, from which the blood flowed in thick streams.

But the young captain had spoken aright: the soldiers' chargers began to flag in speed, spite of the furious digs of their rider's spurs. The officer in command was the only one who seemed to be at all fresh, and that was on account of his being more lightly equipped, and furnished with a better piece of horseflesh than his men; and while he was urging on his guards to follow the daring fugitives, the fugitives took the opportunity afforded them. Altering their course —speaking vulgarly—they bolted in and out of some very dirty back slums of Lambeth, and made their way to the Red Castle.

It was a curious old building, standing on the brow of a hill, and sloping towards the river. A wide moat winding round the Gothic walls had, in the times of war, defended it from the furious ravages, but the moat was partly filled up, and in some parts completely covered to all outward appearance; the north and east wings were defended by two bastion towers, between which, lying back, was a circular arch that formed the entrance, and through this the adventurers entered into a courtyard, or what had formally been one. The clatter of their horses' hoofs brought out several dark and silent figures, who emerged like shadows from some secret crevices, and held the bridles of the fatigued steeds, while the riders dismounted; then one of the mysterious individuals, without being invited, conducted Guy and his friends through a small door that opened in the wall and along an apparently endless subterranean passage.

Guy was evidently known to the mysterious individual. They exchanged signs, which each answered. But his friends were strange it could be easily seen, by the doubtful looks they received as they passed the cloaked personages. Captain Frank began to feel uncomfortable, and he even intimated his intention of making a retreat to Hugh by nudging him in the side with his spiky elbow, and pointing significantly over his shoulder.

Hugh Wardour, who was better acquainted with his comrades' unlawful doings, did not hesitate to follow their guide, though while following he might have felt more cheerful than he did; but he kept his doubts to himself, and nudged Captain Frank, in order to assure him all was right and safe.

Captain French did not think so, but, like his companion, he followed rather than show his fear; and, having one friend with him in whom he could trust with the greatest confidence, he held him tightly for instant use, should there prove an occasion.

> "My trusty steel! my truest friend!
> To friend or foe ye never bend;
> If but drawn in honour's name,
> In weal, in woe, thou art the same,"

muttered Captain Frank; but what he meant is a matter for conjecture.

He was not sorry when they reached the terminus of the long and dreary passage. They now came into a stone gallery dimly lighted by a solitary oil-lamp dangling from a hook in the ceiling. From here they passed through another small aperture, and, after a descent of several flights of stone steps they were ushered into a large hall. The walls were of beautiful polished wood, in parts tastefully carved; from the solid wood stood out in bold relief picturesque scenes from the lives of the ancient Britons. The ceiling was of stone, and splendidly decorated with fret-work; the floor, polished marble; and on one side of the room was a huge fireplace, where several great logs burned brightly, and threw its pleasant glare around. The furniture was not of much account, though what there was had in its time been of a costly nature, and this the conspirators who now inhabited the Red Castle had collected and put together as well as lay in their power for use.

It will, perhaps, be better, ere we go on further, to explain how they came in possession of the grand old pile.

There was a strange legend connected with its history that supplied the superstitious tatlers with food for their inventive imaginations, and many who heard the story felt their flesh creep with horror while they listened, and for nights afterwards their rest was disturbed by wild, unearthly dreams, and they tossed about in bed restlessly, their shaken nerves conjuring up weird objects that peopled their room that held them at times by a peculiar fascination.

The legend ran thus—

Sir Roland Osmond, a baronet by birth and title, had but a small share of his ancestor's fortune allotted to him, for by the time it had descended from one to the other, decreasing step by step, he found it barely sufficient to maintain the few menials requisite for a person of his rank and to support him in a moderate way of life.

He had a brother, a bold, handsome youth, some few years his junior, who, knowing the weak state of Sir Roland's funds, chose his own career, and followed the fortunes of a grand old knight, and soon distinguished himself by his daring deeds on the battle-field.

The old knight with pleasure watched the progress of the youth, though he made no distinction of him from the other men. At any rate, he was observant of Harold's every act, and it warmed his old heart with joy to see the cool courage with which he went about while danger surrounded him.

The knight had a daughter, an only child, just in the blossom of youth, for seventeen summers had not yet come and passed since she first saw light; she was at that age when the heart is most perceptible to the influence of love—at that tender age when young ladies are so prone to indulge in wild dreams of romance, in which they picture their future idols the most noble of men. Eveline had seen and learnt to love hers. Fair and pure as the lily, her mind unsullied by an evil thought, the maiden dared to keep the secret of her love from her sire, though it burned like a torturing fire beneath her fair bosom, she would not reveal it for fear of receiving the cruel refusal to shatter her cherished hope.

And so the lovers lived on, content to remain in their unbroken dream of love for ever. They dwelt in a land of their own creation—a fairy land it was, where there lived but two beings, and these two were themselves.

They thought not of the danger they incurred by their midnight interviews; and when they parted, each with the last kiss lingering on the other's lips, and the last sweet word ringing in their ears, they slept happy that night.

In one terrific encounter with the Normans, in which the English nobles were strongly repulsed and beaten, with fearful loss, the brave old knight got stricken from his saddle and left by his assailant for dead.

Harold Osmond, who ever followed closely the heels of his master, was engaged in combat with a gigantic fellow, who used a huge battle-axe, in a manner that threatened to make short work of his opponent, when he saw the knight struck down.

At that moment he felt a strange sensation take possession of him—a feeling of strong affection, as for a parent, he had never before experienced; and he wanted to save the old man from being trampled to a shapeless mass, although he saw how hopeless would be an attempt, for thousands of soldiers, in strong bodies, were advancing, who must pass over the fallen knight.

Urged on by a peculiar feeling, foreign to his cool nature, he dashed at his enemy, regardless of danger, and seized his upraised arm in time to prevent the battle-axe from descending on his skull, and keeping the warrior's arm in a vice-like grip, he forced the point of his sword between the links of his enemy's armour, he drove it through his breast. Seizing the battle-axe from his relaxing grasp, as he fell mortally wounded, the excited youth, in mad fury, ran his charger full into the body of the advancing troops, fighting like a gladiator. Scattering the soldiers with his formidable weapon, he raised the stricken knight, and, putting spurs to his charger, rode off unscratched.

The blow that felled the knight had been delivered with much force from a battle-axe, and although his helmet showed fearful marks of the blow, the old fellow's pate still remained whole, thanks to the mail he wore.

"I watched thee well, fair youth," the old knight said, in warm gratitude, taking Harold's hands in his own, "and have been much pleased to see thy courage. It was a smashing blow from a coward knave behind that laid me low, and I verily thought I had gotten my death-stroke; an' but for thee, my brave preserver, who, at the peril of thine own gentle life, broke through the enemy's ranks, who trampled me under foot, and saved me from a mutilating death, ere this I should have been mingled with the dust, a shapeless mass. I owe thee my life's gratitude, and anything thou mayst ask for shall readily be thine."

The youth, blushing deeply, bowed low in gratitude.

"Your worship does me more honour than I deserve for my poor services," Harold said. "'Twas an ill-timed blow when the varlet struck thee down; e'en for his knavish trick I sped him to his last account, with my sword quivering in his heart."

"Thou art a noble youth, an' there is nothing thou mayst ask for I would refuse."

Brave as a lion in war, the youth now stood trembling and courageless, held powerless by the influence of the large blue luminous orbs fixed upon him with a tender, encouraging look.

The beautiful Eveline stood by her sire's side as he sat in a grand old chair, with an arm twined affectionately round his neck, her head resting on his shoulder, with her face turned towards her lover, and her eyes fixed upon him with an expression that spoke the language of her heart.

Her father had said he would refuse the noble preserver of his life nothing he might ask for. The maiden's heart bounded with hope. Never had any words been spoken so welcome to her ears as were these.

The time she had so much feared, when the secret of her heart must be known, had come now, like a gladdening sunbeam lingering with its bright hopes of happiness.

Why did her lover stand there so mute and nervous, more like a criminal before a stern judge, than the gallant warrior who had won the laurels of bravery?

The youth stood bound by a spell—the fascinating expression of Eveline's eyes, from which he could not divert his own, held him powerless; the meaning glance she gave him to urge him to ask for that which his heart most yearned for only tended to increase his embarrassment, and unnerve him.

The old knight watched the youth curiously, and his countenance changed pleasingly.

"Is there nothing thou wouldst care for?" he asked.

"There is one great gift thou couldst give me, and yet I dare not ask it of thee, for fear of incurring thy displeasure."

As the youth spoke, his deep, expressive eyes turned towards the lonely Eveline with a look of all tenderness and love.

"There is nought thou mayst ask for I would refuse," said the knight, encouragingly; "nor is there aught thou mayst demand that would give me ill grace towards thee. Ask for what thou wilt, my life, my all, and it shall be thine."

"Thy words inspire me to make bold," the youth said, his voice shaking with emotional gratitude and tears of happiness springing to his eyes. "If I ask too much, I humbly crave thy pardon; condemn me not too harshly if I say I have presumed to love thy gentle daughter. Thou knowest now the great secret of our hearts; my love is bestowed on no barren soil. Eveline returns it with an affection as deep as mine own."

"Is it so?" the knight asked of his daughter.

"Dear father, it is," replied the lovely maiden, burying her blushing face on her sire's shoulder.

"Harold!" the knight said slowly, "Eveline is thine. I could wish for none better than thee for the keeper of her future happiness. Thou art of noble birth, and all noble in nature, 'tis the least I can give thee in return for what thou hast done for me. Take her, my son, and with her the blessing of a grateful parent."

Harold was too overwhelmed with gratitude to say a word, but his look, in mute language, spoke the feelings of his heart.

The old knight joined the lover's hands, and laying a hand on each of their heads, he bestowed upon them a fervent benison.

It was not long after that night of happiness, when the country rested in tranquillity, one bright, glorious morning saw the lover's made man and wife, and never was there seen a more gorgeous company than attended their union.

For some years the old knight lived happily with the young pair, until age claimed its own; then began the long train of sorrow and tragedy which followed.

Harold being affectionately fond of his brother Rowland, and the possessor of the late knight's enormous wealth, and knowing the very scanty means his brother had to keep up his position with, he generously determined to reside at the Red Castle with him, and equally share his fortune.

The baronet expressed his great joy at his brother's proposal of taking up his abode with him in a very ardent manner; but as to sharing his fortune, he would not hear of it.

True, the brothers loved each other very sincerely; and had not Harold brought with him to the castle his lovely bride, their happiness might have remained unmarred, but beauty brings its own sorrows; and the gentle lady was the innocent cause of the great crime which fell upon the ancient castle like a sombre pall.

Sir Rowland Osmond was deeply smitten by the lady's queenly beauty from the day of her arrival at the castle with her gallant young husband, and for his brother's sake he tried to smother the haunting fascination that tormented him day and night.

But his efforts were vain. The less he tried to think of her his passions took deeper root, and at last he became reckless of the affection he bore his brother. This recklessness grew into a selfish ambition.

Harold noticed the change, but knew not the cause; and when he tried to soothe the baronet, thinking that he was not well, Rowland appeared very gloomy and abstracted, and tried to avoid the generous youth.

At times he would sit for hours in his chamber, pondering over events and evil thoughts that rose vividly to his mind.

"Why should I live thus, while *he* is elate with happiness?" he would cogitate. "I, the baronet and representative of an ancient family, to remain in a state of abject poverty, while he, who has degraded his name by his servility as a mean vassal, should possess the fortune of a prince, and a wife of Diana's beauty—a woman, whose very look sets my heart on fire. Too long I have been blind to my own interest, deterred from a course that would have brought everything to my feet but for the tie of affection which held me back; and why should that hold me back, when a powerful feeling urges me on? Did he think of me when he left me, like a coward knave, to fight the battle alone? Was that brotherly love? Bah!" he impatiently exclaimed; and, rising hastily from his chair, he paced the room in a wild state of mind. His thoughts ran in a channel dark and terrible, and his excited imagination conjured up pictures before his mind's eye that curdled his blood with horror; and, in a frenzied manner, giving vent to an unearthly cry, he ran from the chamber, and sought the company of his brother.

Eveline was seated by her husband's side, her hand locked in his, and her sweet face turned up to his, with an angelic expression on her blooming features, when Sir Rowland broke rudely upon their presence. He stopped suddenly on seeing them thus, and his face took a demoniac change.

Harold was startled by the alteration in his brother, and rising, while Eveline cowered back in terror at his piercing glances fixed upon her, he advanced towards the baronet, when, with an impetuous flourish of the hand, Rowland kept him back, and left them alone.

The strange manner of the baronet disturbed the peace of the happy couple, and for several days after his abrupt behaviour he kept from their presence.

But, while absent, his mind was not void of evil thoughts. He was haunted by the vision of the beautiful enchantress rising before his eyes; and day by day he found himself falling helplessly into the terrible vortex that was drawing to a crisis.

One dark and fearful night, the tempest raged with mighty fury, and the pealing thunder rolled round the castle's peaks, shaking roof and casement.

Clap followed clap, dying away in growling anger; the rain fell from the heavy clouds in torrents that soon raised the rivers, and overflowed field and plain.

It swept before its powerful flood trees and habitations, and dealt destruction on every inch of ground.

Spite of its resistless force, there stood a being—a solitary, silent figure—beneath the iron gates of the Red Castle.

Bent on some fell work, for no one but those of evil thought could have remained out in such a night.

Presently the sentry was startled by the distant sound of an approaching horse coming with great speed towards the castle, and he bent his head forward with eagerness in the direction whence the sound came.

In a few moments a youth of noble bearing came tearing up to the castle gates, his horse panting with fatigue, for it had had a long and dangerous journey, and the rider, too, panted with excitement.

He was in the act of dismounting to summon assistance, when suddenly a peal of thunder burst over his head, and went crashing round the castle towers, the very earth seemed to shake beneath his feet. The shock startled him, and his steed pawed the ground uneasily.

A second deafening clap succeeded the dying echoes of the first. Just as he had drawn his leg over the saddle, and while he held the reins hesitatingly, the heavens opened, and poured down a flood of electric light, illuminating all around for a few moments, and revealing to the gaze of the young horseman the crouching form concealed behind the iron gates.

The youth shrank back by an instinct of dread; then, as though ashamed of his weakness, he advanced towards the gate with the reins slung over his arm, and taking the enveloped form for the gatekeeper, he called—

"Ho, there, within, knave! Open the gates and let me pass."

One gate partly opened, and the youth went forward. He was sprung upon by the cloaked figure, and borne to the earth.

A struggle ensued. The youth, by instinct, felt his life was sought, and he fought desperately with his assailant to keep back the gleaming blade raised over him.

The contest did not last long; the long journey he had come had fatigued him, and his feeble strength sank beneath the brute power of his antagonist.

He had no hope now, the wretch kneeling on his chest, with one hand fastened over his throat to stop his cries, his eyes glaring demoniacally on his victim; he seemed to gloat over his fell purpose, and torture the helpless youth by playing with the murderous dagger.

The poor young fellow shuddered with terror. It was a fearful moment for him to lie there with death in all its hideous torture hovering over him.

He breathed a prayer to heaven, and the word Eveline in deep pathos broke from his quivering lips in a whisper.

The simple word breaking on the ear of the evil monster, sent a thrill through him, and his grasp on the youth's throat tightened.

The dagger raised and fell with a thud, burying its thirsty blade deep into its victim's breast.

A piercing shriek of horror escaped from the youth's lips, and with a desperate effort he freed his arms and hung on to his murderer's.

In the struggle the youth got hold of the assassin's heavy beard, and it came off in his hand as the other forced him back.

"My brother!" exclaimed the youth, faintly, recognising the now undisguised murderer. "Rowland, why this?"

"Because thou hast stood between me and the Lady Eveline," said the cold-blooded villain ; "with that thought die content."

As he spoke he raised his murderous arm to deal another cruel blow, but its descent was stayed by his victim clutching his wrist, and the youth looked into his stern, remorseless face imploringly.

He wanted to say something, but his voice had gone with his life's tide flowing from the gaping gash in his breast.

There was no mercy in the callous breast of the fratricide ; he tore the expiring youth's hand off his arm and plunged the thirsty blade thrice into his heart.

A convulsive throb shook the murdered youth's body, and his lingering spirit departed in a faint-drawn sigh.

As the assassin rose from his cruel work the angry tempest burst forth afresh in terrible fury, and the forked lightning played about his retreating form as he tore across the court-yard.

He had barely vanished when a troop of servitors, with the lovely Lady Eviline at their head, came rushing from the castle.

They had heard the youth's death-cry, and had come out to see the cause of it.

Imagine their horror when they found the gallant Harold lying at the castle gates disfigured by the cruel blows that had robbed him of his gentle life, and left him iu a swamp of steaming gore.

Lady Eveline uttered one heartrending cry and fell prone across her husband's bleeding breast.

While the men stood looking on at the deplorable sight, stricken into helplessness by horror, Sir Rowland approached, looking faint and deathly.

"What means this?" he demanded.

The servitors only pointed to the two young and lifeless forms lying at their feet.

Rowland was stooping over them when a flash of light from heaven darted before his eyes, and he went staggering back, weak and trembling, his guilty conscience stricken by the hand of judgment; and he would have fallen, had not one of the men caught him.

"Great Father of heaven help us, 'tis my brother !" the hypocrite gasped.

And he lost all power of his limbs.

His eyes rolled about in their sockets, blazing wildly, and his face worked convulsively while being borne helplessly back into the castle.

For many days after this terrible event the baronet was confined to his bed with a severe fever that brought on frantic ravings, and at times he would give vent to his guilty conscience in the following strain :

"He calls—he beckons—he laughs! Take him away—'tis the fiend! He wants to tear out mine heart! No! no! He shall not torture me in the fire around him ! I did not murder my brother—no, no, I did not ! See ! see ! He stands there, a bleeding shadow, with a dagger quivering in his breast, and I—I—I—"

Here he would generally terminate his ravings, and fall back exhausted.

He was much pitied, and it was thought that the shock of finding his brother in that mutilated state had turned his mind.

His condition was much lamented by his faithful servants, who thought never more to behold their lord in his senses.

But they were mistaken.

It was not long after the interment of the murdered youth when Sir Rowland left his bed.

He was quite calm then, but still a haggard expression lingered about his features, and he was startled by any little noise after dark, and always shut himself up in a room when there was a storm.

The first fierce outbreak had passed, and the consternation caused by the consummation of the horrible deed was slowly abating.

But the baronet swore vengeance on the assassins of his brother.

What was wealth and fame without him to share it ?

Not a place should remain unsearched to bring to light the murderers.

But after the first fruitless search the subject sank into oblivion, and *the* murderer escaped undiscovered.

The baronet was never seen to smile. The fate of his loving brother had left a deep impression on his mind, and he walked about the castle in gloomy silence, shunning all society except the bereaved Lady Eveline, whose grief he tried to soothe by gentle words.

The kindness met with a cool reception. The lady instinctively shunned him as she would have sought to hide from a savage beast of the forest.

Sir Rowland showed evident signs of displeasure at her abhorrence for him. As time wore on he grew more bold, and even dared to press his suit.

This conduct met with the greatest contempt, and the lady declared her intention, if he did not discontinue to persecute her

GUY FAWKES
OR
THE CONSPIRATORS BRIDE

WITH FOLDED ARMS HE STOOD LOOKING COOLLY ON.

with his hateful presence, to return to her own abode, where she could be left to her sorrows in solitude.

This threat rekindled the smouldering fire of crime in all its fury; and he swore that she should not quit even her chamber again until she had consented to become his wife.

He met with a resolution as firm as his own.

"Death would be preferable to me," she said; "and death it shall be, ere I would become the wife of a fratricide. Thy hands are stained with thy brother's blood—he my husband. Thy brother hath told me so, for he hath visited me since he hath been in heaven. Deny the accusation if thou canst. Thou art self-condemning," the excited, lovely lady continued, confronting the quailing wretch in her statuesque beauty; "see how thy limbs shake; thy face is blanched with guilt; and crime is marked in every lineament. Away! leave me, ere I denounce thee!"

"Lady, beautiful enchantress, condemn me as thou wilt," he said; "I am innocent, and my love for thee will be ever the same."

"Impertinent knave, begone, ere I summon thy own vassals, who shall chastise thy insolence."

His wrath burst forth at this threat in great fury.

"I go!" he exclaimed, hotly; "but to-morrow thou shalt be my bride, with thy will or my power; so be ready."

"I shall be prepared," the lady said, calmly, as he quitted the room.

On the morrow everything was prepared for the wedding, which was to take place in the chapel of the Red Castle.

Lady Eveline was ready at the time stated for the ceremony, decked in virgin white, and a wreath of orange blossoms encircled her fair brow.

She was conducted to the chapel with all the honours shown to a princess. Her mien was calm and stately. She had resigned herself to her fate; and the change caused Sir Rowland to marvel much.

Fair, quiet, and beautiful as a saint, she stood upon the altar's step; and, when the sermon began, a heavenly smile rested on her placid features.

The baronet felt uneasy. Her quiet resignation puzzled him; and, when it came for her to repeat the words spoken by the priest, he glanced towards her anxiously.

The lady was silent.

Her face, smiling, was upturned to heaven, and her lips moved as though in prayer.

The priest repeated the sentence, "Wilt thou take this man to be thy wedded husband?"

A hush fell upon the assemblage when the lady turned her head towards the speaker.

"My husband lives in heaven," she said, her voice sweet and plaintive; "and thence I go to join him."

She raised her hand; on her finger glistened a magnificent diamond; this she put to her lips without the least sign of tremour.

The truth flashed to Sir Rowland's mind—it was a poisoned gem she was going to suck—and he sprang forward to stay her hand.

At that moment a rich flood of the sun's golden rays streamed through the skylight of the chapel and fell upon the altar's steps.

The baronet's arm fell listlessly to his side, and he went reeling back void of speech, with a look of fearful agony marking his features.

Between him and the lovely lady stood a distinct visionary form, surrounded by a halo of celestial light, with an arm outstretched towards the guilty, conscience-stricken wretch.

Everyone saw it, and crossed themselves reverently.

"My brother! Harold! do not look upon me in that way!" frantically shrieked Sir Rowland.

The shadowy arm waved at him. Then two forms, the vision of Harold Osmond and Lady Eveline floated through the air and faded from view.

The sun's bright rays vanished, and left a sombre gloom hovering about the chapel.

The form of Lady Eveline lied at the bridal altar lifeless; still there played about the angelic features a gentle smile.

At the hour of trial the vision of her husband had come and called her hence to a brighter and happier home.

The disappointment of losing his much-coveted bride, and the shock he received at the visitation of his departed brother, the baronet never recovered from.

From that time he prowled about like an evil spirit, never resting day or night, and the servants walked about in a mysterious manner, looking at one another doubtfully, and only conversing when they met in the large hall.

At night strange voices were heard in the towers, and it was said that ghosts were seen traversing the corridors in a weird manner.

The baronet grew more depressed in spirits every day, and one night, when every one had retired to rest, they were awoke at the hour of midnight by a succession of frantic, wild shrieks of horror that issued from their master's chamber.

They went to see the cause of the cries, and when they broke open the door, they were nearly choked by a thick, sulphury vapour that filled the chamber.

A wailing shriek for help burst on their ears, then followed a wild, mocking, unearthly laugh—a fiendish, exulting laugh it was—as the servitors advanced in the room to look for their master.

He was nowhere to be found. There were evident signs of a desperate struggle having ensued; but by whom?—their master one, undoubtedly; for it appeared as though he had been attacked in his bed. But, who could have been his assailant, none knew. No one could have got entrance to the castle; besides, even if they had, they could not have carried off the baronet without being seen. It was a mystery none cared to solve; though it was whispered in dread that the lord of the Red Castle had been carried off by Satan.

It was the anniversary night of the fearful tragedy, and, strange to relate, a fierce storm raged with violent fury. There was one person out in the tempest and passed the castle who said he saw the vision of a man prowling about the gates calmly, and from four deep gashes in his breast there seemed to run streams of gore.

From the night of Sir Rowland's strange disappearance, the mysterious voices in the castle were increased, and sepulchural cries and groans, in melancholy moanings, rang through the castle.

This was not the worst. One of the vassals, in a fit of terror, rushed into the room where his fellow-servants were gathered, and declared on his oath that he had seen the spirit of Sir Rowland coming out of the chamber lately occupied by him, followed by his Satanic majesty.

The news soon got spread abroad. The servitors left the castle to its ghastly occupants ; and, from the time of their departure, it was always carefully avoided by everyone who had an occasion to pass it, and so it was left to decay and ruin.

So ends the legend of the Red Castle. For the foundation of its facts we have none, so we cannot assert its truth.

Let it suffice the reader to know that the conspirators did not put too much faith in the wild story ; and, being pressed hard for a place of safety, and knowing no one cared to explore the interior of the Red Castle, they took possession of it, and were determined to fight with the ghostly inhabitants of it for the rights of possession—that is, if there were any ghosts to fight, and as yet they had not seen any, so they remained unmolested.

Guy Fawkes was warmly greeted by his brethren on entering the marble hall, but his friends were eyed suspiciously.

Captain Frank felt that he was not wanted, and, another thing, he did not want to stop, so he did not feel the least grateful for their hospitality. He would have gone had they shown him the way out ; but, as they did not, he was obliged to remain.

Hugh Wardour took things in quite a different light. He felt on principle, as being Guy's friend, he claimed a welcome.

They were evidently recognised as the spies to the conspirator's meeting.

Guy was called aside, and a whispered conference took place between him and his friends.

Captain Frank felt that they were speaking of him.

"Look here," he said, to Hugh. "If they have got anything to say about me, why the devil don't they speak out ? I don't like this sort of thing ; I shall tell them so, too."

"You had better not," Hugh replied.

He was acquainted with Guy's doings—Captain Frank was not—nor did he think it advisable to let him know the secret. The young gallant was heart and soul devoted to his king, and he hated treachery.

Hugh and his comrades had heard him express his feelings very strongly against the Catholics, in a way that informed them that he was no friend of theirs.

It occurred to Captain Frank that he had been hunted about by his own troops.

"And what for ?" he asked himself. Simply because his friends had ran he ran too. He did not feel satisfied with the idea.

"I say," he said to Hugh, "what have we been scurrying about for ?"

"In what way ?" inquired Hugh.

"Why, you know. We've cut away from the trooper, and so on."

"I don't know."

"Nor I. Let's ask Guy ; perhaps he knows."

"All right. By-and-bye. Not here."

"Why not ? Who are all these sulky-looking brutes ?"

Hugh tugged his sleeve to enjoin silence.

"We shall be heard," he said.

"What then ?" Captain Frank asked. "I, as an officer of his Majesty, have a right to question them. It strikes me I have seen them before."

Hugh began to feel uncomfortable for his comrade's sake.

The young soldier was diving deeper into the mystery than Hugh cared him to do.

"Ain't they the men we overheard conspiring against the State ?" Frank asked, curiously.

"I don't think so," Hugh made answer.

"I do ; and if I was sure they were the same——. You know, I have a duty to do as a soldier."

"What mean you ? Wouldst thou betray our friend ?"

"Is he one of them ?"

Hugh was wondering how to evade the answer, when a man rushed into the hall.

"Fly, gentlemen !" he exclaimed. "The castle is approached by four companies of soldiers—the King's chosen guards."

"The King's chosen guards !" iterated Captain Frank. "Gentlemen, what means this ? Explain. Are you guilty of any cause that thou should'st be hunted about thus ? Tell me why it is, for I alone have the influence, as captain of the king's guard, to save you."

His generous proposal did not meet with any gratitude. Greatly to his surprise, he was menaced with scowling looks, and his suspicions were confirmed of their identity.

"Traitors !" he exclaimed, boldly. "Surrender quietly. Attempt to escape, and none of you will survive an hour !"

In an instant he was surrounded by the angry men, and his life was in eminent danger. Long swords and other formidable weapons were brandished near him.

Yet he stood undaunted as ever. His

handsome face flushed with indignant rage, and his hand rested on his sword-hilt.

"Hold !" thundered Guy Fawkes, leaping through his companions. He stood before the fearless youth. "Put back those weapons. The last one to obey, dies !"

Every weapon was lowered simultaneously, but the men murmured, and exchanged dissatisfied glances.

Quiet as was Guy's general mood, he could be dangerous at times. He was dangerous now. His companions' disapproval to his wish had caused the slumbering demon of his nature.

"He who dares to raise a hand against the life of my friend, dies !" he said. And he meant it.

"He is a spy—a traitor !" were the cries that arose from the conspirators.

"I answer for him," Guy said ; "let that suffice."

The men sullenly turned away. They saw it would be dangerous to trifle with the bold, fiery soldier.

"Let them strike," said Captain Frank. "I would show them no mercy ; I want none."

"Go. Thou art safe," Guy said, leading him to a secret entrance in the wall. "As you value your life, keep silence, no matter what you hear."

The young captain went quietly, and Hugh Wardour followed him.

The conspirators all vanished from the marble hall by different ways of exit. Guy was the last to remain.

The soldiers had attacked and broken into the castle. He could hear them distinctly, searching for the recusants, and a cunning smile came over his swarthy face.

The invaders were nearing the hall. Guy thought it time to make a move. He went to the fire-place, and drew a concealed iron ring out of the hearthstone. The slab rose perpendicularly. The burning embers were shot down into a pit beneath. The stone revolved and fell into its former position, leaving not a spark to show that there had been a fire there.

Satisfied with this manœuvre, Guy lighted a torch, extinguished the oil lamps, and sprang through a secret panel just as the soldiers made their way into the marble hall.

CHAPTER XXV.

DEATH FOR LIBERTY.

THE soldiers made a careful search throughout the castle, with sword in one hand and a torch in the other, for the rebels, but no traces of them could be seen.

The rooms showed not the slightest signs of having been inhabited since the day they were left to the ghostly inhabitants, and everything had that desolate dilapidated appearance of decay which fall upon things in time from want of care.

The guards had followed close on the track of the recusants, and only lost sight of them as they neared the castle. Of course the soldiers thought they had sought refuge there, but now they began to think they were mistaken.

"They must be hidden about here somewhere," urged an officer.

"So I thought," replied his brother lieutenant; "we followed them pretty closely, and only lost sight of them as they neared here. But where can they be ? None of the rooms are disturbed, as you see. 'Tis most likely that they have yet a rendezvous in some of those small streets hereabout."

"Most likely," the other answered ; "but let's have a look in the lower regions, and if they are not there, we will search every house in the neighbourhood. They can't be far off."

They had not seen the disappearance of Guy Fawkes, or they might have learned the way of exit from the room to the lower regions.

However, they were not long in finding a way, and, in a body, with sword and fire, they searched every nook and corner, but without making any discovery that led to their concealment.

Once or twice they were very near upon the hidden Catholics, and had it not been for the intense darkness of the subterranean vaults and passages they would certainly have been seen.

One of the guards, who had strolled away from his comrades, unfortunately fell upon the place where Guy lay concealed, crouched up in a corner like a rat.

The glare from the torch the soldier carried fell full upon the conspirator, and revealed him to his searching gaze.

There was a malicious grin on the soldier's face, as he advanced with drawn sword to where Guy lay.

Fawkes saw his design, and, like a tiger hunted down, he sprang on the hunter to escape the fate of death.

He seized the soldier by the throat, tore the torch from his hand, and held him in a grip of iron.

The attack was so sudden, the man was completely thrown off his guard. The sword fell from his hand, and the tightness of his assailant's grip deprived him of all power.

While looking into the blazing orbs of his assailant, the expression of his features was awful to behold. He saw he was doomed.

Guy released him and drew his sword.

The soldier fell against the wall helpless, and gasping to catch his exhaled breath.

"Thou hast sought thy own death," said Guy, in a cold-blooded tone that froze the hearer's blood in his veins.

The conspirator regarded his victim with a pitiless look. His situation made him pitiless. To let the man live would be to sign his own and companion's death.

His hand shook as he raised his weapon to strike the helpless man. The act was brutal and cowardly. He felt loth, but for the safety of himself and companions, it must be.

"Mercy!" gasped the man, in a low breath of horror.

This was spoken with a pitiful accent, and the imploring look for mercy that accompanied it sent a chill of remorse through Gvy, and he recoiled from his deadly purpose. His sword-arm fell to his side listlessly.

The soldier watched him with a malicious gleam. His strength was returning, and while Guy stood in gloomy despondency, his eyes cast on the ground, the man, with sudden desperate energy, sprang to where his weapon lay, and regained it just in time to turn and confront Guy Fawkes, who, ferocious as a tiger, bounded after him.

He aimed a terrific blow at the soldier, and struck the weapon from his hand.

"Spare me," the man implored.

"Thou wouldst have spared me," Guy said, spitefully; and his white teeth gleamed under his shaggy moustaches. "If I spare you I shall consign myself to death. Thou must die for my safety."

The soldier saw there was no hope for him, and he was in the act of shrieking for help, when Guy sent his blade darting forward like a glittering snake, and sent it through his throat.

The soldier fell with a gurgling cry, and Guy, standing over him, said, in a voice of horror—

"It must be death for liberty!"

The soldier closed his eyes as the bloody sword fell and pierced him through the breast.

A low groan, a convulsive throe, and the man died.

At that moment Guy heard people approaching, coming towards him through a long corridor, and he stood over his victim with the blood-stained weapon in his hand and the flashing torch raised above his head.*

He was resolute and savage now. He had sacrificed one life, and he felt that he could have cut his way through a thousand.

"Let them come," he muttered between his set teeth.

They came, but not those he expected.

They were his companions, and they stopped in awe on beholding the stricken corpse at the feet of Guy Fawkes.

"How came this?" asked one.

"He discovered me, and I slew him," said Guy.

"'Tis bad work."

"It would have been worse if he had lived," Fawkes said, angrily; for he felt that his companion's words were a reproach.

"It should be avoided. Strike only when there is an occasion."

"I had an occasion, and I struck. Had I avoided him he would not have avoided us."

"Guy is perhaps right," said another. "He does not kill in wanton wickedness."

"I strike," said Guy, "in self-defence and for thee; had I let him live we should have been discovered.'

"Let us remove the body; 'tis a tell-tale thing to lie about."

"Where are his comrades?" Guy asked.

"Gone," was the answer.

"I heard them say, as they went," said Christopher Wright, "that they did not think we had been here. They know the superstition of our religion and the legend connected with the castle they were certain would keep us away.'

"So much the better," Guy remarked. "They won't trouble us again."

"We don't know," put in Catesby, with a sneer. "Who is that friend of thine thou defended with so much chivalry? If he is allowed to go we shan't remain in safety long."

"I answer for him," said Guy, sternly. "He will not betray us."

Catesby turned away with a sullen brow. There was mischief brewing within him.

Guy watched him go, and his stern face relaxed thoughtfully.

"I like not his look," muttered the Spanish soldier; "there is evil in them."

Wright approached.

"This corpse had better be hidden," he said.

"Yes," replied Guy, "be it so."

"Where can we bury him?"

"Let him be laid to rest in one of the sepulchres of the chapel vault, and show the dead proper respect."

Wright, with several of his companions, removed the body.

Guy Fawkes became dull. He had many thoughts on his mind that troubled him, and to get them explained he sought Robert Catesby.

The conspirator sat occupied in deep thought when Fawkes entered, his elbows rested on his knees, and his face was buried in his hands.

Guy coughed to announce his presence.

Catesby turned sharply, and scowled at the intruder.

"What brings thee hither?" he asked rudely.

"I have much to say," replied Guy.

"But why seek me?"

"Because thou art the person I want."

Catesby's brow darkened with anger. The answer was sharp, and he did not like it. He considered himself the prominent person in the conspiracy, and for Guy to place himself on a par with him mortified his dignity.

"How fares it with Thomas Percy?" Guy asked.

"Better." The answer was abridged.

"Is he in safety?"

---

* This scene is vividly portrayed in No. 5, front piece.

"I left him so."

"Where?"

"In a chamber above."

"Where did he get wounded?"

"In battle."

"By whom?"

"One of Lord Harrington's guests."

"Then 'tis true?"

"What?"

"That thou wert idiot enough to attempt the princess's abduction."

Catesby regarded the speaker sternly.

"Idiot?" he repeated.

"Idiots, I repeat."

"And wherefore?"

"Is that the way to accomplish our scheme?" Fawkes said, severely. "Such a mad outrage will raise the whole country up against us. Think you we shall remain undiscovered? Nay, the King will not rest till he has had us all ferretted out and taken to execution. Then what will become of our enterprise? Our hopes, our ambition, our prize, our all, will crumble to the earth beneath the hand of the despotic tyrant, and through the hasty caprice of one man, whose infernal will will be the cause of sacrificing the lives of our brotherhood. I tell thee, Catesby, 'tis the worst thing that could have happened for our downfall, and had I been present at the time it should not have taken place."

"Talking will not alter it," Catesby said, coolly. "'Tis done, and we have Elizabeth in our power."

"Thou art mistaken, the royal child has been recaptured by her guardian's friends."

Catesby leaped up.

"How know you this?" he demanded, fiercely.

"Because I stopped the carriage which conveyed her back to her guardian."

"And thou didst not attempt to regain her?"

"Not I, faith. I was only too glad to see that she had been rescued."

Catesby bit his shaggy moustache.

"Where was this?" he asked.

"In Mortlake."

The conspirator's countenance changed agreeably.

"'Twas not she, Guy," he said.

"I tell you it was."

"What grounds have you for thy assertion?"

"The word of twelve gentlemen who followed the coach of her abductors, discovered her retreat, and saved her."

"Still, I say, thou art mistaken. Sir Everard Digby has conveyed her some distance hence, totally in another direction to Mortlake."

"To what part?"

"Since thou art so interested about her, I shall keep that to myself."

It was now Guy's turn to bite his moustache, and he did with a vengeance.

Guy began to reflect. What if he was mistaken? What if the cavaliers were mistaken, and had taken Lady Claire of Grace instead of the Princess Elizabeth?

No, that could not be, he argued; gentlemen residing in the same house with her, and seeing her daily, could not make such a blunder. Besides, the princess was so much younger than the Lady Claire of Grace, a mere child beside her.

Catesby watched him closely: he seemed to interpret his thoughts; and he took a savage delight in his doubts, and exulted at him being baffled. He was quite confident that Sir Everard had got safely off with his fair prize.

Fawkes said no more on that subject. He did not want to let Catesby know the secret between him and the Lady Claire.

"Hast thou heard of Guynot of late?" he asked, abruptly.

"Not of late."

"Is he still at Winchester?"

"He was. I know not where he is now."

Here their conversation ended, and Guy went to see his comrade Hugh Wardour.

He found him with Captain Frank in the marble hall. The young soldier met him coolly.

"Signor Fawkes," he said, and his manner was quite sad, "is it as I suspect—as I have heard."

Guy looked at him with interrogative surprise: the truth flashed through his mind: his young friend had heard his secret, and he felt sorry, for he greatly respected the gallant youth.

"What hast thou heard?" he asked.

"That thou art connected with the plot against the State. Is it so?"

Guy hung his head.

"Is such the case, Guy? Tell me," Captain Frank asked, "hast thou turned traitor to thy king?"

"Do not ask me," replied Fawkes, despondingly. "We have suffered. James is no king of mine: I am a Catholic! He has defiled our religion with his bloody hand; destroyed our churches; slaughtered our priests; and we seek revenge!"

"Guy Fawkes, I am sorry for thee." the captain of the king's guard said, deeply moved. "Forego this dangerous exploit as you value your life."

"It cannot be," said the Spanish soldier. "Body and soul I am bound to the cause for the restoration of our Church, and nothing will break my resolution."

"I am deeply grieved," Captain Frank said, and his voice trembled with emotion; "for thy sake, and the remembrance of our friendship; but henceforth we must be strangers. I, as a soldier, have a duty to perform."

"Thou wilt keep the secret?" Guy implored.

"I will not promise."

"Wilt thou betray me?"

"I cannot, Guy; our past friendship

abstains me from that. Farewell! We are strangers from now!"

He turned his head aside, as he put out his hand, to hide a tear that trickled down his cheek.

"'Tis hard to part thus," said Guy, squeezing the captain's hand affectionately. "I would it had been otherwise; but things are ruled by the hand of Fate, and it must be, Farewell! Give me a kind thought sometimes. I shall ever think of thee as a brother. Farewell!"

Guy's voice grew husky, and their hands lingered together for some moments. Then they parted in friendship, not as foes, and each was sorry for the other.

CHAPTER XXVI.

THE DUEL UNDER THE RUINED CHAPEL WALL.

THAT night Guy Fawkes slept at the Red Castle. He did not undress. He could not rest. His mind was troubled by the scene of his parting with Captain Frank. He felt uneasy and restless.

He was glad when morning came. He rose from his couch as the first grey streaks broke through the stained-glass windows.

Hugh, too, had spent a sleepless night. He was troubled about the fair lady left behind him at the Ludlows.

He was glad when Guy called for him. It broke the monotony of the depressing hours.

"Never before have I spent such a wretched night," he said.

"How was that?" asked Guy.

"I could not sleep. Could you?"

"No."

"How was it thou couldst not sleep?"

"I was thinking."

"So was I."

"What wer't thou thinking about?"

"Constance. I don't think she is still in safety."

"And I know Lady Claire is not."

"Art thou going to renew thy search?" Hugh asked.

"Yes. Art thou?"

"Without delay."

"Then let us be off."

They went; and while riding along, Hugh said—

"'Tis a bad job Captain Frank has learned thy secret."

"It is; because I have lost his friendship."

"Think you he can be trusted?"

"I would stake my life on't."

"I wish, Guy, thou would'st forego thy dangerous work," said Hugh Wardour, earnestly. "'Twill be thy ruin if thou dost not give it up in time. Think you 'tis possible for a few men like thy brotherhood to rebel against the nation, and overthrow the State? The idea is ridiculous. Come, Guy; let me beg of thee to give up thy part."

Fawkes shook his head moodily.

"It cannot be," he said, sadly. "If we fail, I shall be content to die. I shall die in a good cause."

"I am grieved to see nothing will alter thy resolution."

"Nothing, Hugh; nothing but the grave can tear me from the course I pursue."

"I am heart sorry to hear thee say so. I wish thee no harm, Guy; I wish thee no success. I hold not with thy undertaking. 'Tis most wicked; and when 'tis too late, thou wilt discover the bottomless purpose for which thou hast sacrificed all for."

"'Tis the will of Fate, Hugh."

"I wish it were not. I did not think to see thee come to this. It would have been better had you never left Spain. We were happy then; we had no cares, we knew no trouble, and in the battle-field, while fighting side by side, we were ready at any moment to die. Thou wilt have much to answer for, man, ere thou canst die in peace. Remember, thou art not only rebelling against thy king, but in the face of God. Thou canst not direct the hand of judgment from falling."

Guy remained silent, his head hung on his breast, and his face was overshadowed with gloomy thought.

"Guy," Hugh said, suddenly.

Fawkes started.

"I must leave thee now."

Guy looked pained.

"You do not go in anger?"

"I am as unchanged as in past years. We part in good friendship, and should you want a helping hand, mine is always ready to strike for thee."

The conspirator expressed his thanks by a good grip on the other's hand.

"We shall meet again," he said.

"Destiny will cast us together," replied Hugh Wardour. "We have not clung together in brotherly affection from the first time we met for nought. And now, adieu, for I am anxious to see after the lady I left at the cottage."

Thus they parted.

Hugh Wardour rode away. Guy was left alone. He watched his comrade fade from view. He sighed heavily; his face grew sad, and something like a tear glittered in his eye.

"Such is my fate," he murmured, and he fell into a whirlpool of abstraction, thinking of the past, the present, and the future.

"Mine is a strange life," he broke out, "my star is a dark one. There is no happiness for me. I was born to be an outcast—a solitary being, with no one to care for me. Fate has been cruel to me. I could have been happy with their friendship, but now they have turned their backs upon me, and I am alone in the world. Why do I live to see the will of our blessed Saint done? When my point is won I can die."

He gathered up the reins, and putting spurs to his steed, rode hastily away.

He had no idea what direction to take for the best. He let the horse choose its own course, and Guy trusted to the turn-up of chance.

The horse seemed to know the confidence placed in it. The animal had kept up a steady pace for some hours, and only began to flag as the day drew in.

They were in a lone part of the country; everything was very still, and even the birds that hopped from branch to branch of the trees seemed hushed in silence.

The horse stopped to drink of the clear running mill stream.

Guy dismounted to give the animal rest; looking around he saw at no great distance the ruined chapel of St. Mary's.

"This is the eve settled for the duel," he muttered. "I wonder if it has yet taken place."

He was going to satisfy his wonderings by looking for any signs under the chapel walls that might give him a clue.

Leaving his jaded steed to graze on the banks of the stream, he went.

He was passing under the left wing of the chapel wall when the sound of voices broke upon his ears.

He stopped and listened.

The voices issued from the rectory.

Guy felt curious to know who were the conversants, and he ventured to the dilapidated door and looked through the crevices.

There were five persons within. Three desperate-looking bravoes, cloaked and masked, who stood together, conversing; the other two were men of rank and fortune.

The younger of the two Guy recognised as the youth who had challenged Captain Frank to meet him at the ruined chapel of St. Mary's.

"Some treachery afloat," thought Guy; "methought when they met his feeling towards Captain Frank was somewhat inveterate for a stranger. I will abide here awhile, it may be that I shall hear something that may be interesting.'

The conversation stopped; he had been heard.

The youth, thinking it was his combatant approaching, looked through the small diamond-shaped windows that overlooked the country towards the main road.

"Has he come?" asked his companion, a handsome man, of middle age, with a cold, cynical expression about his thin lips, and small, piercing eyes.

"I do not see him," returned the youth; "surely I could not have been mistaken; I distinctly heard footsteps without."

"So did I, as plain as I ever heard anything in my life. He might have heard us conversing, and felt curious to know of what we spoke; to make sure, I will reconnoitre without, should I catch an eavesdropper, thou wilt hear of it.'

He said this significantly, and tapped the hilt of his sword.

Guy saw him coming, and concealed himself.

He was effectually hidden, though, from his position, he had a capital view of all around.

He saw the chapel door open, and the nobleman issued forth cautiously, with drawn sword.

He looked about cunningly, and walked round the chapel.

An unpleasant conviction broke suddenly upon Guy Fawkes, that gave him some uneasiness.

He had left his horse strolling about; he wished he had not, but it could not be helped now, though, should it be seen, the nobleman's suspicions would be confirmed that there was an eavesdropper about—a search would be made for the eavesdropper—the eavesdropper would be discovered.

Guy felt extremely uncomfortable—not that he feared the danger of discovery—he was prepared to stand against all who were there; but he did not mean to be discovered, because he felt convinced that there was a mystery connected with the two noblemen and the gallant young soldier, Captain Frank, and he felt desirous to learn the nature of the mystery.

Although Captain Frank, in plain words, had told him they could be no longer friends, he liked the young gallant none the less for it; and, if mischief was meant him, he would prevent it if he could.

Fawkes saw the nobleman return. He looked disappointed; then he had not seen the horse.

He had not; the horse had wandered out of sight.

Guy watched the nobleman re-enter the chapel; then he crept from his hiding-place, and renewed his position at the door.

"Did you see anyone?" asked the youth.

"I did not. We must have been mistaken."

"Think you he has got scent of anything, and is afraid to turn up?"

"I don't think he has heard anything. The secret is known only to ourselves."

"It must remain ours, uncle."

"It shall, Temple. I did not think he still lived. The worse for him that he does."

"The villain," muttered Guy Fawkes, who heard every word, "you mean him harm. He must be warned of thy treachery."

"If he should escape, uncle?" the youth said, interrogatively.

"We have not much to fear, without he learns the secret of his birth."

"And then?"

"We shall be beggared."

"He must die, uncle, I would not resign the luxury we enjoy did six of such stand in our path."

"It would be hard to give it up, now. The earldom is worth a struggle."

THE DUEL UNDER THE CHAPEL WALL.

"Hush, he comes." The youth pointed across a field.

Captain Frank came alone. He did not appear so gay as was his usual habit.

11

GRATIS! with this Number Scene 2 for the New Play of the "Fifth of November; or,

The elder of the two plotters smiled maliciously.

"We shall not have the work we anticipated," he said. "If thou dost not run thy sword through his heart a blow from behind will settle him, an' there will be none to tell the tale."

"Won't there ?" thought Guy. "Methinks thy hopes will be checked."

"Where are the men ?" asked the youth, looking round for his hirelings.

"Here, my lord," said an ill-looking fellow, advancing.

"Be on the alert," the youth said. "You may not be wanted, but in case there should be more than one about, be at hand. You know thy duty."

The bravo inclined his head in assent.

The young noble linked his arm through his uncle's.

"We had better walk round the chapel," he said. "It may be as well not to let him know that we have been waiting."

Fawkes hid again as they came out.

Walking round the chapel they came face to face with Captain Frank under the ruined wall.

Temple raised his hat gallantly.

"Thou art here first," he said. "I hope we have not kept thee waiting."

"Nay," responded the soldier, "I have but just arrived."

"And alone ?"

"No," said Captain Frank.

The youth looked at him inquiringly.

"I have brought a friend with me," the Captain said, and he tapped the hilt of his sword confidently.

The young noble smiled complacently.

"I brought a second," he said.

"I have confidence enough in myself," said Captain Frank, with a slight sneer. "If thou art ready, we may begin."

The youth inclined his head in acquiescence, and stood ready.

They measured swords, and each fell into an attitude of defence.

"I have got one point to get," said Captain Frank, as their weapons crossed. "Shall I disarm or pink thee ?"

"Both, if you can get the chance," replied the youth, and his face flushed indignantly.

"Very well, my friend ; I will do both." That little sadness which had shadowed the soldier's handsome face vanished directly he drew his sword.

He did not meet his opponent with any dire intent, nor did he bear him any ill-feeling. He had kept the appointment because he said he would, and he was delighted to find the youth there.

He would have been much disappointed had his opponent not kept his word.

The youth watched him with a glittering eye, and his small white hand grasped his sword with a murderous clutch.

There was not much difference in the ages of the combatants ; if any, Captain Frank

might have been two years senior. Perhaps he looked a little older on account of his moustache and imperial. His sun-burnt face, too, gave him a more manly appearance, but in other respects there was not much difference between them.

They were both lithe and graceful, and near of a size and build.

But in disposition they varied greatly.

The fair faced youth, who had the delicacy and gentleness of a woman in appearance, possessed a heart black and vengeful of an older and a more crime-stained man.

He tried his every trick and move to send the glittering steel through the breast of his opponent, who had met him in honour, to test his science in a friendly passage of arms, albeit he had received a base insult ; but that he put down as an unguarded speech, said in an impetuous manner.

"You fence admirably well, my friend," said Captain Frank, turning aside a rapid stroke. "Thou hast improved since we last met."

The youth made no answer. He had grown excited with anger. He had been met at every point ; so had his opponent. But he was not angry. Captain Frank admired him the more for his good play. He said it was what he liked. It gave him pleasure to fight with a man who knew how to use his blade.

The young noble was watching carefully for an opening to send in a death-stroke, when his face changed, and he stepped back.

Guy Fawkes had suddenly come round the wall, and stood behind the captain, fixing the impetuous youth with a meaning glance, which he did not mistake.

In an instant he had recovered his self-possession, and was fencing with that treachery which threatened death to his combatant.

Captain Frank, hearing the fall of a foot behind him, slightly turned his head to see who came.

The young noble took the advantage. He made a rapid pass to pin his opponent.

Captain Frank, askance, saw the youth's design, and stepped back to avoid the blow. His foot slipped, and before he could recover his balance the other lunged forward furiously.

The leaping blade flashed through the young soldier's side, and with a cry of agony he staggered back.

Guy Fawkes leaped to the stricken youth's side, caught him on his arm, and, taking the sword from his hand, met the fiery youth as he advanced to renew the cowardly attack.

"Dastard ! coward !" thundered Guy, fiercely.

The youth went back. He did not care about facing the angry soldier.

Guy followed him up.

"Defend thyself, or I strike !" he said, and his sword was raised to deal the blow.

The other noble—who had been watching

the duel with deep interest — seeing the danger of the youth, now drew his sword, and went to his assistance.

He was only in time.

Guy's weapon fell with terrible force in a line for Temple's head; and had the blow not been stopped on the other's sword, it would have cleft his skull in twain.

Guy was not to be foiled of his prey, although the elder nobleman placed himself before the youth. He beat him back, and made the young noble face him.

"Dost thy craven heart fail thee, man?" Guy said, "mean-souled hound that thou art!"

The taunt brought the hot blood to the youth's cheeks.

"Stand aside, uncle," he said; "let me at the knave."

"Come, both of ye," Guy said, working round, getting the two before him in a corner.

The youth faced the conspirator boldly. He fought well, and stood up bravely against the furious onset; but his strength could not last.

His arms already ached from finger point to the shoulder, and each blow he parried benumbed it the more.

Guy fought marvellously to keep off the blows of both assailants. The elder of the two had not half the science of the younger, and a blow now and then sent him back reeling.

It annoyed the Spanish soldier to be opposed so stoutly by such a youth. In quick succession he dealt three rapid down cuts.

The first the young noble guarded, the second struck his weapon to the earth, and the third smote him down, writhing in agony.

The youth's uncle tried to flee, but Guy kept him before him.

"Ho, there!" cried the quailing noble.

His call was answered by the appearance of the three bravoes.

Guy saw them coming. He stood with his back against the wall, and grinned savagely.

"Kill them both," said the nobleman to his hirelings.

"They will have to kill me first," Guy said, drawing Captain Frank closely to his side.

The bravoes rushed upon him with drawn daggers.

Fawkes made a sweeping cut from right to left with his sword.

The bravoes went back.

"Come on," said Guy.

But they didn't see it. His weapon was rather too long for them. It looked dangerous, too, and kept them at a respectful distance.

Though Guy kept the bravoes back, they kept him at bay; for he dared not move, because they would surround him, and he was not able to keep off their thirsty blades both from himself and charge.

To his surprise, Captain Frank suddenly broke from his arm, drew Guy's sword, and sprang amongst the hirelings.

Fawkes followed him.

The bravoes fled panic-stricken; and while Fawkes and Captain Frank gave chase, the nobleman gathered up the stricken youth and made off, leaving the two soldiers victors of the battle-field.

While returning to the chapel to avenge the coward blow, Captain Frank fell at Guy's feet exhausted.

CHAPTER XXVII.

THE ARREST OF CAPTAIN FRANK.

Guy raised the lifeless form, and conveyed it to the chapel. He then hastened to the stream, and, with a drinking-horn he carried about him, returned with some water.

He undid the gallant's coat to examine the wound.

It was not dangerous, though the sword had gone through his side. Little more than the skin over the ribs was touched.

"Half an inch more, and it would have touched his heart," Guy cogitated. "The Blessed Mary be praised 'tis no worse!"

He carefully bathed the hurt, washed off the blood, and with his own handkerchief bound up the wound.

Many hours passed while Fawkes sat watching for returning life, and, when the youth opened his eyes, he was glad.

Frank smiled on him gratefully, and pressed his hand. His lips were parched, and his mouth dry and feverish.

Guy put the goblet of water to his lips, and he drank.

"Thanks," the invalid murmured; "thanks, Guy."

And then he fell back into the soldier's arms.

"He will be better presently," thought Guy, and he knew, for in his time he had had much to do with sick and wounded men. "He is faint from loss of blood only."

When Captain Frank again awoke he was pretty well.

"Guy," he said, "I can never repay thee for thy kind attention. It was most fortunate that thou wert there."

"It was by the will of Providence," said Fawkes. "When I left the Red Castle, this morning, I knew not what course to take for the best. I cast the reins on my horse's neck, willing to go whither it took me. It brought me hither. I remembered when I saw the chapel that this was the place where thou hadst to meet in duel, and not knowing whether thou hadst been, I was approaching when I heard voices within the rectory. I stopped and listened."

"Well?" interrogated Captain Frank.

"Art thou acquainted with thy antagonist?" Guy asked.

"I am not. I never saw him before until the other evening. Why do you ask?"

"I heard much which concerns thee. They are well acquainted with you. Be careful of them."

"Acquainted with me," said Frank, "not to my knowledge."

"They are not thy friends."

"The young one is not, evidently, or he would not have taken the mean advantage to strike when I fell."

"They mean thee harm. Be careful of them."

"Doubtless, but what was it you overheard? Much concerning me, you said. I should like to hear a little of it."

"They recognised thee the other evening. Until then they thought you dead. The discovery has cost them some uneasiness. It appears you stand in their way."

"What way?" asked Frank.

"By what I could make out it seems they have been enjoying that which belongs to thee. They talked about an earldom being worth a struggle, and they said if you lived and discovered the secret of thy birth, they would be beggared."

Captain Frank smiled faintly.

"They have mistaken me for someone else," he said, sadly. "I know the secret of my birth."

"If I knew it, it may be I might be able to comprehend that which I overheard."

"'Tis nought concerning me," Frank said; "and my birth is a secret I keep entirely to myself."

Guy gave up the idea of learning the captain's history as hopeless. He saw that the subject had pained him. It had brought on a sadness which convinced Fawkes that what he had heard had more to do with the young soldier than the young soldier cared to own.

Guy mentally resolved to learn more by cautious watching. There was a sort of mystery in the conversation of the noblemen that interested him, and he wanted to solve the mystery.

"We must part again," said Captain Frank.

"As before?" asked Guy.

"'Tis better for us both to do so.'

"Why?"

"We are better friends apart."

"I don't see it."

"'Tis simple enough. Were we seen together, 'twould place me in a position awkward and dangerous to us both. I should be obliged to divulge the secret, or stand the risk of being shot for treachery to my king."

"I am sorry 'tis so," said Guy, sadly, "I would it could have been otherwise."

"It rests with thyself to alter it."

"I cannot; 'tis too late now, and I must succumb to the ordination of fate."

"There are more paths in life than one, and it is not too late for thee to choose a better one."

"My path is allotted for me by the will of God, and nought can divert me from it.'

"That is thy decision."

"'Tis the decision of a greater will than mine, and I must abide by it."

Captain Frank took up his hat.

"I shall ever be indebted to thee for thy kindly assistance." he said, "an' should we ever meet where thou art in danger you shall not want for a helping hand."

"Many thanks," said Guy. "It may be that thou wilt think different ere long."

"Never! Come what may, I shall always do my best to keep thee out of danger."

They parted thus. Captain Frank went to the chapel door. He walked very unsteadily; he was still weak from loss of blood.

"Take my horse," said Guy, "or thou wilt not get far in thy present state."

"Thanks. If it will not be inconveniencing thee I will accept thy offer."

Guy went after the horse. It's quiet browse had refreshed it.

Captain Frank got in the saddle, grasped the conspirator's hand gratefully, and rode away.

He had not got any great distance when a company of the king's household guard met him vis-a-vis.

"Halt!" cried the commander.

The soldiers drew in line before Captain Frank. Captain Frank drew rein.

"Captain George Frank, of the king's chosen guards," said the commander, coming forward, "we arrest thee as a traitor."

The captain's face flushed at the charge, and he drew himself up with supreme hauteur.

"By whose authority dare you charge me with such a crime?"

"The authority of the king," replied the other, displaying a warrant signed for the apprehension of the young captain. "I arrest thee for aiding to conceal from the servants of the king certain Catholics charged with rebellion."

"The charge is false."

"You must prove that. I have my duty to do, captain, and it will be better for thee to come without resistance."

"By thunder of Jove! this is a nice sort of thing. Lead on, I am thine."

"Your sword, captain," the commander said.

Captain Frank eyed him sternly.

"Be content that I humour thy will by surrendering to a false charge," he said; "but do not dishonour me by taking my sword. No; sooner than I would resign that to be disgraced, I would plunge it deeply into mine heart."

The soldier was silent. He saw that his words had wounded the young captain's feelings, and he felt sorry.

"Keep thy sword, comrade," he said. "I meant no offence when I asked for it. 'Tis the general rule for a prisoner to surrender his arms."

" 'Tis the rule for prisoners, I am aware. I am no prisoner; I humour this whim, as I have before said, for mine own honour's sake. Whose doing is this?"

"I know not, captain. This warrant for thy arrest was sent to me by the king."

"I have some enemy at work," thought the young gallant, while being led to the barracks surrounded by the armed men.

It was very mortifying to the proud spirit of the gay young soldier to be confined in the guard-room for treason, with the men he had had under his command now put over him.

Had it not been for the kind feeling of the old officer, who took much interest in the young fellow's grave position, he would have been consigned to the black hole to await his trial.

As it was, he felt keenly the degradation of such a position, and, with spirits abashed, he awaited, with a heart heavy as lead, for the issue of the coming morrow.

CHAPTER XXVIII.

THE INQUIRY.

HUGH WARDOUR, on leaving Guy Fawkes, made his way straight to the peaceful home where he had left his lady-love, Constance, in the care of the kindly cottagers, little dreaming the blow of disappointment that awaited him.

His mind had been troubled from the time he left when the figure of Father Guynot crossed his path like a shadow of evil, and his suspicions grew stronger when the old lady admitted him. Her eyes were tearful as she looked into his face, and there was a silent sadness about her that caused his heart to sink heavily with sorrowful forebodings.

He looked at her wistfully, and she tried to avoid his gaze. He felt that something had occurred, yet he dared not breathe his suspicions, for fear of hearing the fearful truth his mind predicted.

He took a seat; a painful gloom seemed to pervade the air. He grew chill; his spirits oppressed, and the unbroken silence was torturing to him.

No one attempted to speak; they sat looking from one to the other in awe.

He could bear the suspense no longer. He sprang up, and exclaimed—

"Tell me, has anything happened to the lady?"

"Well, my boy," said the bluff old yeoman, "the lady is not here now, but that's no fault of ours. We did our best to keep back the varlets who stole her away."

"As I thought," exclaimed Hugh; and he sank into a chair. "She has been taken away."

"Yes, my boy, and thou canst not be more sorry than I am, for I liked the lass—I did, as though she were my own daughter; an' should I ever catch the knavish wolf who stole her away, marry, an' it will go hard with him!"

The brave old fellow looked ferocious as a lion; and, clenching his huge fist, brought it down on the table with a bang that loosened every joint.

Hugh wisely concluded that brooding over his misfortunes would not avail him much; he must be prompt to act, and save the lady from any impending danger delay might incur.

Hugh Wardour tried to put a brave face on the painful subject, but he could not banish the sadness that lay so heavily on his heart and spirits.

He did not let things trouble him much in general; he would face danger and misfortune boldly, and an incident like the present, when he had been building up bright hopes, and then to meet with such a disappointment naturally depressed him.

"Canst thou give me any description of the lady's aggressor?" he asked.

"Marry, and 'tis but badly I can portray the rascal," replied the cottager, "though I verily believe the varlet was a priest; and if the fiends don't take him God won't."

"How got he admittance?" Hugh asked.

"Through the window. 'Twas in the night, and I heard the lady cry. I hastened, and was attacked by a half dozen ill-looking knaves, who stretched me at full length on mine own floor, and left me for dead, while they carried off the lady."

"Many thanks for thy kindness to the lady," Hugh said; "and should I be fortunate enough to discover her, thou mayst rely upon seeing her again."

"A fair prospect to thy searching, bold lad!" said Farmer Ludlow, shaking Hugh heartily by the hand; "an' should ye come across the hind who took her hence, I do firmly hope ye will teach him a lesson of prudence."

"Never fear," replied Hugh, "he shall not escape my vengeance."

He left the cottagers with the hope of again being gladdened by the gentle lady's presence under their desolate roof, and bent his steps towards the hostel, known by the appellation of the "Man in the Moon."

He wished to make an inquiry concerning his lost lady-love, and he was confident the worthy landlord knew much concerning her.

He soon entered into the subject of his visit with Ralph Strongbrew, landlord of the "Man in the Moon."

Ralph Strongbrew grew strong with rage, when he heard that the lady had been abducted from Ludlow Cottage.

"Curse 'em! the bastard knaves!" he said, fiercely. "Hast thou any idea where they have taken her to?"

"None," answered Hugh.

"She must be found, Master Hugh."

"That is my intention," responded Hugh. "Thou art acquainted, if I mistake not, with the lady's family history."

"I have lived here for twoscore years or more, an' there ain't much hereabouts that I don't know. I knew Captain Meredith better than I knew thee, and a true, generous-hearted Englishman he was. His like again will never cross the threshold of the Moreland Downs."

"Moreland Downs!" repeated Hugh.

"Ay, that grand old residence ye see standing out boldly yonder is Moreland House."

He took Hugh to a small window at the end of the parlour, and pointed out the mansion indicated. The red sun sinking behind the grey walls threw its dusky glare over the ancient pile, and threw out in bold relief the picturesque scenery.

It was just such a place as lovers would have sought to dwell in, wrapped in the solitude of its wild, romantic surroundings, and Hugh sighed when he thought of the happy home it had been. Left now in desolation to decay, and through the treachery of a false friend.

"That was a happy home once," remarked Ralph Strongbrew.

"So I was just thinking," said Hugh. "A perfect paradise; it was a place for all gladness."

"Faith, friend, 'twas a sad affair when the captain left, the country has not been the same since. He was a good man, as many can tell, and his loss is much lamented."

"By-the-bye," Hugh said, "what became of his wife?"

"Ah, that's a mystery. The lady's sudden disappearance was the cause of the captain going away again."

"Did her husband not know of her intention of leaving?" asked Hugh. He had gained a point of his inquiry by a random shot, and he intended to work all he wanted to know out of the innkeeper by stratagem.

"The lady knew not of it herself, it is my belief," answered Ralph, "although it was said she had eloped with her husband's brother. 'Twas a lie: the lady was too pure and true to dishonour her husband by a thought of wrong. Her disappearance rests entirely with that priestly thief, Father Guynot; and whenever the truth is known, 'twill be seen that he has been the cause of all the unhappiness. Oh, if I only had the traitor in my grasp now! I would wring the truth from his polluted lips, or I would never quit my hold till his last breath was drawn."

Hugh evinced some surprise at the determined manner of the innkeeper.

"Is Constance their only child?" Hugh asked.

"They never had but one, to my knowledge," answered Ralph Strongbrew.

"Then she is sole heiress?"

"Without a doubt."

Hugh thought she was quite enough. He saw himself, perspectively, master of Moreland estate.

"Then she has the right to take possession of it?" he said.

"It wouldn't be good for anyone to say nay to her claim," said the honest host. "Will Kendrick, the captain's gamekeeper, still sticks to his old situation, and he swears it will be death to the first who attempts to usurp his master's domain, without 'tis one of his family, and then they will have to show strong proofs of their claims before he will let them set a foot upon the ground."

"You know him, then?"

"I knew him when he first entered the captain's service. He was a boy then; and now the cold, grey hairs of winter begin to steal over his furrowed brow."

"He is faithful to the memory of his old master. He may be useful. See him, and let him know that we have hopes of restoring one of the family at least."

Hugh heartily hoped one would be the most.

"You think of setting out to find the lady?"

"I shall not rest till I have."

"I would I could accompany thee."

"It may be thou art not wanted." This was said by a third person. As the parlour-door opened, Guy Fawkes entered.

Mine host looked at him inquiringly.

"What mean you by that?" asked the innkeeper.

"I mean," said Guy, "that I am here on a like errand as my comrade. 'Two's company and three's none'—so says the old proverb—not that I should have any objection to thy company, friend."

Ralph Strongbrew smiled. The soldier spoke in jest, and he did not misconstrue his meaning.

Hugh showed evident signs of displeasure at his comrade's presence; his brow lowered, and turning on his heels he went to the window.

Guy went after him.

"What ails thee, comrade?" he asked, and Guy laid his hand on the other's shoulder.

"Nought, friend," answered Hugh. Turning, he observed the expression of pain on the soldier's face; his heart melted instantly, and he felt sorry for his contempt.

"Hugh, comrade, art thou turned against me?" asked Guy, looking earnestly into his face while holding his hand. "Hast thou, like all others, placed a chasm between us?"

"Nay, comrade, 'twas an involuntary act on my part. I would sooner cut off my right hand than cause thee pain."

"Methought it would be strange hadst thou turned thy back upon me, after our long years of deep friendship," Guy said. "I have heard thy parley with mine host, and sorry am I that the lady is lost to thee."

"Say not so, Guy. I may yet bring her back safe."

"With all my heart I hope you may.

'Tis strange that we should both have a like misfortune. Thou art going to set out in search; an' if my company be agreeable to thee, I will follow with thee. It may be that I shall learn something that will lead to the discovery of the fair Lady Grace."

"Right welcome art thou, comrade. It may be that we shall be useful to one another."

"True. We had better lose no time ere we depart, though I know not in what direction to go."

"Nor I; but I have an idea."

Hugh took up a pen, ink, and a piece of paper, which he tore into four parts. "North," "east," "south," and "west" he wrote separately on each piece of paper. Guy, watching curiously, wondered whether that was his idea.

Hugh said it was as he put the four pieces of paper in his hat and held it above his head.

"Draw one piece," he said, "and that shall cast the direction for us to pursue."

Guy put in his hand, and drew out the piece marked "north."

"Then we travel north," Hugh said.

"Do we go now?"

"We had better not delay any more time."

They were about to depart, but on reaching the door they returned. The cause of their returning was the sight of Kit the Keeper and a gang of troopers, who were making straight for the inn.

"Do you think we have been seen?" asked Guy.

"I think so," said Hugh.

"What's the matter?" inquired mine host.

"We have some old friends of ours coming here, and if we are seen and recognised, there will be a scene," Hugh remarked.

"You don't wish to be recognised?"

"We don't; but we shall be, if they come. —and they will."

"I can manage it for you, so that they won't know you."

"And will you?" asked Hugh.

The innkeeper assented by a knowing wink, and leading the two adventurers back into the parlour, he left them.

He was not away many moments, but every moment seemed an endless time to the anxious soldier. His fear of being discovered was painful.

"Slip into these things," said Ralph, throwing a small parcel to each of his guests.

Guy, in a very short time, had made a wonderful alteration in his appearance. A long, white flowing beard hung upon his breast, his dark, curly hair suddenly disappeared, giving place to a scanty supply of silvery locks that fell upon his shoulders, and from a dashing soldier he had changed into an aged pilgrim, with a natural stoop and palsy in every limb.

Hugh Wardour changed into another person quite as quickly as had his comrade, but in character he was different—a robust, ungainly clodhopper he represented, with a frizzy crop of red hair, and a shaggy moustache of the same colour.

"I shall do very well," he said, looking at his small, white hand, "but these are not the sort of paws for one of my representation."

"Half a moment," said the innkeeper, "you are not finished yet."

"What more is there to do?"

"Half a moment," the landlord said.

"That makes a moment," said Hugh, in despair, "and the troopers are coming."

"Halt"——

A look of misery from Hugh stopped the landlord's further speech, and he disappeared.

He brought back a lump of soft clay, which he plastered over Hugh's hands, and heightened the swarthy tint of Hugh in his face by the addition of a little red paint.

When the troopers arrived at the inn and drew up at the door, Ralph Strongbrew put himself before Kit the Keeper.

"I can't accommodate you all," he said.

Kit looked at the speaker cunningly.

"Can't you?" he said; "I think thou canst."

"But I say I haven't got room."

"Plenty of room for the accommodation we want," Kit the Keeper said, with a knowing leer. "Stand aside, and let us pass."

"What for?" The innkeeper didn't budge an inch.

"If you don't move it'll be the worse for you," exclaimed Kit, trying to push his way in.

"Look ye here, hang-dog, if you don't keep back you'll get something." And Ralph shook his big fist in the trooper's malignant face.

Kit glared at him maliciously.

"I tell you I've got a warrant to search thy house," he said, spitefully.

"Why didn't you tell me so before? What do you want?"

"Traitors thou art hiding from the king."

"Be careful," Ralph said, weighing his fist up and down suggestively. "An' now thou don't pass till thou hast shown me the warrant."

Kit found he could not get the best of mine host with "bounce," and it galled him to be compelled to produce proofs of his authority, but he did it.

"You can enter now," said Ralph, stepping aside. "Mind, don't pull the things about when there is no occasion, or I'll pitch thee out of window."

Kit and his myrmidons passed the landlord, and went straight up to the supposed countryman, who sat behind a heap of bread and cheese and a flowing tankard of beer.

"Hi! here! Where didst thou come from?" asked Kit, shaking him by the shoulder.

Hugh looked up at the speaker with a broad grin on his face.

"Eh, eh, eh!" he laughed. "Where did I coom from? Dear noa, mon, where I coom from. Well, well, thee beest a fool! I don' coom from thy country. I bean't that, I noa. Will 'ee 'ave a bit?" And he held up a huge piece of dry bread.

Kit turned away in evident disgust, and went over to the aged pilgrim, who sat by the fire, looking moodily into the glowing embers.

He raised his eyes meekly, and met the searching gaze of the Keeper fixed upon his face.

Guy kept his countenance well, but his heart misgave him; for he thought he saw a cunning leer flit over his enemy's face.

"A pretty pair of"—— the uncultivated brute kept the rest to himself; and, leaving the supposed pilgrim unquestioned, he made his way to the rooms of the inn.

Ralph Strongbrew followed closely behind him.

Every place and everything was minutely examined—cupboards, drawers, and boxes ransacked, boards pulled up, walls sounded, beds and pillows riddled with swords, as though they thought the transgressors were sewn up inside them, and everything done that could be done to bring to light anyone that might be hidden.

But no one was found, much to the disappointment of the cursing trooper, who had fully made up his mind on finding Guy, at least.

He turned savagely upon the landlord, who stood at his elbow, grinning gleefully at his failure.

"Look here!" he said, wrathfully. "Thou art hiding away men, and if you don't produce them, look to it."

"If I have hidden them, you ought to have found them," said the innkeeper, undaunted.

"We won't leave a brick standing, if you don't bring them out."

"All right. Go on."

Kit turned from him with an oath, and began to pull the things off the bed furiously.

"You have looked there once," said Ralph.

The Keeper did not take any notice of him, and began to rip open the bed.

Ralph shook the stuffing of a pillow into one end; bringing it round from his shoulder he brought it down heavily on the back of Kit's head.

Kit went sprawling, full length, on the floor.

"I cautioned thee before you began," said the innkeeper, coolly. "Don't destroy people's property wilfully, or I'll hit you harder next time."

Kit sprang up.

"Seize him! tie him to the bed-post, men."

"The men had better not," Ralph said, standing boldly before them with a pair of huge pistols.

The men didn't.

Kit the Keeper saw it would be dangerous to press the request: and, in a storm of baffled rage, he left the room.

When they reached the bar the pilgrim had gone; so had the clodhopper.

A suspicion that he had been baffled of his prey by the disguise of the aforesaid persons forced itself strongly upon his mind.

"I thought so," he exclaimed. "You will answer for this."

"Oh—certainly. What?" said Ralph, with a quiet grin.

"For cheating us of the malefactors thou hast aided to escape. I thought, when I entered, they were impostors."

"Who?"

"Thou wilt answer for it."

"Certainly."

"You have baffled us this time, but look to it; it won't pass unheeded."

"All right. Good-bye."

Kit the Keeper and his myrmidons rushed from the inn in search of the disguised adventurers.

Ralph Strongbrew chuckled triumphantly as he picked up a parcel in the parlour which contained the disguise worn by our friends.

"It's all right," he thought, "they have got a good start; and I don't think he"—he meant Kit the Keeper—"can prove anything against me."

CHAPTER XXIX.

THE SEARCH.

GUY FAWKES and his comrade had got some distance on their journey due north before their absence from the inn was discovered.

They travelled on foot, it being the surest, though perhaps not the quickest, way for them to go.

Everyone they met on the road was stopped and questioned, but no tidings could be gathered of the stolen lady.

Guy began to think they had taken the wrong route. So thought Hugh; but if they had, he was determined to make a thorough search north, and then work his way round east, south, and west.

"Think you, comrade, the troopers will suspect who we are when they find the pilgrim and the ploughboy gone?" inquired Guy.

"They may," answered Hugh, carelessly, "what matters if they do, they can't travel any faster than we do, and we have had the start."

"They might get horses."

"Not from Ralph Strongbrew they won't."

"They may from somewhere else, though."

"So can we."

"But we had better not."

"That's true," remarked Hugh.

So they went on on foot, and stopped at the first inn they came to.

It was a small roadside beer house with no very grand accommodation for travellers. The travellers didn't want any grand accommodation; they wanted rest and refreshment only, and they got it.

GUY FAWKES; OR, THE CONSPIRATOR'S BRIDE.—No. 11.—PRICE ONE PENNY.—GRATIS! with this Number the Second Scene for the Play of the

CAPTAIN FRANK'S PERIL.—(See No. 10.)

Hugh Wardour called the landlord's daughter to his side. She went to him. A pretty, blooming lass, she was, with a round, well-shaped figure, and a pair of languishing black eyes.

"I want you to tell me something, pretty

one," Hugh said, gliding his arm round her supple waist.

The girl blushed deeply, not with anger, she rather liked the idea of being caressed by the handsome youth, it was not many of his like who visited their comely little inn.

Perhaps the better for her; had their guests been other than the rough countrymen, she would not have been the simple innocent child of nature she was.

Hugh could not resist the impulse to kiss the cherry, pouting lips, and he drew the girl's face to his own.

"That is wrong of thee," she said, simply, though she returned the kiss with an ardent fervour that sent a thrill through the youth.

"Why?" he asked, looking up into her face.

"Had my father seen me, he would have been very angry."

"Never mind; he did not see, and he need not know." Hugh said.

The girl smiled at him confidentially.

"What is it thou wished to ask me?" she inquired. "You must not keep me longer; my father will come after me."

"Well, pretty one, has anyone been here with a lady within the last three or four days?"

The girl looked round to see if her paternal relative was within hearing, and then, bending her head down, she spoke, in a low voice—

"There has been," she said; "but my father said I wasn't to say a word about it. He was a very nasty, wicked-looking man, and he had a poor dear lady with him who had fainted. I wanted to take care of the lady till she got better, but he wouldn't let me; and my father sent me out of the room where they were. "Ah!" she continued, with a sad-drawn sigh, "my father is not too good; and when he sent me out of the room, I thought they were going to talk about something wicked. So I listened."

"And what didst thou hear?" Hugh inquired, anxiously, giving her another kiss for encouragement.

"I heard," she said, in a whisper, close to Hugh's ear, "the man with the evil eyes—he was dressed like a priest, I think—well, I heard him say the lady had been taken from her home, and he had found out where she had been taken to, and saved her; but I didn't believe it—his looks were too untruthful; besides, if what he had said were the fact, why did he deny my assistance to restore the lady? He hired a post-chaise of my father, paid him the full value of it, and told him he could have it by sending for it at the hostel at Framford, about twenty miles from here; but he cautioned my father to keep what he knew to himself, should there be an inquiry for the lady."

"The villain!" exclaimed Hugh. "I will have his heart's blood!"

The girl shuddered, and said—

"Don't talk so horribly."

Just then the door opened, and the gruff voice of mine host called the girl away.

She went, giving the youth a longing look, and even ventured to kiss her hand to him.

"Why didst thou ask the lass?" Guy asked.

"Because I liked not the look of mine host, and I knew, if there was anything to be learnt, 'twould be easier learnt of a woman than a man."

"Think you, comrade, the lass is correct?" asked Guy.

"There exists no doubt about it; the girl's description corresponded too well with that of Father Guynot for one to mistake."

"'Tis curious that we should have pitched upon the right place like this."

"And more curious that I should have thought of asking the girl for the information we required."

"And yet," put in Guy.

The noise of many people entering the inn, the clanking of arms, and the clamour of voices, reached the ears of our friends.

They were seated in a small back parlour, and could not see anyone who entered. They heard, and that was enough for them.

"They have made quick pursuit to be upon us so soon," said Guy. "How are we to get out of here?"

He looked round for a way of escape as he spoke. There was only one way, and that was by the door that led into the bar, where the troopers were who had just entered.

"The window," suggested Hugh.

"How are we to get at it?" Guy asked.

That was a query. The window was over their heads, and high up.

"We shall be taken if we don't get out somehow," Hugh said.

"That's obvious," replied Guy. "They shan't take me alive."

And he drew a pistol.

"What wouldst thou do?" asked Hugh.

"Blow out my brains rather than be taken by them."

"Pooh! put the thing back; that's cowardice."

"Cowardice! How?" demanded Guy.

The landlord's daughter came running into the room in great agitation.

"If you are the men the soldiers seek, fly!" she exclaimed. "Fly, in heaven's name! My father has betrayed thee."

"Fly whither?" queried Guy. "There is no way to get from here but by yonder door, and then that will take us into the arms of our enemies."

"Fasten the door to keep them out," said the girl hurriedly, "and I will show thee a way of safety from here."

Guy did as their fair protectress bid him to do.

The girl looked round her timidly, and pulling the table aside, she raised a trap.

"There," she said, "fly down there while thou art safe."

Hugh Wardour dropped down into the

cellar, while Guy kept his broad back against the door to resist the attack of the troopers, who had made themselves hoarse with shouting threats to the daring fellows. Finding their threats and expostulations were of no avail, they used more forcible means to get at the conspirators.

Every blow aimed at the door with the butt end of a petronal or the hilt of a carbine, sent a stinging sensation running up and down the spine of Guy's back.

The girl thoughtfully—to give Guy an opportunity of following his comrade—pushed all the articles of furniture the room contained against the door, and piled them up one above another as a barricade to keep back the besiegers while she too escaped.

"Now," she said, "help me down the trap, and lose no time in following. We may yet baffle their vigilance and my father's treachery."

Guy took her round the waist and handed her down to Hugh.

Seeing her safely landed, he let himself down and closed the trap as he dropped.

They were lost in the dense obscurity of the cellar.

The girl, taking Hugh's hand, led him forward and told Guy Fawkes to follow.

There was a fearful crash, which announced the invasion of the troopers into the parlour, where they thought to find their prisoners, but they didn't.

The fugitives heard them tearing about and swearing to kill the landlord, whom they said had tricked them. The landlord remonstrated loudly in defence of the charge, but the troopers didn't believe him, and threatened to burn to the ground the thatched wooden inn unless the Papists were given up.

The innkeeper's daughter, trembling lest danger should befall her parent, quite forgot in which direction to take her companions for safety.

Bewildered stood the generous-hearted girl, threatened with danger great as that which lay over the heads of her companions.

Should her father think of opening the trap, she must be discovered with the two fugitives; then what would be his anger? Death for the child who had betrayed his betrayal.

Someone hit upon the trap-door. It was raised. The light of lanterns flashed down. The innkeeper's daughter saw the way to fly now, but it was too late. A pair of legs descended through the aperture, then followed a big body, and a man hanging by the tips of his fingers to the edge of the flooring called for someone to show him a light. He wanted to see how far he had to fall.

Someone brought a light.

Guy recognised Kit the Keeper in the descending man.

"We shall be discovered," he said, in a whisper of intense agony.

"Hide behind some of the barrels," said the girl.

The three had disappeared as Kit the Keeper dropped into the vault.

The troopers followed him two and three at the time, and in a few moments the cellar was swarmed with the armed men.

Fawkes, crouching behind a big barrel perched up on several smaller ones, watched his enemies making a very diligent search.

Fortunately, they only had one light amongst them. Guy thought if he could put it out he might make a retreat.

He didn't think how the retreat was to be made; though, considering the trap was ten feet from the ground, the possibility of escaping that way was very small—so small, indeed, that when Guy did think of it he preferred to leave the man with the light alone, and take his chance.

"Show a light!" The voice came down the hole.

A light was shown.

A rope was lowered, and the worthy landlord, who had more respect for his neck than anyone had for it, slid down into the cellar to look after his property.

To his astonishment, he found no less than five of the troopers hidden in a corner, each with a bottle of his choice old wine, from which they had skilfully dismembered the neck, and were sucking in the delicious juice, as though they rather appreciated its flavour.

His amazement was too much for him; in wild despair he threw up his arms and cried—

"Villains! Is this what you entered my house for?"

"Hold thy prate!" exclaimed one of the five, bringing the empty bottle from his mouth heavily on the little man's head.

The little man staggered back, blinking, and stumbled over a big man who was lying full length on his back, sucking from the tap of a beer-barrel.

"Confound thy lumbering carcase!" bawled the man. Rising to a sitting posture, he seized the little landlord roughly by the collar and shook him.

The landlord was breathless when released. Never, during his long existence, from boyhood (and that was longer than he ever owned), had he received such treatment. Never had he felt so small in his own house —several degrees smaller than he really was (five feet an inch and a half in his boots); so small, in fact, did he appear, too, in the eyes of the trooper, that he was lost in oblivion.

What he lost in estimation he made up for in self-confidence.

"Cowards! miserable knaves! The Council shall know of thy rascally pillaging a poor man of his livelihood!" he said, vehemently.

"Duck him!" suggested one of the troopers.

The suggestion met with general approval, and the little landlord was seized by a dozen hands, eager to carry out the idea.

The top of a big hogshead was hammered

in, the landlord was raised above it, and dropped into his own adulteration.

A wild cry deadened the mirthful laughter as the poor little fellow sank. He rose, hung on to the edge, and yelled to be saved.

His cries reached the ears of his hidden daughter, who, having been a witness to the scene, suddenly sprang out from her place of concealment.

"Save him!" she cried, piteously.

The intoxicated ruffians laughed at her pleadings, and fought with one another for the first kiss.

Guy thought this a capital opportunity to make an effort to escape. He kicked against the big barrel, behind which he was concealed, to bring the man with the light within his reach.

This artifice had the desired effect. The man with the light came sneaking cautiously towards the big barrel, and Kit the Keeper followed him.

This was what Guy wanted.

"There is someone behind here," said the man with the light.

"You go and look," said Kit. "I'll stay here to wait for him if he comes out."

The man went. Guy Fawkes hit him heavily between the eyes with the hilt of his sword, and the man fell. Guy was on him in an instant, gave him a finishing tap to keep him quiet, took the lantern from his hand, blew out the light, and overturned the empty barrel, which fell over Kit the Keeper like a huge extinguisher.

Fawkes, then, in the darkness, rushed amongst the troopers, who were fighting for possession of the landlord's daughter, scattering them right and left.

"Don't be frightened," he said, in a whisper, taking the girl round the waist to conduct her under the trap.

"Now," he resumed, in the same low voice, "hang tightly round my neck, and all will be safe."

Quite a charming position, and Guy seemed to like it, for he was an exceedingly long time climbing hand over hand up the rope; but he succeeded at last.

No sooner had he reached the parlour, when Hugh hurriedly made his way up, with several troopers climbing after him.

"A knife, Guy," he said.

Fawkes didn't ask what he wanted it for. He cut the rope. There was a thud as the men clinging to the rope fell. Then arose from the cellar a succession of oaths.

"Their language is disgraceful," Hugh said.

"It is," replied his comrade. "They may have it all to themselves."

Wherewith he closed the trap-door over them, and didn't forget to fasten it securely, to keep them down.

"Now, my pretty lass," Hugh said, drawing the innkeeper's daughter to his knee, and imprinting a kiss on each of her blushing cheeks. "How are we to repay thee for thy kindness?"

"Oh, don't talk about that," answered the girl. "My father—he will be drowned!"

"Oh, no, he won't. I heard the barrel fall over, and he crawled away.

"Are you sure?"

"Thinkest thou I would tell thee false?"

"Oh, no! Forgive me. But you may have been mistaken."

"I can answer for the truth of my assertion."

"Well, then, you must go; for if he is safe, you will not be so by remaining here."

"Why not, pretty one? Do you want to get rid of us?"

"Oh, no! but there is a way out of the cellar, which leads to the back of the house. It was there that I wanted to take thee."

"Thou art a kind, generous little girl, and I know not how to thank you."

"Do not stay for thanks; delays are dangerous, and I shall think as much of thee without them. Ah! as I thought. Hear you that noise? My father has disclosed the secret entrance to them, and unless thou art away from here within a few moments, 'twill be too late for thy escape. Come, go!"

The girl disengaged his arm from her waist, and pushed him gently from her.

"Go!" she said. "Do not delay another moment."

They went, and the innkeeper's daughter watched them out of sight. Then she sighed heavily, and returned.

"Ah! I may never see him any more," she said, despondently. Falling into a chair she hid her face in her apron.

She fell into a reverie of sweet dreams which she did not enjoy long. The troopers entering in wild disorder from the back of the house startled her, and she sprang up to confront her angry father, who smelt very strong of hops.

"'Tis thy doings, all of this," exclaimed the enraged parent. "Booh! get from my sight, or I'll do thee some mischief."

The frightened girl was only too glad of the opportunity to get out of his way.

"Come back!" he yelled.

The girl stopped.

"What is it, father?" she said.

"What is it, father!" sneered the little man, spitefully; "booh, I feel ready to kill thee, I do. Where are these men you took such an interest in?"

"Gone, father."

"Gone! A pretty thing thy disobedience has done for me."

"What have I done?" asked the girl timidly.

"What have you done?"—the old man always had a way of repeating what any one said, when he was in a rage—"why, brought disgrace and trouble on me, that my life alone can requite, and thou art my murderess!" he added, drawing himself up dramatically, and denouncing the trembling girl.

"Father, father—forgive me!" cried the

poor girl, falling on her knees, and clasping her hands together in supplicating forgiveness.

"Away! Leave me, wretched child!" he said, sternly turning aside with a finger on his lip, and pushing her from him. "Ask not forgiveness of me, whose aged life thou hath consigned to the executioner. When this grey-haired head rolls from the block, severed from its trunk, then think of the wrongs thou hast done thy father, and ask forgiveness of thy Maker."

"No, no, say not so!" cried the heart-stricken girl, clinging to his legs, and looking imploringly up into his rigid face.

"Release thy hold!" he said, tearing her hands from him; "leave me to my fate! Quit my sight, ere I call down a curse from heaven on thee!"

A heartrending cry left her quivering lips, and she fell prone at the feet of her cruel parent.

"Miserable hound!" said one of the troopers, in deep disgust; "what good didst thou derive from thy daughter's misery? Had I my way, thy thick head should be severed from thy trunk, and stuck on the Tower for exhibition. Stand off!"

And the sympathetic fellow hurled the little crestfallen landlord across the room, and stooping down raised the insensible girl in his arms.

"You brutes!—you villains! What have you been doing with my child?"

This was said loudly by the landlady, who came rushing in in an excited state of mind, caught her diminutive husband by the collar as he slid along the floor, and hit the good-natured trooper between the eyes with her clenched hand.

The blow fell on him like a half-hundred-weight, and he went reeling backwards.

"There! there! and there!" said the excited lady, hitting him harder each time. "I'll learn you to insult my daughter!"

"But"—— began the soldier, in remonstrance, when the old party shook her fist in his face, and took the insensible girl from him.

"And that's for thee!" she said, turning to her cringeing husband. "This all comes of your beautiful company! Poor dear child!" she added, in quite a tender voice, kissing the girl's pale brow. "I tell ye what it is, Jacob, if you don't turn these men out, I will, and you, too, that's more. A pretty sneaking thief you are to look after a wife and child, you little wretch!"

Giving him a malicious glare, she departed, with the senseless girl in her arms.

Little Jacob looked round in a timid manner; the departure of his wife relieved him, and he shook his fist at her retreating form.

The troopers burst out into a loud laugh to see the quailing little Jacob shake his fist in vindication.

"You'll get it," said one of the troopers,

clapping him on the back as he went out with his comrades.

"Jacob," said Kit the Keeper, returning; "how many horses have you in the stables?"

"Only one," replied Jacob.

"Prepare it for me instantly."

Jacob regarded him doubtfully.

"Go and do my bidding!" exclaimed Kit, sharply.

Jacob jumped nearly three feet from the ground, startled out of his wits by the sudden loudness of the trooper's voice.

"You want my horse?" he said.

"Immediately."

"I want the money for it."

Kit drew his sword. Little Jacob saw it coming, and made a rapid retreat, grinning cunningly as he went. He meant treachery.

Had Kit seen the grin, he would have been on his guard; but, as he did not, he fell an innocent victim to the snare.

The horse was brought to the door by little Jacob himself. He had saddled it with his own hands; and when Kit was mounted, he chuckled gleefully.

"Follow quickly," said Kit to his myrmidons; "if I ever take the prisoners, I shall shoot them; so be at hand if thou art wanted."

And he rode away in the direction taken by Guy Fawkes and his comrade, Hugh Wardour, with the deadly intent to shoot both.

―――

CHAPTER XXX.

THE CONVENT OF ST. MARK'S.

NIGHT had fallen, like a black shroud, over the earth, by the time Guy Fawkes and Hugh Wardour reached the hostel at Frampton, twenty miles from little Jacob's comely inn.

On inquiry, they found the information the innkeeper's daughter had given them to be correct concerning the arrival of the priest with the insensible lady.

He was not so communicative with mine host of the hostel as he had been with little Jacob. He did not stay even to take refreshment. He merely stopped to change horses.

His manner caused suspicion, and mine host felt inquisitive. He told a smart little lad, whom he employed as a master-of-all-work, to follow the priestly-looking stranger.

The lad made not much ado about the matter. When the priest got on his seat in the chaise, to drive off, the boy hung on to the springs behind, and sat across the hindmost axle-tree. In this position he was taken some twenty-five or twenty-eight miles, when the chaise was drawn up at the convent of St. Mark's. This much he told Hugh; afterwards returning with the horse and chaise, which the priest brought back with him.

Hugh would willingly have set out there

and then, on obtaining the information as to his lady's destination, but his comrade persuaded him to defer it until the morning.

So they agreed to stop at the hostel that night, and truly they required rest.

They had hardly left the parlour to go to their respective quarters for the night when Kit the Keeper was brought in, borne on a litter, by four of his companions.

Haggard, blear-eyed, and savage as a tiger, he laid, writhing in agony.

The vindictive little Jacob had arranged his plan of revenge with clever accuracy.

In harnessing the horse he had so placed the saddle that the motion of riding would unloosen the strappings.

Which it did. The saddle slipped round, and Kit the Keeper suddenly found himself dangling under the horse's belly.

In trying to extricate himself he worried the horse. The horse, being a savage brute, objected to strange riders, began to plunge and kick madly, consequently Kit was so severely injured that, when the horse turned and bolted, he was unable to raise himself from the ground.

He was found lying in the road, groaning in agony, by his companions, who came by shortly afterwards.

It being near the hostel where the catastrophe happened, a litter was made to carry him thither.

Mine host heartily wished the accident had taken place anywhere but near his abode. He felt in no mood to lay his place open to the troop of hungry men, nor did he mince his words in telling them so.

There was a large barn at the back of his place. This he told them they could have at their convenience for the night with his free will.

Some few of the dissatisfied knaves murmured at the offer; but others, who were much fatigued by their long journey on foot, were grateful for any place to rest their weary limbs. So they went, leaving their leader to the attention of the hostess; and, being supplied with plenty of bread and cheese and good ale, they came off very well for that night.

The arrival of Kit the Keeper and his comrades got to the ears of Guy and Hugh. The knowledge did not add to their comfort, though they had a consolation in hearing that Kit was lying in too precarious a state to interfere with them just then; but even that knowledge did not relieve them. They believed strongly in the old maxim, that "self-preservation is the first law of nature," and they acted up to it, too.

At early dawn they quietly departed from the hostel, and journeyed unto Gresham—that's where the convent stood.

Night came on again before they reached the convent.

"The thing is," said Hugh, "how are we to get admittance ?"

"That's one obstacle," answered Guy.

"The next is, if we get admittance, how are we to get the lady ? However, here we are at the convent gates, and if they won't admit us, we will admit ourselves."

Hugh rang the bell.

The summons was answered by a baldpated-monk. He was a crafty, half savage-looking monk, who glared beneath his heavy brows. All monks appear to glare in a crafty manner at strangers, as though they half expected the gentleman from the lower regions had come to fetch them.

"What is thy business ?" he asked.

"With the abbess and not with thee," returned Hugh. He did not like the appearance of the monk, and therefore could not be civil to him.

"That cannot be; the abbess sees no one without she is first made acquainted with the errand on which those come who seek her."

"If that's it, tell her I come to claim the lady Father Guynot brought here.

The monk started, and a cunning leer wreathed his lips.

"The lady entered the cloisters of her own free will and thou canst not see her," he said ; "but I will consult the Superior."

And away he went.

Hugh and his comrade waited outside the gates for more than half-an-hour, in anxious expectation of the monk returning ; but he came not.

"He don't mean to come," said Guy. "Did you not notice the cunning look on his face ?"

"I did ; but all monks have the same cast of features," replied Hugh.

"That's because they are all skilled in the same craft."

"If he don't return in ten minutes, I shall enter. Are you with me ? "

"To the death."

Ten minutes expired ; the monk made no appearance.

"We have waited long enough," said Hugh.

Guy Fawkes was of the same opinion, so they didn't intend to wait any longer.

The gates were of no great height, they were easily surmounted.

The daring intruders now stood in the enclosure.

Hugh knocked at the convent door with the pommel of his sword.

There was no answer.

"Diavolo !" he exclaimed, in anger, "if they don't let us in, we will break the door down."

This threat must have been overheard ; for the door opened quickly, and about half a dozen monks confronted them, holding the holy cross.

"Sacrilege," said one, as Hugh pushed forward.

"To the devil with you !" said the youth. The monks fled, horrified.

Hugh and Guy then made their way to the cells, and looked amongst the lovely nuns for the missing Lady Constance. She was nowhere to be seen, and Hugh, thinking they had been tricked, seized the abbess.

"Answer me truthfully," he said. "Where is Constance Meredith, the lady brought here by Father Guynot? Try any artifice to delude me, and thy life shall pay the fine."

The abbess drew herself up indignantly.

"By whose authority have you dared enter the religious order of the convent?" she demanded. "Thy conduct shall be seen into. This insult and violation you will have to answer for."

The abbess touched a small bell. The tinkle of it brought to her assistance a dozen monks.

"Let these men be removed," she demanded.

Guy drew his sword; Hugh's was already drawn, and they stood ready for an attack.

"I see," said Hugh, "they will try to trick us, if they can. The blood be upon their own heads who try to oppose our search."

He made an attack at the monks. The monks fell back; they were not prepared for an attack of armed men.

"Let 'em follow in our steps," said Hugh, as he marched through the convent with Guy Fawkes, "and those who don't return I will not answer for."

They went on, descended to the lower part of the convent, and searched the cells for Constance Meredith.

Hugh began to despair; he met with the same disappointment in every quarter.

He felt confident that she was hidden there somewhere, and he determined not to leave the place till he found her.

He was suddenly accosted by a nun, a beautiful, fair lady, with a sorrowful countenance.

"Thou art seeking for a lady who was brought here against her will?" she said, timidly.

Hugh was amazed. The other nuns had fled in terror at the sight of him and his friend, yet this one had sought him without fear. No, not without fear; the timid glances she now and then cast round to see that the Superior was not within hearing were full of fear.

He made a reverent bow to the lovely lady, and even the sombre Guy inclined his head and gazed on her with enraptured admiration.

"'Tis so," Hugh answered; "the lady was brought here by a false friend, one who had the confidence of her father."

The lady sighed heavily.

"I," she said, plaintively, "was brought here and forced to wear the veil against my wish. Many persons think me dead," she added, turning pale. "Some think me faithless to my husband. Heaven knows my mind was as far from an impure thought as has been the chastity of my existence while under this holy roof."

The nun had set Hugh thinking; her wrongs had a similar tendency to the disappearance of Captain Meredith's wife.

Yet, thought Hugh, as he closely scanned her pale features, she looked too young to be the mother of Constance.

"Lady, dear, wronged and suffering angel," pleaded Hugh Wardour, on his knees, "tell, oh, tell me, if my surmise is true. Art thou the wife of Captain Meredith?"

Hugh felt the hand he held turn cold, and tremble with agitation.

"My name I must not divulge," she said. "Do not ask me now. I beseech thee go, the abbess comes. If we are seen together my punishment will be severe."

"Lady, lady, do not leave me thus," he said.

"Go, go. Look for the lady you seek in the black hole, for 'tis there I think she has been put, because she would not take the veil."

The nun pulled her hand forcibly from his and vanished as the abbess came striding in a dignified manner towards him.

She had not seen the nun conversing with him, but finding him on his knees as the nun had left him, with outstretched arms, convinced her that an interview had taken place; and she looked round suspiciously for the criminal, for it was a crime if any of the cloistered ladies ever looked upon the face of a man after once being received into the convent.

The monk who had answered the summons at the gate was a privileged guest of the abbess, and it was he who had fetched from the monastery the monks to oppose the strangers; but neither he nor they ever saw the face of any nun—at least, so it was believed.

"Come, comrade!" said Guy Fawkes, tapping him on the shoulders.

The youth jumped up, and looked about him in a stupefied manner, as though suddenly awaking from a dream. His gaze fell upon the Superior standing calmly near him, and he darted towards her in a savage, sullen mood.

Guy Fawkes caught his arm and held him back.

"What wouldst thou, Hugh?" he said. "Keep thy senses, lad!"

"Diavolo!" fiercely hissed Hugh. "It's her doings, that old hag's, there. She is the cause of all my troubles. By the mercy of the saints! if I find harm hath befallen the fair lady, I will run my sword through her black heart!"

"Come, come, Hugh. Let's to the work in hand, and keep thyself cool."

The youth allowed himself to be led quietly away by the hand like a child.

Guy Fawkes seemed to have a better knowledge of the interstices underground than his comrade; he therefore took the lead.

The abbess followed them with the stealth of a cat, her eyes glittering like fire-balls in the dark.

They had to search in the dark vaults and cellars. They carefully reconnoitred every inch of ground.

The low, pitiful wailing of a woman broke upon their ears.

Hugh seized Guy by the arm.

"Hear you that? 'Tis her voice!" he said, in an excited, suppressed whisper.

The two explorers stood breathless for a few moments.

The wailing had ceased.

Presently they heard a very low, melancholy moan.

Hugh, trembling in every limb, staggered with weakness, rather than walked, in the direction from whence the sound came, dragging after him the astonished Guy.

They stopped beneath a low archway.

The abbess stood behind them in silence, meditating a cruel deed, and the youths were unconscious of the danger hanging over them.

The stillness of the tomb reigned throughout the place.

A hard breathing, as of someone gasping for breath, arose, as it were, from the earth at their feet.

Hugh stood in painful hesitation. He was not sure that it might not have been himself or comrade, so he listened to catch the sound again.

It came—a deep-drawn, sobbing sigh.

There was no mistaking now from whence it came.

Hugh stooped to see if anyone were thereabouts, and as he stooped the abbess struck him with a dagger.

He felt the cold steel enter his back.

He turned as the blade was drawn out, and seized Guy by the shoulder.

"God of mercy!" he exclaimed. "Comrade, why this treachery? You have killed me."

He fell prone at Guy's feet.

The Spanish soldier was bewildered with horror. The tragedy had been so quickly enacted that it left him in a state of doubtful suspense to know whether he was dreaming or not.

"Horror!" he murmured, drawing his palsied hand across his sweating brow; "is this a dream, or can it be the fearful truth?"

"'Tis no dream. Take the warning, and go, or you meet with a like fate!" said a whispering voice in his ear.

He turned sharply.

A female form, in white, stood by his side. He made a snatch at the upraised arm with the stained dagger.

"Murderess, I hold thee!" he said.

There was a low, mocking laugh in his ear. He shuddered; the voice was so strangely unearthly and taunting. Turning his head slightly, by an irresistible impulse, he saw the white form sink apparently into the air.

At the same moment the arm he held vanished like a shadow from his grasp.

Yet he held something. What was that something? He brought it down before his eyes.

He staggered back, recoiling with horror. Some agency more than human had been at work.

In his hand he held—and he could not relax his hold—the blood-stained dagger that had stricken down his friend.

There he stood, trembling over his comrade, with the bloody weapon held in his nervous grasp, and he felt as though he had done the deed.

Footsteps he could hear approaching and the clanking of armed men, yet he could not move.

Was he to be found in this damning position with the self-accusing weapon in his hand? Was he to be found thus, and tried for the murder of his friend?

He asked himself these questions, yet he could not move.

CHAPTER XXXI.
THE DISCOVERY.

THE night preceding the departure of the two adventurers from the hostel, there had been in their company a stranger of foreign appearance.

Guy Fawkes took him for a Spaniard, and feeling a pleasure in meeting with one of his countrymen, he tried to draw the stranger out in conversation.

But the stranger didn't believe in it. He apparently enjoyed his own meditations too much to be disturbed by conversation.

There was another peculiarity about this stranger. He kept his head down, and only looked in a scowling manner from beneath his knitted brows, and the hat pulled well over his eyes.

Strange to say, when Hugh and Guy Fawkes retired to rest he raised his head. There was a troubled, yet a cunning expression on his face as he watched them out of the room.

Father Guynot had cleverly disguised himself to baffle recognition on the part of Hugh Wardour, whom he had so often encountered to his remembrance.

Even mine host could not trace the slightest similarity between the foreign stranger and the priest, who had hired a horse.

But the boy who had brought the horse back, fancied he had seen the face before. The boy, like most boys, was endowed with a very quick perception.

"Guvenor," he said, knowingly, to the landlord, "if that ere man ain't the same as I followed, my name ain't Billy, that's all."

"Nonsense, lad," said the landlord, carelessly; "this man's a foreigner, and the one who hired the horse was an English priest."

"Furrin or English, I knows he ain't no more furrin than you or me. Well, look here, guv'nor," said the boy, determinedly,

LADY ST. CLAIRE'S CONFESSION.

bringing one hand down on the other and turning up the corners of his mouth, "tell you what, if that ere furriner, as you calls him, ain't the same man as I followed the other day, why I'll work for you for a month, and give you the wages."

"No, my lad, thou art mistaken," the innkeeper said, smiling good-humouredly.

"Ah, well," muttered the boy, as he walked away, dissatisfied with his master, "say he knows." This was said in a tone of contempt. Jerking his thumb over his shoulder, he began to whistle loudly.

The stranger rang for a light. The boy took it.

"I say, guv'nor, what have you done with the lady?" the boy inquired, putting the light down, and making for the door.

Father Guynot was well on his guard. He had overheard the boy's surmisings with the landlord. Therefore the pointed question did not startle him as it would otherwise have done.

He made no answer, but scowled threateningly at the impudent lad.

There was more meaning in that scowl than the lad had instinct enough to predict—a treacherous, malicious meaning it was, with lurking danger.

It had the power to quiet the lad, and its influence brought on a peculiar uneasiness.

"Why, Billy, what's the matter with thee?" asked a buxom chambermaid, on seeing the boy's white, startled face.

"Oh, Mary! What be the matter with I? Naught that I know of; only that the furriner, as de master calls 'im, give me a turn with one of his ill-looks."

"Come, lad, don't let thee be frightened by that beastly old fellow." And the buxom chambermaid, in her sympathy, hugged the boy round the neck.

If he was not better after that, he ought to have been.

Father Guynot jumped up impulsively as Kit the Keeper was brought in. His intention was to inform the troopers that their prisoners were under the roof; but on second thoughts he sat down again.

He had a better plan to trap them—a plan in which he could satisfy both revenge and hate.

He sat up very late that night; he seemed to be interested in watching the persons as each one ascended to his or her respective quarters.

He followed the boy upstairs; there was a gleam of fire in his eyes when the boy entered his chamber.

"That's a clever lad," mused the evil-minded priest, closing the door. "Clever boys are dangerous; he knows just enough to make it dangerous for me. He is much too dangerous to live." And he grinned murderously as he drew a stiletto from his breast.

"That will do it," he mused, drawing his thumb along the keen edge. "They will be suspected of the crime, and arrested; then my revenge will be satisfied, and I—ha! ha! —master of the Moorland estate."

He undressed and got into bed, but not with the intention of sleeping. Nature having a stronger power than he could resist, she claimed her due, and he fell a victim to repose.

He did not forget to curse his ill-fate for sleeping, when he awoke and found daylight creeping into his room.

He was out of bed before you could say, "Jack Robinson." It was yet early, and he had time to accomplish the foul deed of crime. Like a thief, he silently crept from his chamber, with the weapon of death in his hand.

He paused when outside, and listened.

All was hushed in dead silence; the solemn tick of the big clock on the landing was the only thing that broke the stillness.

The evil-disposed priest stretched one long leg towards the door of the boy Billy's chamber. For a few moments he stood, with his legs outstretched, and again listened, to make sure that all was safe, before he ventured to drag the other leg forward.

Mastering his quailing courage, he reached the door, and got his hand on the handle to turn it, when he was frightened almost out of his life by the creaking of the clock as the weight dropped five minutes before the hour.

He wished all sorts of wicked things against the clock for startling him.

In a few moments he recovered from the shock, and, rousing himself for the desperate deed, he entered the chamber,

The intruder glared like a savage wolf upon the sleeping boy. In cold blood he bared his breast and poised the dagger just above his palpitating heart.

Disturbing the clothes aroused the boy. He started up in bed, and tried to shriek, but his tongue refused utterance, and clove to the roof of his mouth, burning.

"Die, miserable cub, die!" exclaimed the priest, seizing him by the throat, and holding him back, while he accomplished his diabolical task.

The boy struggled, and put up his hands to stay the descending arm of his assailant.

The glittering weapon came down like a flash of lightning, hissed through the palm of the poor boy's hand, and pinned it to his breast, as the cold steel buried itself deeply into his quivering frame.

The wretch was struck with terror for his own safety, by the boy's wailing cries, and tried to fly, but the boy, in desperation, held on to him, and it was only with force he could tear himself away.

The boy's heartrending cries soon aroused the whole house, and in a few moments the room of the fearful tragedy was filled with the persons who came flocking in in great alarm, some half attired—some as they had gone to bed.

There were no lamentable cries or shrieks from the lookers on, their pity for the suffering boy was expressed in their sorrowful looks. The influence of impending death held them quiet, and the hush was only broken by the groans and sudden screams of the stricken youth.

"My poor boy! my poor lad!" said the landlord, sorrowfully, bending over him. "Whose hand hath dealt this cursed blow?"

"The furriner like a soldier," said the youth, speaking between a succession of shrieks.

"The foreigner like a soldier, answers to the description of Guy Fawkes, the man we have been following for several days," said one of the troopers who had been called from the barn by the cries of murder to the tragic scene.

At this moment there was a great stir amongst the assembly, and the buxom chamber-maid came rushing into the room, screaming hysterically.

"Silence, Mary," demanded the landlord, trying to keep her aside.

"Let me see him!" she shrieked. "I will see him?"

And she pushed her way through those who tried to obstruct her, making her way to the bedside. She threw up her hands, giving vent to a lamentable cry.

"Oh! Billy, Billy, Billy!" she exclaimed, pitifully, "tell me who did this for thee?"

Her frantic bewailing seemed to distract the boy. He turned his head from her, giving mine host an imploring look, and pointed to the dagger that pinned his hand to his breast.

The landlord understood what he meant, and, shuddering, he approached to draw the weapon.

When the cruel blade was removed, the blood gushed forth, and the boy fell back exhausted.

The chambermaid, at the sight of the crimson tide flowing over the boy's heaving breast, and dying the sheets, gave way to a cry that rang through the house, and with a convulsive sob, that shook her frame, she fell forward, fainting.

The priest, the cruel perpetrator of the foul crime, had kept back until now, for fear of being recognized by the boy; but now the boy had fainted, he made his appearance amongst the rest, and expressed his horror at such a deed.

"Let the house be well guarded; don't let anyone escape," said the landlord. "If the villain is in the house he shall be brought to light, and made to suffer for the crime to the uttermost of the law."

The troopers immediately left the room to take up their positions around the house, while others of the law myrmidons made a thorough investigation of the house within.

Father Guynot followed the searchers, gloating over his fell scheme, and thinking to trap the slumbering Guy and Hugh in their beds for the bloody deed.

Many others of the landlord's guests took part in the search, but none took such a diligent part as Father Guynot.

A quiet, malicious smile curled his thin lips, as the door of the room, in which Guy and his comrade slept, was burst open.

But what was his surprise when they found the room deserted; the adventurers gone, the window was open; by that way they had gone. They had made a rope to descend by, with a sheet that hung out of window.

Every one stood aghast.

The culprits had escaped. There was no doubt but that they were the men, the evidence of their guilt was too plain to leave the shadow of a doubt now.

The door being found fastened on the inside, the descent from the window by the sheet was evidence of a guilty exit too strong to be questioned, and the innocent were blamed for the crime.

It is the way with poor humanity to throw the censure of crime on the first signs that give suspicions, without going further into the mystery to ferret out the real aggressor. If a crime has been committed some one has to pay the penalty, and the first unfortunate being suspicion falls upon, be he innocent or not, he has to hang.

Father Guynot looked upon the departure of the two adventurers as rather a fortunate occurrence than otherwise.

The merciless hand of suspicion was pointed at them.

"Gone!" said one of the troopers. "But we shall have them yet. Follow, comrades."

The troopers left the house, and traced footprints from under the window, through the garden, and along the road.

The crafty priest followed them. He suspected where Guy and Hugh had gone; but he did think it safe to himself to divulge his suspicion.

"I hope thou wilt find the villains," he said.

"I hope we shall," returned the trooper. And he gave the stranger a curious—a half suspicious glance. "You seem much concerned about it," he added.

"If they are the men I suspect, I can set you on the right track."

"Aha!" muttered the trooper. He fell back and walked with Guynot.

Guynot wished he had kept where he was. The trooper's presence made him feel uncomfortable; it brought unpleasant reflections to his mind. He saw himself handcuffed in the midst of the troopers who were preceding them; and the same cunning man who walked by his side now walked with him, in the passing visions, with drawn sword.

The vision changed. He saw himself standing before a grand tribunal, taking his trial for his treachery and attempt to murder the boy. Constance Meredith and Guy Fawkes stood in the witness-box, and gave evidence of his crimes. The jury, in a solemn voice, pronounced his death.

The third picture vanished, and he saw himself standing on the scaffold, surrounded with armed soldiers. Before him stood the black block, and by his side stood the grim executioner, resting on the gleaming axe.

A groan broke from his lips; it awoke him from the spell, and he turned to meet the cunning face of the trooper looking into his own working features.

"Your mind seemed troubled," said the trooper, artfully.

"The sight of that fearful tragedy has given me a shock I shan't recover readily," murmured the priest.

The man doubted him. He was a keen-witted fellow. The priest's strange manner set him wondering; he thought it strange he should take such an interest in the business. The trooper was determined not to let him escape his notice.

"What know you of the men suspected?" he demanded.

"Nought of them." That was a lie, but Guynot was not particular for a priest.

"You said you overheard something."

"I did."

"What was it?"

"I can't remember the words."

"Then give me the substance."

The men were sitting in the parlour when I entered the hostel last night. They were conversing in an undertone, but I have acute ears, and I caught a few words that opened them wider.

The trooper thought they were wide enough; they stuck out like a pair of sails.

"Well, what did you hear?" he queried.

"They talked of breaking into the convent and taking therefrom a certain nun—a lady of immense wealth."

"That has nothing to do with the assassination of the boy."

"Yes it has."

"Well, come to the point."

"The handle comes first, the point will follow," Guynot said.

"It will if you fool me much more," the trooper said, touching the hilt of his sword significantly. "You say the abduction of the nun has to do with the assassination of the boy. How?"

"Simply thus," answered the crafty intriguing priest. "The boy had played the spy. He knew too much for their safety, so they killed him."

"Canst thou assert this for the truth."

"So far as suspicion goes."

"Thou wouldst condemn men on suspicion then?"

"The evidence of their guilt does not omit a doubt for their vindication."

"Yet they may not be the men," said the trooper, and he looked hard at Guynot.

"Who else could it be?"

"It is not a matter for conjecture. There are so many mysteries about a tragedy of this sort. The poor boy's life could not have done anyone any good. It was a cold-blooded deed, done out of spite."

Father Guynot winced and turned pale, the soldier's words went home.

"It is hardly possible that such a crime could have been done without a purpose," he said.

"I don't see any purpose why it should be done."

"The evidence against these men, thou art after, after their conversation I overheard, is quite plain enough to give a cause why the boy was murdered."

The trooper smiled doubtfully.

Father Guynot became more uncomfortable every moment. There was something so strange about his companions—something in his cold, cynical look, that kept him in a state of perpetual trepidation.

"I don't know," the trooper made answer, and Father Guynot encountered one of his quiet, freezing smiles, that caused him an involuntary shiver. "I don't know; I should not think they would have done it."

"Why?"

"It isn't very likely they did it. I don't think they would be fools enough."

"But why?" asked Guynot, uneasily.

"They are already charged with conspiracy, it isn't likely they would add a murder to the charge."

"I don't know."

"Nor I; but we shall see."

Nothing more was said during the journey to the convent.

They were received at the gates by the abbot, and he conducted them to the vault, where Guy stood over his stricken friend with the reeking dagger in his hand.

The conspirator was paralyzed with horror.

"Another murder," exclaimed the trooper, at once coming to the conclusion that Guy Fawkes had murdered his friend, and of course there was no doubt left about the tragedy at the inn. "Guy Fawkes, I arrest you in the king's name."

Guy Fawkes did not resist. A low groan broke from his lips, and he submitted quietly to be handcuffed by his captors.

Father Guynot held a whispered conference aside with the abbess, while the soldiers proceeded with their duty.

"He is not dead," said the trooper, meaning Hugh Wardour; "he won't cost us much trouble."

"Won't he though?" said one of his comrades. "It strikes me he will; we shall have to carry him all the way back."

"Mind how you handle him," said Kit the Keeper's subordinate to his companions, and he turned to see where Father Guynot had gone.

Father Guynot was out of sight. This incident brought back the suspicions the trooper had formerly entertained of him.

"I shall leave the girl to you, good mother," said the evil-minded priest to the abbess: "thou hast acted admirably. I did not think to find this success."

The abbess smiled wickedly.

"I don't think you need trouble about the girl," she said; I don't think he will recover, and the other will answer for his murder."

"We know not, good mother. I think it will be the safest way to dispose of the girl in the event of the knave recovering. Besides, there may be other contingencies that may arise to thwart our plans, without the girl is effectually got rid of."

"It shall be done," the abbess said. "You know the compact, my son?"

"I do," he answered, with a dark smile, and added, aside, "to silence you when the cards are played into my hands."

"Farewell," said the abbess, hastily. "The soldier comes this way; don't let him see us together. I shall see you again shortly."

"Within a week. Farewell," answered the priest.

They parted.

Guynot turned, and met the soldier.

"Art thou now satisfied?" he asked.

"Well, yes," drawled out the trooper, in an undecided manner. "But I shall want you to accompany me."

Guynot started.

"For what purpose?" he queried.

"To give thy evidence."

"It cannot be. I have urgent business. 'Tis impossible to delay."

"It must be," said the trooper, sternly: "and if you object to come, I must take you by force. Your denial looks very much like guilt."

"What meanest thou, man?" demanded the priest, haughtily, to conceal his confusion.

"Precisely what I say — that if you do not come with me to give thy evidence, I shall take you up on suspicion, as being concerned with the murder of the boy at the inn. 'Twas you I suspected from the first, and that's the truth. Your unusual interest to bring to light the criminal, and your ardent desire to condemn these men, had a very curious appearance for a stranger; besides, you appear to know so much."

Father Guynot stood speechless and helpless as a child. You might have knocked him down with a feather.

A thousand thoughts rushed through his mind. Had he said anything, he wondered, that had caused the trooper to suspect him? Should he fail to bring the murder of the boy against Guy, the trooper, he felt assured, would condemn him.

He bitterly regretted having accompanied the troopers to the convent. Why had he gone with them?—why had he been so indiscreet as to announce Guy and his companions as the murderers?—why? he asked himself; and he cursed his folly.

He looked darkly towards the trooper, and his hand closed over the hilt of a dagger under his cloak. But he did not draw it out — the presence of the trooper's well-armed companions thwarted his design.

The soldier watched him keenly. He saw his dire intent, and smiled a smile of savage satisfaction.

"Will you accompany us?" he asked.

"To-morrow will be time enough for my evidence."

"To-morrow won't do for me," said the trooper. "You can have your choice to walk with us at liberty, or in like manner," and he pointed to Guy Fawkes.

That was enough to stop the argument. Father Garnet did not like the idea of being heavily manacled. He agreed to walk at liberty.

So they left the convent.

The stricken youth was carried by four men; Guy, in a bewildered manner, walked, surrounded by soldiers.

While journeying along, a horseman came thundering down upon them.

The soldiers turned.

"Father Garnet, Papist!" exclaimed the trooper, in command. "Arrest him, my men, he is our prisoner!"

Most of the soldiers drew in line across the road to intercept the priest.

The Jesuit came on at headlong speed.

"Halt!" cried the trooper.

In answer, Garnet urged his charger at quicker speed, drew his sword, and made a circular sweep at the line of soldiers in his path.

The troopers made way, and Garnet passed. A dark, troubled look overspread his face on beholding Guy Fawkes a manacled prisoner in their midst.

"Surrender, or we fire!" shouted the trooper.

Garnet turned in his saddle and made a sign to Fawkes, which the latter understood, and his face brightened up with hope.

"More intriguing going on," said the soldier, spitefully, "but I don't think it will be any good. Guy Fawkes this last deed will settle thy accounts for thee. Bring him down!" he suddenly yelled, as Garnet dashed off again; "bring him down, men, he can't escape. Quick!"

The command was no sooner said, than every piece was discharged at the retreating Jesuit, but he did escape, much to the chagrin of the trooper.

Which was ascertained when the columns of smoke arose. Father Garnet, the principal Jesuit, had ridden out of sight.

CHAPTER XXVII.

SAD TIDINGS.

The time for the consummation of the conspirators' schemes was drawing short.

It was now October, and 1605, and the

had not yet got the powder in the vault of the Parliament House.

Guy Fawkes' prolonged absence caused his comrades some uneasiness; he had been away more than a month, and nothing had been heard of him.

"I know not what to think," Catesby remarked, despairingly. "Nine days have passed since he left us, and none know whither he has gone, or what has become of him. He is a strange being; there is no knowing what to think of him."

"Our secret is safe, wherever he is," said Wright. "Nothing would make Guy Fawkes betray us. "Not the severest tortures of the rack would wring a word from him; he will die a martyr, true to us and true to our great enterprise, whenever it happens, or in any shape."

"I wish I could think so," returned Catesby.

"You may," said Percy. "You bear him malice, through some prejudice only known to thyself. Guy Fawkes is the most zealous member in our brotherhood; he is devoted to it, heart and soul."

Catesby bit his lip.

"That is not saying much for the rest of thy brethren," he said, sneeringly.

"They are all as faithful as thou art," answered the other, sharply; "but none with the ardent zeal of Guy Fawkes. His every thought is for our fallen Church; he has sacrificed everything for this one cause. The world to him is a blank; he lives only to see the restoration of our faith. But this useless prate is only waste of time. Something must be done."

"What is to be done?" demanded Wright.

"Nothing has been heard of Garnet; Guy Fawkes is away; and Sir Everard has not sent to let us know how he has got on since the abduction of the princess."

"That must not hinder us from doing something," said Tresham. "Is it because they are away we are to stand still?"

"No," responded the conspirators.

"Then let us to the dwelling at Westminster, and do what we can. Parliament meets on the fifth of November. There is not much time for us to prepare for their reception."

"Tresham is right," said Percy. "Let us be doing what we can while the others are away; and if nothing is heard of Guy Fawkes within two days, an inquiry must be made. It will not do to desert him if he is in danger."

"Do you suppose Fawkes to be in danger?" asked Catesby.

"There is nothing more likely," returned Percy. "He would not have kept away all this time, had it been otherwise, knowing how urgent it is that we should now get the powder in the cellar."

It was agreed that they should return to the house adjoining Parliament, and there await the issue of two days. If nothing

was heard of Guy Fawkes within that time, a search was to be made for his recovery.

The conspirators then collected together what provisions remained, and left the Red Castle.

Catesby, Percy, and the two Wrights departed together; and the others, in small companies, dispersed in different directions.

The night was a dark one; a thick, hazy fog pervaded the air, and made undiscernable any object at twenty yards' distance.

Catesby and his party found much difficulty on their journey in consequence of the gloom and the stubbled field.

Overcome with fatigue, they were nearing the house at Westminster, when a horseman passed them suddenly.

"Who is that?" asked Catesby, in a strange tone.

The horseman had disappeared before one could discern his features.

"No friend, I vouch," answered Percy. "He takes the direction to the dwelling. Think you we are betrayed?"

"I cannot say. Let's hasten home."

With this they moved on more quickly, and reached their destination. The horseman who had passed them stood at the door with the reins in his hand, as though awaiting to be admitted.

Percy and his companions drew back in some astonishment. The appearance of the stranger at the door of their dwelling instantly put them on their guard against danger.

Catesby glared upon him from his place of concealment like a panther.

In silence he drew his sword.

"That man cannot be a friend of ours," he said, in a hoarse whisper. "We have been betrayed. He is our betrayer, or a spy; and he must die."

"Nay," exclaimed Wright, arresting Catesby by the arm, "this must not be. Let us avoid danger without bloodshed. You may be mistaken. Let us wait and watch him."

Just then the stranger at the door knocked three times upon the panel with his sword, and waited patiently for an answer.

"That is no stranger," remarked the other Wright. "He knows our signal."

"Let us arrest him suddenly," proposed Percy. "We can then satisfy ourselves."

Robert Catesby crept silently forward. Percy and the two Wrights kept close behind him.

Catesby trod upon a piece of dry stick, and the cracking startled the stranger; he turned, and seeing the dark face of the conspirator approaching him, drew his sword.

"Stand off, villain!" he cried.

Catesby bounded upon him, and held down his arms.

The stranger was a man of great strength. He threw his assailant; but before he could do anything to keep him quiet the other three fell upon him.

The scuffle that ensued brought the conspirators out of the dwelling, and they rushed upon the combatants.

"Ah, Percy! what means this?" cried Winter. "Catesby, down! Who is this stranger? Bring him in?"

The stranger was hustled into the house. Winter brought a light to examine him.

"Why," he exclaimed, in breathless surprise, "what the deuce have you been doing? It is Father Garnet."

Percy released him, and asked pardon.

"It was all a mistake," said the principle Jesuit; "the gloom prevented recognition, and you did quite right, though I had to suffer for it. Secure the place—I have been followed, I fancy."

The shutters and the door were securely fastened, and a large room lighted up.

"Are all our brethren here?" inquired the priest.

Catesby looked around. His companions, who had left the Red Castle, had preceded him and his party on their journey, and arrived at the house next to the Parliament houses before him.

"Tresham—where is he?" he asked.

None knew he had left the castle with them, but he was not there.

"He must have left us on our journey," Winter remarked.

"My sons," said Garnet, "you must be careful of that man; do not trust him; he is a friend of Lord Monteagle's, and Monteagle is no friend of ours."

"He must die, then," exclaimed Catesby, fiercely. "We are not safe while we have a traitor amongst us."

"Let him be removed at the first opportunity," said Garnet; "but do not do anything rashly. Now listen; I have much to tell you."

The conspirators gathered around him.

"When I last wrote to you, my son," he began, "I was then about to leave Manchester for London, but such terrible goings on ensued, that I was compelled to stay. Sir William Radcliff was suspected of Papacy. His house was beseiged, the remorseless heathens carried off every article of any value, and laid waste throughout the splendid domain, inflicting the most heinous cruelty upon the poor domestics. Sir William fell by their murderous hands, and his daughter escaped their clutches with Father Oldcorne. I left them on their journey hither, and while I was riding through Framton, I beheld Guy Fawkes in the midst of a gang of troopers."

"A prisoner!" cried Catesby.

"Even so, my son; but he must be rescued."

"Ay!" cried Catesby; "he shall be saved. I will undertake to liberate him. Where do you think they will confine him?"

"In the king's prison," answered Father Garnet. "Six of you may be able to save him. Be careful how you proceed; his life is more to us than aught else."

"Trust me, Father," cried Catesby. "He shall be saved."

At midnight Robert Catesby, with the two Wrights, the two Winters, and Percy of Northumberland, set out on their dangerous mission to liberate Guy Fawkes from the king's prison.

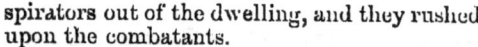

CHAPTER XXXIII.

BROUGHT BACK TO HAPPINESS.

THE troopers, with their prisoners, returned to the hostel. Father Guynot broke out in a cold perspiration. He felt that this visit would seal his fate, and he offered up a prayer for his lost soul.

Kit the Keeper, they found had expired from the severity of his fall. The horse little Jacob had saddled for him had broken several of Kit's ribs and fractured his skull.

The boy had recovered from the danger of his wounds, but still lay in a very precarious state.

Mine host felt more vindictive towards Father Guynot than he did towards Guy Fawkes, who was charged with the brutal crime.

"Thou hast kept thy word," he said, fixing his gaze on the quailing priest, "and brought back the criminal villain."

"I doubt if the one charged is the right one," replied the soldier, "but I have the other, if he is not."

"I am innocent of either crime," said Fawkes. "I swear solemnly by the name of the Holy Virgin, I am innocent."

"Nay," said the soldier; "if thou art innocent of the crime here, you cannot deny having stabbed thy companion? The dagger was found in thy hand, and you standing over him."

"Some one else committed the crime," Guy said. "I caught the assassin's wrist, but whoever it was drew it from my grasp and left the dagger in my hand, and that is how I came by it."

"He is innocent," said Hugh, who had slightly recovered. "He did not strike me, though I condemned him for it at first."

"Then how do you know he is not guilty?" interrogated the trooper.

"Because I remember seeing a female form flit past me as I fell."

"Then you do not think me guilty?" cried Guy, grasping his comrade's hand.

"No, thou art innocent of the coward blow. He who stands there," and Hugh pointed to the priest, "is guilty of the cruel crime committed on the poor boy."

"Can we see the boy?" asked the trooper, "he may be able to identify the right criminal?"

Mine host conducted the soldiers.

Father Guynot and Guy Fawkes were taken up by the troopers.

The treacherous priest nearly fell when the poor boy rose in his bed.

"That was the man who came in the night to kill me!" exclaimed the boy, pointing to the trembling wretch.

"You lie, boy!" screamed the wretch.

"No, no, I bean't lying," said the boy, and he fell back exhausted.

"Clap the irons on him; that's our man," said the soldier.

The troopers surrounded Father Guynot, despite his desperate struggles to resist, and he was secured with the manacles.

"Thou wilt swing for this," said the host, "an' 'tis my belief thou art the same knave my poor boy followed to the convent, and that's why thou wouldst have killed him."

"All's lost!" murmured the priest, despairingly.

The trooper pricked up his ears.

"Oh, oh!" he said, "I thought as much, when he was pitching a tale to me about the boy following Guy Fawkes to the convent."

"No, it warn't the man you call Guy Fawkes that be the man who took the lady to the convent."

"Took the lady to the convent," said the soldier, wonderingly. "What lady? I do not fully understand."

"Well, I will tell you," said Hugh, eagerly, and he related the whole affair word for word.

"Oh! that's it, is it?" the soldier said. "The black-souled villain! I can understand it all now. The abbess of the convent is in league with him, and it was she who stabbed you. We will return to the convent when thou art better. The lady shall be saved. Let the prisoners be conveyed hence," he added to his companions.

"But Guy Fawkes is not thy prisoner," said Hugh.

The trooper displayed a warrant for his apprehension for suspected conspiracy.

Hugh sighed sadly. He knew the suspicions to be too true, and he took a tender farewell of his friend.

All the troopers, except half-a-dozen and their leader, then left the hostel with their prisoners. The others remained until Hugh Wardour should be well enough to accompany them to the convent.

In two days the youth had recovered sufficiently to go on his journey, and, accompanied by the troopers, they proceeded to the convent.

The abbess reeled back when the soldier told her the nature of their visit.

"The ladies have taken the veil of their own free will," she said.

"'Tis false," said Hugh. "Do not attempt to baffle us, or it will be the worse for you. Your confederate, Father Guynot, is now in prison. All is known; and, unless you bring forth the ladies we seek, you will follow him."

"What meanest thou?" she demanded.

"I will tell you," answered the youth.

"I have recovered from the dagger thrust you had inflicted."

The abbess went back, and turned pale as death.

"I will forgive the crime if you bring forth the ladies," Hugh said.

"Follow, then," the abbess cried, and led the way to the dungeon.

"There you will find Constance Meredith," she said, opening a door of a small dark cell.

"Constance!" Hugh cried, in an agitated tone, and stood down.

A low, glad cry broke upon his ears, and the lady sprang out from her cramping place of confinement.

"Hugh—Hugh! Dear Hugh, I am sure," she exclaimed, and threw herself upon his breast.

The abbess had disappeared, but in a few seconds she returned, bringing with her the beautiful woman, who had accosted Hugh on his former visit.

"That is thy daughter, Lady Meredith," said the abbess, pointing to the weeping girl on her lover's breast.

The nun stood stupefied.

The words "Lady Meredith" fell on the ears of Constance like a magic charm. She turned, and cried—

"Lady Meredith! Then it is my dear lost mother. For I am Constance Meredith." And she ran into her mother's arms. A very tender, touching scene, following this happy re-union.

The abbess was forgiven her part in the treachery, the soldiers handsomely rewarded for the part they had taken to bring the ladies once more into the light of the glorious world.

Hugh Wardour and the two ladies then left the convent *en route* for Moreland House, where they took up their abode. There was only one being more wanting to make the home a happy circle, and that was Captain Meredith.

Will Kendrick, the faithful keeper, was leisurely walking through the splendid park, meditating on the return of the lovely lady and her daughter, when a tall, military-looking gentleman stood in his path.

Kendrick looked up. The stranger's handsome face was tanned through long exposure to the tropical sun; his expression was not pleasing, but he tried to smile, and looked kindly upon the gamekeeper.

"Have you forgotten me, Kendrick?" said the stranger, tendering his hand to the keeper, and his gaze wandered to the windows of the mansion.

Kendrick looked hard at the speaker.

"I have seen thy face before, but when or where, I cannot call to mind," Will answered.

"So, Will, you have forgotten your master, cap"——

"My dear master! can it be you?" cried the old man, joyously; and tears sprang to his eyes as he grasped the captain's hand.

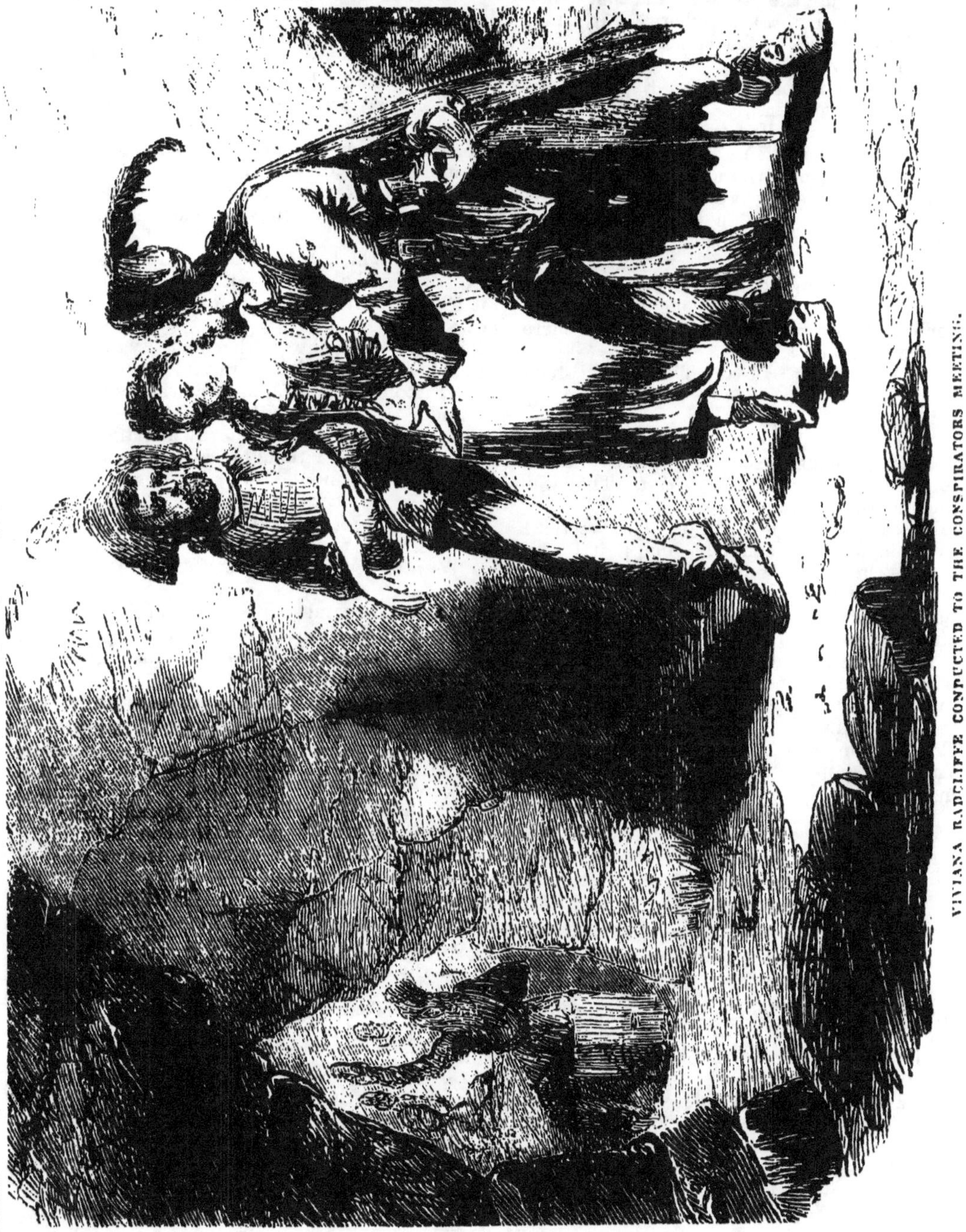

VIVIANA RADCLIFFE CONDUCTED TO THE CONSPIRATORS MEETING.

"Yes, Will, 'tis thy master returned after many years' campaign—returned, I suppose, to the unhappy home I left," he added, sadly.

"Not so," returned the old man; "thy home is more happy. Your wife has only just returned; but she is as pure and unsullied as when she was taken away."

The captain shook his head, and sighed sadly.

"I say 'tis so." And an angry flush rose to the keeper's swarthy cheeks. "I tell you, captain, the lady is as innocent of the charge as I am. The story of her eloping was a base lie of the traitor's, Father Guynot, to hide his own treachery; but, thank God! the knave is held fast now, and his course nearly run."

"What has happened! Explain," exclaimed the captain.

"This, captain. You trusted a traitor who betrayed thy confidence and took thy gentle daughter to Spain where he placed her in a convent; but she was saved by a noble youth, who brought her to England. The villain Guynot followed them back, got the lady in his clutches again, and renewed his fell designs of placing her in the convent of St. Mark's. From there the same youth, at the peril of his life, rescued her; and while there found your wife a nun."

Will Kendrick paused. The captain stood bewildered.

"Go on," he gasped.

"Yes, he found her a nun," repeated the keeper, growing excited: "placed in the convent by your trusted *friend*. That was the affair of the elopement."

"Yes, yes—I understand. The wretch! Tell me where I can find him, that I may requite these wrongs in full."

"He is out of your reach, but he will be justly dealt with. He has been arrested for an attempted murder."

The captain regretted having suspected his wife of wrong; but the gentle lady forgave him, and again the home was happy.

Hugh Wardour had no more to fear now. The captain gave him the hand of the fair Lady Constance, and they were shortly to be married.

CHAPTER XXXIV.
OF MANY INCIDENTS.

On the third day of Captain Frank's confinement he was taken before the court-martial to take his trial.

His late opponent, Temple St. Claire, and his uncle were there.

The young soldier wondered at their presence, and the words of Guy Fawkes flashed across his mind, and he thought there was more truth in the affair than he would own.

He had never known his parents; he had

been brought up in ignorance of who they were by a couple of old people.

Now he began to think there was a dark mystery connected with his life's history.

He was charged with infidelity to his king, and treacherously being connected with a gang of Papists, who were suspected of conspiracy.

"And who condemns me with this infamous charge?" he exclaimed.

"I do?" boldly responded Temple. "I have seen you with certain Catholics I know to be hatching a plot."

"What cause have you for this lie?" asked Captain Frank, fixing the youth with his large dark eyes, "and how know you what Catholics, if there are any, concocting a plot against the State?"

This retort was the cause of everyone turning their eyes upon the hasty youth with suspicion. He moved about uneasily, and, in a stammering voice, began—

"Did you not cowardly attack me when I met you with one, a renowned zealous Catholic, Guy Fawkes."

"No, base liar, I did not. I own that I have been in the company of the said person, but without any knowledge of what or who he was."

"Stay!" cried the youth's uncle; "do not stand there lying with impunity. Did you not set upon him in the most cowardly manner under the chapel wall of St. Mary's?"

"I met him there by his own challenge, and in honour, as I thought, but he took the treacherous advantage to send his sword home when my foot slipped."

Again the youth was regarded with some suspicion.

"'Tis false!" cried the youth's uncle; "did you ——"

"Stop!" demanded a stern voice. And Captain Meredith entered. He was a great favourite with the nobles present, and much honour was shown him.

"What means this?" he asked, angrily, his gaze wandering from the young soldier to the two base villains.

"These gentlemen have charged Captain Frank with being connected with certain Papists, supposed to be carrying on an intrigue against the king," one of the council made answer; "but their evidence is not clear enough to convict him."

Captain Frank's face brightened up; his enemies exchanged uneasy glances.

"Gentlemen!" and Captain Meredith's lip curled scornfully, "usurpers you mean, my lords. That young man there," and he pointed to Temple St. Claire, "is Captain Frank's foster-brother. The man he calls uncle is his father, the murderer of Earl St. Claire, Captain Frank's father, and the seducer of his mother."

The man accused turned deadly pale. He gave the speaker a tigerish glance, and looked towards the door.

The guards left Captain Frank, and closed

around the criminal in time to frustrate his intent to escape.

A dead silence prevailed for some moments.

The terrible disclosure fell like a thunderbolt upon the young captain. He stood bewildered.

Temple St. Claire stood aghast.

"My father!" he gasped. "Base wretch, you have deceived me, and I could tear thine heart out!"

"Let me get at him!" cried Captain Frank; and he made a spring forward, but his comrades held him back.

The council then put many questions to Captain Meredith, which he answered very clearly, and without hesitation.

"Captain Frank is my nephew, I repeat," he said; "the Earl of St. Claire was my wife's brother."

"But in his will," said one of the council, "when he put the Lady Claire of Grace under his Majesty's protection, he mentions but one child."

"True," answered Meredith; "that was on account of his eldest child, Captain Frank, having been stolen away from him while a baby; and knowing the enemies he had at work, he thought it prudent to bequeath all his fortune to his daughter, knowing his wife had had a boy by another man, Charles Moore, her former lover. There he stands," he added, pointing to the daring villain, "and knowing this, he thought if he should fall by any treachery which he felt convinced would be the case, and his forebodings were not wrong, for one day he was found lying in a deserted part of the country with a dagger driven through his heart, the initials on the dagger were "C. M.," which convicted Charles Moore, for the murder; not only that, but he was seen to strike the blow."

"Was it so?" asked one of the gentlemen.

"You may as well tell the truth: there is no hope of your being pardoned, the other offences are too great for that."

"All that Captain Meredith has said is true," answered the assassin, coolly.

"Well," resumed Meredith, "as I have stated, the earl feared something would befall him, and, fearing that if he had said anything about his son Frederick his enemies would keep him back, and bring forward the bastard; so he made everything over to his daughter, whom he placed under the king's protection; but I have a will which he left with me, stating, in the event of his son ever being known to me, I was to put in my claims for him, and I have now done my duty."

Captain Frank listened to the foregoing revelation in deep interest, without evincing the slightest surprise or agitation.

"We do not doubt your assertion of Captain Frank's claims, but we must have stronger proofs—documental evidence."

"That you can get," said Temple's uncle, "by going to the Jesuit, Lady Clair of Grace's guardian."

"Yes," exclaimed Captain Frank's foster-brother, "you must have greater proofs of thy claims than the evidence of Captain Meredith, before you can put in thy claims. How know I that thou art not the illegitimate son of Lord Clair."

"Of that you may be satisfied to-morrow, by going to the Jesuit's house, too," said his uncle.

He was then removed in custody of the soldiers. Captain Frank was acquitted. A note was then written to the Jesuit, informing him to be prepared on the morrow for an examination concerning the Lady Clair of Grace.

Captain Meredith, Captain Frank, and his foster-brother visited the Jesuit. They found him fully prepared for them. The faithless wife of Lord St. Clair and mistress of Charles Moore was there, so was the Lady Claire of Grace.

It will be necessary to say a few words to explain how she again got in her guardian's care.

The reader already knows how she was rescued by the twelve cavaliers by mistake for the Princess Elizabeth.

The mistake was discovered by Lord Harrington, when his noble guests returned with the lady.

The royal guardian interrogated the fair girl upon many subjects, in hopes of learning something that would bring to light the abductors of the princess. Of them she knew nothing, but she revealed to him the designs of her base persecutors, Lord Cecil and his ally, Count Basco.

Lord Harrington had the lady taken back to her guardians, and swore vengeance, deep and dire, against her agressor.

From that time nothing more was heard of Lord Cecil or Count Basco; they thought it prudent to keep out of sight, as their lives stood in great jeopardy should they be seen.

Sir Everard Digby, while flying with the royal maiden to the country, was overtaken by one of the few companies of soldiers.

It being night, he managed to get from them and escape, but without his prize; and the princess was taken back to her guardians.

Having got so far, let us return to the Jesuit and his guests.

The news of Charles Moore's arrest for murder fell a heavy blow to the faithless wife of Lord St. Claire; she stood before the Jesuit with downcast head and quivering look, before her stood her three children—her illegitimate son, Temple, Captain Frank, and the beauty, Lady Grace—the latter was in ignorance that the woman she regarded with so much pity was her mother.

"As you wish for peace with heaven," said Captain Meredith, addressing her, "confess truly which of these two young men is your illegitimate son?"

Lady Claire regarded him studiously ; her looks were pitifully sorrowful : her bosom rose and fell with agitation.

"Captain Frank is the child of my husband," she said, after a struggling effort to speak : "Temple is the child of my paramour. May I—oh ! let me," she added, tearfully, "clasp my child, Grace, to my heart again !"

"Art thou my mother !" exclaimed the lady, gladly.

Captain Frank stood in her path as she went forward.

"Oh, let me go to my mother !" she cried.

"No !" he said, sternly. "Back ! That infamous woman is no longer mother of ours !"

Lady Claire of Grace went reeling back in tears ; it seemed as though her heart would break, so bitterly did she sob with her face hidden in her hands.

"You have nought to cry for," said Temple, spitefully. "'Tis I who have the troubles : born of the same woman as art thou, brought up in luxury and discarded a beggar, and for what ?"

He bit his lip, and laid his hand on her wrist in sympathy—the gentle, beautiful girl's grief touched him to pity.

Lady St. Claire dropped her head on her breast despairingly.

Captain Frank, standing with his uncle Meredith, turned his head in some pity towards his mother.

She had just produced the proofs of his birth, and claims to the title of the Earl St. Claire.

"I have been sinful," she said, "but I have done my duty now, I have repented, and I hope to be forgiven by my children—farewell."

Before anyone could make an attempt to stop her, she was gone none knew whither at the time, but afterwards they learnt that she had entered a convent where she died in penance.

Temple left England to seek a fortune and a good name in a foreign land.

Captain Frank still kept in the king's chosen guards, and strictly forbade his sister ever seeing Guy Fawkes again.

She did not murmur against her brother's will, but time told upon her, and showed how she suffered from internal grief. Nothing that Captain Frank could do would solace her ; but one day a young, daring, handsome, cavalier won her heart, with his sweet voice and the rich music he awoke from his guitar. Soon after heart came her hand in promise of marriage—so she at last was happy.

CHAPTER XXXV.
CLOSING EVENTS.

It was night—midnight, and very dark, when the six conspirators drew up under the wall of the king's prison.

"Give me the line," said Catesby. "We have no time to lose."

Wright gave him a coil of thick rope with a bar of iron almost a foot long fastened to one end.

This Catesby cast over the high prison wall ; the iron bar hitched in the spikes at the top.

"That will do," Catesby said, giving the rope a twitch to try its strength. Then he mounted hand over hand up the rope with the agility of an ape

When on the wall he got the other side of the spikes, lowered himself till his head was in a line with the top of the wall, and then, with both hands, he grasped the iron bar at the end of the rope, and was lowered into the prison yard by his companions on the other side.

Here arose the greatest difficulty. How was he to find in which cell Guy Fawkes was confined ! There were gaolers about, and it would not do for him to be seen.

One of the turnkeys was asleep on his post.

Catesby gagged the man, stripped him of his clothes which he put on himself, and putting the turnkey out of sight, after binding him, took his keys, and went in search of Guy Fawkes.

He found him, liberated him from his cell, and conducted him in silence under the wall where the rope hung.

Catesby gave the rope a pull ; that was the signal for the others on the other side to hold it tight while he mounted.

"Up you go," said Catesby.

"Catesby !" exclaimed Guy, who had been in ignorance of his companion's presence.

"Never mind who I am, do as I tell you. Mount ; your escape is discovered. Haste, or we shall be taken ! "

Guy was up the rope in a few moments. So was Catesby, but he had hardly reached the top, when a body of the prison officials dashed up to the wall, and seized hold of the rope.

Catesby slid down the other side, while they were trying to pull him back.

"Now, all pull together," said Catesby to his companions, "and get the rope out of their hands, or they will get over the same way as we have, and give us a run."

The six conspirators and Guy gave a mighty pull all together.

The rope came up, but it was heavy.

"Pull away," said Catesby, leaving go to prime a caliver.

The rope would not come any further, and while they were pulling one of the gaolers appeared at the top of the wall, hanging on to the end of the rope ; the conspirators had pulled him up.

Catesby just in time, sent him down again by a shot from his caliver, which entered the man's shoulder, and the man uttering a fierce yell of agony, disappeared from the top of the wall.

The conspirators then made off, as they

knew by the confusion they heard going on inside, the whole of the prison officials were aware that a prisoner had escaped, and a pursuit would be certain.

As it was, they had not got far when at least a score of them, armed to the teeth, came trooping after them.

"It's no good running away," said Fawkes, "unless you want your backs riddled."

The conspirators turned and prepared for a fierce contest. As the prison officials came trooping towards them two equestrians came upon the scene.

One was a lady, the other a priest, by his apparel.

"Father Oldcome and Viviana Radcliffe," said Catesby, recognising the two comers.

"Hasten hence, for the lady's sake," cried Fawkes, warning them of their danger.

At the very moment he spoke a volley from the advancing hostile party was fired into them.

A piercing shriek left the lady's lips, and, reeling in the saddle, she fell from the horse, and Fawkes caught her in his arms.

She kept her hand over her left side—a bullet had entered there.

The fall of the fair lady roused the conspirators into action; they met the enemy advancing with furious attack and drove them back.

Fawkes and Catesby being the two most courageous men of the company, took charge of Viviana to convey her to the Red Castle, where the rest of them were to meet.

The illustration on front page pourtrays the wild scene that met the poor exhausted girl's gaze while passing through a subterranean passage to the meeting-hall.

The lady was sent to a chamber, but the lady couldn't rest there; her hurt was but slight after all, and she descended to the hall and concealed herself to listen to the conspirator's plot against the state.

Guy's quiet, melancholy face haunted her, and she was determined to save him from the crime of conspiracy.

It was arranged that they should leave the castle on the morrow for their dwelling at Westminster, and convey, in the dead of night, thirty-six barrels of gunpowder to a cellar under Parliament House, under the very spot where they knew the King and his peers would set on the opening.

Guy was surprised when, on the following day, Viviana stood in his path, with downcast eyes, and blushing cheeks.

"Guy," she said, in a tremulous tone, "do not go on with this fearful work."

Guy was bewildered, but he mastered his agitation, and told her determinedly that nothing would change his resolution.

She listened to him in silent agitation.

"By fate we have been thrown together," she said; "for my sake, for thine own, desist from this monstrous undertaking."

"Viviana," Guy said, strangely impressed by her manner, "it can never be."

"Oh Guy! if you knew all, you would give up this wicked career."

"Nothing on this earth will ever deter me from my path of revenge."

"Guy, Guy, am I to confess!" cried Viviana, falling on her knees. "Can you not see what I mean."

"Lady, you bewilder me."

"Guy, I love you."

"Viviana!" exclaimed Fawkes, reeling back, stricken with surprise and remorse.

"Yes, Guy, I love you. You have wrung the secret from me."

"Sorry I am, Viviana," said the conspirator more calmly, "that you have found no one more worthy of thy love than am I; your affections are thrown away, I can never love you, and if I did, it would only bring unhappiness on your young life; for you could never be my bride."

"I should be content to live if you love me; but you give me no hope," she cried, despairingly. "Farewell!"

And she rushed from him.

In spite of himself he experienced a strange feeling—a feeling that suddenly made the loyal lady very dear to him, and he went after her in some alarm.

She opened a door, and bounded on to a stone terrace overlooking a crystal stream.

Guy followed her, and she mounted the parapet as he passed through the door.

"I cannot live to know you abhor me."

With folded arms he stood looking coolly on. He seemed distracted—lost to all around him.

"Is there any hope, Guy?" she asked.

"None!" he replied, solemnly.

There was a faint cry, and a splash—Viviana had taken the leap.

Fawkes went to the parapet. The lady had disappeared, once she rose, and then he plunged in after her, and saved her from a watery grave.

From that day he learnt to love her as he had never loved before; yet he dared not breathe the thought even to himself, for he knew how hopeless was his life.

One day, while buried in gloomy thought, as was his usual wont when left alone, his reverie was disturbed by the approach of Father Garnet and Viviana.

By the lady's wish the priest took her there to wed her, without delay, to Guy Fawkes. The conspirator was very much astonished at the curious way in which the thing was planned, but he consented; and on the spot was wed, by Father Garnet, to Viviana Radcliffe.

Thirty-six barrels of gunpowder had been secretly conveyed by the conspirators to the cellar under Parliament House, to blow up the king and his cabinet, on the 5th of November, 1606, the date deferred by James for the opening.

But there was a traitor in the band, who

divulged their secret by letter to Lord Mont-eagle, of which we give a copy from the original.

It ran thus:—

"*My Lord,—Out of the love I bear to some of your friends, I have a care of your preserva-tion; therefore I would advise you, as you value your life, to devise some excuse to shift off your attendance at this Parliament, for God and man have resolved to punish the wicked-ness of this time. And think not slightly of this advertisement, but retire yourself into your counties, where you may expect the event in safety; for, though there be no appearance of any stir, yet I say they will receive a terrible blow this Parliament, and yet they shall not see who hurts them. This counsel is not to be contemned, because it may do you good, and can do you no harm, for the danger is past as soon as you have burned the letter, and I hope God will give you the grace to make good use of it, to whose holy protection I commend you.*"

Although Lord Monteagle could not gain any direct information from it—he was in-clined to think it a hoax played upon him for ridicule—he judged it prudent to confer with Lord Salisbury, Secretary of State, upon the matter, and carried the letter to him. Salis-bury did not appear to think much of the matter, till the King returned from Royston, where he had been staying the time.

His sagacious Majesty was prone to think the letter imparted more than they could in-terpret.

From the serious earnestness of the letter he began to think it alluded to some dark and terrible design against the State. Many ex-pressions in it, such as "great," "sudden," and "terrible blow," seemed to conceal some heinous contrivance of gunpowder, and His Majesty was not far out in his conjecture.

The fourth of November drew at hand, and Guy Fawkes, bidding farewell of his companions, left his young wife in ignorance of his design, and repaired to the vault under the House of Lords, where he intended to pass the night till the morrow, when he meant to consummate the terrible deed of blowing the King and his peers into eternity by his hidden treachery.

But, while passing through the vaults with a lantern in one hand and a sword in the other, he was arrested by his bride.

"Viviana!" he said, "you here?"

"Yes, Guy, to save you from this desperate deed."

"Away!" he demanded, sternly. "Go, leave me; or I discard thee for ever."

"Oh! Guy, listen to me, I pray thee. I beseech thee, in the name of the Virgin, to forego this desperate"——

"Begone hence," he demanded.

Sobbing brokenheartedly, the young girl turned from him, when a few muttered words of exultation fell from Guy's lips, which she knew too well the meaning of, and again dared his displeasure by accosting him.

"Guy, Guy, dare not this desperate deed," she said, sadly. Her voice sank, and she fell at his feet insensible.

He conveyed her hence to the house ad-joining the Parliament, and returned to his task.

The clock was just striking twelve when Lord Monteagle, Lord Salisbury, and other nobles, entered the vaults of Parliament House for inspection, under the king's orders, for it was there his suspicions were directed; and Guy Fawkes, seated on a barrel of gun-powder in a dark corner, was seized and carried to Whitehall before the king, despite his remonstrance in trying to pass himself off as Percy of Northumberland's servant.

He was closely examined by the king and his council, who tried very hard to get from the prisoner the names of his confederates; but Guy's lips were sealed, and not all the threats of torture which he afterwards went through at the Tower could wring a word from him.

On the same night as Fawkes was arrested, his brother conspirators heard of the calamity at their rendezvous, and fled in different parts of the country—some to Warwickshire, where Sir Everard Digby was already pre-pared to make a second attempt to seize the Princess Elizabeth.

The attempt was baulked by the officers of justice pursuing and hunting the conspi-rators from place to place, till Robert Catesby and the others, with a great number of Ca-tholic friends they called together, made a stand against the enemy.

A desperate struggle continued for some time between the rebels and the law officers, in which Catesby, Wright, and Percy were sacrificed, all the others captured, and taken to the Tower.

Previous to the apprehension of the con-spirator's league, Guy Fawkes was brought up before the council for examination, and the King offered him pardon, if he would confess all he knew, and give information that would place his confederates in the hands of the law.

But Guy refused. He was true to his oath, and not a word did pass his lips of betrayal.

More forcible means was then resorted to to make him confess.

The first stage of his tortures was the vices that squeezed his limbs up with such pressure that blood broke from almost every joint in his body, and ran from his nose, mouth, and ears freely.

In this state he remained for some hours and when he was found and brought to con-sciousness, he was as firm as ever, and bore his suffering without a murmur.

He was again brought up for examination, but, as before, he refused to say a word that would betray his companions.

He then had to wear iron gauntlets which completely mangled his fingers, and by his hands he was suspended from a beam.

From this he was put on the rack, and

though he felt as though every bone in his body was being snapped, and every joint being rent from its socket, he would not confess.

His last torture was the most cruel of all,—the stone oven heated by a fire under the stones on which he laid writhing in mortal agony.

When taken from here he was half-dead, and it took the doctor some time before he could recover consciousness.

One morning, in February, 1606, Guy Fawkes was conveyed to Old Palace Yard, where a scaffold had been erected for his execution before the House of Lords.

It was so that he should be partly hanged, and while life yet remained in his body his heart was to be cut out, and his body dismembered.

But Guy Fawkes frustrated their designs.

He mounted the gallows with a firm step and a smile on his lips, and directly the rope was placed around his neck he threw himself from the ladder, and when he was cut down life was quite extinct.

His head and limbs were severed from his body and stuck on spikes to excite the population against the Catholics.

All the other conspirators were found guilty, and suffered for their heinous crimes in St. Paul's Churchyard, facing Ludgate-hill.

And Viviana Radcliffe died of broken heart.

So ended the sad tragic story of Guy Fawkes, the conspirator, and his fair bride.

IMPORTANT ANNOUNCEMENT.

NOTICE! NOTICE!

WITH THIS WEEK'S NUMBER OF "GUY FAWKES" IS

PRESENTED GRATIS

No. 1 of the

GRAND SEA STORY,

ENTITLED

TOM NELSON,

ADMIRAL OF THE SEAS.

TO BE CONTINUED IN WEEKLY NUMBERS.

No. 2 (being No. 15 of GUY FAWKES) Now Ready, with a

LARGE ENGRAVING (GRATIS).

NOTICE!

With the New Work will be given to all Subscribers, the remaining Sheets of Characters and Scenes for the Play of

THE FIFTH OF NOVEMBER;

GUNPOWDER, TREASON AND PLOT.

Also will be presented with

TOM NELSON

The continuance of the Prize Cheques, entitling the holder to a Share in the Drawing for the

TEN GOLD WATCHES.

BE SURE TO ASK FOR

TOM NELSON,

ADMIRAL OF THE SEAS.

To be continued Weekly, as the Sequel Story to "GUY FAWKES."

NOTE.—The Index to "GUY FAWKES" will be given with the New Story,

TOM NELSON,

ADMIRAL OF THE SEAS.

WEEKLY, ONE PENNY.